DUST

Dust

YVONNE ADHIAMBO OWUOR

ALFRED A. KNOPF   NEW YORK   2013

THIS IS A BORZOI BOOK
PUBLISHED BY ALFRED A. KNOPF

Copyright © 2014 by Yvonne Adhiambo Owuor

www.aaknopf.com

Knopf, Borzoi Books, and the colophon are registered trademarks of Random House LLC.

Grateful acknowledgment is made to Paulines Publications Africa for permission
to reprint an excerpt from "A Song of the Lion" from *The Gabra: Camel Nomads
of Northern Kenya* by Paul Tablino (Nairobi: Paulines Publications, 1999).
Reprinted by permission of Paulines Publications Africa.

Portions of this work previously appeared, in significantly different form,
in the *Literary Review* (Winter 2009); in *Internazionale Magazine* (December 2010);
and in *McSweeney's Quarterly Concern* (April 2011).

Owuor, Yvonne Adhiambo.
Dust / Yvonne Adhiambo Owuor.
pages cm
ISBN 978-0-307-96120-4
1. Kenya—Fiction.   2. Kenya—Social life and customs—Fiction.
3. Domestic fiction.   I. Title.
PR9381.9.O98D87 2014
823'.92—dc23   2013027871

Jacket design by Linda Huang

Manufactured in the United States of America

First Edition

First, this book is dedicated to you,
La Caridad.

&

Beautiful, beautiful, beloved Tom Diju Owuor
(Couldn't you tarry,
Just a little bit, Daddy?)
1936–2012

&

My dazzling, adored, life-hope-beauty-breathing mama,
Mary Sero Owuor

&

For you my cherished siblings,
Vivian Awiti, Caroline Alango, Genevieve Audi,
Joanne Achieng, Alison Ojany, Chris Ganda, and Patrick Laja;
Joseph Alaro, François Delaroque, Rob de Vries,
and John Primrose. The next generation angels,
Karla, Angelina, Taya, Nyla.
For those gone ahead, for the ones still to come.
Thank you

*"You will hear the voice of my memories
stronger than the voice of my death—that is, if death ever had a voice."*

—JUAN RULFO, *Pedro Páramo*

*Follow my tracks in the sand that lead
Beyond thought and space.*

—HAFEZ

Chon gi lala . . .

—LUO STORY BEGINNINGS

DUST

PROLOGUE

HE LEAPS OVER TWO FIRE-PAINTED BLOSSOMS RESTING ON THE stark cracked city pavement. Roused, these unfurl into late-Christmas-season orange-and-black butterflies that flutter into the violet shade of a smog-encrusted roadside jacaranda tree. A thrum becomes a hum becomes thumping footsteps, and soon he is entangled in a thicket of jeers and tossed gray, black, and brown stones as he flees toward a still-distant night. It is said that in combat some soldiers shoot over their enemies' heads in order to avoid killing them. Some don't even fire at all. Moses Ebewesit Odidi Oganda's fingers tremble on the trigger of an old, shiny AK-47. He hurls the gun away with an *"Urgh!"* The weapon spills across the road—a low-pitched, guttural noise.

From behind Odidi, a wail, *"Odi, man! Cover!"*

Other chords of voices echo:

Hao! There they are.

Waue! Kill them.

Wezi! Thieves.

Odidi runs.

Three weeks ago the rifle was in the hands of a minor Somali warlord turned Eastleigh-based vendor of off-season Turkish designer women's wear. The ex-warlord had given Odidi the weapon as compensation for camel water songs, which Odidi had sung inside the trader's shop while he was picking up lacy feminine things for Justina, his girl. Odidi's music caused wistful chirping sounds to come out of the refugee—lamentations for lost, happy pastoral yesterdays.

The taciturn man had approached Odidi. "You sing as if you know water," he had said.

"I do," Odidi answered.

"These were *our* old songs. . . . How did they find you?"

"A visiting man."

"He has a name?"

Odidi paused. *That* name came with a torrent of buried history. A curt reply: "Ali Dida Hada."

"Degodia," concluded the warlord, naming a clan.

"No. No." Odidi frowned at yellow, pink, black, and red panties and brassieres, his mind struggling. Then he said, "No! A stranger of too many lands." *And faces.*

The trader leaned forward. "You know the song of Kormamaddo, the sky camel?"

Odidi had winked before whistling an overture. The man had pounced on nostalgia's lyrics and belted them out. They had then ventured into and mangled other water songs.

"Desert ghost of yesteryear/Dredge the dunes/Draw sweet truth out."

An hour later, as Odidi was paying half-price for Justina's fripperies, the ex-warlord had muttered, "Wait." He leaned down, hefted up a canvas-and-newspaper-wrapped, hard, four-part object and closed Odidi's hand over it. "From my heart. Open it alone. God shield your songs and your wife." He dabbed tears off his face, partly of relief because he had also offloaded a problem.

Now.

"Waue!" The pursuing Nairobi mob howls.

Odidi runs.

Not feeling the ground. Soaring.

Swish, zip, pop, rattle.

Bullets.

Grunt, *thud.* A man falls.

Ratatatata . . . Screams.

Odidi runs.

Tears flood. Terror-rage-love fuse.

The fallen ones are his men.

Guilt. Fury. Sorrow.

"*Urgh!*" The sound a captain makes when he falters and loses the team. Still, Odidi does not go for the pistol strapped to his chest. Odidi runs. Strength in his arms, his legs pistons, he sprints down Haile Selassie Avenue, jumps over prone, cowering citizens, pities them, the bullets aimed at him raining down upon them. He runs through the stench of decay, the perfume of earth hoping for rain, habits and dreams of Nairobi's people: smoke, rot, trade, worry, residues of laughter, and overbrewed Ketepa tea. Odidi runs.

Incantation: *Justina! Justina!*

Shelter of faith.

The mob screams, *"Hawa!"*

Justina! Faith into sorrow into longing: *I need to go home.*

"Waue!" The answer.

Memory's tricks. Odidi soars into the desiccated terrains of Wuoth Ogik, the home he had abandoned: his people reaching out for him, cowbells, bleating goats, sheep, and far mountains. He sees Kormamaddo, the grumpy family camel, dashing home from pasture. The sky of home, that endless dome. Flood tide in his blood. *I want to go home.* Odidi lifts his feet higher, trying to fly. Odidi runs.

Random humans in this slippery city of ephemeral doings crave his death. *Ua!* Something flutters and falls within Odidi like a startled, broken songbird. *What have I ever done to them?* He just wants to go home.

Justina!

Oasis.

He will cross spiderweb black roads to touch her.

Odidi runs.

He turns down Jogoo Road and glances upward, childhood habit born when Galgalu, the family herdsman, had told him that God was Akuj—Eternity Revealed as Sky. Up there now, orange dusk light's bateleur eagles. Like marabou storks, they are prophet birds. Water in his eyes. Odidi blinks away Nairobi's late-day drizzle. And the earth shivers behind him. A pitiful bellow, a goat protesting the injustice of a butcher's knife. Death stinks of cold emptiness. Omosh: the last of his men. Odidi gulps down vomit. Tastes salt. Tears in his mouth, sticky, wet of hands, as if he has dipped them into blood. Was this the destination of all their wars?

Shadow and regret.

Stumbling.

He must move.

But the city, his city, has all of a sudden changed its shape and turned against him. Roads slither into hard walls; blocks of shadow scurry away to expose his next step to ravenous, carnivorous urban trolls. Faster, Odidi runs.

A whisper from his remote past like a brushstroke on his bare back: *You can't live in the songs of people who don't know your name. . . .* Odidi grabs at his throat, suffocating in a burst-of-fire clarity. *What have I done?* Odidi runs.

Glimpse of his fleeting shadow's reflection on darkened glass panes. What had he done? Odidi runs. Louder: *You can't live in the songs of people who don't know your name.* He understands now that he must protect his family. Odidi runs. He *must* reach a stranger; stop him from boarding a flight from Heathrow to Nairobi. First, he *must* find the labyrinthine alleyways, his escape routes. Pounding steps behind him, sundown's cool breeze on his arm and face. A moan within his throat—*let me go home.* Odidi runs. Damp-fisted hands propel him forward, and the city's twilight rain saturates his skin at the same time that he hears a phone melody from within his coat pocket. Cesária Évora's "Um Pincelada." His sister's calling tune.

Grim grin. Only Arabel Ajany Oganda would phone at a time like this. If he were to answer, he predicts her first words would be "Odi . . . what's wrong?" He would have to say, "Nothing, I'm taking care of it," as she expected him to, and he always did. And he was. Odidi runs. "Um Pincelada" plays. If he could, he would say, *Hello, silly.* After more than ten years of nothing, today he could tell her: *I'm going home.* She would laugh, and he with her. The music stops. *Hello, silly.*

They were chance offspring of northern-Kenya drylands. Growing up, Odidi and Ajany had been hemmed in by arid land geographies and essences. Freed from history, and the interference of Nairobi's government, they had marveled at Anam Ka'alakol, the desert lake that swallowed three rivers—the Omo, Turkwel, and Kerio. They learned the memories of another river—the Ewaso Nyiro—four moody winds, the secret things of parents' fears, throbbing shades of pasts, met assorted transient souls, and painted their existence on a massive canvas of glowing, rocky, heated earth upon which anything could and did happen. They mapped their earth with portions of wind, fire, sky, water, and nothingness, with light, piecing tales from stones, counting footsteps etched into rocks, peering into crevices to spy on the house of red rain. They lived in the absence of elders afflicted with persistent memories: no one to tell the children how *it* had been, what *it* meant, how *it* must be seen, or even what *it* was. Because of this, they re-created myths of beginnings. "The first Oganda was spoken into existence by flame," Odidi once told Ajany. She believed him. His sister trusted everything he said. Glimmer of a smile.

"Hawa!"

He had forgotten where he was.

Odidi runs.

He jumps over mud-stained, crumpled election posters entangled in rotting foliage that show the bright face and pure-white teeth of one of the presidential candidates. *Teeth do not rot in the grave.* Where had he read that? To his left, a plastic-choked alleyway. He ducks into it. Song in his heart, a psalm of glee. This is *his* territory.

Justina!

A glance finds her among a seething mass. He knows most of them—gang associates. Justina is draped in her yellow muumuu with its ridiculous giant pink carnations. He adores that dress on her. He adores her. Her eyes are unusually large, luminous, and hollow. Her howl fragments his heart—Who has wounded her? *Whom must he kill?*—and then flames flare from his heart's soul and engulf him, and after he screams out, he can no longer see Justina.

Odidi limps.

He grips his shattered right shoulder. Protrusion of bone. Blood trail. Trickle from his mouth. It is said that in the throes of battle dying men cry out for their mothers. *Akai-ma,* Odidi groans. She wards off ghouls and bad night entities, wrestles God, casts ancient devils into hell before their time, and kicks aside sea waves so her son will pass unhindered. *Akai-ma.* Throb in the back of Odidi's left leg. Searing that eats the base of his spine. Damp from his chest. And even though his leg is heavier than a tree trunk, he tries to carry it home. He grapples with a thought that keeps sliding away. He seizes it. *Justina!*

The finish line. He will make it because he is Shifta the Winger, rugby finisher, and scorer. His forwards and backs have thrown him the ball. Although they have fallen out of play, they depend on him to end the game. He is the quickest, the trickiest, the best Shifta the Winger, dancing through adversaries. Before Jonah Lomu made it right to have large wingers, there was Shifta the Kenyan Winger, who carried the game into the face of opponents, and who scored try after try after try while crowds chanted *Shifta! Thump, thump! Winger! Thump! Thump!* And later, when he heard the Kenyan national anthem, felt it resound in his spirit, he had wept tears that traveled past his lips and reached the earth.

Shifta! Thump!
Winger! Thump!

Odidi hobbles to the center of a pathway, his twisted leg dragging. Warm liquid runs down, stains his trousers, leaving a visible patch. Piss. Out of his control. *Akai-ma!* She fixes everything. Retrieves those who belong to her. Dim shadows, like bateleur eagles surveying grassy plains, circle in. They herd him into a trap.

A succinct *ratata*.

Odidi's good knee gives out.

He crumbles.

Exhales on a gurgle.

It is said.

That when a person begins to die, all his life races past him in space-less time and timeless space, and he can feel again, only much faster, and with sunlike light, all he has felt before. On the tarmac, Odidi Oganda's knuckles scrape hot stone. His left leg faces the opposite direction. A single spurt of sound becomes a blaze that cuts through Odidi's middle, and his entire existence spirals down a hole that becomes smaller and smaller. His body jerks backward and then forward. He sighs, exhausted now, fingers folding into themselves.

Music.

A replay of Cesária Évora.

Ajany.

His sister.

Words congeal, become blocks of thought. Heart-speak. *Poor 'Jany.* He must warn her. *Poor 'Jany.* Music. Akai-ma will be mad. Flicker of laughter. She *was* mad. *Akai-ma.* Galgalu will be waiting for him. He had said he would watch the sky for signs of Odidi's homecoming. Later, they would travel with the cows to the Chalbi Desert salts and debate life, its loves and crevices.

Music.

Cesária Évora.

Ajany.

His sister.

Once upon a time, long, long ago, when he was only four years old, Odidi, carrying Ajany, had screamed at his mother: *This is my baby!* She was, for he had wandered a long, long way to bring her back home, having, with Galgalu the herdsman, retrieved her from the fixed gaze of five waiting vultures.

Odidi savors the ringing.

It tastes of ordinary things.

Like presence.

He listens.

And listens.

The music stops.

No, he thinks, *No, 'Jany, continue.*

The drone of a million flies now buzzing in his ear. What'll he tell his sister? He'll say, "The land woke up at dusk and said to itself, 'Today I'll be Arabel Ajany. And the lake looked at the land that was Ajany and said, 'Today I'll be Odidi Ebewesit.' That is why we roam. Because sometimes we are places, not people." She would believe him. She always did. He would say . . .

Anonymous murmurs.

Someone moves close to him, kicks at a numbing portion of his body.

"Ameaga?" Is he dead?

"Bado." Not yet.

They arrange objects around Odidi that *ping* when they fall. He squints through an overwhelming dark-red veil at the moving misshapen shapes.

Simpler needs: *Help me.*

Foot on his numb body.

Smaller longings: *Touch me.*

Minuscule hope: *Stay with me.*

Murmurs.

Stay. Odidi hiccups.

Ache becomes pining, every straggling breath now consecrated to presence, a single word bursting through—Baba! The sound dissolves resistance. Baba! Misery pouring out of Odidi's mouth is the color of rotting blood. It stains his coat and T-shirt. Red tears. Streaks make his face a grotesque duo-toned mask.

Odd memory.

Old music.

Fela Kuti.

Moses Odidi Oganda was eighteen years old, a first-year University of Nairobi engineering student, when, in a room full of books and silences in his coral-hued desert home, Wuoth Ogik, he had dived into a story of machines and found, tucked into inner pages, an alien painted vision. He had ripped it from a page that age had glued it into, his breathing all of a sudden disgruntled, pained, and potholed. Before he could further contemplate what the image meant, he heard the hard tread on stone of his father's footsteps. He had returned the piece to its mute page and walked out with the book.

Later, at university, he found Fela Kuti's songs—their compacted rage: *Aye, aye, aye . . . I no go agree make my brother hungry, make I no talk . . .*

He had also appointed himself Thomas Sankara's heir and wore nonprescription lenses shaped like those Patrice Lumumba had once worn.

Three semesters later, Odidi traveled home to Wuoth Ogik. In their third evening as a family, Odidi Oganda brought in the AK-47 that Nyipir, his father, had given him five years ago. He took it apart, then threw the pieces at Nyipir's feet, chanting: *Aye, aye, aye . . . I no go agree make my brother hungry, make I no talk . . .*

Stillness.

Then Nyipir had stooped over the pieces.

Stillness.

Afterward, in the interlude of strokes from a hippo-leather whip that tore at Odidi's body, Nyipir implored, "The only . . . war you fight . . . is for what belongs to you. You can't live the songs of people who don't know your name."

Odidi had tried to shield his body, waiting to execute a rugby side-tackle, forgetting Baba was a seasoned military man. They wrestled across the floor. *Crack.* The breaking of Odidi's left arm, his rugby ellipse-carrying arm. In Odidi's stifled sorrow, the dying of grand rugby hopes that he realized right then he had nourished. He remembers Ajany waving her arms above her head, struggling to scream: "Stop!" Stuttering *Sttttttt* over and over. Akai-ma cursed in Ngaturkana, summoning God and Catholic saints to witness the madness. She also offered to strip and show them her bare behind. A curse. But Galgalu struck the ground between father and son with a long, thick, herdsman's stick. *Thup!*

Then there was silence.

Much, much later.

A father's whispered entreaty to a fleeing son: *Stay. Stay, please.*

The son left.

Never bothered with an answer or even a backward look.

Now, years later, from a bitumen-smelling potholed backstreet, Odidi's heart bleeds out his answer: *Coming home. Wait for me.*

Scent of return.

Burnt acacia-resin incense. Desert essences—dung, salt, milk, smoke, herbs, and ghee, the yearning for rain. Akai-ma said good smells melted bad spirits. *We'll meet our cows at sunset,* Odidi promises. *Home* is the cream of hot milk of their animals, gulped down when Galgalu the herdsman was not looking, chewed-grass, slime-layered goat tongues on skin as they licked the stolen salt he and Ajany fed them with. Small Odidi watches Baba shave, his angular face lost in soft white lather, experiences again the wonder of Baba's smooth-faced re-emergence. Baba winks. He is stretched out on his large, peeling tan leather armchair, head leaning back, a whiff of Old Spice, filled with big laughter. Just when Odidi would have thrown himself into Nyipir's arms, a chill shadow crashes into him, stabbing into his body.

Now.

It stretches over him.

Odidi croaks, *You!*

It stares back, empty-socketed, and as noiseless as when they had first met. *What do you want?* Hollow hunger. Perpetual thirst. *Here I am.* The thing smiles. Odidi understands. *If you touch her . . .* Odidi shivers. *Leave her alone.* Cold tears. If it did not burn to do so, his teeth would chatter. *Please.* The shape watches Odidi's seeping shadow flow into a twisted, dark-red cave, its den. *Not her fault,* Odidi pleads. *I'm here.*

. . .

Odidi and his sister Ajany's December school holiday. Odidi, plotter of adventures, had decreed they should visit the forbidden, damask-stone cave to find the source of a stream they could hear but not see.

"No!" Ajany had stammered. "There's bad in there."

"How do you know?" Odidi scoffed.

"Akai-ma says . . ."

"We'll find water at the base." He had interrupted her. His words had separated and bounced back. *Wa . . . Bassssssss . . . Ter . . . Wa . . . Sssssss . . .*

So Ajany had placed her hand in his and followed him to the cave entrance that opened into a hollowed-out higgledy-piggledy grotto haunted by "God's dazzling darkness" and seeping water. Damp pockets, points of light, and thick shadows that clung. Odidi had squashed his shoulders through trough-like passageways. Ajany followed. Tiny for her age, she could have strolled through. In two places they walked upright. Mostly they slithered on the hard, cold ground, dark skin tones blending in, inching forward on knees and hands. Abrupt left turn into a twisted chamber, into a triangle of light on jutting walls, which revealed yellow-and-red-shaded signs of bleeding spoors and giant footprints heading upward. *There.* The imprint of the world's first record of laughter—open-mouthed toothiness carved into ancient rock. Pictograms. Space shimmering in between icons. They had whirled before the cave wall. "Mhhhhh," Odidi had said, understanding where secrets are born. The too-muchness of experiencing, why silence is the language of last resort. They had laughed and laughed, peals of joy bouncing in the chamber. Ajany had skipped up and down before stumbling backward and falling on her bottom.

Crack! Ajany picked up what had been broken.

Odidi looked at what she carried and saw a white human finger bone, pointing at him. Ajany flung it away from herself. It had struck Odidi on his forehead. And when he had turned his face away, he had spotted the rest of the skeleton. The skull stained, grinning, and missing some teeth. Its sunken sockets stared at him then, as they did now.

"Where has its face gone?" Ajany had wailed, hand facing upward, her feet jumping, crashing down on the thing's left hand. Odidi had stretched forward and picked Ajany up.

She gripped his neck, hiccupping. "It's Obarogo! Odidi, Obarogo!"

And even as his life now leaks out, from the tarmac, Odidi chortles, *He-he!* Bubbles in his gullet. *Obarogo!* His sister consumed every story he fed her. Obarogo, the blind bogeyman born out of Odidi's desire to hear his sister scream. Obarogo, who took life from the wool of darkness. Obarogo, who needed eyes in order to see in the dark and who sought out little girls whose eyes were open when they should have been asleep. Obarogo, of course, avoided boys.

They had raced away from the red cave, he half lifting, half shoving his sister ahead of him. Days after, Ajany, sucking on her two fingers, had dogged Odidi's steps as they pastured livestock. She had yanked at his shorts. "'Didi, I dream of . . . of . . . Obaro . . . Oba . . ."

"Stop it!" Odidi had hissed, and whistled at the herding dogs. When he had looked back, he saw Ajany stabbing the earth with a twig. He shouted, "Soon we go back to school!"

Ajany had looked up at him with large, afraid-of-school eyes. The twig had fallen from her hands.

"We'll go Far Away," Odidi had whispered. Just as he had promised, "We're going to *real* Kenya," when he had learned of Baba's decision to send them down-country to a boarding school south of the Ewaso Nyiro River.

Odidi and Ajany's first vision of the school had been as a space demarcated from the rest of the universe by a massive black gate and an overgrown, almost dark-violet kai-apple fence that covered a thick wall. It was a misshapen world of gray stone edifices, a piteous tribute to an obscure English public school.

The headmistress, Mrs. Karai, M.Ed. Calabash-shaped. Stumpy. Stern. Ice. Yellow-brown, thin legs, faux-pearl necklace, and horn-rimmed spectacles. After her New Year new-student assembly speech, on the morning of their second day, she summoned Odidi and Ajany to her office.

"Stand."

They stood.

"No fighting, no stealing, no politics. Do you know how to use a toilet?"

No answer.

"I take that to mean 'no.' Matron will show you. I warn you. I smell trouble—you'll see. You'll know who I am, you hear?"

Touch and instinct were missing from Mrs. Karai's words. Was reason also a sense? Odidi had gathered every fury that possessed him, had heard his sister grinding her teeth, knew she was unconscious of what she was doing. If he exploded, she might crash. So he had swallowed down rage and touched Ajany's shoulder.

"Dismissed," Mrs. Karai snarled.

They had left the office hand in hand. They had dodged each other's eyes. Later, they focused on study. Ajany learned to paint, covered shame with vivid colors. Books revealed destinations. Huskies in Alaska, pumpkins that become footmen, genteel princes, knights of round tables, and agreeable kings who oversaw holy order. Atlases were a favorite; anything could be imagined to happen between the lines and curves of a journey.

Odidi became a grade-three piano student within a year.

"Come. *Listen. Listen.* Ajany!"

Music and painting bandaged soul-holes.

They forgot teachers whose lip-curling mouths asked, "*Ati*, from where? Is it on the map?" Drowned out classmates: "You people cook dust to eat." Music and painting canceled memories of annual February humiliations when news stories of northern land famines arrived with portraits of emaciated, breast-baring, adorned citizens, and skeletons of livestock. They suffered a flurry of "School Walks" and "Give Your Change, Save a Life" and "Help the Poor Starving People of Northern Kenya" picnics. Ajany, being a useful facsimile for the occasion—reed-thin, small, dark, bushy-haired, with large slanted eyes—was thrust to the school stage to slump over one end of a massive cardboard of a bank check for newsletter photo shoots. Odidi would sit in the audience with eyes shut, dreaming about end of term, when the blessed migration from this Kenya to theirs, via Nairobi, occurred. Nairobi was the oasis where he and Ajany boarded a dilapidated green holiday bus shaped like a triangular loaf and shuttled along ramshackle roads to the trading center. Sometimes they walked; most of the time they got a ride close to Wuoth Ogik, where they purged school from their hearts.

After the red cave, life at school for Odidi and Ajany changed. Odidi acquired bulk, merged it with fury, and, after joining the rugby team, transformed the school's game. In the second season, when the opponents' defense tried to take the ball from him, he broke three sets of teeth and converted twelve tries. Their school, former perennial failures, became School Rugby Cup contenders. In the created songs of worship for their new hero—*Shifta! The Winger!*—Odidi found belonging, and Ajany, reflecting Odidi's glory, was at last left in peace.

Years later, Odidi would command Ajany, "Choose." She did. She left Kenya. He had stayed. To live out a belonging to which he had become accustomed.

Lying on the tarmac, Odidi connects meaning to sounds he hears: a tire squeal, a slammed door, cut-off words, ricochet shouts of once-alive friends. They are where they are because of a green Toyota Prado of which they had tried to relieve its current owner. Wasn't stealing. It had been Odidi's car. He'd bought it, cash. It had been swiped from him. He was just taking it back. He and the car's current driver had once been friends. Schoolmates, business partners, drinking and whoring buddies who had chosen the green car for Odidi to celebrate a life-changing deal gone through. The friend had opted for a brown Jaguar. A few years later, contracts shattered, he was driving Odidi's car. This job was supposed to be easy: stealing from a thief.

When Odidi had told Justina that he was going to take his green car back and give it to her, Justina had begged, "Odi-Ebe, please—why not buy another one?"

He had snapped, "This one's mine."

Justina had placed both her hands over her bulging stomach. "I'm scared."

He had laughed at her, seized her, and lifted her up. She had looked down at him. He had watched her until she managed a smile, the way she always did. "A *kawaida* job like this?" he had whispered as he lowered her. "It's Odidi." And finally she had giggled. This last job was supposed to have been easy.

After this he would marry Justina.

Restart destiny.

He would also find the courage to climb into an airplane. It was time to visit his sister in Brazil. There was so much to say and do. This job should have been so easy. Except, after Odidi and his team had struck, and he had been about to drive off in the car, a police execution squad was waiting for them.

Voices.

More cars.

Whirring of a camera.

Bright light.

Murmurs.

Then.

Five, four, three, two, one, action! A voice, gravelly, pompous, and familiar: "Our *mbrave mboys* returned fire for fire. Two of our men are wounded. The gang leader *mocked* us. Threw abuse. Our *mbrave mboys* gave chase. The climinals *fred* on foot. We persisted. We *forrowed* for two *kirometers*. . . ."

Odidi listens.

"The *climinals* moved with the *plecision* of *rocusts*. They *swarmed* their targets. They have been *stearing*, conning, and *dismantring* vehicles. Have executed bank *rombberies*, *mundered poricemen*, and escaped with ninety *mirrion shirrings*."

Shit!

Odidi understood.

A setup.

The Officer Commanding Police Division, whom they paid every month to look away, and who on three occasions had hired out his gun to the gang, had just sacrificed them.

Sorrow is a universe.

Guilt.

Shame at being fooled. It contains fear because there is no one who will hear what he needs to say.

Such is loneliness.

Tears.

Electric chill-pain.

Odidi shivers.

Blood.

What's happening to me?

Then.

Someone is breathing over him.

Warmth. A voice: "I've looked for you, boy."

Odidi opens his mouth. *Baba?* No sound.

The voice: "I'm here."

Odidi tries to shift toward the presence.

Wants to say, *Didn't rob any bank.*

Attempts a grin. *Knew you'd find me.*

But it is simpler to allow life its rolling sensations.

Above Odidi, the night. Blurred intimacy of twinkling white stars; watching Kormamaddo, the bull camel of the waters.

What's happening to me?

A voice says, "Close your eyes, boy. Go to sleep."
Odidi coughs three times.
Red bubbles spatter.
The voice says, "I'm here."
Odidi breathes in.
Doesn't breathe out.
Becomes still.

The six-foot-tall, professorial, gray-haired, bespectacled man, a high-level plainclothes policeman wearing a nondescript, now bloodied black suit and black shoes, will wait nine minutes to retrieve the pistol strapped to Odidi's chest and a bullet-pierced cell phone. With a tiny, delicate movement, he will pocket these. A squashed scarlet Sportsman cigarette packet with two cigarettes rustles in his shirt pocket. He reaches for one, reconsiders. He can endure, and has endured, the cocktail of stench: blood, shit, gun smoke, and rotten water from a nearby open drain. Eyes empty, he hunkers down. Hand to cheek, he thinks of Nyipir Oganda, the boy's father, while his stained fingers dislodge his bifocals, which then rest crooked on his large nose. He stares into nothing.

1

HERE. SHE COULD PAINT THIS; HOLD THE BRUSH AS A STABBING knife. There. Coloring in landscapes of loss. She could draw this for him, this longing to hear his particular voice, listening for echoes of bloodied footsteps, borrowing dead eyes to help her find him again. Here. Jagged precipices of wounding, and over cliffs, an immense waterfall of yearning, falling and falling into nothingness.

Her father, Aggrey Nyipir Oganda, is a slender, dark stone statue in front of her. Only his eyes roam spaces, taking everything in, the emptiness, too. Eyes reddened and popping out, shadowy tear streaks on an ebony face. His old policeman posture is intact. Straight, stiff, steady, he is old-world dapper in a slightly shabby 1970s coat and 1950s brown leather fedora. Tinged with the gray of age, clandestine wrinkles congregate at the corners of his eyes. As with so many men of Kenya from his time, his manner is genteel English colonial stranded in time's paradoxes.

A twist deforms Ajany's full lips. *Here.* The evidence. They are descendants of a lineage of Living Dead. Breathing in, she shifts her body to stare at a beige coffin, habitat of the new and unquiet dead on a day when distorted election results will set a bucolic country afire. The outside world is drenched with human noises of accusations and coun-teraccusations, election rigging, and the miracle of mathematical votes that multiply and divide themselves. But within their world, in a self-contained, haunted compound with its lone, misshapen grevillea tree, upon which a purple-blue bird tweets, and where death prowls at half past three, Ajany bends forward to listen to and for her brother, Odidi, whose story-words had created vessels that always carried her into safe border.

Hours ago: Inside a morgue with its forgotten dead, the unprepared dead, and the happy dead, a chill had turned all their hands a pale yellow, same shade as Moses Odidi Oganda's long, thick fingers. They had rum-maged among the discarded dead in order to find and retrieve their own.

Post-autopsy, after a smoke-stained attendant had stitched him together again, father and sister had dressed Odidi up: olive khaki suit, black socks, and tan leather shoes, purchases from a half-closed, guarded, nearby mall whose managers balanced the fear of waiting for hell's inev-itable descent with the thirst to milk the last flow of money from panick-ing citizens. By three-thirty, documents signed, all protocol adjusted and therefore observed, Moses Ebewesit Odidi Oganda was officially dead.

Arabel Ajany Oganda stands under gray skies where shadows dart. A pair of bateleur eagles—prophet birds, like marabou storks—survey the ground for cooling bodies. Savanna birds encircling a city that is dash-ing toward an abyss, while here four men advance toward a white hearse with tattered red ribbons fluttering from its front windows.

Ajany breathes into her hands and shivers. Blisters and bruises burst in hidden places within, while her outside eyes glue themselves to Baba's glowing brown shoes that underline his efficient out-of-place-ness. Bile in throat burns, dissolving her screaming. *I hate* . . . What? She swallows, focuses on Nyipir's fixation with the wooden coffin, his guttural breath-ing out of a lullaby. *Oombe, Oombe / Nyathi maywak ondiek chame.* . . . She listens for Odidi. Listens for words that return life into a still body she has seen and touched. *Odi, wake up,* she begs with her breathing.

Nyipir Oganda lifts his hand. Six other eyes have been waiting for his sign. Three men: A mortuary attendant, sinewy and lame, one of his incisors elongated and peeping out of his mouth as if from another existence; his eyes ooze a brown substance and madness. Dr. Mda, police pathologist, a short man of shiny baldness, whose cherubic, pock-marked face carries a too-large mustache set off by big ears and eyes that dart hither and thither; his beige trousers are a size too small. Ali Dida Hada as Ajany had never seen him before—in police uniform, adorned with the insignia of an assistant commissioner of police, carrying a black baton under his arm. An emaciated line, mirroring his strip of mustache, serves as a smile on his mouth. When she was eight years old and the then newly arrived Ali Dida Hada had been pretending to be an itinerant herdsman for her family, she had spied him mesmerizing the family camels with songs sung in a falsetto. She had told Odidi: "He has gold mirrors inside his eyes."

Nyipir signals. The men hoist up the coffin.

It is a short walk to the white hearse.

They fit the box into the runners.

Bruised faces belie outward harmony.

Earlier, there had been a tussle next to the silver autopsy bay.

Nyipir had said, "I'll take my son home now."

Dr. Mda had screeched with moral valor, "A *Mporis* case. The can-daver *brongs* to the state."

His tone had caused Nyipir to grab the rotund man's neck and squeeze as a long python might. Supervising Officer Ali Dida Hada had watched, face placid, head tilted.

"*Heup* me," Mda choked.

Ali Dida Hada had been nonchalant. "Me, I say there's no case."

Dr. Mda bleated, "You *m*brought me here."

"*Eh!* To reveal through science how this *cannot* be a police case."

"Oh!" croaked Mda.

Nyipir had released Mda's neck.

A practical man, Dr. Mda had looked to the mechanics of death for an answer that would not compromise his only partially tainted soul: *exsanguinations caused by pneumothorax and heart failure,* a footnote on a death certificate so that Moses Odidi Oganda could go home.

Distant sirens.

In the compound, near the grevillea and its cheerful bird, life col-lapses into the squeak of the opening door of a hearse, the view of a coffin from a rear window, the deep gaze of other strangers, and more shuf-fling footsteps. No flowers. No cortège—a brother's leave-taking of a sour morgue where other corpses wait for their living. She remembers that the hearse driver's name is Leonard. His thin face bones cast fragile shadows. He has wrapped a white handkerchief around his coat's upper arm and assumed a funereal look. It suits him. Earlier, Leonard had brought Ajany and Nyipir from the airport in a bright-yellow taxi. It is gone now.

Ajany scrubs her face and stares at two sides of the world. *Before-now* was four hours and forty-three minutes ago. Rained-upon earth mingling with smoke and age and dust and sun and cows on a father's coat, and her head tucked into its folds in welcome at the airport, the scent of coming home from all her Far Aways. *But-now* is icy eternity, thick with the terror of the voicelessness of her big brother. But-now is made of the murmured anguish of other strangers—a ragged quartet oozing old-clothes smell. Wet eyes, life-hardened faces, as unadorned as the ill-nailed empty coffin on the cement. Panel-beaten features. The woman's look is a hemorrhage. Wife? Sister? Daughter? Ajany looks away from these other citizens of the sea of absence.

A lethargic white-striped lizard pauses between tiny yellow flowers before lumbering across Ajany's blue-painted toes, which peep out of absurd dark-blue Brazilian high heels. A howling *Where are you?* Resonance of fear, which pounds its hooves, galloping through her soul. Madness neighs. Her fingers press long, painted nails into palms. These bend and break. Groping darkness behind her eyes. Exhaling slowly so as not to disrupt stillness, Ajany breathes, but it is too late. Now is when forgotten ghosts return to claim beginnings. She could paint these arrivals, but for now she is gnawed by the ghastly bawling of a baby that only she could ever hear. Ajany calls for him, her story maker. *Odidi.* He knew water songs that soothed. He always knew what to do.

Outside sounds:

Étude of squealing tires.

Bird chirp.

Machine-gun opening sequence.

A scream.

Fragments of a song from some unseen citizen's room.

Franklin Boukaka's plaintive summons—*Aye Africa . . . kokata koni pasi, soki na kati koteka pasi*—and for a whole minute it overwhelms the frenzied crescendo screams of *Haki yetu,* "Our rights."

It has begun.

Inside Ajany's heart, a sobbing begins. Farther up the road, a prepubescent girl with a tank top, belly ring, and red sneakers hurries off somewhere, clutching her Nakumatt white-and-blue plastic bags. A big hand lands on Ajany's shoulder. She jumps.

Her father croaks, *"Wadhi."* Let's go.

Nyipir and Ajany Oganda approach the hearse. Then they both stop in front of the car door. The veins on Nyipir's neck throb, and sweat pebbles crown his head.

In Ajany, a feeling as if her name had become tactile; she reaches for the sensation and glimpses tendrils of brother, strings thrown into this life from another dimension. She pulls at it and wraps the cord around her wrist. "Come, Odi." A murmur.

Nyipir rubs his eyes before folding himself into the car.

Ajany follows.

They settle in, hugging beige seats, suffused by new-car-in-a-bottle smells. Leonard puts the vehicle into gear. No one acknowledges the pulsating ghost next to them. Like all the others, it is molded out of entombed silences.

Ali Dida Hada, the mortuary attendant, and Dr. Mda watch the white hearse's departure. They also hear the sudden and explosive rhythms of a country shooting its people and tearing out its own heart. The mortuary attendant wrinkles his nose. *"Aieee!* So much work . . . and before the new year. Now, when do I see my ma?"

———

Massive purple clouds rush in from the eastern coast. Ambushed by a warm wind in Nairobi, they scatter, a routed guerrilla force. At Wilson Airport, a *qhat*-carrying eight-seater plane weaves its way off the apron. The last small plane out of Nairobi without top-level permission for the next week. Above the airport din, egrets circle and ibises cry *ngangan-ganga*. Father, daughter, and son are going home.

Dusk is Odidi's time. In the contours of old pasts, Ajany retrieves an image: She is sitting on a black-gray rock, spying on the sun's descent with Odidi. Leaning into his shoulder, trying to read the world as he does, she stammers, "Where's it going?" He says, "Descending into hell," and cackles. She had only just learned the Apostles' Creed.

. . .

The plane lifts off.

The coffin and its keepers are nestled amid bales of green herbs. Straight-backed, stern, silences reordered, Nyipir is a chiseled stone icon again, an archetypal Nilotic male. But there are deep furrows on his forehead. She can paint these, too. Trail markers into absence. Ajany had once believed Baba was omnipotent, like God, ever since he had invoked a black leopard to hunt down the mean and red-eyed inhabitants of her nightmares.

She trembles.

Nyipir asks, "Cold?"

Baba's baritone, Odidi's echo. Dimpled handsomeness. The Oganda men were gifted with soft-edged, rumbling voices.

Ajany turns. The light of the sky bounces on her thin face, all bones and angles. Fresh bloodstains on her sleeves. The frills of her orange skirt are soiled. She is tinier than Nyipir remembers. But she had always been such a small, stuttering thing, all big hair and large eyes. More shadow than person, head slanted as if waiting for answers to ancient riddles. He clears his throat. From the gloom of his soul, Nyipir growls, "Mama . . . er . . . she wanted to . . . uh . . . come to meet you."

Ajany hears the lie. Sucks it in, as if it were venom, sketches invisible circles on the window. Stares at the green of coffee and pineapple plantations below.

"Yes," Nyipir says to himself, already lost, already afraid. He shifts. The dying had started long ago. Long before the murder of prophets named Pio, Tom, Argwings, Ronald, Kungu, Josiah, Ouko, Mbae. The others, the "disappeared unknown." National doors slammed over vaults of secrets. Soon the wise chose cowardice, a way of life: not hearing, not seeing, never asking, because sound, like dreams, could cause death. Sound gave up names, especially those of friends. It co-opted silence as an eavesdropper; casual conversations heard were delivered to the state to murder. In time neighborhood kai-apple fences were urged into thicker and higher growth to shut out the dread-filled nation. But some of the lost, the unseen and unheard, cut tracks into Nyipir's sleep. They stared at him in silence until the day his disordered dreams stepped into daylight with him to become his life:

They had pointed a gun to his head.

Click, click, click.

He had fallen to the ground, slithered on his belly like a snake, hissed, and vomited, because he had forgotten how to talk.

Today.

Sweat on palms, heartbeat quickening, Nyipir swallows. A groan. Ajany hears a father's leaching anguish. She scratches an ache where it itches her skin, gropes inside-places as a tongue probing cavities does. Expecting to be stung.

Today.

The past's beckon is persistent.

From the air, Nyipir peers down at an expanding abyss. His country, his home, is ripping itself apart. Stillborn ballot revolution. These 2007 elections were supposed to be simple, the next small jump into a light-filled Kenyan future. Everything had instead disintegrated into a single, unending howl by the nation's unrequited dead. This country, this haunted ideal, all its poor, broken promises. Nyipir watches, armpits damp. A view of ground-lit smoke. Dry lips. His people had never set their nation on fire before.

On the ground, that night, in a furtive ceremony, beneath a half-moon, a chubby man will mutter an oath that will render him the president of a burning, dying country. The deed will add fuel to an already out-of-control national grieving.

Nyipir turns from the window.

He is flying home with his children.

Yet he is alone.

Memories are solitary ghosts.

He lets them in, traveling with them.

Downcountry.

December 12, 1963.

Lengees, a soldier, hoisted a red, black, green, and white flag up in a park. The flag collected sparks, and visions drifting like clouds. In that arena of spectacle, Nyipir Oganda had led a cavalcade, lugging a smaller red, black, green, and white flag while riding on a high-stepping black horse. He had shrieked as if expelling a fiend:

"Eyeeeeees left!"

Clop-clop-clop-clop. Hooves and blurring vision. Men on a podium, some who he thought had died. Two men he knew had pounded other men to death. Another had been detained for his own safety and been supplied with a stream of world literature and unlovely comfort women, one of whom he married. He had focused on one man—Tom Joseph Mboya, who had colored in the red, green, white, and black flag. He had, years before, scoured the landscape and found promising souls that he sent to America to study, experience, and then come back home with transcendent dreams. The Leader of the Nation had tilted his head at the tracker-policeman carrying the Kenya flag, a dark man on a black horse. In his sweaty palms, the flag had almost slipped as Nyipir had bellowed, "Eyeeeees front!" A mosaic people had cheered. Wanderers, cattlemen, camel herders, fishermen and hunters, dreamers, strangers, gatherers and farmers, trading nations, empire builders, and the forgetful. Such were the people for whom Nyipir had carried the new Kenya flag. There was also the anthem created from a Pokomo mother's lullaby:

Eh Mungu Nguvu Yetu
Ilete Baraka kwetu
Haki iwe ngao na mlinzi. . . .

O God of all creation, Bless this our land and nation, Justice be our shield and defender. . . .

Blended cultures, intoxicating fusion—the new, revised Kenya. Bead *kofia* on his head, cloaked, fly-whisk flicking, the Leader spoke. His voice was a bass drum. Glory! Goodness! Forgiveness! Education! Work hard! Nyipir had tended the fire-lit euphoria inside his body. *Harambee! Harambee!* A nation brought to task in a clarion call that had hauled steel across the land and built a railway. The national summons. Response—a howled *Eeehhhhhh!*

But then came the fear.

It split words into smaller and smaller fragments until words became secret, suffocating, and silent. No one cried when the voracious, frenzied seizing of lives began. A new word slithered into the landscape—*Nyakua*: plunder, possess. Entitled brigandage. But it was cleansed to mean "hard work." In the nation, slow horror, as if all had woken up to a vision of violating, crowing ghouls crowding their beds. Nyipir remembers how bodies started to stoop to contain the shame, the loss, the eclipse. Such eyes-turned-inward silences so that when bodies started showing up mutilated and truly dead, the loudest protests were created out of whispers. To protect new post-independence citizen children, like most new Kenya parents denying soul betrayals, Nyipir built illusions of another Kenya, shouting out the words of the national anthem when he could as if the volume alone would remove the rust eating into national hopes. Keeping mouths, ears, and eyes shut, parents had partitioned sorrow, purchased even more silence, and promised a "better future."

Plane drone, slight turbulence.

They bounce. "Better future." It is a groan in Nyipir's head. He rubs its tautness. His daughter is staring through the plane's window. Below, more greenhouses. Flower farms. Ol Donyo Keri—Mount Kenya, a sentinel that is a revelation.

Nyipir shouts, "The mountain!"

The pilot looks back.

"My son . . . uh . . . he likes . . ." Nyipir's voice cracks.

The pilot scans the horizon and swings the plane right to circumnavigate Mount Kenya. "Batian, Lenana, Macalder," he intones. The late-afternoon sun has colored the sparse snow crimson. Ajany squashes her face against the windowpane and feels their northward swing in her body. Soon the flamingos appear, on oyster-shell-colored water next to the milk-blue Anam Ka'alakol-Lake Turkana. The pilot says, "There's Lake Logipi." They know. This is their territory. Teleki's volcano, a brown bowl, windy landforms. They pass over Loiyangalani, toward Mount Kulal. Shift northeast, toward Kalacha Goda. They level over the salt flats fringing the Chalbi. Hurri Hills in the dusk light, and then, below, a wide unkempt stripe carved into the land. The plane flies through the layers of time, reveals the hollowed brown rock below from which Ajany and Odidi would survey the rustling march of desert locusts, dry golden-brown pastures where livestock browsed, and they would run after homemade kites, eat cactus berries, and curse one of the land's visiting winds, which had ripped the kites to shreds.

Wuoth Ogik.

Home.

Ajany crushes the screaming stuck inside her mouth, clutching a secret string and squashing it in her fist. First landing aborted. They veer upward. Ajany scrunches her eyes shut, grits her teeth, and prays they will stay suspended in space and lost to time. Second descent. She is anticipating the crash. The end. The plane evens out, crabs into a soft landing. Dust twirls on their tail.

———

There were outposts in the world where the sun's rays burned into lingering phantoms of the British Empire. Babu Paratpara Chaudhari was wiping the jar containing his teeth when through the sunlit door of his angry-green-colored store in a crowd of nine, he saw a Caucasian-looking man elevating a shiny object as he approached the shop. Babu always saw the Caucasians first. It was his way of connecting to an England he had imagined, loved, but never experienced directly. Willful journeying to and displacement in a foreign landscape had turned his Brahmin family into merchants. But clinging to sapless straws of caste, Babu Chaudhari had contented himself with assigning his geographical compatriots the place of the *panchamas* while he settled into amorphous, self-stranded being in a Not-England African space. Babu Chaudhari's father's father had set up supply shops through the Kenyan northern lands and then gone to Ethiopia. He lingers with the memory, wondering, as he often did, why he had not joined the rest of the family after they left East Africa for Rushey Mead, Leicester, England, in 1962. He had been left behind to sell the family shops, but when he reached this one, the seventh of seven, a customer and then five more had shown up. He had served each one, intending to close shop at the end of the day. To assure himself that he was only transiting, every January he handcrafted a recruitment notice for a shop manager, which he glued to the door: *Salary negotiable. Accommodation and food provided. Only Hindi, Urdu, or Gujarati speakers should apply with certificate of higher education.* He had not received one suitable applicant. Forty-six years later he was still in the same place.

A fly hovers over a sack of five-year-old turmeric.

"Shhh. Shhh." Babu urges the fly away.

He props up his chin.

Babu barely moved. Gout and gallstones. Glowering was his normal expression. It concealed disenchantment. Settling into his tubbiness, he noted the Caucasian man's carriage—it was proper, the way he felt English posture should be. He frowned at the double-strapped haversack the man carried, relented when he saw it was made of pebble-grain leather and not Chinese plastic. Expensive dark-green army-style cargo trousers, a beige jacket over a loose-fitting cream shirt, all of which, Babu knew, would become red and brown with dyelike dust by the end of that day. The large man was clean-shaven, broad-shouldered, finely muscled, with shaggy dark-gray-flecked hair plastering his forehead. Babu bet to himself that after five days the man would let his beard grow wild. As he waited for the man to speak, his eyes alive, Babu did a mental scan of goods to offload: expired Malariaquin, 1970s curries and spices. He would blend these and hint that the result healed tick fever. If he attached a mantra to the package and proposed that it be consumed while wild sage was being burned, he could imply that this ritual would reveal the image of God. Caucasians appreciated that kind of thing. It would also explain the cost.

Babu chewed on his gums, glared at an aged donkey. Its distressed braying afflicted his days and most of his nights.

Isaiah William Bolton slipped his suddenly dead cell phone into his pocket and strode into the shop, straightening out the creases on his coat, the result of a cramped flight in a four-seater that he suspected was a crop duster. He took in the sardines, garlic, pepper, and Cadbury's chocolate. A giggle behind him. He turned. Two kohl-eyed women looked back. One of them winked as a camel would—long lashes, slow, blink, blink. Isaiah gave a half-grin. This was definitely a world he could get to know.

"Shhh. Shhhh." Babu Chaudhari shooed flies and women away, his mouth downturned. Vile, this threat of tainting genealogies.

Babu Chaudhari's skin was blotched in most of the shades of brown now, but in his prime, he had been cherished for his blond-streaked hair, fair sunburning skin, and almost blue eyes. He was especially fond of his narrow nose—its stern symmetry. From the moment of his emergence from the womb with his golden curls, he had been a favored child, and an instantly desirable prize for families committed to blanching bloodlines.

The visitor speaks: "Afternoon. Could you please tell me how far it is to Kalacha Goda?"

Babu beamed. Definitely English. Dark English, but English nevertheless. "Wery far." A gnashing of gums.

"How far is *very*?"

"Wery, wery, wery far."

"How would I get there?"

"Fertainly not today, or ewen tomorrow."

"I see. Do you know where I might get a room for the night, then?"

"Yef."

"Where?"

"Here."

"Lovely. A single. How much?"

"For you, free fifty." He had doubled the room rate. To be fair, if the visitor had been American, he would have added another zero. Moreover, he was offering this man his best space—mostly insect-free, and reserved for "strictly vegetarians only."

Isaiah pulled out four hundred shillings, eyes transfixed by a jar behind Babu Chaudhari in which teeth were floating.

"No, no, no!" Babu said. "Fay tomorrow." He tilts his head. A coy smile appeared. He could not wait. "England?"

"Yes!"

"Goot. Goat fless fe queen. . . . Do you know Mr. Clark—a fentleman—and Mr. Harry, affofiate of fe Royal Feographical Fofiety, who if right now wif uf?"

"Er, don't think so."

"Tell me, man, fif frime minifter ve hawe . . ."

The visitor paused, laid aside political agnosticism, ignored what ethical orientations a second-tier public-school education had implanted in him, leaned over the counter, and for nearly an hour explained the rise and fall and rise and definite future fall of Gordon Brown.

"A Fcottish fentleman," Babu confided. "Not really Englif."

They shared a knowing and rather contented laugh as twilight crept in.

Outside murmurs. A woman hurled an epithet. Another cackled in response.

"Fey are not af far in fe fourney af ve are," Babu whispers.

"Who?" Isaiah asks.

"Fem. Feofle here. But ve accomfany fem. Carrot and ftick, carrot and ftick."

A donkey brayed, a cock crowed, a thin-voiced and distant muezzin called someone to prayer. Bewilderment engulfed Isaiah and flushed his skin. He had forgotten how far away from home he was.

Later, he would leave Babu's shop with a room for the night, three tins of corned beef, three cartons of milk, a SIM card, a small box of sixty tablets, shaving cream, two razors, a rusted pair of large scissors, two tins of condensed milk, a container of yellow curry with brown and black spices that would destroy parasites in food, water, and the soul, a small green bucket, and the hopeful news that if he did not mind riding with livestock destined for an abattoir, a lorry leaving the following evening was headed in the direction of Wuoth Ogik.

When Isaiah saw his roundish room with its doum-palm ceiling, a safari bed leaning too far to the left, two unlit kerosene lamps, a box-shaped dark-gray creature the size of a small cat fleeing at his approach and escaping through an invisible hole, and a shattered oval mirror above a rudimentary green plastic basin—the bathroom—he was seized by a certainty that he should not have left England.

"I'll be going to Kenya," Isaiah had told his mother, Selene, over two years ago, after an old book had reached him through the post. Its owner's name was etched in the blank page at the front, and a painted image nestled in its inner pages. Selene was at that time being carved up by an odious cancer. She had said nothing while huge tears tumbled down to stain her hospital gown. He canceled his travel plans.

Now here he was in Kenya.

Isaiah dreams that night of cold and gray: the sensation of skimming pinnacles of splendid corporate conquests, just before tumbling down and crashing into the earth, clutching pennies, residues of a big gamble lost. Cold and blue: textures of loss, of seeking and never finding. Abandonment. Cold and red: the color of grasping at air, of hoping to be found or chosen or wanted for more than a season, for more than what he owned. Cold and cracked: the impossible-to-reach broken parts of the soul. Cold and hard: rebuilding. But when he thought he had won again, irascible life currents drove him away and would not let him return, not even once.

Fog—amalgam of mistlike griefs. Fear—the state of being haunted, possessed by unrelenting uncertainties. He had thought to pierce the mists—discovered war zones—and became a voyeur with a camera, but whenever he surfaced for air, Isaiah ran. Streets, beaches, indifferent town marathons; running past finish lines, teeth bared, fists pumping, striving to elude disgrace's phantoms.

He dreams of his mother, her death, its horrid stillness. How, later, he and his stepfather, Raulfe, had taken her life-things and stored them in boxes, swept her closets and cupboards clean and sent her clothes to charity shops. Selene had bequeathed her remaining money and a wedding ring to Isaiah. She had left her other jewelry, letters, and novelty items to the care of Raulfe, who before Isaiah could react, had sealed them all in a safe deposit box, to be opened only after he was dead, and Isaiah had turned sixty.

Isaiah had confronted his stepfather: "Why?"

Raulfe had hobbled away, humming a broken version of "It Is Well with My Soul."

Inside Isaiah a barrage of feeling had exploded: Rage-Hurt-Defiance. Needing to get away, Isaiah chose to cross skyways to retrieve the first ghost he had ever known, and to find a way to bring it back home, where it belonged.

Still.

The fog—amalgam of mistlike griefs, and fear—the state of being haunted, possessed by unrelenting uncertainties.

2

SPARE PASTURES, EPHEMERAL WATERING HOLES. DUST-FILLED
cupules containing red, black, green, and white pebbles speckle the land;
unfinished sand games entice drifters to sit and play. Fresh dung tracks
on gold-flecked violet stones. They zigzag. Pilot, Nyipir, and Ajany, carrying Odidi between them, while Nyipir intones: *March, march, march,
left turn, march, march, halt.* The coffin edge digs into Ajany's right
shoulder. They stumble past two giant milkweed bushes with flamboyant fleshy leaves oozing white life. Beneath a knobby gold-green acacia,
they steady the coffin and lower it to the ground.

Weak-kneed, her hair matted, and unable to let go of tenuous contact, Ajany huddles down right there, studying the dust of home, the
progress of safari ants in an evening that stinks of wretchedness.

Nyipir Oganda looks down at his daughter before trundling away to
retrieve her travel bags. The pilot follows him, clasps and unclasps his
hands before saying, "*Mzee,* condolences. Sorry."

Nyipir nods. He hauls down orange and red luggage and nods at
the pilot over and over. And then Nyipir waits, a solitary form. Soon,
the plane taxies, wobbles, and then lurches skyward. The pilot circles
Wuoth Ogik, offers a lilt and waggle. Nyipir brings his hand up to his
forehead and returns the salute.

Five kilometers away, a slow-moving dust-devil giant lops over the land. Ten minutes later, the formerly green, now rust-colored family Land Rover, long in tooth and loud in rattle, bounds toward the waiting pair. Nyipir faces the car, not breathing. The Land Rover creaks to a stop and emits the smell of a burning clutch. Two people emerge: Galgalu, who had grafted himself onto the family before the children were born, and Nyipir Oganda's wife, Akai Lokorijom.

She flows like magma, every movement considered, as if it has come from the root of the world. Tall, willowy, wasp-waisted, her breasts still large and firm, she is made of and colored by the earth itself. Something ferocious peers out of dark-brown eyes, so that even her most tender glance scalds. Her voice, a bassoon-sounding, gravel-colored after-thought. At unpredictable moments, for nameless reasons, she might erupt with molten-rock fury, belching fire that damaged everything it encountered. Akai was as dark, difficult, and dangerous as one of those few mountains where God shows up, and just as mystifying.

When he sees Akai, Nyipir's hands pour sweat. Ajany's bags slip from his grip and tumble to the ground.

Galgalu, carrying a lit kerosene lamp behind Akai, lifts a hand to Nyipir in greeting, but Nyipir's eyes are fixed on the bald patches on Akai-ma's scalp where she has torn out her hair. Scratches and tear marks on her face. Blood cakes her body in thin strips. One of Nyipir's AK-47s, the four-kilogram 1952 with a wooden butt stock and hand guard, is strapped to her body, cradled in a green kanga with an aphorism written on it: *Udongo uwahi umaji*,"Work with wet clay."

Nyipir shambles toward his wife. He is preparing to steer away from echoes of a conversation that started one day in August 1998, after a distant-living coward detonated a bomb in Nairobi. He should have known it was a forewarning.

"My son!" Akai-ma had wailed at him then, while a BBC Radio news bulletin retold the story of an explosion in Nairobi. "I want my son."

"He's safe," Nyipir had answered.

Akai Lokorijom had said nothing. Disappeared, reappeared—Vaselined and fresh, with a small bag, ready for a journey.

"Now where're you going?" Nyipir had asked.

"To find my son."

Nyipir grunted, "I'll go."

He had started toward Nairobi, the city that had tried to kill him. He'd made it past shifting dunes into the North Horr airstrip when he bumped into Ali Dida Hada, who was also on his way to Nairobi, summoned to the Kenya National Police headquarters at Vigilance House.

"As if we don't have enough fools of our own," Ali Dida Hada griped, not commenting on Nyipir's sweat-bleeding body, his tremulous voice.

"He's my only son," explained Nyipir.

"I'll look."

"Akai would die . . ."

"I'll find him."

"Moses Ebewesit Odidi Oganda."

"I know him."

"She'll break if something has hurt him."

"I know."

A tacit admission of a situation that neither would acknowledge existed. "I'll look. I'll call you," said Ali Dida Hada.

They had parted.

They had not shaken hands.

Nyipir had changed directions, slunk off toward Maralal to monitor the news. Eight days later, with a crackle of the radio, Ali Dida Hada informed Nyipir that Odidi Oganda was safe, and contributing to the after-attack relief efforts. He also said Odidi was a successful Nairobi engineer servicing large contracts.

A pause. "You saw him?

"I did."

"What did he say?"

Silence.

Nyipir now inhales the orange sun, the dry grasslands, and the chirping of early-evening crickets, to escape, for even a second, the horror of the story he must repeat to a mother: the roiling country, the murdered son. The fire in Galgalu's kerosene lamp wavers. Nyipir circles the area, hurries to shield Akai from seeing the coffin.

Her mother. In Ajany, a concentration of absences from seven and a half years twinge in her heart like a torn string clanging lost music. She exhales and bounds over, an eager dog closing in on its mistress. Akai-ma pivots. Another direction. Ajany stops.

Nyipir stretches out his arms. "Akai." He starts his explanation.

Akai shoves him aside.

He stumbles.

She reaches the coffin. Wind hurls dust around, a pair of creamy butterflies. Silence. Soft voice. "Who is it?"

Nyipir enters the breach. "Our son. Odidi." He bows his head.

Akai asks, "Who is it?"

"Odidi."

"Who?"

"Akai . . ." pleads Nyipir.

"No!" she explodes.

She glares at them all, paces up and down a portion of the field, her arms thrown up and then down; then she returns and pinches Nyipir's arm, her eyes sly. "Where's my son?" She won't wait for his reply. She returns to the coffin, clutching her waist, scratching her left arm.

"Mama," Ajany calls.

Akai waves a hand at the noise. "Nyipir, where's my son?"

Nyipir's head swings left, right, left, right. "I tried everything, I tried," he croaks, hands gesturing upward. "Akai . . ."

"Nyipir! I told you, 'Bring my son home.' Didn't you hear me?"

Nyipir's hands move upward again. His mouth opens and closes. Saliva clings to his jaw.

"Nyipir—*where's my child?*" Akai's eyes bulge.

"M-mama?" stutters Ajany.

Akai points at the coffin. "Who?"

Galgalu moves closer. He props the lantern against the tree. Uses his whole arm to wipe tears off his face. He had known it would come to this. He had known.

Akai hobbles past. "Show. Me."

Galgalu unscrews the large bolts and opens the coffin lid.

No time. No space.

Akai-ma falls, arms stretched forward. She crawls, leans over Odidi's body, reaches in, takes it by the shoulders, holding him to her breast, keening in intermittent groans, lips on Odidi's forehead. She rocks her son, strokes his face, rocks her son. *Odidi*, she croons. *Odidi, wake up. Son. Listen. Ebewesit. I'm calling you.*

To name something is to bring it to life.

A churning heat, like heartburn with a rusty aftertaste, grows in Ajany's gullet. *Cry,* Ajany tells herself. An ugly jealousy, of wanting to be the dead one held by her mother, being invoked to life by such sounds. Shame. Akai's whimper. *Cry,* Ajany tells herself. Watches her brother limp in her mother's arms. *Live,* she commands Odidi. But her eyes are dry.

Akai-ma moans furiously. She batters the earth with one hand, while the other grips Odidi. *"Take me. Here, you thing, take me."* Akai holds Odidi with dust-stained hands as if he were just born. She adjusts his shirt, moves his headrest, and swabs invisible drops from his face. She holds him to her breast, her head resting on his. She hums, her voice large, deep, husky, and ancient. She stares at the sky, rubs her face with her son's hands. All of a sudden she looks over her shoulder and stares with intent at Nyipir.

Ajany flinches at what hurtles between them. Nyipir shakes his head, palms out. "Akai." A gray shadow descends around him. From his mouth, a whistling of deflation, and then his face is sunken and old.

Akai-ma turns again to rock Odidi, humming.

Nyipir lumbers toward her.

Ajany kneels, watching them.

Nyipir approaches; Akai lifts up her hands. She screeches, "Don't. Touch. Me. You. Don't. Touch . . ." She points at Nyipir. "Don't."

Nyipir stands still in the middle of an eternal landscape that seems to foreshadow the end of life.

Akai: coded prayers, unrepeatable curses.

Galgalu pleads with her. "Mama, mamama . . ." Akai looks through him.

Galgalu says, "Ma, give me the boy. I'll put him to sleep."

Akai places her head against Odidi's.

Connecting.

Galgalu kneels next to her, his face close to hers, her rifle floating in and out between them. Sticky wet of sorrow tears merging.

"Odidi?" Akai-ma purrs, easing her son, she imagines, into wakefulness.

It is more than an hour before Akai-ma lets Galgalu return Odidi's body to the coffin. She adjusts Odidi's shirt, strokes his sewn-shut eyes. "I can't see," she whispers to Galgalu when he seals the coffin's lid.

Galgalu places the lantern on top, a miniature beacon, then wipes its surface with his shawl and helps Akai up.

Ajany and Nyipir creep closer to her.

"M-mama," Ajany calls.

Akai-ma straightens up and blinks. "You?"

A cold stone inside Ajany's stomach flutters.

"Arabel Ajany," Akai-ma says. "Arabel Ajany." Her voice falters.

Ajany takes four steps toward Akai-ma, a history of longing in the movement. Akai's arms reach out. Ajany steps in, inhales Akai-ma's rancid, sad warmth. Incense, hope, and softness. Almost touching, almost disappearing into her mother. But then Akai shoves Ajany away. She drops her arms; her eyes dart left, up, and right. She groans, "Where's your brother?"

Ajany goes rigid.

Nyipir intervenes. "See, Akai, see, Ajany's home."

Akai-ma sucks air. "Why?" Childlike sound: "Where's Odidi?"

Ajany *not* thinking. Then thinking, *And me?* Thinking, *Where am I?* But before the ground dissolves under her, she throws herself at her mother, grabbing her back. *And me?* The feeling pushes at her mouth. She clings to Akai's neck, an unyielding hold. Mucus and saliva, blood and bitterness from a palate cut.

Akai recoils, tears herself away. Her eyes are thin slits, her nostrils flare, and when Ajany looks again, her mother is a still, steady point with a finger on a trigger and a smile on her face. *Click-clack.* Selector set to burst. Clear gaze. Gun pointed to heart, a glint from the barrel like light on a pathologist's scalpel. *Certainty.* Akai will pull the trigger if Ajany moves in her direction again.

Ajany drops to the ground.

She lies down flat.

Hands scrabble at the earth.

Mind focused and roaming around the barrel of a gun. She senses its position. Tenderness because her mother is at the other end. She hears Nyipir's soft chant. *Akai, Akai, Akai, Akai.* Feels the soft departing of day.

She could paint this. Could even paint the nothing, its sliver of warmth on her skin. Ajany sniffs the earth, dust flecks on her face. She twists her neck to glance at the purpling sky. Not trusting thought. Finding nothing to trust. In that moment, she stops waiting to be born. She is willing to re-enter her half-death, aches for fire that may return her to silence. She rests her head upon her arms and waits.

Shift of pressure, rush of air. Running feet, a question, and the distant slam of doors. Car engine revs, wheel squeal. Nyipir shouting—*Akaaai! Akaaai!*

Akai Lokorijom is leaving.

Ajany waits for her body to come together again, all those parts she had stopped feeling—hands, feet, face. She raises her head to see the lurching, stopping, starting, and stalling green car. She tells herself that she can also leave. She can also go away. And then she is in pursuit of a ramshackle family Land Rover. Behind her, Galgalu also runs. The car jolts ahead of them. Low-lying thornbush scrapes Ajany's feet, stinging. Galgalu overtakes Ajany. Ajany reaches for and drags him back, hanging to his right arm, fighting not to be left behind again, not thinking, she bites into his arm. Galgalu snatches his hand away; he snarls and tumbles. She falls over him. Ajany reaches for Galgalu's hand. She rubs off her saliva and tooth marks. On the coffin, the lantern's flame flickers.

Galgalu pats Ajany's back. *"Ch'uquliisa,"* he croons. *"Ch'uquliisa."* Grasping for clarity. *"Ch'uquliisa,"* Galgalu says, reading Ajany's soundless hiccups. He knows her voices. He had urged Ajany into life from Akai's womb, had sucked mucus out of tiny nostrils, and had understood her stupefied silence when she saw the world she had come to. Later, he had scooped her from beneath a tree where patient vultures watched over her. On that day he had told four-year-old Odidi, while he arranged Ajany in his arms, *"This* is your baby."

Raro Galgalu is an intermediary between fate and desire, a cartographer of unutterable realms. He has lost faith in tangible things. Now he scrutinizes the skies. The portents are cruel. A pale-orange veil shrouds the world. He recites *"La illaha illa 'lla Hu. La illaha illa 'lla Hu."*

Galgalu seeks the mind of his dead father. His father had been *ayyaantuu*—an astrologer, in Hargagbo. After a gruesome drought that he predicted would be the worst—it was—had passed, and a locust invasion he foretold would destroy all pasture had done so, rumors of sorcery slithered across the landscape and followed the family. Mad, the older Galgalu predicted his own death. His son Raro tried to pray him back to life in a season of almost white skies, while his mother sought refuge in herbs and hope. But one moonless night on the day after a total solar eclipse, Galgalu heard his father cough—a rattling sound.

Then Raro saw his father's shadow lift itself from the body on the mat, felt it brush against him as it glided out into the darkness.

"*Ch'uquliisa*," Galgalu sings to Ajany. "*Ch'uquliisa*."
His arms around her.

One wild afternoon, by decree of elders, Raro Galgalu was chosen as scapegoat for all clan guilt. He had been bringing home a kid that had sprained its leg. Its mother bleated behind him while men surged around him and inflicted the ritual curse. He tore at his heart, to pull out the malediction. The scars were curved lines across Galgalu's chest. The kid tumbled from his arms, and his goats cried as he was driven away with sticks, stones, dust, and dung. Driven by billows of unwantedness, he marked his progress by cairns in the daytime and falling stars at night. He wandered, a solitary, bowlegged creature intending to walk itself to death.

Until, that soft dusk of December 12, 1963, when, down in the city, a doleful officer unwrapped the last Union Jack that would ever soar over Kenya, Galgalu stumbled in front of a coral-hued edifice. Wuoth Ogik. A brown-and-black-patched cattle dog that had a lot of hyena in its ancestry had appeared and wagged its tail at him. Galgalu stroked its head. It licked his hand. He would learn that its name was Kulal, after the cherished mountain. By the time he saw the tall, dark, long-limbed spirit flowing toward him, its arms swinging in wide swoops, he was ready to die. *Ekhaara*. A roaming spirit. It carried a headrest and club—things men carried—and a gourd of sour milk, herbs, and grasses. Its feet were dusty in *akala* tire sandals. It had hitched its sarong up on its thighs. Its eyes took in everything. Raro Galgalu had closed his eyes.

Woitogoi! Akai Lokorijom exclaimed when she saw him.
She reached for him.
The dog whined.
Galgalu quivered.
Akai stroked his head. "*Woitogoi!* You're a bone, small boy!" She had clucked. "Your name?" She giggled.
He had wanted to laugh with her. Instead, he wailed, because he understood he might live after all.

Galgalu tells Ajany, "Always, she comes back home."

"We didn't catch her shadow," Ajany replies in between hiccups.

"No," he agrees.

When Ajany and Odidi were children, Galgalu would scoop the soil where their daylight shadows fell and cast the dirt into holes where dusk shadows gathered, so the departing sun would take with it any evil that had threatened them. Galgalu had tried to scrape the earth under Akai-ma's shadow, to try to exorcise those ghosts that made her wander. Ajany and Odidi had colluded with him by trying to make their mother stand still. They always failed. As long as there was sun, Akai jumped from place to place.

Footsteps.

Nyipir hobbles to join them, blinking at the track.

Speaking to Ajany: "Mama . . . she . . . um . . ." Nyipir's voice cracks. "She's happy you're here. Just . . ." He waves in the direction of the coffin.

Ajany nods.

He says, "I tried to . . . but Odidi . . . um."

Ajany nods again.

There is something unnamed and shameful about loneliness created out of rejection. Ajany takes refuge in stillness.

Nyipir says, "Once, when I was a boy, a leopard used to escort me home."

Galgalu and Ajany have heard the story before.

Nyipir continues: "A black leopard used to weave in and out of the shrubs, and his body contained all the nights of the earth. His eyes were made of stars."

"D-did he make a noise?" Ajany asks, as she did when she was ten years old and scared of night.

"Footsteps like silence. When I reached home, the leopard left." A brittle note. "Don't ever call out a leopard's name. Say *gini*, 'this thing,' or *gicha*, 'that thing.' *Kwach, no!*"

Kwach.

Ajany squelches the word on her tongue. The temptation to howl it hurtles around her skull. She presses down on the need, suffocates it with memory.

. . .

One evening, long ago, Nyipir had found Ajany sitting inside the broken courtyard fountain, waiting for him. She had asked, "Baba, did *gicha* come?"

"No. Not today," he replied.

Years later, after Ajany had left Wuoth Ogik and Kenya, she suddenly understood that Nyipir's stories about the black leopard's visits coincided with the seasons of Akai's disappearances.

Now.

Ajany says, "We forgot Odidi's flowers."

Nyipir answers, "Oh!"

Three people listen to four winds creeping through rattling doum palms. Winds cover the car's tracks, sprinkling dust over them. They race southward, to the part of the nation where unsettled ghosts have set the land afire and a gang of men are howling and dancing down a city street, dangling a man's cut-off head. The dead man's fingers, with their stained voter's mark, are scattered around his new blue bicycle, next to his national identity card.

3

TODAY IS THE DAY AFTER LAST NIGHT. THE SUN'S FIRST RAYS strike a mosaic on a covered courtyard to the left of a dried-up water fountain. Dry thunder in this pink morning. Ajany hears sporadic bird twitters interfering with a stillness that scowls like the broody spirit of Genesis. In the dust, skid marks. Footprints. Tire trails. Pathways. Watching over her big brother, listening, feeling that any second he will tell her what she needs to know, how she must move, where she is, and what she must do.

She had told yesterday's mortuary attendant, with his rotten-egg breath and the impatient light in his eyes—a condensation of lessons learned—*This is my brother.*

The man had answered, "*Hii ni kitendawili ya mungu.*"

God's riddle.

Ajany had retched. The attendant had poked her right shoulder. "*Wewe uliyempenda maishani yake utapenda pia kifo chake?*"—You who love his life, can you also love his death?

Blood flakes beneath her nostrils; Ajany's fingers twist her hair into thin braids. *This is my brother.* Today is the day after last night.

. . .

Her nose had started to bleed the moment she recognized Odidi's form. The heavyset pathologist, Dr. Mda, had after a minute pulled her aside and applied small portions of white cotton to her nose. "Lower your head." He had said, "Do you know what 'autopsy' means?" *Ontopsy*, Dr. Mda pronounced it, shifting vowels and consonants, introducing new sounds so that his cadence gave warmth to words and suggested uncomplicated worlds.

Ajany listened.

"'Ontopsy' means 'see for yourself.'" He cleaned her nose. "That's what we'll do."

Today, the day after last night. Ajany watches over her brother. She also draws lines on the earth. In order to see, she sketches.

In dust, an outline, a grooved, leaf-shaped scar. "Every crevice contains a story. Every story points north," Galgalu always says. Odidi repeated this to her when he was telling her how to find a way home.

The scar.

Odidi had fallen on his head. It had been her fault. Ajany was in Standard Six, being molded into a hockey-playing, ethical "future leader." Her tormentor, Ganda, who for the most part regarded her as unworthy of his bullying talent, had, while imitating Ajany's stutter, told his posse that people from northern Kenya could not climb trees because they had no trees to climb. As his acolytes cackled dutifully, Ajany's body moved of its own volition and shimmied to the top of the school's grandest mvule tree.

Easy to climb: feet into furrows, up, up, up, and the next time she looked down, her nemeses were minuscule punctuation marks below. The distance between high up, where she was, and down, where she ought to be, led to her decision to live the rest of her life in the tree.

Could have been an hour, could have been more. A chubby member of Ganda's gang who quietly idolized Odidi, then a rising rugby star, latched on to an excuse to speak to his hero, a need greater than loyalty to the gang. Scuffing his heels, he stood outside the Form One classroom, waiting for the bell to ring the end of the day's lessons.

He accosted Odidi, and garbled the news that Ajany was lost inside a very big tree.

Just as she was praying that it would be painless to turn into a branch, Ajany heard the sweetest voice on earth that day:

"Silly!" Odidi had called.

She wailed, "'Didi!"

Odidi reached her tree. "'Jany, come down. Are you Zaccheus?" Thinking that was especially funny, he screeched off-key, "*There was a man in Jericho called Zaccheus . . .*"

A torrent from Ajany: "G-ganda-said-Turkana-people-d-don't-climb-trees-and-th-then-I-climbed-and-then-he-left-and-th-then-I-was-afraid-and-th-then-you-came."

"Come down."

"Mppph."

"What, silly?"

"C-can't."

"*Whaat?*"

Louder. "Am stuck."

Odidi had bayed with laughter, rolling on the ground. A hyrax somewhere yowled, and in the distance another one answered. Ajany wept in gulps that should have dislodged her.

Odidi answered, "Ajany *yuak-yuak-yuak*."

Hiccups from within the tree.

"'Didi, am stuck." Ajany lisped.

"Try?" Odidi threw pebbles upward. An incentive.

Sobs.

Odidi hastened up the tree, no plan in mind. He got to Ajany, in the Y part of the tree, and sat next to her before hugging her. "Silly goat, I'm here."

And he was.

After a minute, Odidi said, "OK, sit on my back—I'll climb us down."

A slow, sweaty descent. Eight meters from the base of the tree, Odidi miscalculated distances and fell to the ground with Ajany on his back. Rolling to protect her, he had split his forehead in the process. Ajany had used her maroon school sweater to stem the blood flow before racing like a spooked gazelle to get the school nurse, praying *Hail-Mary-full-of-grace-The-Lord-is-with-you* so that *OurHolyMotherMary* would let her die in Odidi's place.

Today, the day after last night, begins with thunder but no rain. Last night three people raised a green tarpaulin over a casket in silence, surrounded it with incense and water, and, five meters away, lit a fire that would witness this death. Last night Ajany had stripped the bed of Odidi's blankets, carried down his pillow, lifted the coffin's lid to tuck her brother in. She had wrapped her body against the desert cold and known she would not fall asleep. She had waited for Odidi to tug on the fragment of string around her body and tell her what to do, when to haul him in.

And today he had appeared when her eyes were closed.

Leaden footsteps.

She turns.

Baba. Nyipir. Hollow-eyed, a new tilt to his body, as if he is fighting gravity. A stone sculpture melting. In its searching eyes, white terror.

Re-entering a ceaseless day.

Meaninglessness is ash in Nyipir's mouth. Swallowing saliva. Failing, falling, clutching at nothings. The compartments into which he parcels his life are broken and leaking. Swallowing, Nyipir stares at sunspots, the contained spaces occupied by pieces of light.

"Baba . . ." his daughter stammers.

He turns.

Father and daughter sit close to each other. Then Nyipir says, "I named him." She leans forward. "Your brother, *Ebewesit.* Akai's father—she expected that. *Oganda* so our name would outlive us."

They wait.

They watch the day walk across their feet. And then it is three hours later and Galgalu is adding tinder to a wake's fire made pale by daylight.

"We'll build a cairn," Nyipir suddenly says, rising and measuring the ground with his eyes. "Seven and a half meters across the base." He picks up black, white, and brown stones, squeezes them in his hands. "A stone garden." Dust strains through Nyipir's fist.

Behind them, a white-fungus-infested chunk of their coral house collapses. The house's water tank has tilted on its roost and yawned open; it is draining its contents through ceilings and down walls.

4

A CONVOLUTED SILENCE WARPS THE LANDSCAPE. NOTHING seems stable, not even the aged acacias. Nyipir Oganda lifts the hoe way above his head, and when it falls it bounces off the ground with a *thwack*! A pause. The sunspots look the same as always. What Nyipir had not considered was the hardness of the ground. Or the fragmenting of hearts during a father-son wrestling match, or the pain of pleading, "Stay. I'm sorry."

To protect new post-independence citizen children, parents like him repainted illusions of a "future Kenya," while shouting out words of the national anthem as if volume alone would re-create reality. *Nyakua*. Mouths, ears, and eyes shut, parents partitioned sorrow, purchased more silences and waited for the "better Kenya" to turn up.

Nyipir's daily covenants with silence had all of a sudden lost their weight. Today the voices of the dead-providing-their-own-witness take over his thoughts with a soundtrack—Babu Kabaselleh's "Lek Wuonda," to remind Nyipir that the dying started long ago. Before Pio, Tom, J.M., Argwings, before the red, black, green, and white flag fluttered one midnight in December.

Eeee . . . lek wuonda. Deceived by dreams.

Nyipir pounds metal to dust, listening helplessly.

Thwack! This is how to beat back seething phantoms.

Thwack! Bury engulfing blackness and its music.

Thwack! How to demand silence.

Aieee!

The usual breeze east of Badda Huri hums over the lava-sprinkled drylands of the Dida Galgalu Desert. Green and beige doum palms at the water point a kilometer away lean west, toward derelict Dida Gola.

Dust in his eyes, inward gaze. Inside Nyipir, secrets stir, and his mouth opens. *"Ona, icembe riugi ni rituhaga,"* he croaks. Witness from fifty-year-old burial grounds. *"Ona icembe riugi ni rituhaga."* Nyipir scrambles for silence. *Ona icembe riugi ni rituhaga*—repetitive, loud-speaking thoughts.

Ajany hears Nyipir. Listens for more. Galgalu hears Nyipir. Knows he is crying. He wanders away, making lines on the earth with his herding stick.

Stillness. Then Nyipir speaks. "A man I knew used to say *Ona icembe riugi ni rituhaga* before we dug the graves."

Ajany hears *"dug the graves."*

Nyipir spits.

He hacks at the ground. Nothing more to add. Glut of shadows. Shadows of phantoms.

What endures?

A disappearing mother, heaving silences, and the desire to vomit out anguish. Head throbs, fists clench and unclench. Ajany teeters on the edges of inside fog. Liquid slides down her lips. Nosebleed, small tears.

She flees.

Dashes into the dimly lit interior of their splintering pink house that at night becomes a sparkle-crackle of parts being chomped down by unseen termites.

———

Wuoth Ogik was once a sanctuary crammed with the music of range-land life: a father's hollow cough, herders' sibilant whistles, day handing over life to the night, a mother's sudden, haunted cry, a brother singing water songs to camels. *What endures?* A father sighing *Aiee!* Talk-ative shadows, crumbling walls, scent of dung and dream, reflections of long-ago clattering of polished Ajua stones falling into a brown wooden board of fourteen holes; the lives of cows, sheep, goats, and camels;

three mangy beige-and-black descendants of a fierce mongrel herding dog with a touch of hyena.

What endures?
    Elastic time.

Another junction. Brazil's Atlantic Ocean, São Salvador da Bahia de Todos os Santos. Five days ago, Ajany had been there, staring at a collage of deep-blue skies, fluffy clouds, and a spread-out view of the beige and frothing ocean. Pre-Christmas exhilaration sprinkled with the beat of a mild pulse of terror attached to dread, of waiting and stillness. She had tried to phone Odidi. She had also been waiting for others, the law keepers, to come for her, had expected up to the end, before the plane strained for high skies, to be stopped and caught. She had expected all these others to reach her first, but instead Nyipir had phoned from Kenya.

"B-baba." Afraid he knew what she had just done.

But he had whispered, "Odidi's gone."

At first she had deleted what she thought she had heard. Did not ask what *gone* meant. Listened when Baba had said, "Come home, *nyara.*" He added, "Come home. Please?" His voice had been low and aged.

She had left Bahia with an orange suitcase and red carry-on half full of mismatched clothes, assorted art supplies, two passports, and three credit cards. A red cell phone and the amethyst necklace she always wore. She had thrown her black MacBook with the tomes of commercial art, her living, into a red shoulder bag and fled.

Also.

In the loneliness of the eastern corner of her all-white, big-windowed room, a space set apart, perched on a black stand sits a half-shaped clay face resting on a plaster skull. White rubber stick tissue-depth markers cut to different lengths, glued in twelve points of the face; the other nine had been removed. The nose and mouth, shaped and reshaped and taken apart over seven years, were half done and gaped in anticipation of a conclusion. The piece's eye orbits had worn and discarded all colors of mannequin eyes. Thin strips of clay connected the white pegs on the face and across the cranium. The lattice spaces had been filled and refilled with clay, everything reconstructed from the dark-lit memory of a skeleton and its last-breath gesture. The form had journeyed with her for seven years, traversed the Americas wrapped in brown paper, waiting for dimensions, nuances, completion, and a name. She had considered it. Stroked the plaster on the unfinished face, the undone muscles. Arabel Ajany had not looked at it when she left.

All departures are layered. Hers was accompanied by fingers of silence on the lips of at least ninety ghosts. Arrivals. Touchdown at Jomo Kenyatta International Airport against a dawn cliché of a postcard Nairobi sunrise, acacia-in-the-morning scene, the sky red, mauve. An exact sensation of life wafted around the passengers. Kaleidoscope flavors, earth scents, for her a tumble of memories. A mother's hand sprinkling mixed herbs into water-keeping sheepskin vessels, spicing hair with ghee, cedar body-washes with desiccated acacia bark and leleshwa leaves. A childhood written in aromas.

At the customs unit, steps toward a queue designated for East African citizens, Ajany was of Kenya again. A dour-looking teak-toned officer with cheap green cuff links on his shirtsleeves stamped the inside page of her blue passport. *Thump.* "You missed the vote." He was gruff. *"Karibu nyumbani."*

Baggage hall, and a circuitous trolley roll. A glance at the waiting people. And then, in front of her, out of place because he was so detached, so elegant and tall, was Baba, who stood where the outside world separated itself from the inside mêlée. She remembers the warm light, the clouds that caught the edge of her left eye, the smell of rained-upon earth mingling with smoke and age and dust and sun and cows on her father's coat. She remembers her head on his shoulder and tears that would not stop. She remembers Baba murmuring, "Ah, *nyathina!* Ah, *nyathina!*" She remembers being safe, and the rhythm of his hands patting her back, a rumbling voice calling her his own.

Arms linked, they had traveled the road from airport to morgue in Leonard's yellow taxi, in silence. Baba watched the road, the vein on the side of his head pulsing. Traffic nervy, bumper-to-bumper. Red brake lights spilled onto the wet road, like escaping blood. Whispery breeze. Above, low-hanging telephone wires swung to, fro, to, fro, tar-paint pole to tar-paint pole. Along the road, leftovers of last month's jacaranda season, the green grass brown-tipped from too-short rains. Next to a lamppost, a purple-pink bougainvillea had wrapped itself around a twisted croton tree. Billboarded faces of presidential candidates and corporate

marketers stained the land; messianic promises on smiley faces, salvation products in shiny packages.

Leonard had turned knobs to increase the radio volume.

They heard a menu of vote counts, rumors, accusations, tallying-hall
disruptions, and even more fantastic numbers. The rest of the world did
not exist. The car swung left, swooped right across an uneven road, and
stopped at a gate of peeling yellow-green paint with a coat of arms. It
read *Nairobi City Mortuary*.

What endures?
    Surprise.
    It is also a question mark.

Now, in the wide-spaced rooms of home, Ajany lunges from spot to spot,
tugging at filaments she can feel, urging Odidi in. *See.*

The room she wanders through has wood shutters that do not close
and is infused with the smell of dung, salt, milk, smoke, herbs, and ghee.
Ajany stumbles over a fourteen-holed Ajua board on the floor, moves
it aside with her feet. On the mantelpiece, two black-and-white photographs, one showing a man on horseback carrying a crooked Kenyan
flag—her father, Nyipir Oganda—the other, in a Sellotaped frame, featuring a broad-faced man, the late minister for economic planning, planner of a pre-independence mass airlift, designer of the national flag, the
murdered Mr. Tom Mboya. Near these, a fading color studio-portrait of
a well-dressed Oganda family, including Galgalu, arranged as if facing a
firing squad.

Beside the photographs, a large seashell with orange lips. Ajany lifts it
up, remembering its weight, the magic of listening to beckoning oceans.
Raises it to her ear. Hears Odidi: *'Jany, you can hear the sound of Far Away.*
She returns the shell to its grimy place. A creak. Ajany looks over her
shoulder. Memory echoes of family feet on stained acacia wood, white-
stoned floors of flaking varnish and gnarled planks. Another framed
picture. Ajany touches the toothless grinning face of Odidi-Eight-Years-
Old. She leans forward and rests her face against the glass. Tightening of
chest as she chokes in all the undone yesterdays. This shade of longing
has a venomous sting: it poisons breath, stretches out time.

Work hard. Study.

Ajany turns to look into the hearth. *Work hard. Study.* Nyipir always tried to be home so that when his children returned from school for the holidays they would find him there. Sometimes he would meet their erratic bus and they would all ride back to Wuoth Ogik in the then-green family Land Rover.

His questions were immediate: *What did you learn?* Odidi told him about rock art, Mozart, Aztecs, and the industrial revolution.

Did you learn about Burma? Nyipir asked every time

Odidi would say, "Not yet."

Odidi. Always one of the top five in his class.

Work hard. Study.

Ajany languished at the bottom, changing places between number twenty-one and number twenty-three in a class of twenty-four.

Until one Christmas holiday when Ajany was eleven and a bit, and had found a new way of speaking what clamored inside her. She drew shapes, forms, and creatures from the space around which the image would be born. Canvas, paper, earth. A yield of unsought rewards: applause from a school she hated, the first prize in the national art show, number seventeen in the class of twenty-four, and the sense that what she felt was what it was like to be born at last.

Her large eyes shone all the way to Wuoth Ogik that December.

She talked and talked all the way to Kalacha.

At the house, she unwrapped her three winning canvases for her parents to see and praise.

Akai-ma and Nyipir saw panels of techno-caricatures of ghosts, the black leopard, and fire makers. They saw the stories as they would see secret nightmares. In the faces and patterns their daughter had conjured, her parents recognized their enemies and some of the devils that haunted them.

At first, there was silence. Then Nyipir had reared back, hands fisted, and he roared, "What's this?" Bulging eyes filled with terror that in Akai-ma's eyes showed itself as sad emptiness. They had glowered at Ajany, as if accusing her of something.

Akai-ma had turned to Odidi. "Go find Galgalu. Take This One with you."

Odidi had rushed Ajany out of the room, leaving her work behind them.

They had run and run. They had made for the rocks where they could look down at the world passing by, where they could sit silent and unseen. Ajany squeezed Odidi's right hand, cutting off its blood supply. She bit hard into her tongue until its blood filled her mouth. Some of the blood seeped out of her mouth; some of the blood she swallowed. And when Odidi saw what she had done to herself, he started to cry. It was the first time she had seen him cry, and the feeling was the worst pain she had ever known in her life.

"See," she lisped, opening her mouth, "Ahh ohhkeh." *I'm OK.*

Below them, the world eased by.

Later that night, after being force-fed by Galgalu, Ajany sat on her bed and waited for the house to become still. She then skulked down the stairs and found the embers of her work in the hearth. The heat evaporated Ajany's tears.

Nothing was ever said about her artwork again. But when Odidi and Ajany returned to school in the middle of January, once they were inside the school gates, Odidi said, "'Jany, you'll paint."

She had stared at the soil.

Odidi shook her. "You must paint."

She had shaken her head.

Odidi pinched her jaw, lifting her face, his eyes deep and clear. He said, "I say you paint, silly, or I take you back to your tree now."

"Can't."

"Can."

"Don't know how to start."

"Try."

"Everything burned."

"Silly, paint a river out of Wuoth Ogik. Then paint an ocean and a ship, and inside the ship, me and you going Far Away."

Ajany had turned and run into the art studio, retrieved last term's unfinished canvases and hardened paint. She could already hear the sound of ocean waves, and inside the waves, she saw the color yellow-white screaming at the color indigo blue.

Now.

Ajany pushes away from the hearth. Racing away from old words, and from the waning memory of the actual pitch of a brother's voice.

A small corridor leads into the narrow kitchen, which opened into a womblike alcove.

Memory maps within an old house.

Details.

Details help with forgetting.

Here was a long-drop toilet with its shower that was open to the elements and also used by bird-sized moths. There, to the left, a gate swung out to uneven stone trails that stopped where food used to be cooked on open fires fueled by livestock dung, paraffin, and desert kindling. Vestiges of numerous herbs and spices and a row of smoked, drying, putrefying flesh. Fodder for so many journeys.

The shelves are empty now.

There, Akai had slaughtered goats, sheep, lambs, cows with the precision of a dispassionate executioner. Cool. Contemptuous of Ajany's penchant for sliding into a mourner's crouch at the sound of a victim's pathetic bleating, the memories of which Ajany would regret as she chomped on and chewed up soft, spiced meat chunks.

No blue fires today.

To the right, a nine-step stone stairway splits into two at the top, separating bedrooms from two windowless bathroom toilets.

Next door, the library-study, a family room with functional furniture, a huge, frayed brown couch, a long oval table of dark wood and hard metal extensions with grooved chinks that held homemade beeswax candles that extended and sometimes replaced the night kerosene lamps' orange light. Memories of long, flickering shadows pouring out of nooks, seduced by naked firelights. A rough shelf laden with the weight of Someone Else's Baudelaire, George Sand, Charles Dickens, the Brontës, Carle Vernet, Flaubert, encyclopedia, and books on engineering, empire, and agriculture. Books on flowers, trees, birds, animals, and hunting. Jack London's *Call of the Wild*. One black-leather-covered Holy Bible. Ajany can select a book and name it by smell alone.

Musty-earthy: *The Flowers of Kenya*.

Fingers run across book spines.

Tactile familiarity.

A gap, an uneven bump; the rhythm is off.

Some books are missing. She looks. Crusty clove and fecund green smells: the engineering and agriculture books—Odidi's preferences. Ajany pulls out a large gray *History of Art* and turns to the first blank page. There "Hugh Bolton" has scrawled his name in semi-cursive script. Most of the books had once belonged to Hugh Bolton. Odidi had nicknamed Hugh Bolton "Someone Else." "Whose books are these?" Odidi asked his parents one day. Akai-ma had snarled, "Someone else's."

Someone Else. As Ajany's hand hovers over the book, her mind replays a humid evening when the family sat in this room. In the armchair, Baba gripped the edges of the Dhouay-Rheims Bible as his lips moved, spelling out words letter by letter, unease furrowing his face, as if he were memorizing a damning verdict in an alien language.

It had been a good time for Ajany to show off her improved reading skills. Drawing in breath, she spelled out: "H-U-G-H, Hugg, Huff . . . Baba, what's a Hug-g B-Bolton?"

Nyipir's head had almost jumped out of his neck. In one move, he dropped the Bible, surged up, strode over, and snatched the book from Ajany's hands, snapping it shut. In a shredding tone he said, "Brush your teeth. Go to sleep. It's late. You, too, Odidi."

Ajany had run out of the room, down the steps, and into the living room and thrown herself behind a settee. Odidi found her there. He crawled in next to her, let her weep into his shoulder. "I c-can't never get the spellings right," she mourned.

Odidi had said, "'Jany, 'Jany, don't cry."

She had wept until she fell asleep in her brother's arms.

Now.

Ajany rustles book pages, sitting cross-legged between a gramophone and a Lamu chest, next to which lie three elephant tusks and moth-eaten sheepskin rugs. In the room, four *lesos* in a heap, a curved horn on which fat white cows with slanted eyes are painted in brown, gold, and white, Ethiopian Orthodox art, wood etchings, and landscape watercolors. A twenty-by-forty-centimeter painting titled *The Last of the Quaggas.* On the eastern wall, a still-flaking depiction of a green robed Saint George conversing with a resigned gold-sashed, golden-fire-sworded Archangel Uriel with only a quarter of his grandeur intact, victim of the brown dirt trails of termite nests.

A creak and grumble from one of two massive water tanks sitting on platforms and posts inside the roof. They had leaked for years, creating a grooved, reliable wide tear line that sustained the life of small things. Ajany disturbs a small cloud of insects as she wanders out. She falters outside Odidi's room.

Odidi.

Crossing time, she trudges in, looks around, glimpsing shadows of brother that slice into her heart, her stomach. No tears. Ajany sits on Odidi's low acacia-wood bed, rearranging its grimy, thin floral cover. Dust of spaces. In the wall recesses that served as his cupboard, emptiness. Ajany folds herself into his old bed and curls into a ball, hands clinging to feet, as she remembers the things that make a brother: Voice. Deep-seeing eyes. His music—old fashioned Afro-rumba. Franklin Boukaka, Fundi Konde, Mzee Ngala. Addiction to water songs—a liturgy of flowing, bubbliness. Even the camels listened to him. Rock-drill laughter, excavating terror; salt in soup; no sugar in tea made from rangeland herbs. Sign of the cross before converting a try—Shifta the Winger's trademark. Soaring out of bed to meet the sun, shaking his sister awake and making her join him in watching sunspots grow and grow. Whistling. Odidi lying on warmed-up stones to witness the evening's departure. Large arms—wings, really—that engulfed fear. Words suggesting Obarogo and then vanquishing the bogeyman in the same breath. Heartbeats. *This is my brother.* And then, in dreams, she has returned to Wuoth Ogik and Odidi is shouting from *akwap a emoit*—the land of antagonists—that she hurry to watch the advent of a moonlit indigo night.

The Kalacha dusk will soon descend in colors borrowed from another country's autumn. Cattle will low their way home, bells clanging; white Galla goat kids in the *boma* will raise a chorus in answer to Galgalu's whistling. Barking herd dogs; bleating fat-tailed, black-faced sheep. Nyipir will watch his animals return, greeting them by name, observing marks, bumps, limps, and moods. He will stroke the head and trained, curved horns of his elegant red dance-ox. When she wakes up, hours later, after remembering where she is, Ajany will join Galgalu in the milking shed.

What endures?

Heat of fresh milk.

A kid butts Ajany's leg. She shoos it away.

What endures?

Galgalu.

What endures?
Fear of lunacy.
But not if she dies first.
Ajany glances at Odidi's coffin.
Nightfall endures.

And when, later, flames sputter inside Galgalu's cracked hurricane lamp, an orange glow appears, the same as that which had assured two desert children that light confounds darkness. That is how they wait for Akai-ma to return home.

5

THE NEW DAY'S MORNING LIGHT DRIPS AND ENGRAVES HUMPS into surfaces. Nyipir stares at his gnarled hands, hands that scrub his face four times a day, and have done so for forty years. Galgalu leaves to pasture the ranch animals. Enshrouding the land a mantle of silence that is vast, feral, and resplendent under naked blue skies in a season that is drier than a dead chameleon's hide. The stillness is interspersed with the buzz-drone of blue flies.

Nyipir now wipes the coffin lid until it shines, and he greets his son: "You look well." Slurred words. Nyipir imagines his son's rock crypt. "I'll build you a home big and strong . . . as you are." New lines on his face: "You're safe now."

When he lifts the hoe to dig, old scars tingle in his hands, burning a silent man from the inside out. Nyipir hits the ground to the tune of one-word thoughts: *Akai!* Her name is a snuffle. And then it is noon, and her name—*Akai*—is a hard, salt tear ball stuck in the back of Nyipir's throat.

———

Within that day, sporadic howls, and Galgalu crashes into the courtyard without the livestock. A jarring *"Wo d'abeela, halale . . ."*

An elderly keeper of ritual turned necromancer, a *d'abeela*, had turned his turban on him—a death curse. Galgalu flings the rusty G3 rifle to the ground, and turns to see if the rabid elder has followed him.

"What? Where?" Nyipir wields the hoe, fight-ready, thinking of his buried arsenal inside the cattle *boma*, of how to reach it, how to distribute arms.

Ajany runs into view. Galgalu stretches out his right thumb to squeeze his tears. He blows his nose with his other hand; the sounds are interrupted by his muddled words: *"Aya! D'abeela . . . wo d'abeela. . . ."*

"Who?" Nyipir shouts.

This is what had happened:

All had been well at the western pastures when Galgalu had blown air into his cupped hands—a whistling—*fuulido*—to summon a bird, a white, long-tailed honeyguide. It appeared. He followed it. As he scrambled through the scrub, he heard bees buzzing. He was reaching for the honeycomb when he heard a piercing cry, thought it was an eagle, and swung around to look. There, standing behind him, was a *d'abeela*.

The disenchanted priest had been prowling the land looking for people upon whom he would incant malice and whom he could afflict with the miserable bile that broiled in his soul. God had abandoned him. He would show God that he was not too old to taint favored souls. Too old! All his five sons had participated in the decision to replace him, as if he were already dead. So he had escaped the boundaries of his vast home, wandered farther, and turned his stiff white turban so its seams were at the front rather than on the left, where they should always be. The gesture was the ritual, the performed curse. So fearful that not even the dying named it, so rare, it had not been seen in five generations. So potent, nothing existed that could halt its malevolent intention. The *d'abeela* had happened upon a honey-seeking fool.

Incessant flies buzz. Kites soar. Ajany's eyes fixate on Galgalu's fallen rifle. "Where are the animals?" she murmurs.

"The animals?" Nyipir repeats to Galgalu.

Galgalu uses his chin to point westward.

Nyipir shouts to Ajany, "Bring your gun."

"Where is it?" Her heart is screaming.

"Galgalu's room."

She pivots, runs toward the adobe hut.

Inside the three-roomed shelter with assorted pictures papering the wall, a sepia photo of Akai-ma, and a Sellotaped copy of the Oganda family photograph, an Ethiopian calendar featuring Orthodox saints, three folding chairs, a slightly raised bed. This had been one of Ajany's childhood sanctuaries. Here she could hide from everything and Galgalu would pretend not to know where she was.

Ajany now crawls under the bed, looks around, retrieves a rifle stored in a broken wooden box.

Baba had called her aside on the day she turned thirteen. "Choose one," he had said.

She had looked at the weaponry. "Which one?"

"The one you like."

She had chosen the prettiest one, an AK-47 with a Type 4B receiver. Baba weighed the rifle, winked at her, and handed it to her. "Now you're ready for your wars."

Ajany had spent three school holidays taking the rifle apart according to the lessons Baba had condensed for her.

Depress magazine catch. Remove magazine. Pull charge handle to rear. Is chamber empty? Press forward retainer button at rear of cover to remove it. Spring assembly forward. Lift, withdraw out of bolt carrier. Pull carrier assembly all the way to rear. Pull away. Push bolt, rotate bolt to clear raceway, pull forward and free. Click, click, and click.

Shooting lessons. Baba taught her how to aim and not move her shoulder back when a cartridge fired.

She lifts the rifle to her shoulder.

Afterward, Odidi had taken over the lessons. She remembers his hands on her shoulders, leveling her. Looking through the sights, she sees his body in the morgue. A bullet's trajectory, and an incomplete statement: *Cause of Death.*

Ajany returns the gun to its hiding place, then races out of the hut, her body damp, mind whirling, and hands trembling.

The ranch gate swings wide.

Baba's gone.

Galgalu the honey seeker sobs in a crouch. Because his soul has been profaned, because when he first saw the *d'abeela* he thought his father had returned to accuse him of all he had not done.

Ajany hunkers down next to him.

Galgalu's horrified eyes—life's layers shorn off.

She touches his shoulders, lifts the amethyst necklace from her neck, and slips it over his head. She touches the stone. Galgalu's fingers close around it. Then, head on knee, Ajany listens to the land. They wait.

In the dusk of that bad day, Isaiah William Bolton arrived with a dust devil under the guardianship of a red-orange sunset that colored the twisted acacia tortilis gold. He showed up on the trail of nonstop weaverbird song, his athletic build drooped, and he reeked of fresh leather, cow dung, cow sweat, and cow saliva. He was unshaven and mottled. His haversack was stained, and his boots were red with dust. He had wrapped his jacket around his head: sun protection. Gray-edged curls were plastered on his forehead, and his lips were caked with white. He had croaked a call, "Is this Wot Ogyek?"

At the horizon, a train of camels, a line of sedate movement. Burbling of water, a brook's language.

Passages.

A scorpion crosses Isaiah's path from left to right, changes its mind, and heads for Isaiah's foot. Isaiah jumps backward. *Ultima Thule,* he thinks. Totters. Tries again, "Er . . . hello, I'm here for Mr. Moses Ebewesit Odidi Oganda."

Returning from the *boma* where he has secured the animals, Nyipir hears the precise pronunciation of Odidi's name. He wipes his hands on his shirt, picks up his herding stick, and crosses the space, his right hand outstretched in greeting. Ajany, who is leaning against Odidi's coffin, listens in.

A voice rumbles, "Afternoon!" With his hand out: "Isaiah William Bolton. I do apologize for showing up like this." He clasps Nyipir's hand, frowns. "Are you Moses?" He had imagined Moses Oganda to be much younger.

Nyipir stiffens, pulls his hand away, and takes a step backward, then another. He lifts and clings to his herding stick, plants it between them, and demands, "Your name?"

"Isaiah. Isaiah Bolton."

Two steps back. "Who?"

Slowly, "Bolton."

Nyipir's side wind. "Bolton?"

"Yes."

Ajany leaps up just as Nyipir zigzags away. "We can't help you," he shouts. He bumps into Ajany on his way to anywhere else, camouflaging his flight. "The camels." He hesitates. "That man . . . there's nothing here for him. Tell him to go away."

Ajany approaches Isaiah, shading her eyes.

The light of the land emphasizes the jagged outline of his face, prominent jaw, symmetry of bones, shape of hazel-tinted eyes, and broad forehead. Gray-and-black hair flecks on powerful arms. He does not look like one who had come hunting for meaning among large East African creatures, nor does he have the messianic glint-in-eyes of "Love Africa" types. Does his haversack contain a problem—the "Mission Statement"? Was he a borehole builder? A poverty eradicator? Yet his look was desolate and distant, with a slight twist of distaste around his mouth. As if he would rather be elsewhere. Enshrouded in the mood of that day, she wants to paint him: movement of space around and about him, presence, hard restlessness, shades of sadness. The man and Odidi share height, broad-chested, muscled, towering maleness framed by a hauteur that is detached from and laughing at the world. Ajany squelches a fleeting urge to tug at the stranger's face muscles. An old habit: it is how she built her knowledge of the shape and texture of faces, which she used to color in shadows that were the frame of a half-finished sculpture now abandoned in her Brazilian studio.

Annoyance.

Ajany chews on her fingernail. *What face was she cursed to seek and never find?* A breeze. She sniffed at the odour of stale cow emanating from the man and scowled. *What did he want?*

The wind tosses dust around.

Isaiah swats an armada of flies with big, impatient hands, flapping them like bat wings. He slaps dead some that had landed on his mouth. His mouth bleeds. Ajany's lips tremble on an almost laugh.

Isaiah hunches. He wipes his forehead. *This woman's stillness perturbs,* he thinks. And the afternoon of this land is much too hot, much too orange. And his thirst has reached such depths of concentrated anguish that even his eyelids ache. *Who is she?* Smallish, curved in the right places, barefoot, dust on shins and ankles, good legs. But under her scrutiny, he feels like a new and sentient specimen. He finds her gaze, an effort, and is transfixed by large, slanted, oval-shaped eyes from which wary questions spark. Hers is one of those faces made to be glimpsed through darkened windows on eerie stormy nights. She's looking into his soul.

Inner shutters come down. He blinks and gestures. "What d-do you want?" he hears her ask, notes her stutter.

Isaiah lifts the coat from his head, noticing the part of the sleeve torn by a wait-a-bit bush. Isaiah picks at the thorns. A low-pitched rasp: "Did I offend him?" He shifts. "Unintentional. Really sorry." Heat-tender skin. He needs to sit. Needs to sleep. Needs a pond to drink down. Had walked more than seventy kilometers. Had underestimated what "near Wuoth Ogik" meant.

He asks Ajany, "Am I at Wot Ogyek?"

"Wuoth Ogik," Ajany corrects. "Who's asking?"

"Isaiah William Bolton. Moses is expecting me."

Rattle of secrets.

A name—*Bolton*. One of the many faces of the Gerasene demoniac, icon of the living dead. With tightness in her chest, Ajany will try to hasten Isaiah's departure. "Moses isn't here."

"What? Oh dear!" Isaiah exhales, wipes his forehead again. "Where is he?"

She says, "You must leave. Before dark."

A crack in his voice. "*Uh* . . . no, please. Water? Please." His eyes are dark with panic. "Please?" Softer-voiced.

Ajany hesitates before aiming for the water pump.

Isaiah walks a few steps behind her, stuffs his jacket into the haversack, and sniffs at the whiff of decay around the decrepit courtyard. Stomach rumble. He had shared three tins of truly awful corned beef and fermenting milk on the lorry, and left behind scissors, a shaving kit, and the remains of his expensive cell phone, which had tumbled out of his pocket and been lost between the hooves of thirty-five humped cattle. He had downed condensed milk on his long walk to Wuoth Ogik, while inside his bag some yellow curry powder and spices moldered. And all the time he traversed the arid district he hallucinated water, pure water, stream water, tap water, rainwater, bottled water, Evian water. Any water.

Ajany now draws water with a calabash. Isaiah licks his dry lips. She offers him the bowl and he quaffs down its contents.

"*Ahh!*" He groans. He can now hear cadences of winds, endlessness of space, changelessness. Infinitesimal beingness. He had never heard anything like this wind before.

The woman says, "Now you can leave."

He asks, "Where's Moses?"

"You must go."

"Where's Moses?"

"Gone."

"Where?"

Her intense gaze, craters inside her eyes. She could be half wraith.

She says, "Leave before dark." A tinge of threat.

Despair in spite of himself: "I've come such a long way." He touches her forearm. "Please."

When she lifts her eyes to meet his, he finds the details he had missed before: redness of eyes, puffy, damp face, the thick aura of sadness, an edge as if she did not give a damn.

"You friends?" she asks.

A whisper, "Friends?"

"Moses?"

"We've been in touch for a while." He hands over the calabash. "Shared interest in my father, Hugh Bolton . . . and"—an expansive hand gesture—"Wot Ogyek."

"Wuoth Ogik." Her hands flutter.

"Moses said I would find what I needed here." Isaiah rests his hands over his chest. "Here I am. To see Moses." A pause. He leans forward. "I've been looking for my father for a long, long time."

A migrating bird's glissando—they angle their heads at the same time to listen. Ajany hesitates. And then she moves her body the better to point out a coffin resting under a green tarpaulin. Isaiah follows her look.

He will forever remember the texture of the wind at that moment, how it was a witness. He will remember how he stopped breathing. He will remember the flavor of sorrow blended with fear against the backdrop of pale bonsai thornbushes, sand, a doum-palm tree, Bayonet aloes, cacti, fleshy giant milkweed, myriad acacia sentinels rooted in loam, sand, and lava. He will remember that the singing bird stopped mid-reprise.

Incense drifting.

By the time he was touching the coffin, all color had drained from his face. He knew better than to speak.

He is bending over the box, hand on lid, lines written into his face. Time shifts, a chain of moments leading him across thresholds. An intrusive urge moves his hand. He watches himself raise the coffin's lid to look. *Moses*. A stiff, graying clay man, stained cotton in his nostrils, an olive safari-suit collar beneath a yellow-and-red blanket that covers him as if he were merely asleep. Last mood recorded in eyebrows that point in different directions; the left one, slightly raised, conveys last-second amusement. A man about his age.

He lowers the lid, not able to look at Ajany.

An impatient long-bodied creature whirrs between them.

A loud thought: "What do I do now?"

Ajany shrugs her *Don't know, don't care*. Her head throbs. Nose aches. *Bleeding?* Wanting relief from persistent and invading ghouls, she looks above Isaiah's head, registers the place of red caves and labyrinthine secrets. Drained, she stutters, "You leave b-before it gets dark. Not safe here." She hugs her body.

"You are Moses's . . . ?" Isaiah tugs at his brows.

"Sister." She anticipates his next question. "Arabel Ajany Oganda. I'll point a way to the next town." The insect departs.

"Moses wrote to me. Told me to come to Wot Ogyek." Isaiah moves close to Ajany.

Ajany looks back at her brother's box.

Isaiah touches her wrist. "Sorry."

Ajany lowers her hands, her armpits drenched, wanting a dark hiding place where she can bleed unseen. Her nose tickles. If she sneezes, the bleeding will start. She looks to the ground.

Isaiah reaches for his haversack, unzips a pocket. Next to a battered-looking camera, he pulls out Odidi's *Engineer's Field Guide* book, taken from Wuoth Ogik's library. Ajany already knows the first blank page has a name inked in: *Hugh Bolton*. Isaiah opens the book to the page and shows it to her. "Moses sent me this."

Ajany takes the thick, musty book and lifts it to her nose, waiting for the fragrance of Odidi.

A cheerless recognition: *the same ghost that haunted her had taunted Odidi*. "How did my brother find you?" she asks.

Isaiah wipes sweat from his face. "Three times a year, every year for the past five years, I've posted a request for information in East African newspapers. Moses was also looking, as it turns out. Over two years ago, I received a postcard asking for an address to which he could send a parcel that would be of interest to me."

Ajany inclines her head, listens. "The package came: this book." Isaiah takes the book from Ajany. He browses the pages. "The sight of my father's name in his handwriting . . ." His voice breaks. "Here—my father." From out of his black wallet he pulls a sepia-stained black-and-white square of an ascetic-looking man with smallish eyes, neat hair, and a fine mustache.

"Also, found this inside the book that Moses sent."

This. A seven-by-eight-centimeter, oversized bookmark, canvas material with an image.

Ajany takes it.

Reads the neat script—*Finn diri*—beneath a watercolor of a nude woman whose eyes glower. The woman, not just naked, exposed, raw to the soul. Intricate body scars jump off the small canvas. Languid. Indolent. Poured out woman. Etched into it, sorrow, hunger, beauty, anguish, worship, and defiance. One hand on her knees, the other beneath her head; something arcane suggested in the fecund, swollen belly. Details—a beaded wrist bracelet. *This is a soul.* Worlds slipping, a giddy wondering. Ajany glares at the artist's signature: *H. Bolton.*

The bookmark is clammy in Ajany's hands.

She averts her face, moves toward her brother to shield him and to conceal herself. She places her head against the coffin lid, striking it. Suffers the throb. Fatigue and dread compete. She scrutinizes the bookmark again.

To scare them, Galgalu had threatened her and Odidi with a ritual of malice, which he said vacuumed the essence of a person's life through a circle of fire. Its potency slithered out of a seductive song that lured the target's soul into a confined aperture where it becomes perpetually entranced by the song keeper. Right now, if she knew any such song, she would sing it to own the soul of the artist who blended shades of black with velvety violet strokes, infused with red and spots of gold-yellow, and touched them so that a woman's life was incarnated on a page. She would sing the song to consume what she had just seen and disintegrate what she now knew. Quivers start inside her stomach. Heart palpitations. Breathing is an effort. Here, now, is the tune of underworld streams feeding murky marshes. Ajany studies the woman. An overwhelming tension eats into her, then leaves in a burst of light. She sees why Odidi had fled Wuoth Ogik's enchantment with silence. Silence would never explain why and how Akai Lokorijom, their mother, came to be the naked, potent, pregnant subject of Hugh Bolton's art.

Cicadas and beetles chirp night into being. Ajany crushes the bookmark, fingers cutting into her palm. Ten meters away, Galgalu limps in with two lanterns, dried meat, and two metal jugs of sour milk.

Isaiah watches Ajany's approach, tries to forestall her demand that he leave. "I was hoping to be able to . . ."

Ajany touches his right hand, at his wrist. Soft-voiced, she says, "Why don't you c-come into the house?" A pause. "Wash up, eat, there's a room upstairs where you can sleep. You'll find more of your father's books there."

Isaiah focuses on the warmth of her hand, her delicate touch on his pulse, embracing words. He almost smiles, is closer to tears of relief. He is unaware that a family's citadel woven from infinite secrets has just been breached. He clears his throat and nods three times, clutching Ajany's hand. He lets go.

The throbbing inside Ajany's head ebbs.

6

AJANY COULD PAINT OVER THE SLICE OF CANVAS, COLOR OUT
her mother. She chooses, instead, to bring the image into Nyipir's dimly
lit arena. She lifts the *boma*'s thorn fence where Nyipir sits against his
red dance-ox next to a small fire, propping up his head. The animal
chews its cud. Nyipir inclines his head toward a teensy sound emerging
from his medium-sized transistor radio. From time to time a phrase is
strangled out. Piecemeal news. Ajany has carried a red blanket for him.
She drops it around his shoulders.

"Ah!" he says, huddles into it.

Ajany says, "B-baba?"

"Mhh?"

A geyser of questions, a rushed tone. "His name's Isaiah Bolton. . . .
His father . . ."

"I know," says Nyipir; he rubs his head and slouches.

Ajany crouches.

Nyipir indicates the radio. "Down-country, they're chasing people
from their homes. The ones who stay are being cut up and burned."

No logic. Her mind grasps nothing. Her heart lurches.

Tears crease Nyipir's face. His left hand hides them. "*Wuod* Annan
is here—listen—to help us."

The radio spews static. Ajany strains to listen, draws her knees up. She hears minuscule sounds: the radio, her father, jumbled thoughts, the silent night. Perverse desolation. She shudders. More ghosts circling. Static. Kofi Annan's voice weaving through in words that don't connect: *Parties . . . eminent persons . . . bloodshed . . . peace . . . violence . . . Peace . . . spoken . . . Honorable gentlemen . . . war . . . tribal . . . politics . . .*

Nyipir says, voice crackling, "They know when a body is cooling."

"Who?"

"Vultures."

Within a dark nook in Nyipir's heart, a long-ago man whispers, "By the time I'm done with you, you'll become another. You'll become mad. To live." Nyipir shivers.

"Vultures." Nyipir wipes his face with the blanket. "Baba?" Nyipir hears Ajany. He resurfaces. Stars fill the sky, maize meal white against dark violet.

Ajany asks, "Who's Hugh Bolton? His books are in the house."

Nyipir hesitates. Then, "We worked together long ago. Police."

"The photograph . . ." she says, remembering the picture of Baba in uniform carrying the Kenyan flag, riding on a black horse.

"No, before." Baba tilts his head back. "We shared . . . *trouble.*"

Fireflies land on memories. Images. Baba coming home from secret journeys, bearing gifts of livestock and assorted weapons like a fourth magus. Ritual display of changes in gun sizes, shapes, and weights. Concealment before sales. Plots and plans. Progression into steelier glints, smoother mechanisms. Smaller, lighter, more compact, faster off the mark, with and without silencers.

"Trouble?"

Baba's voice is as parched as the Chalbi Desert. "The thing . . . Mau Mau . . ."

Ajany shifts, brows puckering. *What?*

Creaky-voiced: *"And if I should speak, may the oath kill me. . . ."*

"What?" she asks again.

Silence's oaths, slow-dripping venom with their seductive promise of memory loss. Erasure of secrets, as long as the oath was fed in intermittent seasons with spilled human blood. "Ahhh! We bury evil with covenants of silence." Nyipir says, "For the good of the country." He explains, "We know, *nyara*, that to name the unnameable is a curse."

Ajany hears his words, the spoken ones, those unspoken.

Nyipir adds, fingers gesturing, "Even if you plant another story into silence, see, the buried thing returns to ask for its blood from the living." Nyipir's laugh is short and dry. "Death does not keep its secrets well."

Ajany rubs her eyes. When she had left Kenya, she had imagined an amputation from its riptide of murky things. But here they were again, expecting her reply. What was she now supposed to be? A memory. Odidi scaring her with stories of misshapen demons jealous of humanity that invade the earth scouring for human spare parts to use to replace their defects. Obarogo shopping for little girls' eyes. She could paint this darkness and ogres emerging from petrified silence as she and Baba waded across swamps between life and the underworld.

Dung and heat; heady rain-on-earth tang.

Next to them, the red dance-ox grunts.

Nyipir's silences have summoned the Forgotten. He wrestles, but in spite of his contortions, the Forgotten frog-march him into a lake of histories to retrieve rotting stories. "*They'll* return." Nyipir supports his head with shaking hands; fingers shield his eyes.

"Who?" she asks, smelling Nyipir's anguish.

"Aloys, Tom. Aloys and Tom." Then he pleads, "Others are voiceless."

Ajany picks a ghost: "Hugh Bolton?"

Nyipir gurgles.

"Bolton?" she repeats.

Nyipir is brusque. "I was going to Burma. Then I met him."

Ajany draws circles into the ground with fingers. "What's in Burma?"

Soft-voiced: "Our people. Went for King George's war. Didn't come back."

Ajany draws lines. Listens.

"Was bringing them home." Nyipir wipes his eyes.

Ajany scans black spaces between stars. She finds Kormamaddo, the bull camel of the waters, Odidi's sky marker. "Myanmar," she mutters.

"Mhh?"

"Burma is Myanmar."

"*Myanmar*," Baba says. "Mandalay, 21° 59′ N 96° 6′ E, Rangoon, 16° 47′ N 96° 9′ E."

From the sky, Kormamaddo looks down on them.

"Yangon," she adds.

"Who?"

"Rangoon is now Yangon."

Nyipir sighs.

He asks, "This Isaiah . . . he's gone?"

Ajany says, "No."

"Tomorrow?"

She shakes her head.

"Where is he?"

"The house."

A high-octave pitch. "*My* house?"

Ajany is curt: "Odidi's guest."

Nyipir exhales, a whistling sound.

Ajany continues, "Odidi was coming here to meet him. . . ." A pause. "Odidi was coming home."

Nyipir breathes into fresh tears. *Rhhhhhhh.*

An aging man dreams what could have been the right end of a broken-off conversation:

Where's my son, my boy?

Here. Here he is.

Baba.

In dreams.

Odidi had wanted to subvert Nyipir's hopes for his destiny. He had succeeded. Yet Odidi had been coming home. Nyipir no longer hears BBC's World Service struggling through static to reach him. His son *had* come home.

Then.

Odidi's absence seizes them both like an unconfessable sin. They peer through a night steeped in other silences. The unraveling.

Ajany opens her mouth to ask, *Why is my brother dead?* Nyipir opens his to beg her to leave the past behind.

They shut their mouths and eyes.

Then.

Nyipir tells Ajany, "Akai-ma must be on her way home. She'll wonder where we are."

They rise.

Nyipir says, "He must go."

"Who?"

"*Musungu cha.* Give him water, make him go."

"Baba," she replies, "Isaiah . . . he's come with . . . Odidi gave him things. Books ... and *this* ..." She lifts the small canvas rectangle to Nyipir's face. "Akai-ma."

Nyipir becomes a wooden monolith.

He does not touch the piece.

He lurches away, minuet in movement, holding himself intact, leaving Ajany behind. Nyipir hums, *"Par Oganda odong nono."* Sounds as if cawing crows are trapped inside him: "There's nothing left of Oganda's home."

The canvas is damp in her hand. She stuffs it into her skirt pocket. She hurries to keep up with Nyipir, deluged with the fear of being left alone. Nose tickle. Fire in lungs. She spits. Wants to apologize for Odidi's absence, for still living, for Akai-ma's nakedness on a piece of canvas.

They approach the house and discover two things:

Akai-ma has not come home.

Odidi has not returned from the dead.

"Par Oganda odong nono. . . ." Nyipir hums to an emptiness that stretches even further out.

"Baba," Ajany groans.

Par Oganda odong nono. . . .

"Why d-did my brother die?"

Nyipir halts. Then a staccato answer: "Police." *Let it suffice.*

But he speaks to dark-violet skies. "I begged them, knelt down. Searched for him. Begged them to save my child."

Ajany would now haul back every question if she could. Bulldoze guilt, shame, and the loneliness made out of a father crying out for his son's return. Sorrow is admitting to a mother's loathing for one's existence. Terror is the knowledge that a persistent phone call could have saved an only brother's life. Horror is a vision of blood on her hands. Powerlessness is hearing a father's deep voice become a wail. One question crosses wires with another so that from out of her memory a deliberately suppressed phantom now bounds into Wuoth Ogik.

. . .

It is a musician from Salvador de Bahia, and his spectre looms in her mind, and plunders her soul again. What had she done? The echo of a howl, the vision of blood spurting from a jagged wound on the same date as that which was scrawled on a brother's death certificate. In seeing, inside Ajany, something at last detonates.

There is a minuscule space into which sanity may slip without turning into chaos, an intimate line that should not be crossed by unbearable memory. At last, she is stumbling down cliffs. Mind is black, body melts into massive silent waterfalls that cascade into endless chasms, falling and falling. Her spirit whispers to her soul that Ajany is now dead.

———

Isaiah had paused outside the house to watch the coral tints that darkened as the light's mood shifted. Colored tiles, mostly brown. Walls of termite-mound soil, wood mixed with crushed coral. He had wandered into the house and strolled through its two levels. He lay on the floor, the better to appreciate the high roof that nestled on broad, rough wooden beams. He imagined that the style was a paring down of a Kenyan bush aesthetic—made of a palette of colors from the stark landscape. There were glimpses of outside vastness wherever he stood, startling portals designed to sneak the landscape in. He had shut his eyes before one such entryway, and four shrieking winds emerged in a resonant cascade. The house paid homage to water.

Now a fly weaves in between fault-lined pillars. Isaiah's eyes follow the insect as it navigates wall fissures that start at the base of the house and disappear into eaves. The house creaks. Musk of neglect, and something else—as if the inhabitants whose memories drenched the walls had lived their lives within the house, but not *in* the house, and the house had never participated in the ebb and flow of their existence.

Isaiah finds a place for himself in the library, to which he has been directed. He stops before the shelf filled with his father's books. He turns, sits on a dust-dotted sisal mat, and draws up his knees. He invokes his mother, Selene. *I'm here.*

Nobody sees his tears.

Later, he would browse through book pages, count the number of times *Hugh Bolton* was written into the first leaf: sixty-one. Trace squiggles in margins, mountains, water, trees, and stick figures, feeling for messages, imagining warmth. He has brought books to his nose and thought he detected a whiff of old cigar smoke. Brushing fingers on black fountain-pen strokes, lingering on a twisted old-fashioned "g," imagining that he was touching his father's hand.

7

OUTSIDE, DAY BECOMES NIGHT. INSIDE HER DREAMING, ODIDI and Ajany run from the red cave and its skeleton that oozes resentment. They scamper over large black, red, and brown rocks and spill over spidery, sandy trails, a camel track. Tear through small thornbushes that grab at and leave blood stripes on their bodies, cross a damp *laga,* past a Morengo and Mareer tree, through an abandoned cattle *boma,* and crash into flowering acacia thickets, from where they can hear Kalacha springs murmur, the prattle of buffalo weavers and golden pipits.

The shadow of Wuoth Ogik.

Line of blood on Odidi's face.

Ajany spits on her hands and wipes Odidi's forehead where blood has clotted. Odidi winces. "Sorry, Odi."

He pulls at her hair. "Is it showing?"

Ajany nods. "Sorry, Odi."

"We say a wait-a-bit branch got me, OK?"

Ajany asks, "We pray?"

Odidi pinches her arm. "Silly!"

She sobs, "Where's Obarogo's face?"

Odidi's fingers nip her upper arm. "Shhh."

A falsetto trill seduces cows and camels to water. Water songs.

"Sprinkled life

Unshackle journeys,
Respite. Rest.
Drink-Drink, flat-footed, sand-dreamer. . . ."

The two children wait for after dusk, when lanterns are lit. They tremble with the wind. The night is as jumpy as they are.

Odidi's voice is slow and solemn: "Never, never, never shall we talk about this, never to remember the cave. We forget, and if we tell, the earth must gobble us up. Swear?"

Fear inserted itself between them.

It breathed.

It was in Odidi's hiss, "You must *swear.*" Grabbing earth: "Hold this soil."

The oath inflamed Ajany's little throat, and she choked.

"Why m-me?"

"'Cause you're a cry-*dudu*-water-mouth silly."

"Not."

"You scare easy."

"Don't."

"So?"

With watery eyes, Ajany ground out the words "I swear," clinging to the dirt, and something elemental inside her flowed away, just like the soil she held in her hands.

The woman glided toward the gate. Her AK-47 pointing downward. Not threat—vigilance. A sunset silhouette. Akai-ma. Baba was not home.

Two pairs of eyes followed Akai-ma as she inspected the patterns of the land, looking for something.

Ajany clutched her brother.

Her stammer worsened in Akai's presence: Akai-ma's all-seeing eyes, a temper distilled into condensed, burning, tearing words with the impact of a curse.

"Odi, I'm afraid."

Ajany felt herself to be a shadow that flickered at the edge of her mother's gaze. It was rare for her mother to call her by her name. *"That One!"* Akai-ma might yell until Ajany emerged, already protecting herself from physical blows that were implied but never came.

Odidi said, "We go. I talk, you shut up." Which was the normal way of things between them. "And stop shivering, *idjut!*"

Sniffle.

Odidi's harsh whisper, "Silly *dudu*. Can't take you Far Away if you cry. Such a baby."

Ajany forced herself to let the crickets' chirping fill her thoughts.

She wiped her face and sniffed twice more.

"OK," Ajany said.

They crawled out of the bushes.

"I anger."

Akai-ma's English, pockmarked, dragged through moonscapes, propped up by gesture and hacked into low-droned present-tense portions into which any number of languages were inserted.

Akai: I *anger* you.

Though Odidi dared a quiet snigger, Ajany had long understood that Akai rendered words as they were made to be—soldier verbs, constructed for action and war. Ajany cowered in front of them.

Akai breathing in Ngaturkana: "Where did you go?" She would say, "Etch!" And spit a long distance away.

Every time Ajany practiced spitting, she would end up with great globs of saliva spattering her feet.

"*Etch!* Where did you go?" Akai-ma asked.

Odidi leaned back on one foot and looked back at his mother. A chin gesture indicated west, the place of the rock shelter.

A furrow on Akai's forehead.

Odidi said, "Far behind the red stone. Where smoke and water come from the ground. I showed Ajany."

Dangerous. But not forbidden. Not like the rock shelter.

The creases on Akai-ma's face disappeared. Light lost to sky darkness above them. Akai-ma and Ajany shivered at the same time, night haloes atop their heads.

"*Italeo akitap,*" Akai-ma started. "That part is forbidden!"

A light flashed in the sky.

Akai-ma's eyes bright, voice low. "There's a python," she warned. "There's a python. And all the red stone belongs to it." She glowered at Ajany. "It sucks spirit out and leaves shadows for you to rot in."

An incantation.

Akai-ma's eyes met Ajany's.

Oddly, for the first time in both their lives, Akai-ma's eyes slid away first.

Later that night.

Odidi and Ajany had washed, eaten fermented meat soup, crawled into their beds, and drifted to sleep. Both woke mid-rest and discovered there were new ways of being afraid. Separately, they longed for day-light. From that day, their days were stuffed with choked fear, suffocated by the family habit of silence. At night, when wind jolted doum palms, nightmares made of white bones, teeth-filled mouths, and indecipher-able words showed up. Twice in the night, Ajany woke up to find that the shadows from within her dreams had become a presence that stood over her. Behind the presence, a baby's long wail, the sorrow of which made Ajany cover her head. The presence dissolved; the unseen child and its incessant wailing lingered.

One night, four days later, Ajany tore out of her room and jumped onto Odidi's bed. "Odi . . . Obarogo came. He wants my face."

Odidi said, "I'll fight him. I'll punch his bones until *he* has a face."

Ajany had not laughed. "Promise, 'Didi?"

"Promise forever, 'Jany." Odidi turned down his coverlet.

Ajany snuggled down next to him and grabbed his hand. She was drifting to sleep when she thought she heard him whisper, "Good you're here, silly. Me, too, I was scared." She could have heard wrong, because she knew Odidi was not afraid of anything.

Under a harvest moon, a woman now sleeps. Childhood pillows do not offer simple dreams. Before dawn, a new name explodes from out of her underworld. *"Bernardo!"* she howls.

To name the unnameable is a curse.

Bernardo! The entity rips at her heart and she arches her back, away from the sense of salted wounds that still bleed, still seethe, still yearn, still make her moan. She tugs at air, fighting portions of her life that are trying to disintegrate into Bernardo again. She clings to another name for protection: a talisman. He has always known what to do.

——

A bird somewhere cackles with a hint of hysteria. In the library, a cold feeling starts at the base of Isaiah's spine and rushes to his head, making his hair stand on end. *Is the night watching me?* He blinks away the mad idea. *What time is it?* He touches his watch. Wuoth Ogik. Not just words anymore. He gropes for and finds a window chair, falls into it. His bag falls by his feet. He touches it, relishing the cool of its leather against his palms.

The house shivers when its old tanks creak.

Isaiah recoils.

Aggravated insomnia. Isaiah has not slept for two days. Jet lag. That is the problem. Explains the whisperings he hears in the land's nights, the return of nightmares, those things he thought he was finished with. For more than three years, he has been unable to sleep without all-night radio chatter or a night light. He had started experimenting with being in total darkness six months ago, and it had been successful. But now, in this space of no boundaries, the darkness has a throbbing, dense menace to it. He feels safer watching it.

He also needs to talk to someone about Hugh. A day earlier, Isaiah had retrieved sheets of paper with more of Hugh's signatures—plans, sketches, designed spaces, lines, curves, and outlines of this house, which had been tucked into some large books. He had sat for a long time on the edge of a couch, reconciling exhaustion with the bittersweetness of a conviction that he was in his father's home.

Old man Oganda stiffens every time he approaches. Spends his days digging a hole, and pretends not to speak English. *No understand.* Sure.

Isaiah paces. The ghastly creature cackles again. Echoes. A skin-chilling *aaaaado!*

He stops. He needed a break from his obsession with frontlines and transition zones of terrible absences. Outside, a clattering of doum palm leaves. Isaiah glares. *When do the bloody winds end their garbled groaning?* Too much life; everything breathes here, even the damn stones. Too much space. But being in the house is like being crammed into a too-slow metal lift with no light. He hates the startling creaks of many unseen things here.

A hyena's guffaw; he shivers. This land, its awful age—here time hums an ancient, eerie tune. The hyena cackles, and all of a sudden Isaiah is deluged by a need to see the wide sky. He leans out of the window.

. . . *aaado!*

He sprints out of the room.

In Wuoth Ogik's courtyard, a pang as if he, the outsider, walking toward this *outside,* will never find his way back to *normal.* But he is hungry to experience his lost father. This *was* Hugh's house—a certainty. Isaiah wonders about his five pages of questions: *Who to ask when nothing answers back?* A groan.

Up.

So many wild stars in the night.

———

Whirling backward in time, becoming Arabel again, finding that blood still congealed on a Christmas Eve white silk robe. It left the imprint of an oryx's face mask. Whirling, and all life whirled. She was just Arabel, the way Bernardo sang her. Arabel Ajany writhing around a steel pole, accompanying Bernardo's seven-minute story, which he sang in a throbbing bass. Her life in stark light twice a week, working so hard to show Bernardo how necessary she was to him.

Except that she was replaced on Christmas Eve.

Before the blood, she had dialed Odidi's number. He would know what to do. But she had switched off the phone after the fourth ring.

After.

From under her bed, she had dialed Odidi's number again. She would tell him what she had done. She would beg him to come and get her. She heard Odidi's phone ringing. It rang until it returned with a message in two languages: *Mteja hapatikani kwa sasa; the mobile subscriber cannot be reached.*

And then, a day later, after midnight, Nyipir Oganda had phoned her and said, "Odidi is gone."

A strange idea: *Gone. Where?*

Ajany laughed out loud then.

Ajany laughs now.

———

Isaiah watches the fire that burns close to a woman who barely breathes on her tattered mat.

"May I help?" he had asked Nyipir a day and a half ago.

"No."

Isaiah said, "She's unconscious."

"Really?" Nyipir's brow had gone up.

Isaiah was convinced that, given the smallest chance, the silly bug-ger would have clouted him on the skull to make him disappear. A grim grin—he would leave only when he was ready.

Isaiah had persisted, "She needs help?"

Nyipir's terse "Someone's coming."

Three days later, nobody had shown up yet.

Not his problem.

Doum palms rattle; he hears the woman laugh, so he moves closer to see if she is conscious. He finds stillness, a reclining caryatid. Isaiah stares. Stirring of recognition besieged by flickering images, song por-tions, and old words, almost knowing . . . *what?* The night fire sputters. When Isaiah turns, he sees through its embers a mirror of the scorching hole in his heart. A muted groan: *What in hell am I doing here? What has my mother to do with this forsaken realm?*

8

THE TRADER, WUOTH OGIK'S NEWEST VISITOR, HICCUPS *"THEE-thee-thee-thee"* over a joke he alone grasps. He had returned with Galgalu, who had shambled over to his corner of the land and told him the current season's story in six lines:

Police in down-country Kenya had murdered Moses Odidi Oganda.

Akai Lokorijom had fled Wuoth Ogik with the old car.

A rabid *d'abeela* had implanted a death wound into Galgalu's soul, which needed to be exorcised.

Nyipir was breaking rocks to build a cairn for Odidi, who could not be buried until Akai-ma had returned.

Sorrow had swallowed Arabel Ajany, who was now like one of the dead.

A man named Bolton had shown up at Wuoth Ogik with a question: *Where's my father?*

The Trader is a bald-headed, medium-sized harlequin with jutting-out ears and a straggling beard like the land's thornbushes. He templed his fingers and considered the wealth of events. He wondered how to weave himself into the center of the tales. Pouring words into his ears was a beige-leather-covered shortwave radio that seemed to have been cemented into his shoulder. He listened, he considered everything, and then he packed in haste, eager to get to Wuoth Ogik.

The Trader knows neither where he was born nor who his father was. He has hazel eyes and a skin tone that changes with the seasons, place, and circumstances in which he finds himself. He suspects his father might be the old Kenyan Punjabi trader who once lived in Ethiopia, or the embittered illegitimate son of a murderous and psychotic Greek trader. He knows about one of his great-great-grandfathers on his mother's side, a failed Arab slaver whose human cargo had died of dehydration in Bagamoyo, and who, to escape creditors, had fled northward until he collapsed and was saved by a widow whom he married. The Trader was raised as a shared son among the twilight women of Garissa, who skirted borders of orthodoxy and hypocrisy in a blur of clove-oil scents and cinnamon gestures, *mwarubaini* portions and *oud*. He went to the school under the Mareer tree. Because his genealogy stank, his head teacher ignored him. He preferred herding goats anyway. He left school at fourteen, stole his first radio from the stuffed bag of a nervous passenger, and found two things: a porthole to a universe, and the realization that by listening deeply he could manage the world.

He became *duddaani-nyaatte*, a desert peddler who carried goods on his back. His wanderings brought him a deep and wide relationship network. Because he listened, he discovered what people wanted to hear. He also had money to lend at exorbitant interest rates. Shamed borrowers sold him secrets for relief. One of them, a former Coptic priest, had given him nine formulae for blending coffee, nine secrets of intent that delivered the scent to nine places of the distressed soul. He also started to change and retell some of the stories he had heard on the radio. In time, people came to him to confirm or deny what they had heard in the news. He had already obtained four passports by then, two of which were Kenyan. He spoke all the tongues of the desert, mimicked accents and postures, dialogued in the gist of some European languages, including Croatian, adjusting words to suit his hearing, and adopted so many names that, except for him, almost everyone forgot he used to be Zaman Nawfal. Nyipir does not know he was Zaman Nawfal, and Nyipir knows most of everything in those northern lands.

· · ·

He showed up at Wuoth Ogik that day on a Rendille camel bearing assorted goods, including a Chinese-made Uzi and a five-stringed Spanish guitar. Now his *thee-thee-thee-thee* jounces his shoulders. From time to time he tilts his head and nods as if picking up an old conversation from his radio, before returning to his audience. He tells his audience that a man from Ghana named Choffeur had sent another, named Kofi Annan, to save Kenya. Kofi had in turn invited "Haninant Parsons."

Galgalu wonders, "So many to save a country—there must be something good here."

"*Thee-thee-thee-thee.*"

Nyipir leans forward, "What news of Agwambo? Is he alive?"

The Trader lays out his paraphernalia and stops to tap his chin. "It is possible. Me, I only repeat what the radio says."

Galgalu asks, "Chibaki—you know him?"

The Trader purses his lips, his eyes narrow. "I sold him two camels—no, no, three."

"If a man knows camels, he must be agreeable," Galgalu suggests.

The Trader nods. "But here is a question: are the camels still living?" The Trader sighs. "*Aieee!* Godless news."

His audience waits.

"A fisherman left his home on the day after the counting. He went to Lake Naivasha. You know the one I mean? He left his wives—there were two, and eight children in their house. But when he was on the water, neighbors wrote out his name and those of his wives and children. Neighbors whom he brought fish. They wrote out his name and gave it to demons that came to seal his house, pour petrol, strike a match, and dance while the family inside died screaming. Those neighbors watched. They ate food."

Red glow of desert light.

Silence made of revulsion.

Nyipir sits very still.

He has seen this before.

Touched it.

Hidden it.

His mind tumbles back to a different time, when brother, son, mother, father sealed family members in rooms and huts and set these alight in honor of covenants of terror that guaranteed silence: *If I speak, may the oath kill me.* Much later, the horror was painted over and replaced with myths of triumph, repeated, repeated again, then adorned in all seasons of retelling. Nyipir waited for the inheritors of these silences to call out the names of their undead dead. Not a word. Now, fifty years later, the murdered were shrieking from earth tombs of enforced, timeless stillness, wailing for their forgotten, chopped-up lives. They seemed to accuse every citizen inheritors of their hemorrhaging. Nyipir shivers, chilled. He looks over his shoulder.

The Trader continues. "When those firestarters opened the door to see what they had done, the first one in witnessed the bursting open of the second wife's womb. And the child leaned out to look at the man. It turned its head. It died." The Trader says, "Now that one runs up and down looking for priests to cleanse him."

"Who delivers men like those?" Galgalu covers his mouth.

A hum in his ears, Nyipir mutters a confession: "Long ago, I carried Kenya's flag. It was not so heavy then."

The Trader nods.

The Trader is a gatherer and carrier of stories. He collects secrets, a source of income, a pleasurable economy. He cannot endure not knowing. Every memory, even borrowed ones, are his. Sometimes he distributes these when he needs to, and always for a profit. The Trader trades in names, but never with his.

Misery had brought Nyipir to the Trader, in 1970. Over fourteen lucent nights, the Trader had sung soft songs to return the right rhythm to Nyipir's heartbeat, and then convinced Nyipir's soul to trust human life again, explaining that what had happened was not Nyipir's fault. Afterward, the Trader had taken names Nyipir had known and written and made him recite these until they became soft to the taste, which meant that Nyipir was no longer indebted to the disappeared.

Later.

Nyipir declared, "I owe allegiance to no nation or people."

The Trader had guffawed. "Now, brother, we are of the same race."

Time.

The two men would end up trading in information as Nyipir expanded his gun-trading and cattle-rustling enterprises across the northern territories and into the Horn of Africa. Years later, the Trader would help Nyipir dissolve his circuits and turn assets into cash and gems, after rogue politicians with private armies leapt into the game.

Nyipir owed the Trader one other valuable thing: his nonexistence. The Trader had arranged to purge references to Nyipir's life from all official records. An uncommon debt, one of the Trader's favorites. The Trader now faces Nyipir. "I'm sorry—your son."

Nyipir nods.

"His life has changed."

Nyipir nods.

"This road is a circle. We'll meet again," the Trader says.

Silences.

Isaiah stares at the man. He imagines a silenus with a face that might have been sketched by El Greco. Watches a set of skeletal fingers move, play with air, communicating story, implying conspiracies. He wonders why a guitar juts out of a gunnysack. Sees the man adjusts a blue-and-white kanga hovering around his waist. Isaiah reads the legend on the cloth: *Light of All Nations.*

The Trader shakes sand off his sandals. Stands, uses the moment to scrutinize those present. He regrets Odidi Oganda's death. Knows he might have helped, had he known in time. God's will. *Maybe.* He, too, has lost a son. Does not often think about it. Still, he can explain how the cosmos of grief is another land. It is territory he traverses in silence.

He sizes up the outsider. Watches agitated hands, and searching eyes that reveal the homesickness of eternal wanderers. *Bolton.* He maps Isaiah's body. Reads strained muscles, a throbbing vein. Sadness etched into skin, hardness in downturn of eye and mouth. This man has seen death and lived, a good beginning. The Trader grins, adjusts his features, and reshapes his body to attract response. He sidles next to Isaiah. "Are you a vulture?"

Isaiah turns.

"I say!" the Trader says, a broadcaster's voice, mocking Isaiah. "I say . . . you here to suckle our violence . . . you like?"

Isaiah's hands rise. "Think what you want . . ." *Asshole.*

"Journalist, project manager, philanthropist, messiah, job seeker—which are you?"

Isaiah retreats to the far end of the fire, tenses.

A tap on his right shoulder.

Isaiah sighs.

The Trader says, "I sell secrets. I buy secrets." He grins. "Which do you need?"

Sweat beads Isaiah's forehead.

"A secret for a secret."

Isaiah snaps, "Don't have any. Don't *need* any."

The Trader tips forward. "Everyone has at least four secrets."

"You don't say." Lack of interest bleeds through every word.

"Thee-thee-thee-thee."

The heat of morning and scents oozing from the Trader overwhelm Isaiah, making him dizzy. He looks skyward.

"Ah . . . some coffee." The Trader grins. "Real coffee. Then we talk about your secrets."

Isaiah's brows shoot up. "I've none."

"I've none," mimics the Trader, using Isaiah's voice.

Feeling hunted, Isaiah heads out of the courtyard.

The Trader chants, "One secret can be repeated only to God."

Isaiah walks forward.

The Trader glides after him. "Your evidence against His goodness."

"Absurd," Isaiah mutters.

"*Thee-thee-thee* . . . The second is buried in between life and death, to be retrieved at the time of a man's most important life decision."

The Trader dances in front of Isaiah, walking backward.

"Excuse me." Isaiah tries to sidestep the pest.

The Trader trills his next words. "The third is the one you sell to buy your oldest longing."

Humidity suffuses Isaiah's body as he listens in spite of himself. Waits. Nothing. "There is a fourth, you said."

"Did I?" the Trader asks.

Isaiah turns and sees the Trader's broad, yellow-toothed smirk. Blue flies whirl between them.

A chortle. "I knew you'd want to know."

A stain of red on Isaiah's skin, a tic above his right eye.

"I'm not irritating you," says the Trader.

"You are," replies Isaiah.

"No. Statement. I'm not irritating you. The irritation is already inside of you. *Thee-thee-thee.*"

Nyipir, listening, turns a sudden laugh into a cough as Isaiah jumps. The Trader has spoken straight into Isaiah's ear, the voice seeming to spring from within his own body. Isaiah watches the Trader's mouth.

The man's mouth has not moved. *Bloody hell.* Isaiah turns away. *Ventriloquism in the armpit of Africa?*

The Trader persists, "What's your name?"

Isaiah is desperate to escape. "Isaiah Bolton."

"Ah! You want the fourth secret?"

Isaiah oozes aversion. He cannot give the hobgoblin the satisfaction of an admission.

The Trader exudes warmth.

Isaiah, confused, frowns.

"The fourth one . . ." the Trader starts.

Isaiah listens.

"The fourth is the name you baptize your death with." The Trader laughs out loud, offers an expansive hand gesture. "This name, when spoken out loud, can even *kill* you . . . *thee-thee-thee!*"

Isaiah lurches back, aware that his hands are shaking and the world is receding. Just then Galgalu steps out with a camphor-and-clove-scented burning censer. Isaiah sucks in the perfumed air. The sinister sensation that assailed him fades.

"*Isaiah!*" the Trader whispers. Isaiah's head swivels. "Never trade in a name. Trade in everything else, but not a name. Nothing like a name. For example . . . *Bol-ton.* I heard that a man came very close to this place of fire."

The Trader about-turns, salutes Nyipir, and slow-marches toward him.

Isaiah rubs his arms, feeling as if grimy hands have manhandled his soul. He needs to scrub out the man's voice from his body.

Nyipir looks over at Isaiah.

Isaiah holds his gaze.

Nyipir turns away.

Isaiah knows a clue to his question has been dropped. *Everything spits out fucking riddles.* He spins and strides toward the livestock enclosure, his thoughts everywhere, fists clenching and unclenching. What would happen if he held the scrawny peasant in a choke hold? *Secrets? I'll squeeze out secrets!*

Engulfing loneliness.

Will I ever return home? He stops mid-stride, leans over the *boma* fence. His agitation subsides as he watches the placid livestock.

When Isaiah returns to the others, he finds that the Trader is covering Ajany with orange-blossom-scented smoke and broken tunes. Isaiah watches the Trader blow smoke down Ajany's nostrils. He closes his eyes. Was this the doctor they had all been waiting for? A tic pulses near his left eye. He reminds himself that he does have *normal* to go back to. A gust of pleasure—it would soon be spring in England. He might even be home before the emergence of new leaves on winter-denuded oak trees. He would also try harder to make peace with Raulfe, his stepfather—a surge of fondness for the fragile man who had tried so very hard to raise him right, *dear Raulfe.*

9

TWO AND A HALF YEARS EARLIER.

Soft lights. Night obscured life's details. The emaciated woman limped around the bathroom of her hospice room in Sussex, easing a cramp in her right thigh. She used to be a marcher when she was not dying, when she was not seventy-eight years old. Touched her hair. Meager where it existed, once ink-black, worn pageboy-style. She winced. Breathing was a chore. The cancer had spread. Curved spine. How tall was she now?

Her nose twisted. "I'm old."

Dying has a ghastly smell.

She had been fragile until the visit.

Her son.

She had dreaded this, had hoped to avoid it.

Now it had happened, adrenaline urgency.

All these invasions, she thought. *One eats the body; the other deranges the soul.*

Agitation.

Now engrossed with praying to the night through a wide bathroom window. Night obscured reality's details. *I love this dark.* Not primeval, concealing, and heavy, like other darknesses. *Leave my child alone,* she tells those other nights. *Let him alone.*

A word: *Uncontained.*

Isaiah William, her son.

Uncontained, like . . . She snapped off her thoughts.

"I want my truest daddy!" the toddler had once screamed, and afterward his longing had become a suffocating mania, which she had ignored, waiting for the day he would outgrow it. The yearning wounded him, infected others, ate at him. But because she had erased the name, neither he nor she dared voice it. It had no room in their renewed existence. "Raulfe is your daddy."

Bloody Kenya. Bloody.

Not blasphemy.

Bloody.

Blood had seemed to leak from too many holes there. A cut bled. Sunset bled. Sheep bled. Red mud roads bled. Sunset-sunrise bleeding. Oozing life, seeping death. The full moon bled on water.

She was not afraid of death. She had a list of her intimate dead, friends, people she once knew, beloved strangers. But she had also lived through an odd internecine war, seen bleeding headless bodies, bleeding bodiless heads, miscarried old love, watched practice fireworks of hope-to-be-better Kenya.

She had escaped to England from Kenya long before Kenya's Independence Day. At Heathrow she almost flung herself on the tarmac in foaming glee. Home. Where death was wrapped in decorous packages—very well-mannered.

Now, glaring at the night, she snarls, "I'll win." She informs Kenya, "This one's mine."

Then.

Head over the sink, knees trembling, head pounding. The morphine wearing off into memories of crimson Nandi-flame-tree flowers lying crushed on earth roads. A smile. Even if she would not speak the name, she could write it.

Selene creeps over to a small blue desk.

Hospital notepaper, a faux fountain pen, and cramped fingers stretch out, stoking memory's fire:

Darling Isaiah,

There is a story behind every no, every maybe. Make of this what you will. One of the loveliest of patients here signs off his chemotherapy sessions by declaring, "When the wells are dry, men seek to drink at a mirage." Keeps us laughing. This is a story about a dry well. If you look—I pray you don't—you will find it close to a house of gargantuan pretensions, a pink folly. This is a small part of the story of the man who dreamed it, built it, and offered it to me: Hugh Bolton. You've idolized him as your father. I fled his desert, left him with his gift, for I had found you, and for you I would have forsaken my life.

Hugh.

We were as young as our generation could be in the sad season after the war when we met. We eloped eleven days later, certain, in the way of fools, that we had been created for one another. We sought adventure in blank-slate kingdoms where we owned the rules and would remake a country in our image. Your generation, son, so easily discards the burdens of history and its mind-the-gap strictures. For us, leaving was a bold act, and we left England, with its weary nostalgia for a past that had been burned to ash with our far too many war dead. Hugh and I skipped into a ship that was heading out to the Kenya Colony. . . .

That year, 1950, Hugh and Selene had berthed in Mombasa. As they walked up the pier at Kilindini Harbour, a deluge of sights, scents, and sounds startled Selene. Stiff, she followed instructions. Half an hour later, on the boat rowing them ashore, laden with steamer trunks and luggage, she turned and stared at the ship, flapped at the cloud of insects, noticed that the sky was overcast, and thought: *Let's go back, Hugh.* She turned to tell him. He was laughing; he touched her face and gestured widely. "We are home, my love, we're home."

On Mackinnon Square, the Union Jack fluttered. Later, the noontime train chugged with them over three hundred miles on a narrow-gauge track up to Nairobi. Selene retreated into nonengaged observation after the train stopped at the railway station. There, in the bustle of a pompous, gentrified swamp, she felt that everything and everyone existed for the entertainment of this pulsating, living, breathing landscape. *It's toying with us,* she thought.

It had started to rain. *Is this a sign?* It had been raining in Cambridgeshire when Hugh and Selene met. Because they were preoccupied with escaping the damp, their umbrellas had bumped and got entangled. They had exchanged umbrellas as they giggled. They swapped stories of origin. Hugh was a soldier who had skimmed through war's amphitheater, a disgusted and detached witness. She was an Anglo-Indian—more Indian than Anglo, truth be told, but that had been streamlined by very English picnics, books, parties, and music, the latter made a torment by a mother who played "Flight of the Bumblebee" when Selene had been naughty. Old but suspect money, world travelers with lost secrets, a swarthy-skinned father obsessed with keeping his three daughters' skins fair and lovely. On impulse, eleven days later, Selene and Hugh got married in a rained-out civil ceremony with a retired butler and cleaner as witnesses.

When Selene summoned the courage to take Hugh home and introduce him, Selene's mother scrutinized his ginger hair, insipid features, a complexion that if he had been a woman would have rendered him an English rose. "Good choice," her mother had said. "He is adequately English." And even though she played "Flight of the Bumblebee" afterward, it was *con allegria*.

On a steam train traveling through the Kenyan landscape, she discovered pure air and light, a proliferation of life, and the might of the Rift Valley. Hugh and Selene got out in Naivasha and found their plot of land, with its view of a hippo-inhabited, bird-filled lake.

They smelled roasting calves at parties to which they had not yet been invited. They reveled in the sight of a lake of myriad moods around which assorted species gathered, with seasonal pastoralists bringing livestock down to drink. Vestiges of paradise.

There was so much to do. They needed a home. They needed to make money. They started by camping out, and laughed and danced, and made love under starlight next to lemon-green thorn trees within earshot of moaning hyenas. They built a temporary shelter and were found by the right kind of servants, who bowed at every turn of phrase.

Hugh started work on their five-bedroom stone bungalow. Selene researched horticultural options after she had ruled out long-haired sheep and Jersey cows. When the house was done, Hugh started to paint as he once did at the university. His watercolors were vibrant and defied lines to cavort on the canvases. Needlepoint was Selene's skill, and the flowers that she wove were brilliant and fecund. Together, they studied the soil, experimenting with crops, failing, waiting for rain, digging and planting, and mobilizing human beings whose lives, dreams, and cultures were as far away from their own as universes can be. Loam, clay, sand. Blending soils. Planting grass, herbs, and flowers. Some took root. Hugh had an idea. They could become vintners. Selene agreed. So they ordered vines from Italy and South Africa. Hugh had hired a tractor with borrowed money and prepared the ground. They worked with fifteen shamba boys to plant vines. They waited.

The vines thrived.

Neighbors would call in to exclaim at the sproutings and plot their own wineries. They had already sized Hugh and Selene up and found them acceptable. An exhilarating beginning, full of hard work, experiments, dreams, plans, building, borrowing, and always starting again. Genial neighbors, the Thompsons: middle-class accents, plump, proper, Anglican, and polite. They had named their four children after animals, rivers, and trees: Topi, Oryx, Tana, and Acacia. They played backgammon, listened to Wagner, and wondered what other crops might take in this glorious land. Selene drank down glasses of champagne mixed with Guinness, and later, with Hugh, she laughed at the proper Thompsons and their untamed children.

After the rains, at their five-course dinner, Selene asked, "Wouldn't it be lovely to have a child?"

Hugh had leapt across the table, knocking over the flower vase to land on her lap, his arms around her, clinging. "A son! My son!"

The first of Hugh's "my"s.

Kenya was seeping into Hugh. His eyes had deepened, gone grayer, bolder, older. His cheeks were sunken, contoured, scarred, tinged with heat, his skin mottled. He laughed much louder, head thrown back.

Selene watched him.

Uncontained.

In time, whatever Hugh desired, he touched and claimed.

The houseboy: my Kavirondo.

The Waliangulu hunter: my tracker.

The cook: my *mpishi*.

The all-purpose repairman: my Indian fundi.

The boatman: my Lamu oarsman.

The dead elephant: my trophy.

Kenya: my country.

Selene: *my wife*.

One day, Hugh told her, "Darling, James Thompson says he'll introduce us to the Colfields over at the Muthaiga Country Club. They can present our names for membership." He beamed at Selene.

No, she prayed.

"Civilized company to keep, good for us," said Hugh.

"Kenya," declared Hugh one afternoon as he bounced into the house, returning from one of his spontaneous bush forays, and peeling off rain-dampened clothes, "Maasai. Means 'ancient place of eternal purpose.'" He paused to point to an invisible space beyond the lake. "My Mkamba told me that 'Kenia' means gleaming substance. Like jewels, darling, though my tracker—odd chap—did contend that 'Kenya' was a word for 'ostrich.' But think, what a delectable convergence is our Kenya, dear, eternity glitters. As we shall."

Yes, Hugh.

Selene sought refuge in decorating the home, adding throws, changing wall colors, surrounded by the servants who kept the rhythm of the day ticking.

Mwihaki, the maid.

Karanja, the gardener.

Noormohamed, the head cook, whose shepherd's pies were of legendary repute.

Lisabeta, the assistant cook.

Linus, the kitchen toto, who synchronized his moods to Selene's signs of pleasure or displeasure.

Lazaro Agwaro, houseboy, who had been a signal man in Burma.

"Boy, what was Burma like?"

"Hard, memsahib."

"What did you do?"

"Nothing good, memsahib."

"What did you see?"

"Bad things, memsahib."

Penina, ayah and housekeeper, employed in anticipation of children-to-come, was still underutilized.

Two Labradors.

One feral cat.

A mongoose.

One Sykes's monkey.

A troop of colobus monkeys.

Several duikers.

Five giraffes.

And Hugh.

Selene started to call herself a *collector*. Picking up and fitting pieces and things to life. She also changed. Head tilted, eyes lucid, she would listen, even to concealed messages in tapping fingers, and inhale a truth, which she stored for later use, in her dreams.

An unexpected massive storm rode into Naivasha over Easter, three years later, expanding the lakeshore. It had started as a spitting, back-lit gray cloud. It blasted the landscape for five weeks nonstop. Selene and Hugh waited, one of their infinite Kenya waitings. Hugh set up an easel on the porch facing the lake and imagined the temper of the storm in, over, within the lake, in fierce colors and shades. A column of vodka and gin bottles memorialized this interlude. Then they watched the vines rot. Some hardy stems loitered but eventually turned feral.

Uncontained.

It should have been paradise. Selene had asked, "Hugh, what do we do now?" It was sensible to return to England.

"Start again!" said Hugh, guffawing. "Bloody good storm, what?"

Selene deflated.

He can no longer see the small things.

Resolution. She would outwait this country.

The tempest unshackled Hugh, and he roamed deeper territories. Safari after safari, and an assortment of guns entered the house, as did a parade of slaughtered creatures—heads, skins, tusks. All those things they had never needed until they came to Kenya.

Selene abhorred the look of dead animals. Hugh the predator made her nervous. She decided to stay behind in Naivasha to wait out Hugh's hunts.

The first birth: a girl, at Nanyuki Cottage Hospital—a late-term miscarriage. Selene named her Elise, and when they had taken her away, she wondered how a mere turn in a footpath could lead to a woman lying on her back alone in a hospital bed staring at a stark white high-vaulted ceiling.

I'm becoming smaller.

Hugh! Selene called out before covering her mouth, crushing need into tears. Hugh was, as always now, somewhere else in Kenya. She had stopped asking where he was going, with whom and why. Selene checked herself out of the hospital. Traveled overnight back to Naivasha, where, the next day, Penina administered chicken soup and a green soup made of unknown ingredients, until her body recovered. Selene started to garden, planting dahlias. She tilled the land and purchased a pair of long-haired milk-producing goats. They thrived and produced more goats. Every night she dreamed of the stark, honest blast of an English winter.

Hugh came home hauling the tusks of four dead elephants. "Where's the baby? What is it?"

"*She* died," Selene says. "Tea, dear?"

"Thank you. Died? Oh, bugger!"

For five seconds Selene hoped Hugh would cry. He wrestled a torment, which puffed and then deflated his face, and said, "Was looking forward to raising a real Kenya lad. Must not wallow, though. We'll try again."

"Yes, dear. Scones?"

Refuge in caricature. Play-acting.

She was good at this.

Selene waited.

The ferment was not long in coming.

Restlessness.

She plucked news from the frothing landscape.

National happenings.

A death.

Mission-reject Lucas Pkiech in a battle with British forces. *Postwar dinis.* Hugh relished the phrase. Intimate details of battle, as if he had been there. "The color of blood drying in Kenya's sun is more intense than at other battlegrounds, darling. Copper and something in between."

Lovely. Selene winced. *How do you know all this?* She clutched the battle scars of her womb, their empty bounty. Hugh mixed copper on his palette. Color of blood from a hemorrhaging miscarriage, one spectacle Hugh had missed.

The duke of Gloucester came and baptized Nairobi a city.

"Must go home," she told Hugh.

"You *are* home, darling. Start a craft, get busy. Cheer up!"

"Must go home." Selene's arms clasped her body. Her voice sounded whiny, and Hugh turned his head, eyes slit, mouth firm.

Nothing more said.

Yet she prevailed.

Selene landed in London. Another damp and disappointing spring was under way. She and her sister watched black swans glide by on a park's pond. Her two nieces played with their brand-new brother. Pieces of grass smeared Selene's fingers. Selene brought the fingers to her nose and inhaled home. Ached. Hugh's absence was a sorrow.

So Selene returned to Kenya in tears, just as the Nandi flame trees were in crimson blossom. Outbreak of luxuriant redness; *Spathodea campanulata* in glory. She reached her Naivasha gates under the light of a dry-season full moon.

"You are lovely," Hugh said, when he saw her. "Missed you so, old girl."

A blur of battling dreams—Kenya hopes in ceaseless conversations. What would the country be? Half a year later, as Hugh stood, neat gin and *Flowers of Kenya* book in his hand, he caught Selene's eye. "I love this country."

A warning?

Kenya had since added muscles and height to Hugh.

His sudden excited boy's laugh in a grown man's body. She loved that laugh.

Time.

Princess Elizabeth and the duke of Edinburgh came to Kenya.

The princess became a queen.

A rhythm.

Friends, farming, dreams; parties, music, drink, and barbiturates to ease the unease. Two weeks later, Selene was tending the Naivasha garden in the dry heat and watching as herdsmen sheared the new sheep.

"Hereditary ineptitude," Hugh burst out.

English class-system rules rigorously applied in the colony had refused Hugh's application for membership at the Muthaiga Club. It meant he despised the governor, Mitchell.

Months slogged on.

Nairobi and Naivasha Club weekends. Selene danced. Got drunk. Flirted. Would have committed adultery if her target of affection had not spotted more youthful prey. Danced some more, played backgammon, gossiped about an English social season she had no part in, and hosted teas for the Thompsons.

In the early part of 1952, the *Kenya Weekly News* sustained Governor Mitchell's perspective that *"the general political feeling in Kenya was better than he had ever known it for many years."*

Hugh had thrown the newspaper down. "The fool has a wooden skull and a forked tongue." He threw Selene's saucer at the wall, where it smashed up.

More of Hugh's "my"s:

My country. My land. My dream.

My people.

"My people built this land, named it, toiled, built, and died for it. Won't let that bugger destroy it."

"What're you going to do?" Selene muttered, the question a waste of breath.

Governor Mitchell left.

Hugh was a guest at the good-riddance party held at the club. He gave the third toast to Acting Governor Potter. Selene drank down the toast and then some more. She tried to fox-trot, because Hugh had disappeared with a boy-figured woman on his arm, and she was not the only one who had noticed how he had slithered out through the kitchen door.

New favorite dinner topic: Mau Mau.

Subtheme: *kiapu*—the oath, the covenant.

Its dreadful mystery, the herald of shadows.

Favorite rumor: insurrection.

Favorite fear: death of the European.

The unspoken: loss of a nation, nowhere else to go.

The fear: requiem for an ideal.

Selene thought: *I told you so.*

She waited for Hugh to return to her.

News: The murder of a settler family in the Aberdare Range, children included. Crop fires, and the threat to Hugh's perfect plans for the perfect country where they could live out perfect lives.

Mau Mau. Acrid fear.

Mwihaki saw threat everywhere. "Memsahib, we must be careful."

Sundowner gin-and-tonics filled with cigar smoke and, suddenly, numerous plans to leave, head south or north. A woman named Rosaline who kept Arabian horses distributed *Save Our Country* doilies. When Hugh returned to their Naivasha home, Selene concentrated on pouring his cup of tea and counting the blotches on his skin. Dark tints. Her father would be appalled. She observed herself splitting, wondered which one of her different selves restrained itself from poking holes in Hugh's body before splitting his stomach with a machete and shearing his skin. She smiled at Hugh, prized milling thoughts apart, brushed away the variety of insects that attempted to bite, perch, and crawl on and feed off them.

Like the country.

This is my country. Foolish Hughie. The country chose its prey. Seduced them, made them believe they owned it, and then it gobbled them down, often in the most tender of ways—like a python. When Selene was alone, she laughed and laughed, tears marking her face. Despair. She needed to go back home.

In Nairobi. An idea—Kenyatta. A rally. A metaphor. Sugarcane. Unease. Chaos fluttered. *Kenya News Weekly,* October 7. Senior Chief Waruhiu wa Kungu's car had been forced off the road and he was shot four times at close range. Rumors. Three battalions of the King's African Rifles garrisoned. And the Fourth Battalion from Uganda. And two companies of the Twenty-sixth Battalion from Mauritius.

A wind-whiny gloaming. A chill seeped into Selene's room. Agwaro fidgeted near the door until Selene asked, "What is it, boy?"

"Memsa'p . . ." He entered and stood at attention. "Something bad's on its way."

"Don't be foolish," snapped Selene with a shiver, and huddled into her pink-striped cardigan.

Husky-voiced answer: "*It* wants human blood."

"A soldier like you," Selene mocked, "afraid?"

A hesitation, as if he had something more to say. Reconsidered: "No memsa'p," Agwaro answered, and slunk away.

Selene stared at a large spot above her door. She had long sensed the footfall of advancing predatory shadows.

Twelve Hastings aircraft were making their way to Kenya. Mid-conversation at night in Naivasha on October 21, 1952, Hugh, red-faced and bright-eyed, plowed to Selene's side and whispered, "The Lancashire Fusiliers are here."

The next morning, the new Governor Baring's radio voice: a state of emergency had been declared in Kenya. The previous night, Operation Jock Scott: 183 arrest-and-detention warrants. The fusiliers patrolled Nairobi's streets. The Kenya Police Reserves and Kenya Regiment were summoned to active duty. Two days later, Senior Chief Nderi was hacked into meat-sized chunks by pangas in the hands of his people. The next day, *Kenya*, the Royal Navy cruiser, docked in Mombasa. There were men on board.

A week later, the solitary Eric Bower was taking a bath when he was slaughtered with his servants. It was difficult to tell where his body ended and those of his servants' began.

One balmy dusk, a few days later, Hugh donned a nondescript uniform, waltzed up to Selene, and swung her in his arms. "Our country needs us," he intoned.

Our country? "Where are you going?"

She should have asked that question long, long ago.

He was going to Central Headquarters, Special Branch, to attend a meeting with Sir Percy Sillitoe.

"Sillitoe?" Selene said, frowning. "Director-general of the British Security Service?" Her voice ended in a screech. "What're you doing with those people, darling?"

"For heaven's sake, Selene, be an adult!" He rubbed his head, a perplexed boy's gesture. "This is my work. You know that."

She did not.

"You never said . . ."

"Didn't I?"

She sat down.

Didn't ask, she conceded to herself. *We do not talk anymore, Hugh.* She looked through him, not seeing him.

Felt his kiss—warm, hard lips against her forehead.

She breathed him.

"*Power is useless if it cannot be expressed,*" Hugh murmured.

Leave him alone, she pleaded with the land. *Forgive him.* She looked over her shoulder at the red setting sun, its light bleeding into plump clouds. Waited.

Selene tallied the State of Emergency dead.

Picked up smoking to mark time.

Operation Anvil.

Operation Hammer.

Relocated lives.

Operation First Flute.

Lari Massacre.

Manipulation of the insurgent's generals.

Terrains of waiting.

Selene stole forgetfulness with music and etched scratch grooves into her two Patti Page albums. The songs became indecipherable from the outside screeching of Naivasha's seasonal winds. She latched onto Perry Como and his "cute little cottage" in "Hot Diggity," as she created a sound turret that was aloof from Kenya's happenings. In the late evenings, music from the servants' quarters swarmed over her sleeplessness: Griff's Mambo, replays of Machito's swinging Afro-Cuban *Kenya,* every sixth song Lord Flea's "Shake Shake Sonora." There was rumba she learned by melody, and not name, Congolese sounds she could hum to if she chose, but did not. Her resistance to the forced intimacy of shared aesthetic sentiment with alien servants.

This country.

Next day, news of a raid on the Naivasha police station.

Good, cheered Selene. *About time. Hit the installations. Make it a real insurrection so I can go home.* She wanted to read about the disruption of the railway system, public works, the water works, detonations in the city, an uprising by the population, the basics of an insurgency, real combat, and, finally, evacuations.

Nothing.

Selene sobbed into her sewing.

A sound. She turned, clutched her throat. The servants: Noormohamed, Agwaro, Mwihaki.

Noormohamed said, "Memsahib, no one will hurt you, we are here."

More tears. "Thank you," she managed.

Agwaro nodded.

She wondered, *Behind those placid faces, what lurks? Would they drink human blood to emphasize their separation from our lives?* That night, Selene went to sleep with one of Hugh's hunting rifles within her reach, under the bed.

. . .

A collection of Hugh's new words:

Pseudo-gangs. Economical. Effective. Population Sweep. Flogging the forest.

Whispered words at night: *My people created this country. I'll be damned if I'll be forced out. This is my country. . . .*

What "my" am I? Selene wondered.

She needed the lake, its frazzled ediginess. The insurgency had imploded. Disappointment. *You will still die.* She answered her own whispers: *I know,* she said, *but first I want* . . . to belong to something real, like truth. Erase unspoken things, like Hola—a work camp where an unnamed man goes berserk and pounds eleven inmates into pulp. Men are redeployed, Hugh one of those. *Why?*

Silence.

Hugh was transferred to Athi River to lead some of the mopping-up operations. As weeks went by, he turned florid with fury about what he called *covert shenanigans.* He wrote letters she never saw, crisscrossed Nairobi without her, returned to Naivasha pale and drooping. "They're selling out."

Selene did not ask what had been sold, and to whom.

Hugh annoyed enough people, who then arranged to dispatch him to the Northern Frontier District, a closed district and an official destination for exiles.

"With the Turkana?" Selene asked, thinking of District Officer Kennaway, conforming to the demands of heat-filled lands, walking the district naked save for sandals and an official topi helmet.

"They're hoping I'll resign." Hugh's eyes had glittered.

He left for the north. Selene had called out to Hugh as he drove away, "Say hello to Kennaway for me, would you?" She listened for Hugh's gust of laughter. She loved his laugh.

10

A PUNGENT SCENT SHAKES AJANY OGANDA FROM HER THICK wool of sleep. From the doorway of wakefulness, she stares at the Trader as if from far away. His eyes carry the shimmering image of the house, of blue flames, orange sparks. Of fire and light.

You'll burn black-black.

A resonant voice returning.

She turns away.

"You'll burn black-black," Bernardo had once rasped at her.

As then, she now saw herself from the outside in.

"We're lost in the same song, we're the same lost song."

Speaking to her tears: "Don't cry. I'm the son of a witch." He had licked each tear sliding down: *"Não sou eu. É a música."* *Not me, it's the music.* Yet, compelled by his life, which had taken over something inside her, a madness that she offered and he needed, she still danced naked for him, stripped down to her soul. His hands cupping her breasts: "You alone? *"Não, meu amor."* She should have fled then.

Now two of four winds pound the doum palms.

Ajany mumbles.

"There!" the Trader says, his voice as serrated as a musical saw.

She sways as if drunk as he helps her up. He offers her a brew: "*Ka-ha-wa?*"

Ajany peers at him through hair that covers her eyes.

Galgalu reaches forward. "*Ch'uquliisa?*"

Ajany listens to the Trader's hum. An ache along her spine, in her stomach; a hammering in her head. Something niggles.

The Trader says, "Ka-*ha*-wa . . . Wash the night off your body with blue water, my soul."

Shoveling. Grating pebbles. A memory of . . . *what?* Ajany's eyes stare into the Trader's. *Inside here, something is bleeding.*

The Trader strokes Ajany's head.

A shout: "*Ehh!*"

They turn.

Nyipir. "*Nyaaaara!*"

A hope-filled bellow.

Ajany grasps her father's voice. Walks a few steps toward him, sniffs a faint eucalyptus scent. What was it again? Something terrifying. She sees the green tarpaulin. Eucalyptus pungency. Hint of putrefaction. The territory of infinite pain.

Odidi.

She runs.

Past Nyipir.

Arms flailing, feet gliding above the ground, she runs.

Beguiled by her rush, the gathered gawk. By the time Nyipir kicks aside the gate to try to stop her, the darkness has already swallowed Ajany.

Isaiah shakes his head to dislodge the lost-in-dreaming sensation that suffuses him.

The Trader stares into nothing with a finger across his face. "It's out," he explains. "Now it roams."

Silence.

———

When Ajany was fifteen and lost—a drought had run for two years, and the old nanny goat simply lay down and died. Galgalu found her and shouted, "You'll save those tears. Crying is for when camels fall."

Ajany-jany yuak, yuak, yuak, Odidi used to taunt.

Now she leans into cave walls, clinging to stone. *Odidi Oganda,* she etches, and then she touches his name. When she scrapes the cave walls with her palms, she feels.

Eeeeoiiiiahaaa!

After that, as should be expected, there is stillness. It is the time of false dawn and red, purple, and blue smudges in the sky. Small moths flit in between fireflies and shadows of conical mountains. Among the sojourners there, it is understood that *ekhera,* the restless dead, might show up and shout around encampments at night. The most tormented sounds are the *ekhera* avoided by other ghosts—those exiled and lonely dead.

That night.

Eeeeoiiiiahaaa!

A hideous lament.

It contains the kernel of all their deepest yearnings.

"Eeeeoiiiiahaaa!"

The notes find and burrow into secret wounds of the hearers. Peel away scars. Goose bumps at Wuoth Ogik; even the livestock moan. Gut ache, heart murmur. Nyipir paces back and forth, a leopard caged. Paralysis starts with a popping stab in his right eye. More losing. He cannot move.

Weary.

Of waiting.

For Akai.

Where was she?

This woman.

His no-center-of-gravity war.

Weary.

Of battle losses.

Of fighting alone.

Memories are ghosts.

Akai, even wandering herdsmen come home at sunset.

Even the house was dying.

Galgalu tries to light an incense stick, fumbles. The stick drops. He picks it up again. Glances at the scented clouds to see if they show whether his mother is still alive. He cannot look at the answer.

· · ·

The Trader's hands are claws; there are tension lines on his face. He has clamped his teeth over images of faces once caressed, which as the years have passed have become more and more beloved, more and more blurred.

Isaiah strides—left, right—haunted and hunted, clutching his head as the wail bounces inside him. He *will not* die like this. Not here. Stops. *I'll leave,* Isaiah reassures himself. *Go home.* Stoops. Knuckles to the ground, wanting to vomit. He grinds his teeth.

Hands on Isaiah's shoulders. Isaiah does not see his comforter, but he bounds away, too many questions after him. "I want *my* daddy. *My* daddy." A child's tantrum. Selene had spanked him. Fury in her arms, face distorted in horror, as if he had become evil. He had cowered. "Sorry, Mummy. Sorry." Selene had gathered him to her, covering his body with kisses and tears, whispering, "Oh, my poor, poor baby."

His questions had dissolved, only to re-emerge as asthma. The asthma evaporated when he found something beautiful of his own to save—a woman who would one day walk definitively away from him. With her disappearance, the compulsion to find his lost souls returned to possess him.

Soon after, he and Moses Oganda found each other, and Moses had called him to Kenya. He had shown up a few days too late to find Moses out of his reach. Another of his lost.

Something flutters past Isaiah's ear. He swings at it. The Trader's droll voice: "Giant moth."

A lantern shakes in Galgalu's hand. Nyipir looks in the direction of the red caves. The Trader watches Nyipir standing guard over shadows. "What did you do to her?" Isaiah asks the Trader.

"*Ka-ha-wa?*" the Trader suggests, pointing at the coffee beans drying on the fire.

Isaiah says, "Good night." Amid his father's books, he can salvage sanity.

"*Isaiah!*" the Trader calls. "They'll come."

Isaiah stops. "Who?"

"Your dead."

Isaiah walks away.

The Trader wheezes "Good night" and stomps his feet for warmth. The night was cold—wrong temperatures for this season. A random arc of light from Galgalu's lantern shines on the wet on the Trader's face. The Trader blows into his hands. The hyena that normally crossed Wuoth Ogik to get to the watering hole avoids it. It waits by the acacia tree as echoes of a lone spirit's wail are swept away by Wuoth Ogik's four winds.

Drenched in so many feelings, losing himself, Isaiah puts his head in his arms; bile rising, he swallows. What was he still doing here? His mother had been right. Ghosts were best left undisturbed. What did his father want here?

———

Late 1961, at about midday, a native aide to Hugh, a recruit of the Tribal Police, drove Hugh's black car up to the Naivasha farmhouse. The man was square-faced, tall, and thin. His Hitler mustache set off high cheekbones. His skin was ebony velvet, and when he spoke, his voice rumbled. When he looked at people as he did Selene, they wondered what he saw that they themselves could not recognize. *What're you looking at?* Selene almost snarled.

Hugh jumped out of the car. His head was bandaged, left arm in a sling, and no explanation. No questions. "Darling!" he droned.

Selene sauntered over and laid her cheek against his.

"Your head?"

"Little cut. Healing well."

"Who's that?" Her eyes on the aide.

"My new man. Aggrey Oganda. Good boy. A very clever Kavirondo."

She watched as the aide parked the car. Smooth, swift turns. No movement wasted. He got out of the car, wiped the door handle with a white cloth, flicked invisible particles from the windscreen, checked the tires, tucked the cloth into his pocket, turned, and saluted Hugh: "Sir." He stood at attention, waiting for instructions.

Hugh waved him off without a glance.

Aggrey Nyipir Oganda lowered his cap at Selene. "Madam," he said, and then about-turned in the direction of the servants' quarters.

Not *memsahib*, Selene observed. "You ought to feed your boy, Hugh. Rather scraggy, isn't he?"

"He'll fill up. What've you been up to, old girl?"

"I *have* missed you," she told Hugh.

He patted her bottom.

That night, in bed, Selene curled next to Hugh as he told her he had decided to build her the perfect house near a perfect oasis in Kalacha. He told her about pink and coral stones being carted across the arid lands. "From Dar es Salaam."

Tanganyika? She asked, "Frightfully far, isn't it?"

"No, darling," hooted Hugh. "Dar es Salaam—below Somaliland. On our side of the map."

Our side. "I see," said Selene, for a moment certain that she would die from her longing to return home to England.

Hugh spoke of the northern lands, of birds and desert plants, of transient peoples and wild horses. He spoke, and in his words there were gaps and new silences.

Before dawn, Hugh got out of their bed. Selene counted his pacing steps. One . . . three . . . nine . . . eighteen . . . thirty-two . . . a hundred and thirteen. *Who are you when you're there?* Selene wondered.

Hugh struggled to recompose an interest in their Naivasha life, but at any time of the day Selene found that he had stepped onto the porch to stare at horizons beyond the lake.

When he was not painting, he was going for long walks with Nyipir, journeys that started at dawn and ended after dusk.

Who are you when you're there?

Selene served tea and an experimental tangerine sponge cake. She studied Hugh and his clear-eyed insouciance. A wild laugh, organic. She startled a rare raw hunger in his eyes as he watched her. He muted the gleam. Selene avoided her husband's gaze, but now, if she brushed against his body or touched him, it was with the mild titillation of taking liberties with a stranger. Committing adultery with one's own husband. *Committing idolatry*—a wry grin.

When he was on one of his walks, she returned to the scene of his drying artwork. Her fingers hovered over the thick, dark brushstrokes, as her eyes studied the jagged lines. His finished work: impressions of heat on black rock, and something else, a shimmering form. Selene stared at it for a long time.

At night, one hand cradling her jaw, the other lifting a cigarette to and from her mouth, Selene watched Hugh read, and picked out his edited phrases. *What is true?* she wondered.

Every day, Hugh spoke of the place he had just come from. He said there were different notes to the "whistling thorn." That each of the four winds up north carried its own song. That the clatter of the doum palms evoked the rush of a freight train. He said water evaporated before it reached the ground. That he had gone to the South, North, and Central Islands in Lake Rudolf. Quiver of awareness.

He guffawed at her reaction to his assurance that the islands were indeed inhabited by demons and evil winds. He told her he saw the giant python in the crater on the east end of the North Island. Said his boat had stumbled into a lake storm. Said he screamed at the wind, that it stopped only after he dared it to kill him: "Like a faucet turned off." Hugh's nostrils had flared, his eyes narrowed, he was back on the lake. *Crocodilian,* Selene felt.

Death's grim grin.

The next day, without her expecting it, Hugh left with Nyipir for his Northern Frontier District.

Selene listened to the clock tick. Brooded before the canvas with the impression of heat. The remaining dog sat close to her, shivering. The other older Labrador had died after a tangle with a poisonous snake. Today, everything Selene touched or thought seemed ready to crumble. She breathed. She walked. She gardened, planting herbs and hydrangeas, and turning the soil with her hands. Selene waited.

A month later, Hugh returned to Naivasha without Nyipir.

Deep in Selene's womb, twisting anxiety.

He came with a new stillness that menaced her.

After dinner, Hugh sat brooding, oozing solitude.

Selene went to brush her teeth.

Turned when she sensed Hugh.

Found him staring at her.

Memorizing me.

Her lips trembled. Her skin tingled. He opened his mouth to say something. She pre-empted him. Rushed to lock her arms around him, pressed her body into his, cupping his face, seeking a return to familiar silences.

Bed.

A frenetic and furious slippery mating, in which his teeth bruised her nipples, they tore at each other again and again—clinging, clawing, marking—and, in the midst of the craving, sudden stillness. Hugh stroked her back, drawing lines with the back of his hand.

Later.

"Darling, my darling."

Selene tensed.

Then.

"The home Hugh's built is perfect for his dear darling thing," he spoke into her neck. "What does she say?"

God, dear God, no. But Selene faked an animated laugh. "For me?" she said. "However will I thank you, *sweetheart?*" Dread in her voice. She hunted for the pretense of joy.

"We'll have to find a home for the dog," Hugh said. "Or maybe let's braise and eat him? Or stuff him so he'll always be with us?"

Selene stopped breathing until Hugh poked her back and sniggered. "So solemn, my love?"

She yawned, murmured, and pretended to become drowsy.

Selene stayed awake all night, head pressed into the pillow to absorb streaming tears. *Let us go back home,* she wept to the country.

Two months later, on the eve of the day they were to set off, Hugh went to the nearby club for a drink. Selene wandered into his workspace. On the easel, a half-done art piece; on the table, rolled-up canvases. She reached for one of these and unwrapped it.

She dropped it.

A moan.

She retrieved it from the floor, body shaking. She stretched out the charcoal portrait of a fiery-eyed, long-limbed, crop-haired, full-lipped, dark-brown-skinned woman. Harsh lines, clear, old eyes. Hands sweating, she picked up another canvas. The same woman was stretched in a pose that might have been lewd if it were not for fine details—a beaded bracelet, intricately patterned stomach scars—which made the work an intimate ode to visceral femininity. Three small pieces, a triptych, making a medium-sized rectangular piece, made blood rush from Selene's head, forced her to catch her breath, sit on the floor, and breathe hard. The woman, her belly rounded, pregnant, legs stretched out, watching the artist, the universal lover's gaze, hand beneath her head, a half-smile.

Hugh used to mock portraiture—*icon making for ghastly paper gods.* Questions arrived and left. Inside no-thought, Selene restored Hugh's art to its place. Left it at that.

The next day, she left with Hugh for a stark otherworldliness where the sky dominated everything. *This is how the land crushes its refugees.* Selene stared at broody mountains, the rockscape. *Drought is profligate.* She fanned her face. Sweated streams, struggled to breathe, visualized winter. They reached Kalacha. Everywhere she looked, there were camels and goats, cows and donkeys and sheep. Oryx, gerenuks, giraffes, elephants, gazelles, impalas, and snakes. Horses. Mules. Everywhere she looked, she craved verdant greenness. Organic green.

Hugh hugged her. "For you." The house. Almost ready. A pink mouth made out of the land's eclectic matter.

Selene thought, *Not mine. Yours.* She compressed her lips.

Hugh dangled a bunch of keys above her head.

She dragged out a smile, took them, and, with a quick step to the front door, inserted the wrong key into the lock. Unsteady fingers searched for the right one. The keys fell. Hugh picked them up. He unclenched her fist and placed the keys on her palm, closed her hand over them, and kissed each of her fingers.

Another kind of heat: *Touch me,* followed by an impulse to flee as only the preyed-upon can. Lifting her hand, Hugh inserted the right key into the lock. The door opened into a large, cool room where a gap in the wall brought air in and revealed a splendid view of the desert.

Selene sighed. Glazed stone tiles, plastered walls and floor, Ethiopian Orthodox icons. A green-robed Saint George accompanied by a glowering angel carrying a flaming sword—Hugh's work. Etching in the wall. It read: *Crux sancta sit mihi lux / Non draco sit mihi dux / Vade retro satana | Numquam suade mihi vana | Sunt mala quae libas | Ipse venena bibas.* She remembered, "Let not the dragon be my guide / Get thee behind me, Satan. . . ." And gasped, "Hugh?"

Hugh's lavish laughter. "No *shetanis* here."

Aggrey Nyipir Oganda stood a few paces behind them.

Selene turned.

He looked at the floor.

She would wonder that his face had been distorted by pity.

If all houses had resident spirits, Selene knew the ones here regarded her as an invading entity. Her nails cut into her palms as she looked through the screen window into the landscape, its sleight-of-hand mounds over vast horizons. The winds slithered in through the doum palms. She slapped her arms, imagining insects.

A sensation.

She was being watched.

She turned to look.

The light's sublime, Hugh was saying.

Inside, Selene wept.

But Kenya had given her the ability to wear the right face for the right time. To proceed as if nothing had happened, as if she had not been changed, was not being changed all the time.

That first night at Wuoth Ogik, the face of the painted woman haunted Selene's sleep. *Who is she?* Mouthed in silence to a darkness that scared her. She clung to Hugh. *Who is she?* she thought as she got out of bed. Stepped into the library, strode around the room, counting footsteps. Eighty-two. She struggled to light a kerosene lamp, scorched the tips of her fingers as the lantern wick burned. She wandered downstairs and outside and found herself in a courtyard. She sat on the edge of the fountain, leaning back until the water's coolness soaked her body. *Very, very civilized fountain,* she told the water. She listened to the murmur of spring water.

Wuoth Ogik: Journey's End.

Sensation of being watched.

Then.

A movement, a strangled-off voice, scuffling.

A minute later, Aggrey the aide appeared carrying a calabash of water, which he offered her at once.

"*Ni nini?*" Selene gasped. What is it?

"*Paka tu,* madam." A cat.

The gourd smelled of use and sour milk. Selene took the vessel with both hands and sipped water. *Who is she?* she needed to ask. "Thank you. You may go now," she said instead, handing over the gourd.

The aide bowed and left.

Who is she? The wind screeched among doum palms; Selene covered her ears. *Enough.* She dashed into the house—leaving the lantern behind, gulping down a scream.

Upstairs, she peeled off her wet gown, crawled naked into bed, and snuggled into Hugh. His large hands adjusted her body to his. He muttered in his sleep. Selene ignored the shadows that had entered the room with her.

A pink haze over the land lit up their room. Selene woke up in tears. Hugh was sleeping faceup. He had raised his left knee. Selene studied his naked body. Seamlessly brown, as if the sun had delicately turned him on a spit over its fires.

Till death do us part.

Which death? Many kinds on offer here.

She moved so that she was on top of Hugh. He opened his eyes and smiled a lopsided smile, tightened his arms around her. She lowered her head, her hair covering his face. Memories of another couple named Selene and Hugh nestling in each other's arms, people from a Pleistocene epoch, far away from the Selene and Hugh they had since become. She tasted his sweat. The scars on his chest, on his head. The chest hair. Rubbed her face against his stubble, inhaling silent lines of too many hidden stories. Scratches, bites, bullet wound, the faint mark of a garrote beneath his chin.

She should have asked the questions. *Who is she?* Painter hands, hard, elongated, denuded of excess fat. *Who are you?* Open-mouthed breathing. *Who is she?* Her tongue hunted the Hugh she remembered. He was there. He was there. *Who is she?* A long kiss made of grief. Hugh moved his body so she was under him. He bit her nose, half in jest, stroked her leg. Selene moaned instead. Hated the memory of buzzing blue flies. How could she live with these flies? Hated Hugh. Loved Hugh. Craved Hugh. Arched into Hugh, who used to gasp but now grunted. She placed his hands around her neck and squeezed. Soft. Gentle. Loving. Loathing. Tears.

She did not know how long Hugh had been watching her. He touched her sweating body. She turned to him, her face unmasked. He kissed her mouth. He whispered, "You don't like it here."

Hugh's disappointment scalded Selene's soul. She knelt, reaching down him, fingers fluttering, touching his face. Willing to forgive and forget everything. "Let's go home, let's go back home."

Hugh played with her hair. "We *are* home, darling."

She left the Northern Frontier District.
She left alone.

———

Almost a year later, volcanic shifts within Selene were interspersed with the outside rising babble of new-Kenya tunes: *"Kenya, Kenya, Kenya nchi yetu . . . wapi wale wabeberu waone haya . . ."* Gloating hymns overpowered her, their deafness to intimate losses, as if she had no right to desire, as if the years of work and ash-strewn dreams meant nothing, as if she had not struggled to love this land even though it had tried to take everything from her. A secret. In the darkness she had seized something from it, and now, like a jewel thief, she was fleeing the scene of her heist. Destination England. To save a life, to have a life.

Unease.

The baby moved. She shielded her stomach, exhaled, and then smiled a mother's smile.

11

IN THE MORNING, AFTER AJANY STAGGERED BACK INTO WUOTH
Ogik from the caves, she saw gold-and-red daylight on stone. She lurched
to the edge of her brother's half-finished grave, sniffed the putrid smell
of dying, and jumped in.

Light swathes. It warms her skin. She clambers out to stand near
her brother. Contemplates the gray, placid face inside the coffin. Its stillness and absence are a new palette. She knows how to paint with darkness. She knows shadows, too. Absence is new. She must chase after it
until it takes her to Odidi's Somewhere Else.

Shadows shift.

Ajany pushes open the doors of the falling coral house. Hearing the
sound, Galgalu hobbles in, fingers knuckled against his chest where
it throbs. He starts when he finds Ajany staring at family pictures.
"Ch'uquliisa?" he whispers, fingering the amethyst she had given him.

She is wiping the picture frames.

Galgalu takes Ajany's blood-streaked palms and turns them over,
touches entangled hair, smells sweat, rot, and coldness. There is bright-
ness in her eyes, and her body thrums. She had turned herself over to
something. *Madness?* Galgalu trembles.

"'Galu," Ajany says as if in a dream, "tell . . . Baba I've gone to find
Odidi."

Galgalu mutters, "Remember the moon." Ajany stares. Galgalu says, "It falls to pieces. It becomes whole again."

She hears his words in patches.

Galgalu tiptoes out of the room pulled apart by two desires, to seize Ajany and shake her back to lucidity, and to protect Nyipir from this, the image and likeness of lunacy. *If a man has nothing to live for . . .*

Akai Lokorijom had not come home yet.

Galgalu pinches his chin, then twists the amethyst this way and that. He must return to the Trader. There was a formula for exorcising everything. The Trader always said so.

Ajany pulls out clothes from her still-packed bag until she can carry it with one hand. She places Hugh's painting in the library for Isaiah to find. Nothing to do with her now.

Wind-marked solitude. A goatskin water bag. Ajany's orange carry-on swings in counterpoint to her steps. She scans the earth for signs of water, wells, damp soil, mud, dew-storing stones, and scraggly grass. Mount Kulal—the storykeeper of this land. She listens for songs of the terrain that Odidi would have been singing by now.

He had started it, Odidi had. Their homelessness. He had conjured up stories of Elsewhere—imagined siblings, aunties, uncles, cousins, and grandparents, a web of doting dream relations into which he and Ajany inserted their longing to leave. Those relatives never did come.

Ajany walks over scallops molded into a black, pimply earth. Her stride lengthens. A view of mountains shaped like music notations, and six cairns. She crosses two *lagas*, gawks where foreigners have planted a forest of white windmills, implants in a land made for silence. There are other strangers elsewhere building giant rigs, prospecting for oil in margins without a sound.

Blue sky. Memory of cattle drives across this land to markets and to *jilali* safe pasture. Toward Turbi, distances and destiny. Heat, dust, and hope; murmurs and songs; whistling, laughter, and spare words. The last time they had walked she had been ten, still sucked her two fingers, and lurked in Odidi's shadows. Not wanting to be left behind with Akai-ma, she had sneaked after Galgalu, Nyipir, and Odidi after they had left with the cattle for sale. Galgalu knew she was in the shadow of their trail, but he had not given her away. She showed herself after two and a half days.

Baba had frowned down at her. Then he sighed and asked, "Akai-ma?"

Ajany had looked back at Nyipir, as unworried as a favorite cat, while Odidi made throat-cutting gestures at her behind his father's back.

"What do I do?" Nyipir's brow had gone up.

Nothing, she hoped.

Nyipir contemplated her.

He nodded.

They resumed their trek.

Odidi moved close to pull her hair. *"Olwenda,"* he hissed.

So what if she was a cockroach? She stuck her tongue out at him. "Baba," Odidi announced, "everyone does their share of work."

Nyipir looked over his shoulder at Ajany.

She smiled at him. He laughed, stooped so she could ride on his shoulders in their northward journey.

"Olwenda!" mouthed Odidi.

She stuck fingers into her mouth, stretched it, and crossed her eyes at him.

Ajany learned from Galgalu how to bind the camels' feet; she milked the camels and mimicked him as he murmured to the animals' secret anxieties. At night, under the stars, Odidi, whose stomach served as her pillow, showed her Kormamaddo, the camel of the skies, and as he did, she knew she was as safe as a seed enclosed in a warm, thick pod.

The Turbi market. Even now she remembered the smell of moneymaking, life's tensions abandoned to bargaining in an exchange of wit and energy. Trust extended. Wall Street heated up, and the commodities bleated. They left with a well-bred Boran bull, probably rustled off someone's farm, five top-grade cows, two Somali camels, and four Rendille camels, placed on a lorry and driven to Wuoth Ogik. When they returned to the ranch fifteen days later, Akai-ma did not scold. She seemed not to have noticed that Ajany had gone. They quarantined the new animals. Later, the men branded them with the ξ family sign before introducing the newcomers to the family herd.

Memory of bare feet squishing the *boma* earth. Intoxicating smells of life. Peering through holes in the thorny fence at a horizon that spilled into a shimmering dome. The longing for her people is a sudden sizzling ache. *What if I had stayed?* Damp eyes blink at the thought. Ajany walks and imagines Odidi's water songs. They should have gone together Far Away.

In the middle of her first year at the University of Nairobi, into which she had scraped with the lowest grade allowed, she had hidden in the design lab, reading design magazines from other corners of the globe. There she had spotted a small advertisement. A Nova Scotia–based center of fine arts sought candidates from all over the world to infuse soul into a two-year art, design-in-landscape, and new-technology experiment. The only African applicant, Ajany was accepted by default. She fit the exotic indigenous-person profile.

Odidi had scrutinized the document before screwing up his face. "The *shags* of Canada—nothing there that you can't do here." Odidi added, "Here, we belong." Ajany had stared at the black of the road next to which they stood. "Us. We stay here, 'Jany."

She waited a moment. Stammered, "'Didi, don't see it. Can't see it here." She tapped her chest.

He had said, "Not about seeing."

Teardrops in lashes. She thought a little about that, her face contorting under doubt. With fright in her eyes, she whispered, "Let's go, Odi." Heart pounding: "Let's go, Odi. . . . Thh-th-this . . ." She grunted to a stop.

"This," emphasized Odidi, his hand up in the air, "*this* is home." Tears in his gaze, voice firm. "Home."

"How?" She would do anything to feel as he felt.

Odidi watched her, rocking on his heels.

She pleaded, "You p-promised, 'Didi." She coughed, stared at the concrete pavement. A frown creased her face. Was it possible that two separate feelings of place could exist between them? What if she stayed? Instant nausea. So she had shivered, turned, and watched the confident braggadocio of other students, those who had been given coordinates to destinations to which she would never be invited. The noisy weight of a hundred silent terrors that she could escape—here was her chance. Odidi. She saw his rootedness, compared it with her floundering. A panicked question had burst through her lips: "Why does Obarogo need eyes? What's he looking for inside darkness?"

Shadows crisscrossed her brother's face. He almost said something, uttered a plea. But shutters fell, and instead he barked, "Choose."

Ajany saw herself inside Odidi's eyes, paused before she tore at the convoluted cords that entwined their lives, felt every cut in her bones and being. She had stood close to him, almost on his shoes. Not touching him, but keeping her face close to his chest. Realizing this was how death happened, this loneliness. She had closed her eyes, and murmured *Odidi,* while inside her heart a cool breeze floated. She had held on to her brother, memorized the sensation of his securing arms; she pulled down his head and kissed the leaf scar on his forehead. *He'll find me,* she had told herself. He always did. She had said, "You said we'd go Far Away. You said 'together.'"

He waited.

She waited.

Nothing.

She let him go and drifted into Elsewhere alone.

The funereal silence of her departure was colored by a tinge of shame, of giving up. Impulse of flight, its red-eye rimmed guilt, like she was a haunted bird. "Peace," she thought. That is how she soothed herself. "Peace." Except it wasn't.

She did not know then of the riddles Odidi had discovered in a book off a shelf in Wuoth Ogik until now.

———

Three children ambling home with family goats and sheep, the sun against the mountains, and white birds singing as they circle a destination. A yellow van hurtles across the landscape. The same potholed sliver of road that had rattled Ajany's body almost twenty years ago does so again, the same kind of policeman manning inconvenient roadblocks, waylaying wayfarers. Travel companions still reek of rancid butter, the desert's special sweat. Pulse of language—Kiswahili for trade, English spots, and fifteen murmured dialects—this was how they crossed worlds. The bus sways. View from a dust-dotted window. Stunted flame trees, yellow-blooming cassias, and giant milkweed with white, purple, and pink flower clusters. A child cries; the bus stops. *Qhat* and livestock traders gather.

The bus conductor is squat, round-shouldered, and bouncy-haired, like a French pop star. The bus is his stage. He pleads for passengers to board in the voice of a frustrated muezzin. *"Waabiria wapenzi . . ."* Beloved passengers. A woman screeches last-second instructions laden with "don't"s—*Msi . . . Usi*—and heaves herself into the bus. Her translucent buibui shimmers, slips off her caramel shoulders with their henna patterns of whorls and flowers. She targets a stern red-bearded passenger immersed in an intricately scripted book of wisdom, and says she is menopausal and must have a window seat. The red-bearded man dives for the back of the bus, squashes himself next to baskets of live chickens. Goats are secured to the roof of the bus.

They are on their way.

And then it is 4:50 a.m.

Welcome to the City of Nairobi. A scarred sign hangs lopsided. The morning leaches multicolored chill. The bus conductor, now a fussy grandmother, tells passengers about Nairobi's breed of *majambazi*, *wahuni*. Wait for the eye of the sun, he suggests.

As if it is reborn in the city, Ajany's mobile phone clicks into life with a tune. Downloads in Portuguese. Her fingers hover over the "delete" button. She depresses it. The messages disappear. Cold breeze on Ajany's face, tantalizing promise: She will find Odidi. Listen to his stories. If he says, *Stay*, she will this time.

———

Places are ghosts, too. The clouds above Nyipir's head are shaped like an anvil. Light squeezes through a tongue of cloud sparkling mauve, purple, yellow, and green. Distant cowbells. Seven days have passed since he returned from a night search to discover that his daughter had left Wuoth Ogik.

Galgalu said, *"Ah . . .* she went to bring . . . *uh . . .* flowers."

"Flowers?"

"For Odidi."

"Flowers. And you didn't stop her?"

"Ah . . . no."

"She didn't tell me?"

Galgalu looked miserable.

"Why?" cried Nyipir. "Kenya's treacherous. She doesn't know it."

Galgalu had crept away.

Nyipir had rushed to the boundary fence, looking and looking and seeing nothing.

Isaiah hears voices. Heaviness in his body; he does not want to move. So he closes his eyes and sleeps through the day and night.

12

NYIPIR STARES AT THE GAP THAT WILL CONTAIN ODIDI'S CASKET.
Around him the emptiness. The coral house. A temptation: to set alight
walls inhabited by unseen termites that are eating it to the ground. He
could stay at the center of the fire.

A heavy sigh. *Memories are ghosts.*

Nyipir was Kenyan once. Then Kenya had torn Akai away from him.
Memories are ghosts. The day after Independence Day, Nyipir became
one of the newly independent warrior-men stepping in array into Hurri
like locusts. Invading the nation. Marching, marching, and not seeing
then that he and his kind were the new scapegoats, so that a freshly
haunted people would never ask *why*. Marching, marching. Myth of
valor spun to explain the desecration of a nation; oaths of silence; Nyipir
marched and marched to whispers of blood oaths that had been made
for him.

Against Mount Forola's shimmering, the platoon split into squads
to scour territory, move northeastward, read trees and bushes, pore over
ground marks for freshness, watch the movement of birds, the slither of
lizards. A white-bellied go-away-bird warned them.

A three-day trail flecked with blood: jackal's meal. Next to a black
boulder, five zebras had been disturbed. Farther to the left, human footprints headed northeast. Thirteen, no, seventeen separate prints. Man

hunting man in comradeship. Predatory subtlety; soft, no-fuss walking. Silent gestures—a look could say everything. Muscular wakefulness, essential manliness, as if this were how it had always been. Hypnotic life, a clarity of worlds so that he could see even past the clouds. Close-target reconnaissance work. He was in a platoon fanning out in the northern terrain, tracking scents. Women, children, and elderly equaled prey, equaled game. Blasting hapless homesteaders, AK-47–ing camel herds to encourage cooperation. They mowed down elephant families, loaded tusks into lorries with blacked-out number plates. Destination, Singapore via State House.

The national economy of secrets.

One night, a human screams, "Am I now the enemy, *afande*?"

Nyipir remembered that despised things also cried.

But.

Thou shalt not kill? That was for another season. It was simpler to obey commands for the good of the nation. No questions asked.

Later, Nyipir, like others, marched up to receive his Head of State Commendation. Listened to citations for "Tactical excellence. Intelligence. Agility. Service beyond the call of duty." *Ushujaa*—heroism. Discretion—which mostly meant, *Keeps secrets.*

He was rewarded. Nyipir moved to the Anti-Stock Theft Police Unit, as trainer and supervisor of horses, mules, camels, and people. A journeying man who rode for weeks, chasing down rustlers and bringing Kenya's livestock home. Great work.

Memories are ghosts.

Now Nyipir strikes the ground with all his strength.

From the top of the hole a voice he despises.

"Excuse me."

Nyipir ignores it.

"Sir . . ." Isaiah repeats. Papers crinkle, and he leans forward.

"What, Bolton?"

"About this house . . . I found some plans in the library, here, hope you don't mind. . . ." Isaiah shows Nyipir a yellowing sheet with penned sketches. Portions of the paper break off. "The house, Wot Ogyek."

"Wuoth Ogik."

"Yes."

"No," says Nyipir.

"My father . . ."

"Go away."

"My father, Hugh . . ."

Nyipir returns to digging, sorts out the bigger rocks from the smaller. Isaiah stoops over the hole again. "Might you know who the woman in my father's work is?" He steadies the bookmark in front of Nyipir's eyes. Nyipir brushes away the paper. Isaiah pushes it forward. Nyipir slaps it away.

Yes. He *knows* the day, time, and emotion of the making of the painting. By the time he raises his head from the pit, a red-eyed meanness owns him. Rage. He has killed men before. He could kill again. "And if I do?" Nyipir asks, a thin twitching of lips, darkening of pupils.

Isaiah backs away. "Your son, Moses, sent me this."

Nyipir wags a finger. "You'll not say his name. You'll not *speak* his name!" Nyipir throws his shovel at Isaiah.

Isaiah's arms jut out, ready to fight, but he chooses flight. He hurls himself at the house and kicks the low couch twice. He will stay. He hates this place, but damned if he will leave without getting what he has come to find. He blinks, rubs his eyes; in the silence, he hears the sound of his thumping heart.

———

That afternoon, in the landscape, a multinational smattering of voices and the BBC World News signal as the Trader crosses the land. Today, for him, the voices are ambient noise. When he left Wuoth Ogik, leaving his camel and goods behind, he gave himself over to a dream in which his wives and children were still with him and his grandchildren played amid fat cows, green grass, and weekly rain.

The Trader walks until he reaches the white picket fence that is the mission where the Jacobses live and preach a version of their Gospel, teaching, healing, and baptizing in the name of God. It is a rectangular white house, a larger version of a Mississippi sharecropper's house, surrounded by purple and yellow flowers hanging in little pink boxes around the fence. Spikes like sentries around a formerly communal watering hole. New cement on a foundation that is to become a worship center. The Trader stares at the half-adobe, half-canvas medical center. The fly trap, he calls it.

The Trader stakes out the place, not moving for almost two hours, until the sun-blotched pastor, an angular man, trots out. His watery, pink, pale-blue-eyed wife watches from the door. In a loud, smiley voice, in a new dialect of Kisetla, the man announces, *"Hapa kwetu ni ufalme ya Mungu."* He flaps his hands in all directions, delineating the territory of the Kingdom of God. The action swats flies, and he swivels his neck like a pretty giraffe.

The Trader wants the freckled man to recognize him. He remembers gray eyes that were suspicious and intense.

"Medicine," creaks the Trader, slouching so as to meet the missionary's low expectations about the meaning of his life. The wind tosses sand at them. The Trader clutches his chest, in the place in his heart that is being cut into pieces.

Within three hours, the Trader has surrendered his radio, taken the prerequisite disinfected shower, been photographed for the mission's fund-raising Web site, and chosen Sila for his baptismal name. These gain him admission and a safari bed with a thin mattress. His heartbeat is measured, blood pressure noted; aspirins are administered; he is encouraged to rest.

"You'll be fed," Mrs. Jacobs says in slow, loud nasal sounds. "And, Sila, as a new lamb in the Kingdom of God, you shall pray."

Sila cries. "The devil is conquered. The perfidious liar! Praise God!" concludes Mrs. Jacobs.

Dawn. Before breakfast, the Jacobses and three acolytes gather to pray around the Trader's bed. Their prayers include a sequence in which the Trader gets a chance to renounce Satan again, his works, pomps, and empty promises. "You are a free soul now, Sila." Pastor Jacobs gives him a watery smile. "Rejoice."

The Trader closes his eyes and heaves a sigh, tempted by the simplicity of being Sila, of being thought for and hoped for.

The prayer warriors leave to have breakfast.

When some time has passed, the Trader tosses off the sheet, throws on clothes, grabs his radio, and escapes the mission through the window. His body shivering, he heads toward his *tukul*, a six-hour run from the mission.

——

Not too far from Wuoth Ogik, near a green-stained waterhole where two years ago a pair of hippos had been seen, a crazed *d'abeela* waits for another soul to frighten to death.

Radio crackle.

The Trader turns the corner and glimpses a man's silhouette. He sees the snow-white hair, the flecks on the man's face mirroring the creases hacked into his heart. The Trader knows the meaning of the misshapen turban and the dance of the devil in the wide, red, and furious eyes glaring at him.

The Trader sings, feather-light, "*D'abeela, maan feeti?* You're awake?"

He gets an answer that is arcane, succinct, and crude from a voice that is like a thin flute's song carving fleeting presences into the soul. But the *d'abeela*'s eyes fill with tears.

Over radio chatter, the Trader reaches over and readjusts the seams of the *d'abeela*'s turban.

"Sit. *We are ravens*," the Trader explains. "*We pluck fallen color. We barter. With dreams, incense, secrets, animals, and stolen sunsets.*" The Trader plucks out a small sealed bag from inside his robe and counts out eight beans. "*Ka-ha-wa?*"

The *d'abeela* offers him a two-tooth partial grin.

They chew beans.

The Trader says, "*We are bees. We touch two million scattered moments, reaping the small nectar of things.*"

The day passes over them.

From the back of the *d'abeela*'s throat a harsh purging sound. He spits out phlegm, mucus, and ugliness. "*We are stones.*" The old man stirs and twists his neck to contemplate the Trader.

No chattering radio now. The Trader sniffs the breeze. A wind lumbers past like an ancient wizard. They chew beans. The Trader says, "*We taste sweet smoke inside bitterness.*"

They chew coffee. The Trader speaks because he must, and because an unshared story can break a heart that carries it alone for too long:

Eleven years ago.

"The drought," the *d'abeela* says.

"The drought," the Trader confirms.

Ceaseless dryness, as if there were no God. Nine half-moons of waterlessness. Even the camels died. It was a bad time. The Trader, who was still answering to the name Zaman, had left his wife, mistress, children, and suffering livestock at Hurran Hura to go for water, identify pastures, and obtain help from other supportive clans. Three weeks later, outside Kargi, he received two messages, which had been passed down from trading post to watering hole to trading post. First his fickle mistress, Rehana, had seduced a visiting Malaysian prospector and, in the thrall of new love, had disappeared from the district with him. She had combined her greetings and goodbye and conveyed them through a stranger. Second, his wife and his children were now on their way to Kargi. Irritation. His wife was an insecure nag. They spent their time together raging about one or another of his many misdeeds. Yet her fragile beauty still made him sing, and he could try to summon down the best stars for her. And when he tried, she would laugh like a chime caught in a soft wind.

The children must be exhausted after a long walk.

He raged.

Women. Insensible camels.

He shook himself and readied to meet them.

Zaman approached the town center, now milling with escapees from the drought, afflicted by empty eyes and potbellied fragility. He searched for his family. He found them gathered around a stripped-down tree.

All his life and its hopes collapsed there. He crawled over and touched the gaunt, desiccated frames that were already disintegrating. They lay wrapped and small in the garish colors of the Somali cloth he traded with. A tide of fury at the yellow-red-orange and blues. He smelled death. Saw vultures and *bambaloona* waiting in trees.

"*Biche naisi,*" moaned his wife. Water, please.

"Yes. Yes. Yes."

And he had run.

Run thirty kilometers.

Run as if a hungry lion were at his heels.

The watering holes were stink ponds, filled with green poison.

He ran another twelve kilometers to the beat of *Biche naisi*. He flagged down a lorry carrying fluorspar. The driver shared a drop of water with him. He promised the man a milk cow so he could borrow a mid-sized round yellow plastic container. At Kalama he jumped down, fought off livestock and other herders at a green-water oasis, groaning, *"Biche naisi,"* and because he looked crazed and unkempt they let him scoop the sludge.

He was trudging back when he heard the sound of a car charging along the track.

The Jacobses' four by four, *Light of the Nations* emblazoned in pale blue. It would have scuttled past him if he had not thrown himself across its path. Scrunch-on-the-ground brakes. All six Jacobses stared at Zaman, who waved at them from the front. The cacophony of an amplified car horn and Pastor Jacobs's big red face leaned out of the window as he screamed at Zaman in a twang that infused words with curves and elongated vowels. "Heathen, in God's name, what do you intend?"

Zaman pleaded. His wife and children needed the water he carried. He had lifted the container for Pastor Jacobs to see. In the name of God, he needed a ride to Kargi. In the name of God. It was less than a day away. In the name of God, Whom they both served.

The pastor's nasal prodding: "Son, are you Bible-believin' and saved? Do you serve the living God, the true God, the only God?"

"Yes, yes, yes."

"Do you know our Lord as your personal Savior?"

"Yes."

"John 3:16?"

"What, sir?"

"John 3:16? Confirm your faith, son."

"The Lord is my . . . uh . . . shepherd in . . . uh . . . heaven?"

Pastor Jacobs's pale wife leaned over to the driver's side. "Tch-tch-tch," she said, wagging a finger.

Pastor Jacobs withdrew his face from the window, his mouth firmed up. He put the car into gear and sped off, gunning the engine as Zaman raced after them. Zaman threw the jerrican at them with all his strength. The lid burst open, and the foul water spilled out to the ground. He heard the earth quaffing down his family's life, and then he wailed.

Eeeeeeeeoiiiiaaaa!

Zaman stretched out his arms, fell forward, lay on the ground, his face and arms bruised. After half an hour, with ants clinging to his arms, he wiped his face, cleaned the dust off his clothes, and walked back to the foul oasis with the yellow can. The people saw him; they said nothing. They watched him fill the container again. He restarted his journey to Kargi on foot. Got there in the late evening of the day after that. Remarkable speed.

A wheezing part-time imam approached Zaman as he shuffled to the tree where he had last seen his family. He stopped.

"God be praised," exhorted the imam.

"Yes."

And he told Zaman the truth. In keeping with burial customs, all bodies were buried just before sunset. The prayer man said, "It is God's will." He told Zaman that they would all meet in paradise, thanks be to God. He said they were in a better place.

Zaman heard the words.

He said nothing in reply.

Nothing.

Had not spoken about the events to another human being until now.

Eleven years later, the Jacobses were still plowing seeds of light across unheeding desert people of Kenya. In keeping with the times, they had also become spotters of terrorists and pirates. Their medical center was a web, a rich pond for mass baptisms and extraordinary renditions.

Close to dusk. The Trader gets up. He is trundling away when the *d'abeela* calls after him, *"We are ravens . . ."* the Trader gurgles. The voices on the radio tell him about the chaos that followed the murder of a Pakistani woman leader.

13

OLD COFFEE AND A CONVERSATION IN THE WUOTH OGIK *BOMA*
—two men and a cramped eavesdropper. Galgalu had taken to lying under the sky so his nightmares had greater distances to cover before they reached him. Galgalu had seen that the Trader's eyes were cold and his voice like breaking glass. His spirit shivered as the man spoke.

The Trader was saying, "In the places of water, where stories are left to be found, long-ago tales of a man named Hugh Bolton linger. It is said, one day he left. Was he looking for the house of red rain?"

Nyipir squirms, blows his nose, and allows himself a grunt.

The Trader says, "I feel there's something you need."

"Nothing."

"Anything?"

Nyipir gestures toward the coffin. "Bring him back to life."

The Trader grabs Nyipir's forearm. Nyipir's muscles shudder and then relax. He emits a groan.

The Trader leans close. "I met a friend of the family."

"Who?"

"A *d'abeela*."

"What do you want?"

The Trader pulls out coffee beans and shrugs. *"Ka-ha-wa?"*

Nyipir looks away.

"*Truuut—rat-a-tat-tat,*" sings the Trader.

Nyipir answers, "I don't trade anymore."

"It's what *I* want."

"I don't trade."

Silence.

"I can help."

"What?"

"Eliminate poisonous snakes that infest a quiet house."

Silence.

"He'll leave."

The Trader looks over at Wuoth Ogik.

"Maybe. Akai is frightened of snakes. The venom . . . could kill her. . . ."

"He'll leave."

"When?"

Nyipir shifts.

The Trader leans his head against his shoulder. "I can make watering holes forget everything."

Nyipir mutters, "It's not like that."

"As you say."

"What do you want?"

The Trader snorts, "You were a terrifying man before. Now we only pray for you."

Nyipir glares.

The Trader says, "Costs much to make a man disappear."

"I paid."

"A discounted rate."

Nyipir exhales; his nose flares; he grits his teeth. "I'm grateful."

The Trader smiles. "So?" He extends a quarter-filled pot. "I've added four drops of clove oil and a cinnamon twig. Try it. Clears the head, helps the mind to retrieve its silence." A ravening grin. "A great feat, to cause a man or men to disappear—*paff*—or bring them back!"

"What do you want?" Nyipir's eyes blink rapidly, and his hands shake.

"Very little," says the Trader.

Outside, a small wind eases past a thorn tree. Inside, the scent of ghee, smoke, and warm leather. It saturates skin, cloth, blood, grime, and sadness. In the dark, Galgalu slithers into the room where Isaiah snores. In his hand, the Trader's potion—it is shaped like a fist-sized incense lump. Simple instructions given with a glimmer in the eye: *Light this in the room where he sleeps. You, you must leave when the smoke rises.*

"What's this?" Galgalu asked.

"A gift for the home," the Trader said, and giggled.

Lump in one hand, Galgalu watches Isaiah's chest rise and fall. He wonders at the haplessness of sleeping souls. Swallowing saliva. "Isaiah?" Galgalu tugs at the coverlet with the free hand. "Isaiah!" A hiss.

Isaiah jumps awake, stands naked, swaying. "What is it?"

Galgalu puts a finger to his mouth, listens for something outside, and then throws Isaiah's trousers at him. "Go." Tosses his shirt.

"You can't just come in here and . . ."

"Leave."

"Why?"

"Go to Nairobi. Find Ajany. She'll tell you everything. Go." Desperation. "Save your life."

"I'll leave after I speak to the old man." Isaiah pulls on the unclean shirt, khakis.

"Wait and die, Isaiah," Galgalu says, lucid. And then, "You want to die? Stay!" Galgalu pushes Isaiah's chest. "Go! Go! Go!"

Isaiah grabs his things, more shaken by Galgalu's urgent gestures than by what he's saying. Immortality's veil cracks. Icy fright. He is so far away from home.

Galgalu spits resentment: "You open quiet graves and think the dead won't also look for you?" He shoves Isaiah's chest. "Go, with your sickness."

"Why not just kill me?" asks Isaiah.

"Too much work." The death nugget feels hot within his palms.

Isaiah squeezes his eyes shut. In between wondering and deciding, an image shows up: the death-destruction-fear-night-of-death goddess Kalaratri. A shudder slithers through Isaiah's body. He succumbs. "How do I leave? Here, I've got a map."

Galgalu rolls his eyes. "Leave the house, walk a straight line from the door. Don't stop till you see many, many black rocks that are the shape of many, many breasts. Wait there. I'll come with the cows. Listen for bells. Go. In Nairobi, find Ali Dida Hada. Police headquarters. In your map, write 'Ali Dida Hada.'"

"Who's he?"

"Police. He was looking for Bolton."

"What?"

"Yes."

Galgalu disintegrates into darkness, leaving Isaiah alone after he has tossed the poisoned lump onto the bookshelf.

Fear's moldering stench. Isaiah listens for movement. *Is this an ambush?* The water tank creaks. Isaiah craves a place where tea shops sit next door to Covent Garden ballets. He misses the disembodied voice nagging, "Mind the gap." He wants to hear Christmas bells and dull sermons from apologetic vicars. Isaiah grabs his bag, stuffs in some books, stares at the night, greedy to live. Terrifying Kalaratri. She is also a mother. So he prays. *Help me!* He is not running away. *Help me, Kalaratri.* Needing to live, promising to live.

14

THE LAND'S ROCKS CANNOT DECIDE WHAT COLOR TO BE. THE
splendid Mount Kulal is violet, then a pink-edged blue. An oryx herd gal-
livants and leaps. Someone's scattered camels huddle, and a weaver colony strain the branches of an acacia, chattering with intent. The morning
stillness enhances desert murmurs. Isaiah has walked for exactly four
days, using the landmarks Galgalu had crafted on the ground. The long,
brown, beaded gourd of milk that Galgalu had also left behind dangles
from his wrist.

Isaiah had written out *Ali Dida Hada* on his map. He had also transferred Galgalu's earth map, created when Galgalu met him that morning. With a thin stick, Galgalu had pointed to the sentinel to their left,
"Kulal." He indicated a sketched area of earth. An "X." And he used
the tip of the stick to move black pebbles. "You walk here . . . here . . .
here . . ."

Lines and holes on the ground, a curve to show a *laga*, a hump for
a mountain, small holes to indicate valleys, ridges, watering holes, and
sand dunes. Galgalu said "North Horr, OK?" and went quiet.

"OK," Isaiah replied.

He has retraced the earth map to the hum of flies. Such insects. Horrible heat.

He wanted to stay close to another human being, but he was too embarrassed to plead for Galgalu's company. "What's the name of God here?" Isaiah asked instead.

"Sometimes Waaqa, sometimes Akuj." Galgalu's finger pointed upward, and then swept in all the directions of the world. The sky was a dome over everything.

Galgalu tossed his herding stick at Isaiah.

Isaiah gave it back. "Yours."

Galgalu thrust it at him.

A hesitation. Isaiah grasped it. A nod.

They turned their backs on each other, stepped in opposite directions.

Isaiah struck out, dry-mouthed, wet-palmed, walked as if he were being chased, glancing back every few meters along pathways with panoramic views of sculpted volcanic disarray and scattered boulders of all shades and sizes. *Mount Kulal to the left,* he told himself. A burst of yellow and black first alarms and then amazes him. It soars skyward, lands on a flat-headed tree, where it spreads out its wings and, like a butterfly, flitters: a supernal bird. Then, at night, the stars. A discovery: here, the moon was the other way round. He had lost his north. *Think, Isaiah.* He was startled by his own voice. He licked dry, cracking lips. He walked on soft, crumbling sand. Then hard rock. Sand again. Pebbles. Treacly sweat, scented with salt. The milk became a tart paste. Isaiah chewed it down anyway.

A slender red line lacerates the sky. A night insect stings Isaiah's face. He scratches the place. A lone jackal watches him, lets him pass, golden gaze puzzled. Small blue insects get a free ride on Isaiah's body. The silence. Old presences appear, like the floral perfume that a woman he loved used to wear. Delicate, hopeful, like tender dreaming. He wonders again why he still lives. He reads the new sky, tests wind direction and the position of stars. Finds pattern and rhythm. God-roamed-land. He might start singing litanies to nomadic deities. Later, dog-tired and fiercely fed up with loneliness, he just stops walking, sits down dust drenched, curls into himself, and sleeps.

A high-pitched wind that night.

"*Eeeoiiiah!*" A cry pours out of Isaiah.

He sits up and hears echoes of the howl of a wounded beast.

15

A TAXI DRIVER'S RECOMMENDATION HAD BROUGHT AJANY TO A
guesthouse hidden in a Nairobi suburb. A Kenya colonial-style bungalow with wooden floors. Few guests. The round-faced chef, built like a
cheerful wrestler, offered Ajany strawberry crêpes and cream at once.
His name was Calisto, and his crêpes were the best in the world. The day
Ajany arrived, she crawled into bed, and then screamed and screamed
into her pillow.

By way of the window into Nairobi night skies, memory had dragged
her back into the terrain in Brazil called "Saudade." Its acual name was
"Clube Dorival." It was evolved by a few of the assorted casualties of
music's broken promises. Saudade's men showed up in suits and ties
and two-toned shoes; its wild-haired women in recycled evening wear
that flowed and shed light and molded cloth to all-shape bodies. Desire
was communicated through still moments: a way of glaring, for example. Saudade was a crossroads peopled by remnants of the colonized.
Portugal-infused Africans, vagabond refugees, wounded immigrants, all
in-betweeners, representatives of nations' detritus, those who had disappeared into "lost" and the merely curious. It was a place of meeting,

and sometimes a bordello. Ajany found it five years ago, on an evening of drizzles, after a disheveled woman stepped into her homeward path, palm out, and snarled *"Menina"* in a too-high voice. A slithery sensation had assailed Ajany, who turned and fled, until the string of the woman's voice roiling in her head snapped.

She had rushed through a doorway around which elegant Luso-phone men stood.

A breathed-out song reached her—*Estes braços eternos, curvados sobre as penas*—and she followed it into Saudade.

Dark-brown décor, coffee, wine, voices into music, over music, as music, russet mustiness. A blend of spice and perfume, night jasmine too. Aphrodisiac melodies. Chico Buarque and other tunes. It was always dusk there. They were five, the music makers. A slender guitarist, playing with his eyes closed. A percussionist channeling Neguinho do Samba. Singers: two women, plump coquettes in sparkling high heels, who slapped their thighs, clutched breasts, and rolled and rolled their hips. A big man, a blue-black man, seated, a guitar's stem to his face, right ear pressed close to hear the chords he sometimes gave voice to, crisscrossing scales in clean lament. Bernardo gestured for music from his one-eyed guitarist. Ajany watched a woman in a shiny brown satin dress. The woman moved, climbed the stage, grabbed Bernardo's arm, and leaned into his ear. He leapt off the creaking stage. He prowled across the room, a pathway creating itself for him while, in a large, gruff voice, sewn together with laughter, he called for drinks all round.

Ajany was still staring from a stool in the back of the room. And then he was there.

He said, *"Mulhere!"*

She tried to leave.

Before he touched her.

Her body shook.

He grinned, put both his arms around her. "I'm taking you home with me."

She shivered next to him.

"Cold?" He spoke into her ear.

She said nothing.

"Wait for me." He laughed.

He had gone.

Ajany left.

Ajany would paint him that night. Furious violet and dark-blue hues, rubbed into paper with fingers.

She returned the next evening.

Bernardo found her.

They left together.

She did not care.

And for an entire season she forgot about Wuoth Ogik.

Then she wrote home.

Dear Odidi, I am happy.

Bernardo said, "Song is sorcery."

He said, "You are the voice of my dark."

He said, "I called you into my madness."

She listened. It did not occur to either of them that she, too, might speak. Laughter, anguish, moans of relentless, endless, deep filling. Feeling. He played her body, too. He loved her, he said. "Loving you, I live." And her body opened a way for her soul to fall into his.

She wrote. *Dear Odidi, I love. I am loved.*

Bernardo said her madness was not African enough. "I feel . . . authenticity. . . . That's your dilemma." It was the first time she would cry because of him.

But.

Seduction: the house of forgetfulness.

She did not write home.

Ajany opens her eyes and discovers she is in Nairobi. Sun-sprinkled pale-orange light through white veils. Ajany jumps out of bed, lands on the floor a meter away. A habit devised to avoid Obarogo.

Calisto the chef offers mulberry crêpes.

"No," says Ajany.

"English breakfast?" His hands clasped partly in prayer.

"No," she stutters. "Just tea."

His jaw sags. "Is my food bad?"

Ajany murmurs, "Crêpes."

Calisto grins.

Other people's English breakfast. Bacon. The meat smell evokes the morgue. Ajany gets up, grabs the orange juice, and heads for the garden. A cold morning, but she can eat her crêpes there.

She calls up yesterday's taxi driver. His name is Peter. He communes with God. He says he has to. "Not all passengers are good."

She can understand.

He asks, "You're from where, madam?"

"Here."

"Where?"

"N-north."

"Where?"

"Kalacha . . ."

"Where?"

"Northern Kenya."

"*Ngai!* That's far. . . . You don't look like you're from those sides."

She turns.

"What do they look like?"

Peter frowns.

They stop in front of a sweating policeman who is choreographing the traffic flow and creating a logjam.

"Business in Nairobi?"

"Yes," she sighs, staring out of the window.

The policeman points, and they crawl into their lane on the roundabout. Destination, the University of Nairobi, Department of Civil Engineering and Material Sciences, near the street where Ajany last smelled Odidi's student-budget cologne.

16

ENGINEER OPIRR IS A BAG-EYED MAN WITH A BIG OVAL FACE ON which a verdant sprouting of white-streaked hairs flourish on an elongated jaw. His crimson suspenders lift dark-blue trousers above his stomach. A large oval ring set with turquoise and coral bulges from his third left-hand finger. Odidi's former tutor. He ushers Ajany into his book-choked, paper-filled office.

"Odidi's little sister! Aha-ha, indeed, indeed!" A flourish. "What can I do for her?"

"I'm . . . uh . . . looking for Odidi."

They sit down. Between them a perfect round dark-brown table weighed down with books about bridges, notepads, written papers, five rectangular containers stuffed with cards, and an incongruous delicate pink-blue flowered china cup, with its saucer and a thin, etched silver spoon.

"I graduated the boy, you know." Odidi as a theme gave him warm feelings. A most excellent student.

Ajany waits.

"In this age of technology, would've thought . . . ?"

"Lost contact."

Opirr plucks at his face, eyes missing little. "Mhh."

"Just came home," she elaborates, "Looking for him."

She believed it.

Engineer Opirr observes the structural dysfunction in the otherwise well-put-together frame of the female in front of him. Leaking from her eyes. "Tea? Hard times for our blessed nation, what? Must have faith. Our young are still unsullied, eh?" Opirr pours out liquid into another floral cup. "Oolong tea," Opirr confides. "Mix leaves with crushed *dek*, food for the heart. Sandwich?"

"No, thank you," Ajany replies.

Engineer Opirr plunks himself down on a ratty couch. "Lost touch myself."

Silence.

A white wall lined up with framed certificates of overachievement. Pictures of Opirr in assorted robes carrying scrolls and other artifacts of accolade. Seven pictures of Opirr with a plump, happy giantess, presumably his wife, and their nine children lined up for a photographer, adorned in different-colored academic gowns.

But it is a silver-edged, elegantly inscribed framed text, beneath which a small square of the Kenya flag is glued, on which Ajany focuses. She reads:

> "I heard my country calling, away across the sea,
> Across the waste of waters she calls and calls to me . . .
> I haste to thee my mother, a son among thy sons."

Opirr follows her gaze. "A reminder, for when I forget." He says.

"Sir?" Ajany asks.

"Why I'm here. Y'know, was in the first of the Mboya-Kennedy airlifts. Excelled, of course. The Americans had never met anyone like me. Top of my school, of course. Much courted. Abandoned the banquet of Western tables to come home. Yes. Y'know the anthem from which I borrow these lines? Cherished by our English friends?" He begins to croak, "*I vow to thee my country, all earthly things above. . . .*" He stops and clears his throat with a trumpeting sound. "Ah! Odidi." He frowns.

Opirr and Ajany sip tea. Opirr booms, "Musali!"

Odidi's competitor turned friend.

Ajany remembers the nervy, loud youth whose jumpy presence discomfited her. Musali had been the heckling cheer-song conductor to Odidi's rugby turnout.

Odidi had once told her about his rivalry with Musali. Musali had mocked Odidi's private-school accent. Odidi had let him get away with it for a week. "Then I sorted him out," Odidi boasted.

Opirr recounts the tale.

"The very next week, Odidi became Musali. Dress, accent, and walk. Uproar in class and campus." He chuckles. "After three days, the two young men called a truce. Learned to share projects, plans. Yes. Mad about water, both of them, what?" Opirr pauses. "First-class honors. In the top ten best marks in the university's history." A broad smile. "Two of the best. Both in my class."

Opirr fishes out details from a tattered fat black pocket planner. "Moses Odidi. Infatuated with the geometry of life. Loved beautiful things. An aesthete—do you love beautiful things? Do you know the boy redesigned a ditch carrying effluent into the Nairobi River so that it generated potable water? Very grateful slum people." A hand gesture, light on the turquoise ring. "They renamed the ditch for him, what? K'Ebewesit in Korogocho or one of those other ridiculous Nairobi 'K' settlements—Korogocho or Katina—no, Kawangware. KKK . . . Kibera? That ditch rebuilt under the nose of a city councillor who vowed to *behead* him. Who are these sociopaths? Such *calicoes*. Behead? What ugliness." Pursed lips. "M'fraid when they killed Tom we lost all sense of our . . . *elegance*. Whatever given in exchange for his soul—poor man—opened gates for a viscid, stygian presence to roam our land unfettered, trading in baubles, lies, and blood for lives." He frowns. "Do you understand?" He drifts, muttering an incoherent phrase before stirring himself alert.

Heart jolt inside Ajany.

"Anyway. Heard our Odidi went off with Musali and some members of his rugby team to confront that terribly foolish man. Called him out, gave him a sharpened panga, told him to try." Opirr chortles. "Another truce called. Odidi. A character."

"Musali and Odidi. Good team. Final-year project became Tich Lich Engineers, a company." A frown. Opirr's jowls collapse in a downward movement, eyes whiten with subtle unhappiness. "Oh, what do you do when you are made to wade through political sludge? Terrifyingly ugly, Odidi's little sister. Soul-corroding." He looks into his book, then turns to search through one of the containers on the table overflowing with business cards. "No moral gumption among men today, m'fraid, few noble testicles around—forgive the crudity—we're spawning tawdry thieves, hitmen, and gigolos who love nothing!" Opirr wheezes, plucks out a card, and hands it over to Ajany. "Little sister, when you find Moses, tell him his old teacher would be so pleased to meet him, what?"

Ajany studies the black card, the white text that reads, "Tich Lich Engineers. Bespoke Engineering Consultants." No names, just an address. She slips it into her handbag.

Opirr leans forward to grab Ajany's hand.

She stares at the shape, color, and size of his ring. A finger sneaks out to feel its texture. "Tell him, you hear me?" An urgent edge in Engineer Opirr's tone.

Tears in Ajany's eyes. She clings to and then drops his hands to pick up her bag and glances at the room one more time. "He was happy here?"

"Delirious. Never saw a child thrive as he did, once given the tools, the time and space. A treasure."

Ajany gives Engineer Opirr her first real smile since her return to Kenya.

She walks faster than the unmoving traffic all the way to City Park, where someone's loud, bombastic praise music—*pakruok*—fills the air. Lively food, touchable juiciness. Two hopeful vervet monkeys peek through doors. Cashew nuts, aubergines, and chili-tomato sauce. Braised meat, braised chicken, and fish. Dried fish. Ohangla music next door to Mzee Ngala's sedate bango beats. Ajany eats with her fingers, tasting flavors for the first time as portions of Odidi accumulate around her. *A treasure.* She pauses and smiles.

———

Isaiah walks the landscape unseen and unknown, as if he might not even exist except to himself. It is toward the end of the fifth day when rectangles of shimmering corrugated iron roofs strike his squinting eyes. A white Land Rover drives past him, and the silence that has been his companion evaporates.

Now.

A bevy of beautiful lorries, contemplative humped cows, a small market made of color and dung. Sheep and goats bleat. A large van with a red cross parks parallel to a decrepit curb laden with gunnysacks next to a green Kenyan army truck whose driver is attempting to reverse in quicksand. Under twin Acacias, three supercilious camels rest. They are flanked by six white boxes bearing a blue-yellow sign with the legend: *Reading Is Knowledge*. The Kenya National Library Services Camel caravan pitching camp for the night. A youthful camel handler with dark gold skin and a splendid dome of a head is sprawled on a grass mat spluttering away at the contents of Enid Blyton's *Five Run Away Together*, the only one in the series Isaiah had not read. With dusk plodding in and scarring the sky with yellow-orange trails, the crescendo of a hundred different home-going birds, blue-note winds, variegated shadows, invisible balsam-scented things, and the multi-toned buzz of assorted insects, within a flat, hard land with neither beginning nor end, in this surreal grandeur, Isaiah's shabby, bearded, thirsty, shimmering appearance from a place just beyond sight, hands propped on a herding stick balanced on his shoulders, is a small part of "normal."

The drone of a plane preparing to land. A beatific grin transforms Isaiah's face. He watches the Piper circle the patch of earth serving as the airfield. His way into Nairobi. He will buy the plane if he has to.

Isaiah returns to Babu Chaudhari.

A toothless grin: "Fou're back!"

"I am."

"Fou're wery brown."

"Thank you."

"Not good. Here . . ." Babu shuffles to the back of the shop and returns with a brown plastic bottle. Suntan lotion. Presents it to Isaiah, who does not recognize the manufacturer.

"Not sunscreen." Isaiah frowns.

"S'OK."

Isaiah sighs. He wants a room, a shower. Wants to go home.

The suddenness of night.

Behind a column, with a view of everything and the door, the District Officer drums fingers over a very old newspaper, the football section his source of irritation. The story of the Harambee Stars' ignoble retreat and their subsequent five-to-one annihilation. The D.O. carries the bug-eyed

aura of solitude of the forgotten person consigned to the northern fron-
tiers by indifferent superiors. The tips of his hair are brassy blond—this
land's heat and saline.

"Kwaheri." The traveling librarians wave at the D.O. on their way out
of the bar-restaurant. They are turning in early so they can resume their
wanderings before dawn. The D.O. turns to count the regulars, a relief
from reflecting on the outrage that is the national football team. Was
the long-haired Japanese water engineer turned herdsman who played
solitary Ajua already in? They sometimes shared silent drinks together.
He was not. Pity. He could have done with uncomplicated silence today.
The Harambee Stars had twisted his heart.

Clut-clut-clut. The bald-headed, six-foot-tall, short-skirted woman of
indifferent reputation who wears a red ring on her small hawk-beak
nose and presides over the billiard table. Wide-eyed craziness. Her skirt
is something she made out of a military general's coat.

The D.O. looks away before she can see him.

Notes that six of the town's other night women cling to strangers
like extra limbs. Apart from an intermittent pawing, the men ignore
their transitory mates. The women keep proprietary hands on the men's
thighs. They speak through smoke, pick meat and *ugali* from trays,
quaff beer, and chew *qhat*. The D.O. understands the facts of children to
feed. He recognizes a buxom woman who he had sought out in the early
days of his posting when the silences had been unbearable. He knows
of other dreams behind kohled eyes and Vaseline-tinted lips. *Our poor
mothers.* He hears the laughter of the no longer deceived.

The shaggy-haired Estonian with the look of an anxious hoopoe
walks in. Hunter of tales. He waves to two of his type. A Scottish
explorer—that is what he says he is, a stranger who had driven into
town four months back, would make mad forays into parts of the lake,
return days later, desiring silence, and the German company man who,
daily, dashed from landscape to landscape, plucking plants, leaves, gathering berries, scraping barks, and digging out roots. The Estonian sizes
everyone up before nodding at the new arrival, a broad-shouldered, sun-
darkened stranger who had walked in at dusk.

The watching D.O. rumbles at the male ritual posturing, teeth baring, and muscle-strength testing through hard handshakes.

The owner of the space, a double-chinned sometime bartender and
indifferent cook, also owner of the only abattoir in town, waddles to his
clients with drinks. Eyes dart; they miss nothing.

Isaiah is dressed in a formerly white T-shirt with a frayed collar and dark-brown khakis that may have once been beige. After greeting the strangers at the table, his hands tremble next to a warm Tusker bottle. His hands have been shaking ever since he settled in his room.

He takes in the bar. Eyes rest on the broken television set on a wooden stand.

Thinks.

Wuoth Ogik.

He must restrategize.

He will.

In Nairobi.

Reflections of patrons bob on the blank screen.

Tuskers and sodas on a round table. Eight lanterns cast a brownish-orange glow into the room. Isaiah turns to the curious gathering of European men at his table, indulges the tribal feeling coiling around them. Yet not one of them will admit to the pleasure of finding the others' company in the belly of Timeless Nowhere. They share vices; a nameless woman is attached to each. He speaks to a glow-lipped woman whose Bint El Sudan perfume corrodes his nostrils.

"What'll you have?"

"Martini," she answers.

"Who's paying?" His eyes are half-slits.

"Tusker." She readjusts.

Isaiah watches somebody else's cigarette smoke rise.

What he needs. To feel skin, heat. Needs a body to lose himself in. Any body. He strokes his stubble, wraps an arm around the perfumed woman with the baby-girl voice. Squeezes flesh, inundated by perfume. His thoughts scatter. They gather at Wuoth Ogik.

And skid away.

Inside, chairs scraping the cement floor. The sound of wood on wood. A shout outside. A donkey brays. A fourth round of beers.

The shaggy-haired Estonian filmmaker is trying to use special lights to capture relics of a past he hopes he can make an exclusive future with. He is an apprentice, a student at the foot of a one-legged Turkana rainmaker-healer-spiritualist. To Isaiah: "Where from?"

Isaiah answers: "Here. There."

The Estonian shifts.

The German oil-prospecting-company ecologist, cultivating a stringy gray ponytail which roosts like a bushy tail above his neck, scrutinizes Isaiah. He leans forward and demands, "Vot do you do?"

"This"—Isaiah looks to the ceiling—"and that."

The Scot trying to solve the mystery of Sir Vivian Fuchs's lost Lake Rudolph expedition-team members watches Isaiah. "Bloody Internet wasteland here." Isaiah raises his brows. "Must upload my blog. Where you from?"

"South," drawls Isaiah. His temples pound, and from inside the bar comes the sound, solid against solid: *clut-clut-clut-clut.*

The Estonian insists. "What're you doing here?"

"Safari."

The Estonian growls, "No one comes this far *just* for safari."

"No?"

The explorer watches.

"Another beer?" offers Isaiah. No need to start a fight.

They speak of landscapes crossed.

"Going to Nairobi," Isaiah concedes.

"Is zeir trival vor finished?" asks the German. "I hear, and I vas at vance understanding a pis festival, ja? Viz ze lake, by ze lake, near ze lake. I vill speak to my embassy and ve shall gazer ze desert tribes." His voice crescendos: "Zey vill sing, zey vill dance. Togezer, ja. Zey vill illuminate metaphorical pis and from ze lake pis vill be a mirror, like ze memory." His smile is determined.

The explorer's tone is droll. "And yet the desert nations' work schedules might not coincide with your 'peace' plans—animals to pasture, journeys to make, people to meet, that sort of thing."

"But *ve* must insist. Zey must conform." A frown. Sarcasm missed.

Isaiah stares hard at the tableau. Headache. He shrugs. *Clut-clut-clut-clut.* Isaiah turns toward the sound and sees her. A vision of presence, of curves within which a hundred thousand sorrows can be deeply forgotten. He pushes away from the table, Tusker in hand.

The Scottish explorer's low voice: "Don't look, lad. Don't touch."

The splendid vision leans backward against the table and cues the ball.

The Estonian. "With her, you lose."

The German continues, "A trival pis festival vizin ze allegorical oasis . . ."

Isaiah saunters over and leans against the table just as the woman strikes a billiard ball across the table into its pocket.

The explorer, voice overloud: "I say, can we get some Tusker *baridis hapa sasa hivi?*"

The large, double-chinned bar owner toddles over.

The bald-headed woman rearranges the balls, ignores Isaiah.

The D.O. rereads the football score on the paper under lantern light. Sips ginger ale. Glances out when a night bird calls out in staccato warbles.

Clud-click.

Isaiah strikes a billiard ball on the warped table. Tattered cloth, tilting leftward. Isaiah plays until only two striped balls are left. The woman plays the plain balls to the last, a dance of strikes. Isaiah pulls out and drops a thousand shillings on the table before she can play the last black ball.

She watches him.

He pulls out a five-hundred-shilling note. It falls across the thousand. She gives him a slow smile. Direct gaze. She picks up the money, rolls it, and sticks it behind her ear. Leaves the black ball on the table. Isaiah takes his cue and plays it. It crashes down the table, and bounces off a pocket into the opposite end, and bounces across the table, then into the middle pocket. It clatters inside. The woman leans over the table and stares at Isaiah.

She indicates the bar door with her head.

Isaiah downs his Tusker.

Waves at the others and swaggers out after her.

"Poor bugger," mutters the explorer-blogger.

The D.O. focuses his hatred on the photograph of the Harambee Stars' coach: a scummy, overpaid charlatan with a foreign accent.

The next day, a generation of marabou storks have taken position on available trees in the landscape. Babu Chaudhari watches Isaiah stumble into view. Disheveled hair, bloody face scratched, a haggard, glazed look. He appears smaller than he was yesterday.

Isaiah pulls out four hundred shillings.

"Nine hunred," lisps Babu.

"What? You said three hundred and . . ."

"Nine hunred or folice. Nine hunred for two."

Isaiah peels nine hundred shillings from his shrinking wad. "You're a thief."

Babu takes and holds each of the notes to the light. The threat of receiving fake money was a constant. "And you, fir, are a frostitute." Babu grins.

Heat rises and sears Isaiah's gullet, burns through and out his nostrils. Roar in his throat, and the need to reach over and squeeze the gums out of the bloody dolt. He grunts instead.

Babu Chaudhari titters, rheumy eyes damp.

A desire to dry-clean his soul engulfs Isaiah. Mourn the lost, kill the sordid taste of bad booze, angry sex, and sullied memories. *Did I actually . . . ?* A shudder.

"How much for aspirin?"

"For you, forty fer two taflets."

Isaiah pays his penance and drags himself back to the small room. He sits on the unmade bed. Gets up. The mirror above the faucet is small, broken, and framed in pink plastic. It reflects the round room. Light-daubed water reflecting shifting moods. He shaves off his beard. Leaves Galgalu's herding stick in the room.

Outside, the marabou storks gaze back at Isaiah as he shambles to the edge of the town and tries to orient himself with Mount Kulal. He reaches the shade of a tree on a little incline. Sits down, facing the mountain; he sees barbets on scraggly trees. He skulks into an instant of last night. Had he actually wept against the scarred back of a bald-headed harlot?

His tears had come from nowhere. The woman had tolerated it for five minutes, then slapped away his hand, picked up her clothes, and, still naked, opened the door. "Tch!" she had clucked on her way out, and let the night peer at him.

———

Destination Nairobi. Southward flight. The police pilot rests his right arm against the window. The colors of the land change from gray to deep, dark green, show-off Kenyan dusk lights and shadows. Cars on the ground like jumbled bricks scattered on the uneven black road. Evening light bounces off corrugated roofs. Seven minutes past five. The pilot pushes the throttle up. A gray hangar appears to the left. The tarmac of the aerodrome looms.

They taxi to a stop.

Isaiah sighs.

A floral fragrance pierces his senses.

Uneasy calm. *Was the post-election thing over?*

The taxi driver with whom he haggles a day rate is a hearty man called Kalela. Their car is a rehabilitated Subaru.

On the road.

Film of shabbiness. The city's tensions in crunched-up shoulders. *Honk, honk.* Breathing. Movement. A noise jam. A hand-cart jam. A traffic jam. Two men strain at the handlebars of one *mkokoteni* cart. A woman in a small red T-shirt and white pedal pushers tiptoes across the street in pink high heels. Short-haired gentlemen in gray suits carrying briefcases weave through the traffic. Music boom-booms from a bucking *matatu*, which a driver steers along a broken island that separates roads, his body leaning outward. *"Jinga huyo."* Kalela spits at the empty patch where a matatu used to be.

Two a.m. The bed light is on; Isaiah watches the ceiling fan rotate.

He is certain it is a late-in-the-day version of jet lag.

No sleep.

Hakuna matata. "Only tourists say that," Kalela had scoffed earlier. "Say *hamna mtatizo.*"

No worries.

In the morning, at breakfast, he browses through *The Rough Guide to Kenya,* before trying to sleep again.

Much later, Isaiah will prowl the city's streets, witnessing its surreal radiance. Nairobi's night music will draw him in. Pulsing lights, shrieking conversations, and boom-boom beats in a club he has found filled with a multicultural class lamenting the nation's halfhearted attempt at civil war, seedy diplomats, and do-gooders—an alarming rash of these. Isaiah squints. What was it with the men and their long wavy hair, unshaven look, indoor sunglasses, even tan, sneakers, and Jesus sandals?

The stale-breathed club Anzigane is easy to get into, harder to leave. Dance. Music. Cocktails. Hookahs and hookers. Double brandy in hand, Isaiah barely flinches when a thin woman, just out of school, squeezes his testicles. "Go away," he grumbles. Blond-wigged, long-legged females—thin, fat, mostly in between—wiggling flesh, grabbing his thighs, drooping over him, with fucked-up suggestiveness. Wanting a different kind of world. Hybrid lusciousness; in more receptive lands, they would be starlets and über-models. They give shape to his expanding Nairobi vocabulary: *malaya.*

Restless, insomniac, and pissed off, Isaiah wants to start a fight. He is irritated by the existence of a pebble-spectacled, weedy Swiss man who plows through the night's women like a predatory combine harvester. In a more just place, this watery specimen of manhood would have had to slit his wrists to save himself the ignominy of perpetual rejection. Isaiah's nose flares as the European export scurries about like a popular rodent. He wills the man to reach his corner of the bar. Three hopeful females flutter their lashes at him. He downs another caipirinha, gets up, and flees the bar, weighed down by this nocturnal character of exile, the incessant darkness of no-place-ness.

17

NYIPIR LIMPS ACROSS THE COMPOUND, SPRINTS, DARING IMAG-
inary foes—*goyo sira*—but his tear ducts are blocked:

> *Ochamo ka Oganda ma ji oluoro.*
> *Dede ochamo ka Oganda ma ji oluoro*
> *Ere? Ochamo ka Oganda ma yande riek.*
> *Par Oganda odong' nono ma wuon dhok.*

> Locusts have consumed Oganda's realm,
> A once-splendid realm is emptied
> Where? Oganda, who was once wise.
> Nothing remains for this guardian of cattle.

The dread becomes sweat that heats up his body, broils his thoughts so that, as a young boy would, he reaches for his father, Agoro Patrobus Oganda, and his big brother, Theophilus Paulus Oganda.

"Burma." Nyipir mutters to himself, "Mandalay, 21° 59′ N 96° 6′ E, Rangoon, 16° 47′ N 96° 9′ E." He recited this as an invocation for them.

. . .

By the time able-bodied men in Nyanza were summoned for King George's war by persuasion of the paramount chief, and a trumpet-voiced member of the regiment-recruiting safaris offered King George's shillings, thumbprint-on-paper, and reduced taxes for the prestige, honor, power, and glory of membership in the King's African Rifles, Agoro and Theophilus had both left for training in Maseno.

The steam train taking men to foreign battlefields stopped in Kisumu. Petronilla, his mother, who was pregnant, had held on to Nyipir's arms as Nyipir's body twisted toward his father. *"Adwaro dhi kodi!"* I want to go with you.

Petronilla's counterpoint: "Leave me this one—leave me this one—leave me this one at least."

"Theo!" Nyipir's brother had turned, faced him, and raised his hand in salute.

"Owadwa adwogo." I'll return, bro.

The train had gained speed. Petronilla let Nyipir run after it as far as he could. It left him far behind. He stared at the rails until the station-master chased him away. Nyipir memorized journeys his brother and father took: Madagascar, to fight against Vichy France. Back to Kenya. Mombasa to Burma and the 1944 Monsoon Campaign.

And then a period came that was woven from sorrow alone. Petronilla Ajany, his mother, died—snakebite when she was washing in the river. Nyipir's uncle took over the family's goods and lives. He commanded Nyipir to tend to his baby sister, Akoth.

One night, six months after his mother had died, Akoth, who had been restless and hot, coughed, looked at him, and, even as he clung to her, became very, very still.

Uncle took Nyipir away from school, told him to herd the family live-stock. Nyipir reread old schoolbooks, prayed, and waited for his father and brother to come home. They did not, not with the men march-ing back home from war fronts. Changed men like Baba Jimmy, who brought a Spanish guitar that he plucked like the *nyatiti*. Baba Jimmy was a giant with a hoarse, tearing voice, a descendant of musicians who make the lyre weep. Gangrene had eaten Baba Jimmy's toes during the war, and now he hobbled. He never explained why his body lurched in twisted angles as he moved.

Nyipir had run to him: *"Ere baba, ere Theo?"* Where are they?

Baba Jimmy shuffled ahead, his guitar swinging on his back, told Nyipir to direct his questions to God. He relented. "*Gi biro.*" They are on their way.

Nyipir heard the condensed sadness in Baba Jimmy's voice, the source of music.

"Come, boy, sing," Baba Jimmy suggested. He wanted to stop Nyipir's no-answer questions. From within the army coat he still wore, he dug out a brown-and-silver mouth organ. Baba Jimmy dangled it on the tips of his fingers and let it fall into Nyipir's open hands.

"Inhale, exhale." Hollow laugh, cheerless eyes.

Nyipir counted sixteen holes before lifting the instrument to his lips, eyes on Baba Jimmy.

"Breathe in, breathe out."

Nyipir did.

"Open your mouth, whistle. With your lips, cover these holes; don't move until you know the name of the sound."

They had turned old stories into songs without words.

It was the evening of a cold day in Kisumu; Nyipir milked the animals and settled them in for the night. He went to his hut. And then his uncle came to count the Oganda animals. Two goats that had eaten poisonous weeds died that evening. Uncle returned with *boka rao*. He raised the length of whip. It connected with the side of Nyipir's face the first time. By the second blow, Nyipir had picked up the hoe next to his mat and swung it at his uncle. The hoe hit its mark with a crunch. Maybe it split Uncle's head, because there was a small, spurting fountain of blood, which in the dimness looked very black, and Uncle whimpered.

Nyipir did not wait.

He ran. And when he stopped, he found he had crawled into Baba Jimmy's granary. The next afternoon, when Baba Jimmy found Nyipir hiding there, he said nothing, closed the door, returned with a calabash of water, and closed the granary door again.

Three days later, Baba Jimmy told Nyipir a story, which they would turn to melody:

"Listen. . . . *Chon gi lala,* a greedy hyena, had a brother. The brother was a warrior and went on a journey. This hyena opened its big mouth to swallow his brother's home. He also tried to swallow the brother's son, except this son was bigger than the hyena's open mouth. . . ."

Baba Jimmy played. Nyipir listened, he cried, and then he wiped his face with his arms.

"*Thu tinda* . . ." concluded Baba Jimmy. The end.

"Baba Jimmy, how do I go to Burma?" Nyipir asked seconds later.

Two weeks later, Baba Jimmy and Nyipir left for the Catholic Mission Orphanage and School that was in a village in Kisii. Dressed in their Sunday best, Baba Jimmy wearing his two war medals, footsteps on dusty roads. They walked for four hours to meet the blue bus. Nyipir walked backward, ahead of Baba Jimmy, staring at the gleaming medals.

They had approached a forested patch, the green so different from the dust of the plains that it caused Nyipir to tremble.

He told Baba Jimmy, "I want to go back home with you."

"You want to go to Burma?" Baba Jimmy demanded.

"Yes!" Nyipir yelled.

"Boy"—he pulled away his hands—"when you get out of this bus, after your feet reach the ground, don't look back. Only a hyena travels the same road twice."

18

AJANY READS THAT IN 2006 ENGINEER JEREMIAH MUSALI OF Tich Lich Engineers received the Gedo Award—a red-and-green rhino-horn-shaped protuberance—for regional engineering excellence and innovation. Ajany rereads the bronze plate in the pale-yellow-and-rust-red T. L. Associates Engineering offices in Lavington.

A cursory glance. In an alcove, a glimpse of a blown-up picture. Ajany moves closer. Five men in white-and-yellow hard hats. Behind them, the Kiambere power plant. In the middle, a man taller, broader, more muscular, and darker than all the others, with a thin mustache, his hair cropped close to the skull, his coat stretched over his body. Moses Ebewesit Odidi Oganda in a charcoal-gray suit, with a gap-toothed grin.

"Odidi!" Ajany cries.

She stands dry-mouthed. Hears a car slowing down outside. *Petrol engine, four-liter engine.* Smell of sprayed-on, bottled newness everywhere. The photograph. Odidi.

A woman in a flowing green dress walks in.

"Hello," she says. "May I help you?"

Ajany grabs her arms, points at the picture. "My b-brother . . ."

"Sorry, madam?"

"Moses Odidi Oganda. I'm his sister!"

The woman pulls away.

"*Eh* . . . wait here." She points at green chairs nearby, seizes a handset, and spits into the receiver.

Ajany stands next to the chair, gripping the armrest, eyes focused on the photograph, her heart beating.

A turbaned man of medium height in a tight German suit hurries in. The receptionist calls to him. They exchange quiet words, and he turns toward Ajany. "Odidi's sister?" He rushes over to pump her hand. "I'm Joginder. Uh, you know, uh . . . he left . . . maybe two years . . . maybe . . . ago. He . . . uh . . . hasn't, uhhh, called since. . . ."

Ajany stares.

He says, "Uhhh . . . wait."

He turns. Neat, hurried steps down a corridor.

Ajany's hands are damp. She wipes them on her skirt. The receptionist is answering phone calls.

Coffee appears.

Ten minutes.

Half an hour.

At four-twenty-two, Engineer Jeremiah Musali appears. He is not as thin, highly strung, or twinkly as he used to be. There are, however, traces from the past. Musali practically leaps into Ajany's arms. High-pitched voice, more fashion than steel; well-oiled, short hair with little waves. Manicured hands. Still handsome, he wears round glasses, like Gandhi's. Copper skin, ocher highlights. A brace around his neck.

"Arabel 'A. J.' Oganda! *Ei!* Let me see you," He looks her up and down. "Such a ka-lady! Brazil! You went *faaaar*!"

Ajany takes two steps back. "Yes . . . uhm . . . Musali, was wondering about my b-brother?"

Musali's eyebrows make small movements across his forehead. They are subtly plucked. His facial bones hold his muscles close to their structure. And, like an old person's, his ears are longer than his nose. Time seemed to have rubbed out the tiny lights that used to make his face a most mobile presence, fascinating to watch. Still, his would be a curious face to sculpt. Musali exhales hard, looks at the carpet. "Hasn't he contacted you?"

"Should he have?"

"Sit down. . . . Tea?"

Tea, the national balm of Gilead. She sits. "Your neck?" She watches his face.

"Some stupid *jamas* tried to jack me. I was lucky. Cops *twanga*-ed them."

Ajany studies the floor, biting inner lips.

Musali looks away, tea in hand; he says, "Odi, man. I'll tell you."

Silence.

"That *jama*, man, AJ, everything black and white for him. *Shit*, look, I feel bad. Y'know, we started this thing together. After campo." He glances over his shoulder.

"Where's my brother?"

"Don't know, man."

"Your friend?"

"Long ago."

"What, friendship?"

Musali sighs. "There was a deal."

A time in the life of Kenya when the long and short rains failed. El Niño. Odidi had chased after a contract for the repair of the nation's dams. He had lobbied, argued, and dazzled. Their company, Tich Lich Engineers, had won the contract with the power company. A two-hundred-and-seventy-five-million-shilling job.

They had "made it." Doing what they loved, designing with water. They had signed the bottom line, signed nondisclosure agreements—part of the procedure. Dated everything. Received a quarter of the money. Bought guzzling cars and started to dredge the dams. One day, they were summoned for an urgent meeting. They waited in the board-room for half an hour until a senior magistrate came in.

They were given a paragraph to recite. An oath of secrecy, subject to the Official Secrecy Act. A man in the proverbial black suit witnessed it all. A week later, Odidi, as chief engineer, received top-secret instructions to silt the dams. Contract to "service the turbines"—in other words, render them incapable of delivering power to the public.

At the same time, news of the sudden flooding of the lower reaches of the Tana River. Traveling to the dam site, they found the dam gates opened.

"We knew what was happening. Told that *jama* to back down and shut up. Why be martyrs, man?"

Odidi had insisted on talking to the managing director, who was in another meeting. Odidi had left a note, setting out what he had seen and asking for an explanation.

"Who did he think he was? It wasn't rugby, y'know?"

A few days later, the managing director was on national television, showing journalists how low the levels of water in the dam had fallen. In sorrowful tones he announced an imminent power-shortage emergency and the enforcement of a power-rationing plan. As if by coincidence, obsolete diesel generators from Europe and Asia happened to be aboard cargo ships on their way to Kenya. They would take care of the shortfall in power at 3,000 percent above the usual cost. A company to administer the supply of power from these generators had already been registered. Tich Lich had been contracted to install and service the equipment.

Odidi barged into the minister of energy's offices the next day.

"Something's wrong," he shouted.

Musali smiles as he remembers.

"The minister listened, then said, 'put it in writing.' "

So Odidi wrote a letter to the minister headed *Acts of Treason Against the People and Nation of Kenya,* backed with data and evidence, dates and figures.

When there was no response from the minister's office, he circulated it to the dailies. It was not published. Musali grimaces when he recalls Odidi rushing to record a statement with the police. "He even wanted to see the president." He wipes his eyes.

A minor functionary told Odidi to record another statement, and as he did so, more diesel generators were brought into the country. Tax-free. To cope with the national emergency caused by the power shortages.

"We were offered five percent of profits for ten years, y'know?" Musali says. "Odidi called a board meeting to demand that we resign the job and expose everything."

Musali sips his tea. "I told him, 'We have to survive. This thing of mahonour ama patriotism, man—you must be practical. Mortgages, *mbesha.* Y'know?" Musali rubs the edge of his bandages.

"This was big. Really big. When you see something like this, man, you say yes or you die, y'know?"

Ajany reads in Musali's shiftiness the extent of her brother's isolation.

"What happened?"

"We voted."

"And?"

"Opted to stay with the job. Odi took it badly, man." Musali leans over. "Went crazy!"

Ajany flinches.

Odidi broke into the office of the managing director, having driven through the company gates in his new green Prado. He shouted that this was treason. Everyone who gathered to hear him watched and did nothing. The managing director's bodyguards hustled Odidi out, tearing his shirt in the process. In an hour's time, a board meeting was called.

"The chairman called for a vote. We voted out Odidi." Silence. "He was being difficult. Wouldn't listen. We're talking billions, man. Y'know?" Musali pushes out his lower lip.

Tich Lich's partners received instructions to reregister the company under a different name if they still wanted the contract. Within two hours, an oily Ivy League university–graduated lawyer who represented the establishment personalities turned up with relevant documents extracted from his brown, black, and gold python-leather case. As they looked through the documents, the lawyer played classical music from a small device, hummed musical phrases, and witnessed the signing of the company reregistration documents.

"That man," Musali says, giggling. "Insane! After we sign, he speaks *mara* Beethoven *mara* Heili-Heiligenstadt Testament. Imagine." Musali adds that he had looked up the testament and learned to say *Heiligenstadt* properly.

Tich Lich was renamed T. L. Associates Engineering.

Odidi was no longer a partner.

Ajany's whole body has been shivering; her teeth chatter.

Musali touches her shoulder.

Ajany shrugs his hand away, ducking her head.

Musali asks, "Which Kenya did Odi grow up in? That *jama* could be so, so, so stupid, y'know?" Ajany hisses. "Sorry, man, just that, you know . . ." Musali shrugs, a practical man.

When he showed up for work, it was Musali who told Odidi what they had done.

"Tough day, that." Musali shivers at the memory of Odidi's look.

He had told Odidi to leave the premises. Urged him to take a break until the contract was serviced. Promised him that when it was over Tich Lich would return. "You know what he said?"

Ajany glances up.

"Nothing."

Musali stares at the carpet.

"He just left."

Ajany asks, "Where's my b-brother, Musali?"

Silence. Then, "Don't know." Adds, "Lost touch." A tinge of malice. "Heard he'd been moving from office to office with a petition form for citizens to sign."

Musali stops short of revealing to Ajany that Odidi had once been spotted speaking on street corners. Cannot tell her that, seven months after he had walked away from the offices, Odidi had phoned Musali for money and a place to stay. The bank had all of a sudden recalled his mortgage and had then thrown him out with his things. They were auctioning the house. No lawyer would take up the case against the state. Odidi was threatened, followed, summoned, booked for loitering with intent. Some NGOs he visited made the right sympathetic noise but emphasized to him that AIDS, women, malaria, girl children, and boreholes were priorities.

Musali gives Ajany a direct look. She sees the cold glimmer of a green mamba's stare. "We silted the dams. No choice. We have our money."

National power shortages worsened.

Companies closed down.

Utility bills exploded.

Citizens paid up.

The managing director held a party to celebrate his first personal billion shillings. Others were more discreet. T. L. Associate Engineers thrived.

"After you make money, you can afford to be an activist."

Musali stares at the carpet. "We deposited a year's salary into his account."

Musali leans back. "Last December, when I was carjacked"—Musali rubs the brace—"I thought ... it was late. . . ." He looks at Ajany's stricken face. "Ah! Man. When you see that *jama,* tell him we're in business again. We can do those *ka* sweet, sweet projects he wanted."

All of a sudden, shoulders heaving, Musali starts to cry. His teacup topples over. Everything within Ajany is set to melt. She stares at the tea-cup spilling its rust-colored tea, hears her own breathing, how creaky it sounds. Listens to Musali say, "I heard him." Pauses. "A year ago? Odidi came to my house. *Kedu* eleven o'clock at night, banging the gate."

Ajany waits.

"Ah! Man, don't look at me like that." Musali is cotton-voiced. "I was afraid . . . and my family . . . Then the carjacking . . . shot in the neck . . ."

"And?" prompts Ajany.

"It was late."

"And?"

Musali lowers his head.

He had called the police.

He was not going to tell Ajany that.

Nor that Odidi had shouted, "Musali, bro, help me."

Ajany's mouth is wooden, her head heavy. She absorbs the story and everything that has not been said. She needs a body scrub.

Musali rubs his eyes. "Don't look at me like that."

She surveys his manicured layers.

"I'm sorry." He gets up and trundles through a door. Minutes later, he returns with a copy of the picture on the reception wall. "Here."

Ajany takes the picture with both hands.

"I miss Shifta, man," he says.

Musali's hand hovers over Ajany's shoulder, tentative. No intellectual sparring partner had ever matched Odidi. Without Odidi, even rugby had lost meaning for him. He and Odidi had been among the first to paint their faces with Kenyan colors during the game. They had helped spread the lewd, loud compositions that fans sung even when the Kenyan team was losing. "Who's your father, who's your father, who's your father, referee . . ."

He says, "We used to be happy."

She stammers, "Wasn't that enough?"

Musali pauses. "No."

Ajany stands up, grabs her handbag.

"I . . ." Musali starts.

Ajany raises her hand, screws up her face; her whole body says no. She sucks air in. *Why hadn't she known her brother's suffering?*

Suffocating, she lurches for the exit, stumbling over a low table. Her body tingles in places. She focuses on the daylight. She had forgotten that time existed.

The receptionist shouts, "I'll pray for you."

Ajany halts, turns. "Why?" Lifeless eyes.

Stiff walk into the parking lot.

A gray-uniformed, cheerful, burly man waves at her. "*Sa'a*, madam!" He sprays water on a parked green Prado.

Ajany asks, "Whose car is that?" Her legs feel so heavy, she is unable to move.

"Engineer Musali."

Nails bite into skin. "Moses Odidi Oganda's car?"

"Er . . ." The man drops the cleaning cloth. "*Ehhh . . .*"

Thunder in Ajany's ears, acid on her tongue. "You know you'll die? You'll all die," she explains to the luckless driver.

Shadows of her brother's footsteps in Ajany's exit. She finds Peter the taxi man stretched out on his seat, napping. When she drags open the door, he snaps awake. Ajany collapses on her seat, forces breath in; there is blood on her nose. She clutches the picture frame.

Silence as they drive back to the guesthouse.

Peter says, "I'll fast for you."

What's the point?

She pays him for his prayers anyway.

Inside her room, numb. Weary of scrubbing tears away. She needs a destination. Maps made from the matter of memory. And that is when the walls start to close in. And she runs out of the room, out of the guest-house, out of the gates, into a darkening city.

She breathes in audible gasps. Speaking to Odidi, of Odidi, for Odidi. Passersby see a smallish woman in a yellow dress. Some watch her tilt her head as her hands open in question. Others hurry past in wide arcs with single, cautious sideways glances. She does not see any of them.

19

LONG AGO, IN HIS NEW CLASS, WITHIN A SMELLY ATLAS ON A brown square desk, Nyipir had located Burma. "Burma." Nyipir learned, "Mandalay, 21° 59′ N 96° 6′ E, Rangoon, 16° 47′ N 96° 9′ E."

After he got his primary certificate, Nyipir should have gone on to secondary school, except there was little spare money, and nobody was ready to exchange livestock for school fees for him. A priest at the mission in Kisii decided to send Nyipir to Fort Hall. Nyipir could earn money there and complete his education, as he wanted.

Fort Hall, in the Central Province, had asked for a reliable Christian good boy, a non-Kikuyu, to help with the gardening and other chores. "For a short while," Father Paul had assured him.

Nyipir left on a train, in long trousers and a hat, to start lessons in high culture by planting gardenias and watching them grow. He left in hope.

He settled in at Fort Hall. Entered into the rhythm of work: whitewash stones, cook, wash clothes, clean and polish shoes and boots, set the table, dust, and wait tables. He had sneaked textbooks from the wooden shelves next to the chapel to read by candlelight, preparing for school and wondering what to do so that he could go to Burma and bring his father and brother home.

Next door to the mission was the makeshift army camp. Nyipir would peer through the fence and watch men march in array. He heard the howling of a sergeant major as he screamed men into order. *'Eft, 'ight, 'eft, 'ight,* about-turn. When there was no one about, Nyipir tried to practice what he saw.

If he had not met Warui the gravedigger, he would not have met Aloys Kamau, and maybe he would have gone to Burma as he had intended.

Warui made bodies disappear for the Crown, and anyone else who paid for it. Deep-sunken eyes, tattered gunnysack, stained brown coat. One clipped thumb. Warui had stopped outside the mission gate, hat in his hand, glaring at Nyipir, pointing at his mouth, his way of asking for water. Nyipir glanced around—nobody looking—and led Warui to a tap, where he crouched and drank. When he finished, Warui lifted his hat and slunk away.

Five days later, Warui returned. Over the gate, he pursed his lips at Nyipir. In Kikuyu he said, "If you want to make more money, get ready tonight."

Nyipir sneaked from the mission hut, already counting the money he would earn.

He did not yet understand the state of the nation, or that interrogation units were generating far too many bodies for one man to bury alone under the blanket of night. Bodies in *gunia* leaked liquids into the ground, over his hands, the stench of invisible human beings, smashed up and nameless, lowered into grounds that he then leveled.

"What's this work called?" asked Nyipir.

"Vulturing."

"Who are these?"

Silence.

"Don't they have people of their own?"

Stillness, and the sound of metal hitting earth.

"How is it possible?"

Warui said, "Too many questions; work."

They did, in silence. Except for the times Warui would say, "Sssssssssssss" into the ground. Planting secrets. Warui also said, *"Ona icembe riugi ni rituhaga."* The sharpened hoe gets blunt. When Warui said it, he implied many things.

Nyipir planted grass atop burial sites. Unlike Nyipir's gardenias, the grass grew thick, green, and healthy.

After every hour, Warui gave Nyipir ten cents as well as half a tin of maize meal for the evening's work.

Nyipir said, *"Ona icembe riugi ni rituhaga."*

Warui spat, "Speak what you know, better still, don't speak at all, you hear?"

They worked into the deep of night.

Few witnesses.

The inarticulate dead buried by mute gravediggers.

Warui once peered into the forest canopy and whispered, "It watches."

Nyipir looked. "What?"

"Too many questions. Dig, dig."

Nyipir returned to his real post at the mission hours before dawn, bathed his body with a pot of cold water, and went to huddle among the plants. They were stunted and stubborn but had gained a grudging root-hold. He also wondered why his body was trembling. All of a sudden he remembered that he had been handling human remains. He knelt over, head close to the earth, and vomited into the soil. Nothing left in his stomach. He stared at the mess and then covered it. *Fifty cents.* He told himself that every coin brought him closer to Burma and his father and brother.

Nyipir slept until cock's crow.

The coins piled up.

But there was still not enough to even buy a train ticket to Nairobi.

The mission had told him that his food and board were payment enough, with a token two shillings a month for savings.

He needed more money.

When he asked Warui to increase his pay to twenty cents an hour, Warui laughed before clouting him in the ear.

"Work!"

One chilled night, Warui helped Nyipir bury a sack. The end of the sack burst open when they tossed it into a hole. Bloody hands and shriveled male genitals poured out. Nyipir gasped and turned to run; Warui barked at him once.

Nyipir stumbled and fell to the ground. Warui spat. "It's better if your eyes are blind. Hear?"

Nyipir nodded, still dizzy.

They returned to seal the hole in the ground.

That night, needing to clear his head, Nyipir switched paths, walked into and through the safe forest fringes. He walked through cobwebs, the tingle on his face spreading all over his body. He marched on. The ground of Nyipir's mind opened, and he spoke to the dead and their broken parts. And his father and brother walked with him. His mother joined them, as did his sister.

After he had wiped away tears, Nyipir saw that the forest unveiled a path. He stopped next to a mountain olive tree and waited before doubling back. He did not sleep at all. He knew there was a reward for giving information that led to the capture of rebels. That amount, added to what he already had, might be sufficient so he could take a train to Nairobi, and from there he knew he would find a way to Burma.

Nyipir woke up early to water the plants in the garden, long before morning Mass. He skipped breakfast, slipped out of the gate, and went next door, where the soldiers' camp was.

After the parade, Nyipir approached a corporal and told him what he had seen in the forest the previous night. The corporal went and told an officer, who beckoned to Nyipir. The officer stood next to a fading white-washed stone—a fierce son of a struggling empire leaning against the mast upon which the Union Jack quivered. "What do you want?"

Nyipir stuttered the story of a covered diversion waiting in the forest. The field officer was a wiry, medium-height man with a ragged strawberry-blond beard. He listened to Nyipir, dolorous eyes becoming smaller and smaller.

The man said, "Right, boy! I'll arrange things with the padres."

That night, Nyipir rode in a Land Rover for the first time in his life and decided that this was all he would ever drive. Four others, one informant, a young soldier who had blackened his face, whose lips gleamed pale, and three armed home guards, in the car. The road was bumpy. The Land Rover slid down slippery grooves, then halted. The men leapt out. Nyipir led the way to the path he had seen. The men crawled through the thick undergrowth.

An advance tracking squad had brought in a man on suspicion of being an oath giver. Nyipir was standing next to a guard when the man looked straight at him and said, "I surrender. And you?"

Nyipir puzzled over that.

The men eased their way into the concealed path, rifles at the ready, as silent as hunting cats. Nyipir, who had been ordered up a massive Wild Olive tree to wait and whistle an alarm if he saw anything untoward, ached to be part of the fierce band of men. Within the branches of the tree, Nyipir made a pistol shape with his right hand: two fingers pointing out, thumb up, two fingers in his palm. He waited up there until the hunters reappeared at dawn.

The following afternoon, Nyipir was redeployed from the mission to the camp—more of the same work but with guard duties thrown in and better pay. He became the camp's odd-jobs boy, until two months later, on a frost-cold day, he was ordered by the commandant to join a group of men sent to retrieve bodies from a hut: a beheaded old man, a hanged youth about his age, a toddler, and two split-apart young women. The attempts to torch the hut had failed. Only the doors and windows were scorched.

So *this* was war? Nyipir had pressed his face into the soil and screamed until he blacked out. Cold water and invective revived him, supplemented by a kick on his rear.

He imagined he could leave. *"Afande,"* he pleaded with a tow-headed junior officer, "this is sickness. If I stay, I'll surely die."

The man had guffawed and pounded Nyipir's back twice. "Gets easier, boy, don't worry."

It didn't.

And then Aloys Kamau.

More collecting of hacked-to-death human casualties of a small war.

A convulsing Italian priest drenching the site of death with holy water and incense, chanting, "Aloys Kamau," instead of prayers.

The priest was long-faced, dark-haired, as bony as an Ankole cow in the drought. His cassock was disheveled; he had a swollen face from a cracked, pus-filled molar.

He had grabbed onto the police officer who had turned gray at the human mess scattered around. In a bass voice the priest howled, "*This is a teacher of children—oh God—of children.*"

Much later, the priest, chewing sour tobacco, attempted to seize sense through staccato phrases. "That oath," he growled, "that . . . black sacrament . . . that cursed, roaming architect of sin . . . this vile landlord . . ." He swallowed the tobacco instead of spitting it out. Choking, crying.

"Aloys abjured the oath."

A week later, the children he taught gathered to spit on him as one. "*Oh! Miei bambini.*" The priest groaned. "Their poor souls." He sputtered his knowledge, and his hearers, Nyipir included, understood that Aloys Kamau had tried to save another teacher's life, a man who was being chopped up by seven men in front of his students. Aloys had intervened. He could have escaped. He did not.

Silence.

Then a palpable existential dread invaded the landscape, and the men moved closer together while the priest bayed, "Why are we here?" over and over. No birds sang. The priest howled at silent clouds, "We are simpletons. What can we do? Send exorcists, for God's sake. Send them exorcists!"

No birds sang.

Later, Nyipir would scrape the ground, looking around. *This is a body,* he thought as he waited for the brooding dread to materialize and crush them all. He gathered everything he could that was once Aloys—pieces of body in the sack. A wide dark spot marked the ground where Aloys had fallen. The priest stared at the site, paralyzed, and Nyipir thought, *This is blood,* and waited for the rumble that would surely end a world confronted by this horror.

It didn't come.

The world rolled on, but not before consecrating Nyipir to its whims, Nyipir, who clutched a bloodied sack, as if it contained all the densities of night. Much, much later, Nyipir's mind watched life shutting down on itself inside the pitch of human screams: *Ngai, Ngai, Ngai.* God, God, God. Of passes issued to souls with blank eyes who volunteered names in exchange for peace, peace alone (the pass read, "*Mwigito wa kwiho-nokia ukineana . . . uyu ukuuite 'bathi' ino arinda*"—The bearer of this pass wishes to surrender). Of wondering how a people could harbor a malignant presence that would devour children, and not scream out, not even once. Of trying not to scratch himself out of his skin, because *this* could not be the meaning of life.

Yet.

He knew he might endure all this so that he could go to Burma and bring his father and brother home. He could endure this world, he realized, so that, in defiance of intent, a murdered dreamer named Aloys Kamau might borrow eyes to still look upon a life that had been severed from him.

Months later, a special "processing" station was built to manage the national crisis. The base at Athi River sought trustworthy hands. An officer slapped a band on Nyipir's upper arm and sent him over to the plains. On his way to Athi River by train, Nyipir glimpsed Nairobi at sunset and thought of Burma.

At the secretly located Athi River station, Nyipir's tasks were simple: join seven other men and stare at inmates in cells, no words.

"What kind of job is this?" he asked a short man.

"Are you being paid?" the man asked.

"Yes, sir," said Nyipir.

"Then why question?"

Concentrated silence drowned the hardest of men.

Faces he contemplated every day burned themselves into Nyipir's nights, and would start conversations as he slept that had not been possible during the day. He began to dread both day and night. Some nights, to postpone sleep, Nyipir wrote long letters to Baba Jimmy. He told of stages of light in human eyes. *Akia kata nying' gi*, he wrote. *The body of a human cannot live without kindness. When it meets hatred, it stops trusting its life. This is what weakens men.* Nyipir did not write that because of the ugliness in the stillness of the plains, he was unable to play the mouth organ and had kept it away in a crevice of his suitcase. He wrote, *I will find Baba and Theo. To be so far from home cannot be good. I'll go to Burma.* He did not write that Burma meant he could forget the things he had seen and done. Nyipir signed off his letter. *An wuodi, Nyipir.* If Baba Jimmy sent a reply, Nyipir never got it.

"*Mwigito wa kwihonokia ukineana . . . uyu ukuuite 'bathi' ino arinda*"— The bearer of this pass wishes to surrender. A new man, an officer named Hugh Bolton, came to join the study of lives belonging to the documentation Nyipir issued: "*Ne ûndû wa kûhonokia ûtûro wake*"—For the salvation of his soul.

In the Kalacha heat, within a partly dug grave, gasping for air, for the first time Nyipir wonders where the pass holders went after the compromises had been made and the names they had listed had been made dead. *If I should speak, may the oath kill me.*

Sipping air.

Some silences cut off breath.

Even under oath.

20

THE CITY'S SUN IS SOFT AND WHISPERY. BEAUTIFUL NAIROBI people dodge the newspaperman burdened with four versions of the previous day's news. At the Book Centre, Ajany has filled a supermarket trolley with watercolors, pastels, paper, brushes, molding clay, anything and everything arty. She had already made photocopies of a zoomed-in portion of a photograph. She pursed her lips at the one hundred copies of Odidi.

On her way out of the mall, she slips into the ladies' toilet. Shifting feet. A cubicle becomes vacant. Out steps a buxom, fluffy-haired, expertly painted, open-mouthed woman in a too-tight white sweater dress. Agalo? Ajany dives into the stall. She has no energy to summon school-day memories. The sound of an air freshener being sprayed. Ten minutes. The woman should have gone. Ajany opens the door, makes for the faucets. Blueberry liquid soap. Rubs her hands.

The outside door squeaks open.

The woman pounces. *"Araaaabel!"* A squeal.

Face in the mirror.

Ajany blinks at it. "Agalo?" She suppresses a flicker of terror when she confirms the presence of one of a clique of popular girls she had spent her school years avoiding.

The woman lurches toward Ajany, and they squeeze each other in an insincere hug.

Agalo, who still speaks with exclamation marks, yells, "You! Came back! Must tell Alfred! Remember Alf! Where's Odidi! What do you do! I've three sons! You?!"

A breeze of mint-scented spirits.

It is not yet noon.

Ajany considers the window. They are on the third floor. It would be a long way down.

"Are my eyes red?" Agalo spins toward the mirror, sniffs. "Nairobi flu."

Ajany edges toward the door.

Agalo grabs her arms. "A quick coffee? Dormans?"

Ajany pulls away. "I-I w-was . . ." Ajany points in a vague direction.

"Oh, one cup." Agalo rushes Ajany down escalators, talking all the time. They come to a stop where three other women lounge. One of them, with red talons—there is no other way to describe what she has done to her nails—is in the middle of an argument. Agalo interrupts. "Look who I found! Arabel. Remember Shifta the Winger? His sister!"

"Ohhhhh!"

They look past Ajany into recollections of respective teen crushes on Odidi. "Where's Shifta now?" drawls a woman whom Ajany cannot remember.

"Traveling," Ajany says. She plunks down her bags of art materials and inhales.

Agalo trills, "What'll you have, hon?"

"Masala tea." Ajany slumps into the chair, planning her escape, just as she used to when this same gang of girls stopped her at school under one pretext or another, usually to do with access to Odidi as his star ascended. She scrunches her nose. Exhales at the unrepaired past. Notes the paraphernalia of their present lives: small technology idols—phones, beeping, purring, bleeping objects that expect to be fondled mid-conversation, pieces of a shape-changing land with grand fiber-optic tentacles plugging into old histories that refuse to rest in peace. Ajany listens. One woman's words are fringed with New Age positivity as she debates an activist. "If we breathed more and grounded our being, connecting to the womb of the earth, and looked upon each other with kind eyes, we would feel that we are already one."

"Are you 'one' with me?" the thick-dreadlocked activist chortles as she drops an effervescent tablet into her concoction. She lifts the blend to her mouth. "Yeah, so visualize *shit* as gold, gaze at the red bums of baboon politicians and imagine them as dung beetles!" She gulps down her mixture in one long swallow and burps.

The Nairobi New Ager says, "Eat more greens, you'll be less angry . . . and . . . *raw*." She pulls out a tiny leleshwa-and-jasmine scent bottle and sprays the blended essence on her wrists, inhaling the pungent goodness. It wafts over everyone.

The activist sneezes and continues as if with the quotation marks of irony. "Sister," she says, her arms curving into the shape of an Ankole cow's horn, "even when a cockerel wears a turban it'll never be a Sikh!" An exclamation mark's triumph. "Greens! Kenya's choking, and you, with your *ati*—'lavender essence'—she makes two air-scratching movements—"and *hordohordo* English . . . you . . . blood-drinker, as if we don't know about your secret oath-gobbling covens. Eat greens, you tell the rest of us?" She glares at everybody around the table, mouth working as if she were a gasping fish. She drops her head and plows into her salad with endless fingers that dangle on too-thin wrists.

Perfect tears hover in the perfumed aura-reader's eyes.

Agalo pats her head.

Ajany watches and senses the scratching of unrepudiated ghosts here. An image of her father huddled over a radio. She winces. Tilts her head to search for other intimate signs on skin, within eyes. Truth signals. Like those shadow marks on Akai-ma's wrists. Scars—resistance against suffering.

The activist was humming. Sounded like hiccupping. Ajany glances at her. She had once read that the activist had been arrested by irritated law enforcers. That she had worn sackcloth and ashes over one cause, been treated for allergic reactions to tear gas in another demonstration, and already been charged in court six times under different public-nuisance statutes. There was a photograph of her walking down Uhuru Highway wearing a large elephant mask, and yet another of her returning on the same route wearing a brown rhino-horn costume complete with a tragic white horn. She had once stood in the back of a van with a loudspeaker, simulating wails for Kenya's dying forests, and stolen pastoralist lands. There was no cause she did not champion, no protest she did not join. She was also seeking her "Unique African Voice" for "Global Climate Change Conversations."

Agalo breathed in the leleshwa-and-jasmine perfume, sneezed, and beamed upon all, a blinkered look on her face. She was used to such confrontations among her friends. She encouraged the whingeing. It was how they dressed up the rancid issues that agitated their otherwise ordered Nairobi lives.

Securing their universe.

Ajany watched.

Here they were, the "better future" their parents, teachers, and leaders talked about, drinking Kenyan coffee (with milk), tree-tomato and minty pineapple juice, and one Masala tea. Post–Kenyan independence, older women, lines beneath eyes, enmeshed by national subtexts, still hiding from anonymous bogeymen, still trying to plaster, with easy words, the fetid moral swamps engorged by the sludge of what a nation does, or does not do, with its freedom.

Ajany watched. Overloud laughter and performed rage on the outside, but inside, labyrinthine crevices dense with debris from personal, surreptitious, and very quiet wars.

Agalo leans toward Ajany. "What do you see?"

Ajany's eyes dart away. She says nothing.

Agalo takes Ajany's hand. "Did you vote?"

Shake of head.

"Good for you! Oh! No ring? Unattached?"

Ajany shrugs.

Agalo gives a sympathetic eye roll. "Life happens."

They had exhausted the boundary of permitted rediscoveries.

Across the room, a man leans into his phone. Whoever is on the other side convulses him with sultry laughter. Its soft heat blends with the leleshwa-and-jasmine fragrance drifting around the women's table.

Stillness.

Ajany stammers, "The time! Must go." She drags out two hundred shillings from her wallet and, at the same time, tries to shake hands, air-kisses, picks up her shopping, and nods to the chorus of *Let's do this again—do come visit—good to see you again.*

Agalo retrieves a bleached business card from the depths of her handbag. As she enfolds Ajany in a one-handed squeeze, she whispers, "Tell Odidi to phone me."

Ajany takes the card and hurries away. *Odidi,* she thinks as she reads the card. *Regional Director,* it says, beneath a logo that belongs to a global conglomerate—and, written quickly, *Agalo's expecting your call.*

Breathing easy in her room, Ajany lays out her purchases. She then lies on the bed and cleans out her mind. She pulls out Agalo's card and rips it into small pieces, which she tosses into the wastebasket.

Later, she pastes seven images and likenesses on her wall. She surveys her work, stretching out on the floor. Images of Odidi look down at her. She crawls across the room, takes a ballpoint pen from the table, and returns to tear open the art paper. She will draw tales she has heard. Her drawing hand shakes on the page.

———

Past the city center, the jumble of anonymous sky-scratching steel-glass-stone edifices, toward the railway station. Architectural devolution—squat, steady, older, defiant frameworks. Agrovet centers, rubble and tattered clothes, Gospel enterprises, Mutigwo Iganjo Hotel, street vendors selling tomatoes, shoes, Jesus-Mary-and-Joseph clocks, and windshield wipers. A school sports field. Smog-stained grevillea trees, flame trees, survivors of a day when that landscape had been lovely. Art Deco rooftops, a proliferation of buildings—blocks shooting up, a story a day; satellite devices like a thousand giant insect feelers probing exotic realms for truths. Single-pump petrol stations that were always three shillings below the city center's pump prices. Air and water for sale.

Views from a square window.

Ajany is in a *matatu,* heading out into the city's inner worlds. Servicing a new addiction, that of collecting her brother's shadows.

Some people listen to her questions.

She has posters to support her query: "My brother, Moses Ebewesit Odidi Oganda, is lost. Have you seen him?" Some people tell her others have also been lost in the post-election violence. Others say they, too, will print and distribute images of their lost. Many take her aside and tell her to leave these things in the hands of God.

Ajany crosses the railway tracks and walks, reaching a culvert opposite a plastic-and-wood hair salon, with braids drying on outdoor poles, called Gloria's God Gives Hair Design. A loud, stocky woman whose breasts spread way out there shouts to someone upstairs and reaches with her hands to disentangle used braids. Their eyes meet. Her red braids fall over the black ink-stain mark covering the left half of her face.

The woman shouts, "Babi!"

Translation: daughter of Babylon.

Ajany thinks: *Whore.*

This city.

Outside of a used-shoe booth where stylish right-foot shoes dangle, a sublime cologne flits past. Ajany breathes. The dirt and flowing sewage superimpose their odor on the moment. And then it is dusk, and Ajany is one of many complacent souls who have been stuffed into a *matatu* while Franklin Boukaka harangues a lumberjack in song: . . . *Aye Africa, Eh Africa, O Dipanda* . . .

The piercing blare of a distant, late-arriving train, dust-on-shoe solitudes, questions that were prayers, the past's interference: it would come as memory, and she would have to kneel where she was until midriff-splitting sorrow passed. Some days would be better than others.

Good evening, Ms. Oganda?

Good evening, Jos.

Jos is at the reception desk most evenings.

Ajany rushes for the shower, strips off her clothes, and washes the day off her. She hobbles as if her body were a borrowed, oversized dress. Shapeless mists brood; there are welts in her heart. Overnight, acne has appeared on her face and covered the sides of her neck, too. She falls into bed and sleeps at once.

Morning. Incursions into Nairobi's dark-light worlds, treading the banks of the putrid soup that is the Nairobi River. From Ngong to Komarock, asking existences-in-squalor if they have ever seen her brother, Moses

Odidi Oganda. She has pictures to show and share. No one acts as if her questions are strange. A few think it is funny to send her looking where there is nothing.

Traders: information in exchange for cash or phone credit, or a fuck. She says, "Bring me my brother first, I'll do anything."

And she would.

The desperate and mad believe in magic.

So she throws bones, as she is told.

Carries tainted feathers and the claw of a crow.

Wears a blessed medallion of Saint Gerard.

Kills a white cockerel to appease an unknown, malignant ancestor. She is praying for more shadows, and her patron saint, Moses Ebewesit Odidi Oganda. Some warn her of the times in which they live: "Others, too, are lost," they say.

She listens.

"Many are dying."

She listens.

"Nothing special about you."

"He's my brother," she says.

"Others have brothers, too."

"This one's mine."

Good evening, Ms. Oganda?
  Good evening, Jos.

One day, in Baba Dogo, Ajany becomes a face in a mob staring down at a man shot in the head by policemen for impersonating a policeman. A man in a blue-and-red shirt laughs and points at the bleeding corpse. No one to affirm dignity in the bleeding out of a former man.

She starts to sob aloud.

She runs away.

Stumbles across the railway lines into a now familiar space. There is Gloria's God Gives's buxom owner.

"Babi!" She screams at Ajany.

Ajany, wiping her face, thinks, *Shitty city.*

. . .

Good evening, Ms. Oganda?
Good evening, Jos.

Next day, she peers into and out of misshapen shelters that are cafés, res-
taurants, temporary morgues, clinics with discredited doctors, medicine
men, exorcists from Lubumbashi, Lagos, and Mombasa. Pornographic
video dens, brothels, churches, bars—spaces of encounter and paradox.

Reads the name of a nearby butcher shop: Soma Lebo.

Chapped lips, bitten through. Bad habit.

A story-less day.

Good evening, Jos.

Jos is gesticulating madly, nose wrinkling, eyes rolling, pointing at
a bespectacled, well-aged man with straight eyebrows and a squarish
head, whose large hands are leafing through a women's magazine.

The man sees Ajany, smiles, flips a couple of pages before toss-
ing down the journal. Soft-voiced. Luo-tinged English, a husky but
clear articulation of words, a downward-shifting cadence with sibilant
sounds enphasized. "Apparently, green is the new black." He rises and
stretches out his hand. "Assistant Commissioner of Police Petrus Keah,
and I'm ahead of my time." He lifts his trouser leg to reveal lime-green
socks.

Ajany looks up at the big, very tall man, in his oversized dark-blue
designer suit. Arms like giant boat oars, a large face, hard bloodshot
eyes behind metal-framed spectacles.

Contrived insouciance.

Petrus says, "How's your father, my brother *Wuod* Oganda?"

Ajany, head tilted, asks, "What're you to him?"

"Friend of the family." Petrus's brows gather.

Ajany, light-headed: "Something's happened."

"No, just looking for you."

Fainthearted: "Why?"

"For your father."

"What's happened?" Break in voice.

"We shared time, a room, and a cigarette, long ago. Ah! Your friend
the youthful Ali Dida Hada"—Ajany whirls—"wanted me to give you
his salaams. . . ."

Sweat beads on Ajany's face; she tugs at her sleeves until they cover her hands.

Petrus watches her, moves closer. "*Nyar* Oganda, we're very concerned. Correction, I'm concerned. This." He retrieves a folded document. With a shake it unfolds. Odidi's image.

Ajany breathes in slow sips. "So?"

"Why?" asks Petrus.

Ajany sits down, her knees shaking. "I'm looking for him."

"The truth is not as you saw it?"

She stares at Petrus. Ice-voiced, she says, "No."

Petrus looks at her above his spectacles. Her smallness, her defiance, questions that furrow her forehead. "Go back home, *nyako*." He sighs. "No truth here'll set you free. Go, rest."

A sliver of insight from Petrus's pitying look—*was it madness to want to build a bridge into Odidi's underworld?* Ajany glances away, hands touching the place of the sheet of sorrow that covers her heart and cohabits with the shard of shame that she was still alive.

Petrus savors the end of the unlit cigarette, the illusion of smoke to battle a nicotine craving. A pang. Ajany's presence is like an accusation. He *had* raced out when he heard a dispatch about a gang being accosted on Nairobi's streets. How had he been bypassed? Such accosting was usually his prerogative. He had reached Odidi's side seven minutes after the bullets that mortally wounded him had been fired. *Am I too old for this?*

Petrus had reached retirement age eight years ago, but ever since then, he would ignore all requests to submit a retirement date. He could. Kenya regimes had come and gone, but Petrus had stayed around long enough to build cauldrons of knowledge about the sins of many, including those who tried to threaten the continuation of his work life. His targets were paralyzed by his genial unpredictability and the intimate knowledge he brooded over, which, as he explained when date-of-retirement issues were suggested as a meeting agenda item, would hatch, soar, and circulate worldwide in the event of his untimely retirement, death, especially by accident, "mistaken-identity" shootout, poisoning, or sudden illness. Silence afterward. Yet ever since he had reached Odidi just in time to see him die, an unexpected sag in the heart and a persistent inflow of sorrow were driving him to accept his own decline and increasing irrelevance to the only life that he knew. A quick glance sideways, mouth downturned. But he had so much to offer. Petrus throws back his shoulders, flicks his soggy cigarette stick into a bin shaped like a goose, pulls out a rumpled, red cigarette package and reads the warning: *Cigarette smoking can kill a fetus.* He eases out another cigarette. Doesn't light it. Dangles it in his mouth. "Why?" he finally asks.

Ajany says, "He's my b-brother."

"And you, *naturally,* his keeper."

Ajany buries her head in her arms. "He's my brother."

Petrus moves near her. "Do you understand what you're trifling with, Ms. Oganda?"

Petrus pushes at the space between his eyes, pushes at the feeling that besieges him more often now—that of being a minuscule bit actor in an invisible force's movie. A quiver. *Odidi.* A stabbing sensation accompanies his recollection of the young man's wasted blood.

Stupid boy.

Over a year and a half back, a *matatu tout* informant he was squeezing for information about a spate of robberies in the city had told him of an urban gang named Jokadhok, all-purpose criminals who were the forerunners of the city's cyber-crime networks. They made the police look foolish. Petrus knew that some of his officers had likely been compromised. That was always the case. Petrus had evolved a profile and acquired a grumpy respect for the criminals. He soon had a grainy picture from an ATM heist, and connected the image to that of a man gone amok who years back had damaged the dam authorities' offices: Moses Ebewesit Odidi Oganda.

Petrus had at once sought out Ali Dida Hada to deliver a warning to the Oganda family, which he did. But, to Petrus's shock, a face that had plagued his forty-year memory had sought him out to plead for his son's life. Aggrey Nyipir Oganda came to the city he had sworn off, to fall on his knees in Petrus's office.

"Save my boy," he said, through tears falling into deformed hands, which he, Petrus, had reshaped. "You can save my only son."

Petrus had fled Nyipir that day, escaped the re-emergence of violent memories, of doubt, of the accumulated voices of a thousand bleating citizen-victims.

Crinkle of cigarette pack.

Petrus glances at Ajany.

Does she know this part of the story?

She is huddled within her sweater even as rage skulks in her eyes. *No,* he concludes. He munches on his cigarette.

Stupid boy.

If the lad had needed easy money, he should have become a parliamentarian; he could have raised his salary daily. Petrus blinks. He *had* tried. Had even arranged for Ali Dida Hada to move into police headquarters on a promotion, the better to monitor the case, locate Odidi, and spirit him back to Wuoth Ogik. *A life for a life,* he had intended to write to Nyipir after Odidi reached home. *There are now no transactions pending between us.*

Atonement denied by seven minutes.

Stupid boy!

Petrus studies Ajany's bony face, the sunken, dark-rimmed eyes. He resumes his pacing, feeling sweat patches on his body, stopping to touch the wall tiles, then curtains, picking up another magazine. A twinge. So he frowns at Jos, who knocks over a file. Colorful papers flutter to the ground. Petrus grins. Human beings! Usually guilty about something or other. Usually afraid their secret had been discovered. Funny creatures.

A gnawing sensation in Ajany's stomach as she watches Petrus.

He turns. "Gun battle; Odidi lost."

Stillness. Her arms cradle her body.

A whisper: "You murdered my brother?"

"No."

"Then who?"

Petrus pops his knuckle. "Some police."

"You *are* p-police."

"Yes."

"So?"

"Odidi was a key figure in a crime situation."

"My brother?" Scorn in every word. "Think again!"

"We did."

"And?" Ajany glowers, standing.

Petrus gesticulates. "Sit down."

Jos's papers rustle.

Teeth gritted, Ajany says, "Yesterday, I saw a man shot for wearing a p-policeman's uniform. He died on a cement pavement alone, surrounded by people treating him as they might an insect. He c-cried tears of blood. Nobody wept with him. He was—what?—twenty-four, and k-killed for wearing a p-police uniform." Her voice descends an octave. "Erased, as if he n-never existed. *Why?* Doesn't his life matter?" Her voice breaks. She stops, her breathing shallow.

Petrus's eyes slant. "He chose death."

"That's it?"

"Every crime story begins with a decision."

"And a finale that is a d-death sentence?"

"It happens." Petrus positions his hands behind his head.

"A summary execution."

"Maybe he attacked our officers. Maybe he was resisting arrest. Maybe he was a mad dog? A terrorist. Maybe he was planning a raid. We have a million reasons, *nyar* Oganda. And we can apply these to you, too." In his soft voice, Petrus asks, "Therefore, madam . . . would you like to make an official statement about everything you know about this police impersonator?"

Stillness.

Ajany's knees shake. She reaches for the chair. Her ear aches. The world looks foggy now.

"Would you?"

Ajany's shoulders droop.

"We can go to the station now. I'll say we have a witness, a person of interest who has details about a criminal who has been impersonating policemen with a view to committing heinous crimes. Come with me."

"N-no."

"No what?" Petrus asks.

"I d-don't want to make an official statement." Her nose is bleeding. She shields her face. Ebb and flow of shame: humiliated by this hideous solitude. "He must have had dreams. . . ." Her voice is tiny.

"Who?"

Silence.

Petrus wipes his forehead. "We all do . . . at some point."

Petrus had turned up seven minutes after the ambush against Odidi had been sprung and an unnecessary gun battle had reached its end. He had watched Odidi struggle to get up. Then the media had shown up, as did the Officer Commanding Police Division, reciting from an unchanging script. When the show was over, Petrus had pulled rank and taken charge of Odidi's body.

He had spoken to the young man, lying with blood-streaming eyes half open, limbs twitching, and mouth open: "I've looked for you, boy."

The boy had attempted a laugh.

"I'm here," Petrus had said.

The boy's look had scorched Petrus's soul and punctured an inner sac of buried tears. "Go to sleep," he had told him, had called him "son," and had come close to praying right there.

Afterward, when he stood up, Petrus's first thought was to make the corpse disappear and spare Nyipir Oganda the news of his son's death.

He had escorted the body to the mortuary and had it tagged, *Unknown African Male*. Petrus had then wandered into a downtown bar behind River Road where accordions played *mugithi* tunes, rising and falling, while gibbering patrons took on the character of shadows.

Later.

A gargantuan brown-box 1970s television had sputtered the signature tune for the 7:00 p.m. news bulletin while he studied the beer froth. A protuberant nose had appeared, a most stupendous organ, which collapsed on a pockmarked face, darkened to blue by bad lighting. With eyes bulging, a chunky neck popped out of the gray khaki uniform of the state's potbellied police spokesman. Gloveless, he cradled a rifle, fondled a bullet; sleight of hand revealed the black .45 that had served such occasions for more than twenty years.

The spokesman's blurring and piercing words, displacing consonants with microtones unheard of before or since—he had left no vowel unturned. "Our *mboys*"—the man had pounced upon phrases, made an adjustment—"our 'eroic *mboys* accosted a *notolious*, viorent *gang*. . . ."

The image on the screen. A green Toyota Prado, banged up by bullets, windscreen shattered, bloodstains on the driver's seat. A commentator's hysterical voice-over: "The victim, a prominent businessman who owns an engineering firm, is recovering from bullet wounds to his neck at a private hospital in Nairobi."

"Our *mboys* . . ." attempted the police spokesman.

Petrus, the drinking man, had glimpsed the distorted shape of a man leaning against a white saloon on television, and then spilled his beer when he recognized himself. Petrus had stared at the image of tarmac, two AK-47s, rounds of ammunition, and two pistols on the scene and listened to the OCPD's tale: "These *climinals* moved with the *plecision* of *rocusts*. They *swarmed* their targets." A swarming gesture. The image cut to blue socks on the soles of Odidi's feet. Showed a stained white tight-fitting T-shirt. Blood pooled, and there was the shoelessness of a big man's muscular body.

An open palm, the slow curling of fingers inward.

It had been so many years since Petrus had cried. *This is how we lose the country, one child at a time.* Two hours before dawn, breathing off the bliss of several downed Tuskers, a normally hypervigilant security man walked in an unnaturally straight line. All the way to the top of Kirinyaga Street, he howled in off-key, an unlit cigarette clinging to the insides of his mouth: *Hasira za nini wee bwana . . . wataka kuniua bure baba . . . sina makosa, wee bwana. . . .* What's this rage? Why kill me for nothing? I'm not at fault, man.

He had thought, *All my life I've been enforcing silence by chopping off noisy human parts.* His face was distorted by a rictus of self-mockery. *A mere class prefect,* fwakni, *in a derelict school where every headmaster is a murderous pickpocket.*

Even as Petrus leaned over the ramparts of the bridge over the Nairobi River and dropped a pistol and broken phone into the murky waters, he improvised: *Petrus is not at fault, bwana. . . .* Voice fades to silence. The braying of a distant, late arriving city-bound train. Petrus walks. He steps over a creature pressed like black cardboard into the road, and for a moment remembers Nairobi's extinct hedgehogs—why they had not survived the city's infested sprawling.

Three hours later, bleary-eyed and raspy-voiced, Petrus retrieved Ali Dida Hada's personal mobile number from one of his four phones.

"Rotting on the job," Petrus had accused him when he answered. "Where were you?" he asked. "The boy died last night—where were you?" He hiccupped.

Ali Dida Hada asked, "Who?"

"Oganda, who else?" slurred Petrus.

Ali Dida Hada had not spoken for about a minute. Then he swallowed audibly. After that, he had switched off his phone.

Ajany memorizes the details she would need to carve Petrus's profile into black-ice stone. She would pound in jagged craters to reveal ravenous eyes of fathomless reach. Black holes.

Petrus senses her gaze probing his mind. Refuge in an image. "I'll keep this." Petrus folds Odidi's poster and tucks it back into his coat. This is a dense land, he thinks, its memories a deluge that crave atonement. Petrus blinks himself alert. Now he is going mad.

A weary "Go home, Ms. Ajany, leave us alone. Go to your Brazil, today, tomorrow, but go away, please."

Heavy exiting footsteps. At the reception, Petrus points at Jos with a snappy *"Kijana!"* Young man! On impulse, he bares his teeth: *"Wee!"*

Everything on Jos's desk drops to the floor.

Petrus grins.

People!

He is sniggering when he unlocks his car door.

A pause. From his shirt pocket, he tugs at a small black notebook with a red pencil tucked inside. He chooses a blank page and carefully tears out a piece. He sketches something in. "*Kijana!"* he bellows in the direction of Jos, who dashes to him in a half-crouch.

He has gone, but Petrus's shadow is a trap. Cold sensations crowd Ajany. *Fear is a presence,* Bernardo had hurled at her one night. *"It penetrates beauty to deform it."* He had sung, *"Eu quero que sejas bela"*—I want you to be beautiful. Now a vile cord, woven out of writhing shadows, wraps itself around her neck. Bile throttles even the not many words she can speak. She is motionless in her chair.

21

A ROUGH, CRUMPLED MAP DRAWN ON A SCRAP OF PAPER.

She has found the place.

She scrapes fragments of her brother's dried, rusted blood onto a small piece of paper. She scratches the potholed, gray-black tarmac of a Nairobi side road into which a driver has squashed a fat, mottled bull-frog. The frog's life has contaminated the scene-of-crime. Does not matter. No witnesses apart from those who are consumed by an eternal vow of silence. The frog's entrails poke out of the ground like a portent. She has just noticed the sullied petals of a crushed lily when the acrid loathing surges from her body, gushes out of her mouth, and mingles with the chaos on the ground.

A solitary wind trots in and brings a chill with it. She hears the echoes of a herdsman's prayer after every one of his remaining sheep and goats had been torn apart by leopards in a horrible season of drought: *The day I meet God, I'll throw my spear at him.*

She has poured water onto the wound in the ground, and scrubbed with her fingers and hands. But before she poured the water, she had bent over, rested her head on the warm tarmac, touched the memory blood with her face. Ears to the ground, listening and waiting. Becoming Odidi. Waiting, toppling over the limits of space, and as she stares at the below, she can see Odidi's footsteps and they are turned toward Wuoth Ogik. *Odidi!* she whimpers.

Silence answers.

It bursts inside her.

Passersby, exhausted from running battles with false policemen, murderous gangs, double-tongued politicians, and priests of sorrow, think the smallish woman lying on the road is another of the well-dressed insane who from season to season appear from nowhere. Moreover, in an unreasonable season—when a nation has smoldered inside the small egos of broken men who would be kings, and when rabid men with spiked clubs circumcised small boys to death, and seventeen heads without bodies were roadblocks across a national highway, and people used ballpoint pens to accuse next-door neighbors who would then be slaughtered and burned while they sorted out the earthly goods they wanted from their homes—a small woman scrubbing blood off a potholed road is nothing to marvel at.

She will keep vigil over a spot of road. Wash it. Cleanse the condemnation, the persistent loneliness of a brother. Savoring hatred. An approaching orange cement lorry honks. Seeing it, she admits to helplessness before this thing that has no words.

Honk!

Simple thing, this lying down: dropping it all, even the anger. Allow, become tarmac. Become nothing.

From the inside of a red kiosk, seated on a high stool, a pregnant woman spies on Ajany, her hand resting on her rounded stomach. The woman has come to the site of Odidi's death daily. At her first visit, she was furtive and frightened, but now this pilgrimage is just one of the things she does with her life, like drinking tea at ten o'clock. It was she who had left the lily there. For her, Odidi is not fully out of reach. When she can sleep, in the middle of dreaming, she knows his arms envelop her, her head is tucked into his chest, and she hears his heart beating. She did not know that death could be this hemorrhaging sob that makes opening her eyes a daily battle.

She knows who the woman crawling on the tarmac is. Does not trust her. His blood should belong to *her*, hers to decide when to clean. Eyes squint. She watches Ajany. She makes a decision. She leans forward on her stool to tap the kiosk owner's shoulder.

.   .   .

A stocky hairdresser with big arms grabs Ajany by the upper arm. "Babi!" she yells, dragging her from the approaching orange lorry, which groans past them. *"Saitan!"* spits the woman. *"Ashindwe!"*

Ajany focuses on the thick grizzle covering the woman's chin, how it disappears into her neck. The big woman tugs at the ends of Ajany's hair, stretches out her lips, and makes a sucking sound.

"Mbaya. Mbayaaaa!" she tuts.

Firm, warm, hard hands lead Ajany into the salon she spurned before.

Water drains through a hole in a black plastic sink beneath which a cracked blue bucket waits. Ajany watches the escape of a blend of unknown shampoo, butter-smelling conditioner, hair dirt, and warm water. Large, tough, firm hands press her neck down. Ajany cannot move. Rub and twist and comb and rinse. Soap in her eyes. The sting is good. Water in her eyes. Smell of black-woman hair things, smoke, liquids, heat, and strands. Chatter in the room.

Politics, where politicians have names linked to habits: The drunkard whose wife beats him? The slut who has three children with his secretary? The drug dealer running after the newsreader who is younger than his daughter? Which one? The fool who shot his driver? The election bandit? The murderer found dead in his pool? Mocking laughter. If-these-men-cannot-keep-their-families-how-will-they-keep-the country? The question boomerangs. They retreat to the theme of fashion. A new clothing-and-shoe shop. Fallen-off-a-ship designer wear. Crime. *Ayayayaya!* Whispered, *"Walimpata."* They got him. "Good." "The betraying insect."

The big woman rubs Ajany's hair dry, reaches for a clothesline of hair pieces, and picks a thin strand to twist into it. Another young woman, with doe-brown eyes, walks in and pulls a strand, starts on the left side of Ajany's head. Ajany's head, swung this way and that, tingles.

"Songa Aunty."

Not "Babi" anymore.

The woman stands in between Ajany's legs to braid the center of her head. Tilts her roughly so that another woman, who has moved a white stool close to her low chair, can roll hair strands on a darkened and hardened thigh. Casual intimacy.

. . .

Four and a half hours later, minute braids that curl red on the edges run down Ajany's back. It costs a thousand shillings. The stocky woman plucks the money from Ajany's hands, tucks it into her brassiere. She winks at their truce. Today Ajany had gained a passage out of Babylon.

Ajany leaves the salon, her head aching, heart melting.

She walks past a red kiosk, toward the *matatu* stop, wondering if she should call her taxi man instead.

The kiosk man calls her: "*He!* You! Babi?"

Ajany focuses on the crowd at the terminal. She could curse as her mother would. Kick down the ramshackle red shop. Her eyes are fire when she glowers at the man, who is gesturing with chin and eyes. "Go to Justina." He points at her. "Go."

"Me?" she stammers.

"*Kwani,* you see anyone else? Go!" he says. "Go!" A furtive look.

A customer approaches the shop.

He wants a sachet of milk and oil.

"Mluyia!"

The kiosk man snaps, "*Ati,* Mluyia!" Like most citizens, he is now careful about small, unconsidered talk. New sensitivities. His cultural roots had not mattered before the chaos—not in the city. Now most citizens understated ethnic roots, overemphasizing Kenyan-ness in brash Kiswahili and even louder English. Renegotiating belonging, desperate faith in One Kenya.

Ajany returns to her quest for a ride home.

The kiosk man shouts, "*Weh!* Oganda, *umenisikia?*"

Ajany pivots; her new braids swirl. "How do you know my name?"

"Go to Justina." He glares at her.

Ajany heart pounds. "Who's J-justina?"

The man shuffles objects on his narrow shelf.

She says, "So where's this Justina?"

"Ask that woman." Chin points toward the Gloria's God Gives salon, where the stocky hairdresser beckons her back.

22

JUSTINA'S DARK-BLUE CORRUGATED IRON DOOR IS OPEN. AJANY
pushes it inward and finds a pregnant woman painting lines on a canvas
that is perched on a sturdy wooden stand. The air in the room is stuffy,
smoky, and tense, as if an argument has been interrupted. Ajany frowns
when she sees the Windsor canvases that fill the room.

A stove reeks of paraffin. Cabbage in a small *sufuria* on the boil,
as a hen cackles under a large wooden bed with a cheap purple velvet
headboard.

Ajany's eyes adjust to the dimness. "Justina?"

The woman gives her a side glance, offers nothing.

Justina is a long woman, no other way to describe her. Long fingers,
long nose, long thin earlobes, and long limbs. Her muumuu is yellow,
her lipstick too dark. She waves her squirrel-fur brush at Ajany. Nib-
bling her nails, she tilts her head at the canvas with its slash of red, its
airbrushed-looking violet horizons.

The hovel's door eases shut behind Ajany and locks into place. Ajany
then notices a pair of a man's dark-brown leather shoes placed behind
the door. She reaches for them.

"Don't . . ." starts Justina.

Ajany picks up the shoes anyway, eyes closed. Lifts them to her face,
inhales the residue of sweat and dust. The smells become life, acquire a

voice. A dog yaps. New grief creeps in. *The day I meet God, I'll throw my spear at him. . . .*

Justina paints.

Time evaporates.

Justina dips her brush into a metal mug. She tells Ajany, with a sudden side look, "I saw you."

Ajany lowers the shoes, arranges them where they had been.

Justina says, "Saw you looking for Odi." She scatters the excess liquid from the brush across the concrete floor. Red color splatters on concrete. A drop lands on an Ajua board set on a table.

An unfinished game.

Ajany stares at the board.

"*Un tem fé, si un tem fê . . . mh, mh, mh . . . medo e confians . . .*" Justina hums, "*lalalala . . .*"

Cesária Évora.

Ajany's eyes fixate on the board.

Two rows, six cups. Forty-eight seed "cattle."

Two extra holes.

Cattle storage areas.

She walks toward it, squats.

Sows seeds counterclockwise on the board, one at a time.

The aim of the game—practicing brigandage.

Take cattle, retain your own.

Justina approaches. "Only you may touch that, nobody else."

Ajany almost slumps to the ground.

"Before he went that day, we played."

Ajany rocks on her heels, hands covering her face.

"Don't . . ." says Justina.

The hen clucks.

Justina bends and tugs at Ajany's left hand, lifts it, and places it on her stomach. Fluttering movements within. Her baby stirs.

Ajany's eyes meet Justina's. Justina gives her a half smile, a tiny nod. A small sound as Ajany rises at once and presses her head to Justina's stomach.

Justina cradles Ajany's face, paintbrush in hand. She touches her brush to Ajany's tears. "He wanted to tell you himself."

"Odidi?" She needed to speak his name here.

Justina's voice is low, with a touch of mischief. "I hooked him. He came to Twilight 333. I was there. I saw him. I wanted him. I got him."

Justina is watching Ajany's reactions. Ajany stares at the ground.

Twilight 333. The dome-shaped go-go lap-dance magnet. Floor shows, and rooms on the side for assignations and deals.

Justina's lashes flutter.

"He came with me. He never left." She looks into the distance, and a smile appears on her mouth, revealing a dimple in her left cheek. "He paid a daily no-service fee."

Ajany asks, "And you p-paint?"

"Sex for oils and canvas." Justina's eyes harden; the ends of her mouth turn down. "Odi-Ebe—he wasn't supposed to die."

They take in the canvases, oils, paint powder, turpentine. Justina rubs her face, in fear of tears.

Silence.

Justina says, "He told me you painted." A laugh. "We were coming to see you, Arabel."

Ajany lowers her head.

"He got tablets—-see—to help him sleep in the plane. . . ."

The room was closing in. Ajany's body collapses in uncontrollable weakness, she is on her knees, her head drops to the floor. She lifts her arms to support her head, face turned toward a wall. *Paint a river out of Wuoth Ogik.*

"Do you like this?" Justina points to a canvas on the wall. Next to one of the photocopies of Odidi that Ajany had distributed, Odidi's eyes, a triptych in four shades of rust. Next to the eyes, a square canvas on which a dancer in blue shadow leans against a copper-colored pole; she has exaggerated eyes. The gaze.

Ajany looks.

She asks, "What's the tint?"

"Henna." Justina turns to Ajany, stroking her face. "I'll paint you."

Ajany whimpers.

Justina whispers, "He wasn't supposed to die, Arabel." She drops her brush. "I wanted to see you."

"Why?"

"To know what it would do to me."

"And?"

Justina examines Ajany, eyes half lidded. "You're nothing to me."

Ajany steps back, gasps, recovers, tugs at a sudden sharp ache within her heart.

Justina grunts and says, looking at nothing, "Where is he?"

"Who?"
A whisper now: "Odidi, where is he?"
Silence.

Two years ago, Odidi had stepped into the frenzied friendliness of Twilight 333, away from cold city streets and the growing list of friends who could no longer abide his presence. He walked in for the music; it was something Angolan, and at once he wondered if he should call his sister. He walked in because he was exhausted by his helplessness, and the uselessness of his crying out to citizens, trying to alert them to the reasons they were paying six times the price for bread, fuel, milk, and sugar. Why their shilling had plunged, and why there were now multibillionaires shopping for helicopters in their midst. He understood that as long as there was enough to move the day, beyond a grumble, people really didn't care to know why their lives had become harder. They prayed. They organized themselves into cooperatives. They prayed. They wanted good things for their children. Worn out. He had tried.

Then he had seen the gangly girl with the big Afro wig, limbs dangling, as skinny as a reed, wearing a sparkly red top and black tights. She was haranguing bouncers in a dark-timbred voice while threatening men twice her size with a squirrel-hair paintbrush that she had drawn out of her oversized black handbag as if it were a knife.

He strolled over. "Is there a problem?" he asked; his voice was growly.

One of the bouncers whirled on him and lifted a hand, which he stopped easily. The bouncer looked closely at him, "Shifta? You?"

Odidi raised a brow.

"Oh, man! No problem, man, you don't remember me, man, you left and, man, after that, rugger *mbovu*! Oh, man! Oh, man, can I buy you a beer? Where did you go? Shifta!"

And Justina—that was her name—had swirled, and tilted her head.

"I like your voice," she said.

Odidi smiled.

She reached for his shoulders and measured them with her hands. "Strong. Are you rich?" she asked.

"No."

"Can you make money?"

"Yes."

"Come dance with me."

They had danced together until the pain of his illusions of Kenya numbed, and when the music ended, at dawn, Justina knew she would never leave Odidi behind.

A sobbing cough from Ajany.

"I fed him," Justina says. "He was so hungry."

Ajany looks back at her brother's eyes on the wall. Eyes lift toward a wooden cupboard. She sees it. Odidi's brown leather rugby ball. She knows it is the one with a squiggle in blue, some Springbok player's signature. From the day at the university when he had received it, just before Ajany left, Odidi had carried it with him. It had rested on his pillow.

"Leave that," shouts Justina.

Ajany has to jump to reach the ball. It bounces off her hand and onto the ground. She grabs it, clutches it to her body. Gnashing teeth. Suffocated keening. Now she tries to gather her shattered selves by putting together pieces of Odidi.

Nothing happens.

Clutching the ball, Ajany cries.

Nightfall.

"I'm going to work," says Justina.

"Now?" Ajany sniffs.

"When?"

Ajany walks in the direction of the door and sits on the ground in front of it. She watches Justina.

"A prostitute's child needs the same things other babies have," Justina says. "Stay or go. I've got work to do. If you stay, inside that box are his clothes."

"He lived here?"

"Those dogs could never find him." Pride. "I protected him."

Studying Justina, Ajany wonders, *Why her? Why this place?* Bitter taste. Ajany looks around. Flickering lights, stench of yesterday's cabbage, brooding chicken, children playing football outside. Ceaseless noise. *Why this?*

Justina strips off her yellow muumuu, digs around for a loose-fitting black-lace spaghetti top. A quiet laugh. "Sometimes, Odi-Ebe used to dress up as an old woman to pass through police roadblocks. They never caught him." She squeezes into skintight shiny red trousers. "This is our world. Odi's world. Tomorrow, when you come back to look for Justina, you may find there was no Justina. Maybe there will even be no house."

Justina retrieves platform wedges and weighs them in her hand. Her head bends. "He almost made it home."

"What happened?"

Justina leans against the bed.

"*Uhaini.*"

Betrayal.

"Who?"

"A diseased dog we were paying. He's gone now."

"Gone?"

"Someone got him."

"So this is normal?"

Justina's head goes up. "What's wrong? Your brother was a thief? So what? Ebe organized us, he organized everyone. We do—did—do everything for our men. Even die." She wipes her eyes. Throws her hand up. "Go away. Odi-Ebe didn't want you here. Go away."

Ajany looks at the ball. Tosses it up, catches it. "How much?"

"What?"

Ajany stares, eyes clear. "For your time?"

Justina whistles. "What do you want me to do?"

"Talk."

Justina ponders Ajany, lips curling. "Anything else?"

Ajany glares.

Justina says, "Money first."

"How much?"

"Five thousand shillings, for the night." Justina sticks out her lower lip.

Ajany pulls out the notes from inside her coat. "Here's what I have, three thousand and fifty. I'll bring the rest tomorrow."

"Keep your stupid money." Tears slither down Justina's top.

"Take it."

Justina hits Ajany's hand; the money scatters.

"May I feel the baby again?"

"For the money?"

"For Odidi."

Justina lowers her head.

Ajany places her hands over Justina's belly.

Closes her eyes.

The baby kicks.

Odidi, Ajany calls with all her heart, *Odidi*.

She exhales.

This she can paint.

Today, filling in the name of loss.

The color is red.

It has a name.

Odi-Ebe, pronounced in the breathy voice of a pregnant woman named Justina. She could sketch hope living in a womb, the best portions of a brother's life—shoes, football, a woman, and an unborn child.

Small things.

Justina touches Ajany's hair, leaves her hand on her back. They cry. Outside, thunder rumbles; there is a scattering of rain on the tin shack. Two women crying while the beloved unborn and the now dead listen.

They sleep on opposite ends of the bed.

They are only able to speak of Odidi at dawn.

The small universe inside is apart from the outside world. It is a place with Odidi at its heart and his sister guzzles down what she learns from the woman who had known this part of his life. She hears something of this woman's life too. Family from Mombasa, Nairobi railway workers, father a polygamous train driver in the last days of the steam engines, Justina growing up contented in the city with assorted brothers and sisters, then a series of misfortunes that devastated, decimated, and dispersed the family. Disease. Job loss. Death. Dropping out of school, where Justina had excelled in art and mathematics, to take care of her sick mother, who had been the youngest and later abandoned wife. Justina's little joys: timing the Mombasa–Nairobi train as it chugged along the railroad close to her shack, running after it and listening for the sound of its loud horn.

Crows caw outside. Footsteps—life in a hurry. Somewhere a dog barks and then whines. Inside, endless cups of ginger tea, and *mandazi*, and then it is six-thirty in the evening and Justina is adjusting a blond wig, while disentangling yellow neck-length earrings from the hair.

Ajany says, "I'll come with you."

She looks Ajany up and down. Her lips curl. "You?"

"Odidi went."

"Yah! He could dance."

"I dance."

"You?" Justina laughs.

"I'm going."

"So I can look after you, yah?"

Ajany picks up her handbag. "I'm not asking."

"*Haiya!* But change those *shagsmudo* clothes. *Haki,* you can't go dressed like that to shame me."

———

That same night, under remote northern-land lights, a woman who has run away from home to outsprint death, shreds her clothes. She has traveled two hundred and fourteen kilometers to do this. She knows the enchantment of fire just as her daughter does. Red flames soar. Two drowsy goats sulk. Healing and insight. A spirit problem. A spirit solution requires a forfeit. A scapegoat. What is she willing to offer? Soul healing needs sacrifice. Given the extent of the problem—she agrees, death is a problem—to appease its hunger, something beloved and of blood must be offered. Something that will endure awfulness. "What could that be?" She thinks about it for a long time.

———

Ajany cannot stop moving. When she dances, the dread dies. When she moves, she is not lost. When she moves, there is no absence. When the music moves her, there is such life she laughs. The antics of a firefly caught in the memory of a once-perfect flame. Ajany dances. She dances with a hard-bodied Namibian doctor who is in town and looking for a good time. His arms wrap around her; her head is pinned on his shoulder. She dances away until she is three steps from the DJ. There she sways until it is daylight, the last one on the dance floor. Then she just stops. Justina, who abandoned her once they walked through the door of the club, is long gone.

Ajany, shoes in hand, handbag strapped across her body, saunters out the door, squinting at the light. A passing early-morning watchman's wrapped-up radio plays: *Maua mazuri yapendeza / Ukiyatazama utachekelea / Hakuna mmoja asiye yapenda / . . . Zum zum nyuki lia wee. . . .* Nairobi's flamboyant trees are in bloom. Ajany stoops to pick a floppy crimson flower, her feet soft on the cold, hard tarmac, feeling her way to the guesthouse, where she will eat the chef's strawberry crêpes and, afterward, sleep the day away.

Ajany slumbers through the morning, still savoring yesterday, which was the opposite of limbo. Yesterday was Far Away. Yesterday she discovered that the shadow tendrils wrapped around her body had loosened and she had lost the will to tie herself up in them.

23

AJANY RETREATS INTO A RESTAURANT TO COMPOSE A NEWSPA-
per item. She drinks milk-filled coffee and, pen in mouth, stares through
a table of huddling black-suited men, two women looking silently into
cups, and another woman gesticulating. Undated recycled post-election
violence scenes on CNN, panga-wielding Kenyans setting their country alight explained in the voice of an "Africa specialist" from Louisi-
ana, whose accent clangs all over his disapproval. Cut to news from tidy
Anglo-Saxon worlds—a sequence of pretty, orderly spaces explained
with tender adjectives.

Sniggering from another table.

Ajany overhears the tail end of a joke: "We were terrified the country was going to the dogs. But it was worse; it was given to the Africans." She turns. The joker is a scruffy foreign-correspondent type
wearing scuffed leather sandals. His eyes carry the ravenous gawk of
Must-Become-Authoritative-Protagonist-of-Bad-African-Happening
types. His bespectacled companions are a droopy man, something of
the I-speak-for-Africa worthiness of Bono about him, and a woman with
thigh-length brown hair, whose painted nails adhere to his tanned arm.
Catching Ajany's look, she turns a brutal shade of violet. "Shhh, Shhh."
She makes it sound foreign.

The waiter says to them, "Anything else, sir?" He is unperturbed in a Nairobi way. *Surprise me,* the look says. *Surprise me and witness my indifference.*

Ajany signals to the waiter as she finishes her message for the newspaper, takes out her payment. She departs. On the streets, a traffic-busting, police-avoiding *matatu* brakes. Emblazoned on its side, its name, *Monica Lewinsky.* It is cruising down the wrong end of the street. At the top of the street stands the rotund structure of the newspaper office.

At the crossroads leading to the Nation House, a group of turbaned Bohra men sweep past in robes. A lanky, dark-toned man with shattered glasses, his hair uncombed, stands in a washed-out brown coat that covers a frayed blue shirt. His shoes are so worn they tilt to the edge. He trots after the men, yelling, *Osama, Osama.* He stops and laughs out loud and long; his laughter punctures Ajany's senses. The Bohra men increase their pace, robes flapping, and turn down a corner. Ajany's spine prickles. The raw laugh, its concentrated mischief, is pure Odidi. She glimpses the man among milling passersby. Unthinking, Ajany runs across and into Kenyatta Avenue, where a hawker furtively peddles new and old lace underwear, nail cutters, and chewing gum. She runs. A car screeches. Three p.m. cathedral bells, book vendors' glossies. Opposite the Parliament buildings, a street preacher in a yellow-brown shirt and belly-high trousers is selling insurance against sulfur and hellfire. There, Ajany sidles as close to the charcoal-stained street man as she can. Laughter suffuses his voice as he screeches at a passerby, *Go to hell!* As Odidi would have.

———

Two nights later, a dust squall warped Wuoth Ogik's destiny. It came on the tail of a cattle raid when livestock, it is said, tiptoed out of Wuoth Ogik. Not even a moo of distress. Not even Nyipir's pampered dance-ox tried to find its way home after it wandered away from the main herd of camels, cows, sheep, and goats heading northward. The news flew across watering holes. The rustler has been rustled.

The night before, Wuoth Ogik had been wrapped in a rare white mist made of dust. When, at 2 a.m., the house's large water tank cracked completely with a metal yawn, Galgalu had staggered awake, picked up a short *rungu,* and left, barefooted. Inside the house, he waded through small streams. In the dark, they look red, like blood trails He clucked, "Tch."

A woolly quiet broken by the muffled grunting of animals in the *boma.* Galgalu made his way there, thinking of adding logs to the hearth, wondering about Akai and when she would come back home.

Electric awareness, his hair stood on end, shadowed rapid movement behind him. Burning vegetation.

He knew . . . he knew the size of the fire eating the Wuoth Ogik drought grass before he turned. A soft hiss became a sting, and the world bright and burning. Galgalu tasted redness, and blackness. Too late to call out for help, he fell. A long shadow bent over him—he knew its scent. It touched his forehead and murmured something. It rested its face against his. He smelled nettles, sweat-dust softness.

For the first time since he had brought his son home, Nyipir slept straight into the morning. He woke up to abnormal silence. He rolled off his mat, wrapped a *kikoi* around his body, and dashed outside. A ghost scorpion scrambled away. Above him, the sky had turned up as strings of violet clouds. It was then that Nyipir knew that a portion of his everyday horizon was gone.

A single white butterfly.

Scattered rocks, red dust, and heat. Burning grass. The fire had left a trail. A mishmash of tracks, churned-up soil, leading out of the homestead.

Absence.

Hitching up his wrap, he ran through a thorn fence, which cut shallow strips into his body. Feet scraped dung through fire-infused earthiness. Nyipir scoured corners, hunting for the crevice into which his camels, cattle, donkeys, sheep, goats, and herding dogs had fallen. The dung was still warm. Nyipir circled the place where the *boma* hearth's fire still smoldered. Arms sagged. Knees genuflected. Hand touched soil. Nothing. This absence, like that of his son, was absurd, and anything that was left of his heart had become dust.

He saw that Galgalu had crawled as far as he could.

"Gaalgalu!" Nyipir had howled. *"Ahhhhh."*

Nyipir held Galgalu's body, touched his sticky face. Leaned toward his nostrils. Soft air in and out. Head wound. The blood around it was coagulated. Blue flies, a buzzing cloud over him, on him.

That morning, Nyipir carried Galgalu, his first journey toward the mission. Blood spots on a hard road. A disjointed wind kicked dust around them. It took a day and a bit of night to reach the Jacobses' medical center. He talked to Galgalu about the past, to keep Galgalu conscious.

Nyipir had started an alternate existence by bartering intelligence. Sudan, Somalia, Ethiopia, Eritrea, and Uganda paid for Nyipir's knowledge. He had trained ragtag platoons, sold secret passageways through the northern frontier, used his windfall to buy the first set of guns, which he sold at the border for a 2,500-percent markup, with which he bought more guns.

Galgalu had been the message carrier, the chameleon who changed colors and helped distract Nyipir's pursuers. It was easy, their first cattle raid. They returned with a hundred head of Karamojong cows. Half were dispatched on lorries to middlemen who turned them into supermarket beef. An escalation of rustling. New tactics, new routes, new keeping areas out of the reach of the state. The rustling diverted attention from the business of helping arms flow across boundaries and landscapes. He had launched his reprisals against Kenya. This was a private war that had its center in Wuoth Ogik. "Remember, Galgalu?" Panting, Nyipir only stopped murmuring when he reached the mission's white gate.

With Galgalu being treated, Nyipir Oganda embarked on another journey, changing into one of his old police uniforms for this. He stumbled, a weary man navigating the vastness. The uniform hung loosely on his body. He walked and walked until, eighty-eight kilometers later, he reached Ali Dida Hada's former police post. It was just more than a day and half later.

Aaron Chache, Ali Dida Hada's replacement at the police post, was a lugubrious, long-jawed officer-in-exile who started to sweat when he saw Nyipir shimmer into view, dust behind him, a curtain of flies ahead of him. In that moment when day struggles not to relinquish light to darkness, Aaron had raised his hands in surrender, submitting to unfair fates even before they had stated their purpose, the extent of his defense a choked *"Ashindwe!"*

Begone, Satan!

He had not planned for this in his career strategy. He had not anticipated needing to cling to sanity in an arid land. The previous morning, Aaron had dreamed of a banana salad. Just as he was about to put a spoon of pineapple, mango, and banana into his mouth, he woke up. The sun had reminded him that his fruit of the day, of every day, was the doum-palm nut.

The apparition spoke. "I am retired senior sergeant Aggrey Nyipir Oganda. I'm here to report a crime."

"Aaron Chache." A broad, gum-revealing grin of gratitude that it was a human being addressing him. *"Karibu, karibu, karibu."* He wrung Nyipir's hand. "Where did you serve? Shall we go inside?"

Nyipir, dully: "ASTU."

"Eh!" Aaron's eyes shone with awe. "Anti-Stock Theft Unit!"

Inside the tin shack, with sparse thatch on its roof, Aaron shoved a pile of assorted confiscated items and cultural paraphernalia to the ground, hunting for his imitation pith helmet, adjusted its insignia, and wiped his wrinkled uniform. Law-by-correspondence-school books were on the floor against the metal walls. A sixteen-year undertaking. The holes in the tin allowed in a rare breeze. The heat was already unbearable. A faded Kenyan flag slouched on a too-small brass pole. A framed map of Kenya with colorful pins sticking in a perpendicular pattern barely hangs onto the wall. A shelf with some school and world literature stood in the back of the room, and two blue lanterns, one with a broken glass cover, sat on a table next to it. The color portraits of three presidents formed a triumvirate. Next to this was a picture of Aaron in a topi hat, with a hand on his blue-frocked wife and two boys and three girls, who wore maroon-and-white school uniforms. The camera had captured the sense of family occasion.

"Sit! Sit! Sir!"

Nyipir took the wooden stool, adjusted it, and sat. No preamble. "My home was invaded, my animals stolen, dry season grass burned. Nothing left. If we leave now, we can find the animals."

Aaron's cleaning efforts ceased as he retreated into a torrent of regret, self-pity on its heels. He had been reduced to serving in this wind-wailing blot of landscape. His chief purpose was to hunt for lost cows. Being here had amplified his aversion to cows. The way they looked, chewed grass, and mooed. Their sense of entitlement, ambling around and expecting people to move or worship them, their gross dung. He would use his salary to import ravenous lions from Amboseli and dispatch these to every homestead. He also despised camels—they looked down on him with a superior grin. He longed to pluck out their eyelashes before setting them alight. He would soak the beasts with paraffin first. And if he could without being lynched, he would stomp every goat he met to death. He regretted their existence. He detested sheep, their dumb silliness and stupid, startled looks. He had to check his pistol every time one of those things crossed his path. Sheep shooting could be a national sport. He was indifferent to donkeys, even though he considered their braying diabolical. He was confused about his unresponsiveness to donkeys; he thought about it a lot. Maybe they were a last-resort means of trotting out of town.

Aaron had plenty of time to regret many things. The absence of regular fruit. Few opportunities to speak proper English, no one with whom to explore motivations in the poetry of Elizabeth Barrett Browning. He found great solace in the words of Browning's "Chorus of Eden Spirits," but he regretted that there was nobody to tell about the meaning of this relief. Most of all, he regretted that Thursday in August, on an extension of the Naivasha–Nakuru road, when he, a traffic policeman, and three others, who had prosecuted random traffic offenders without a receipt book for three years undiscovered, were found out.

In the three honeyed years, he had reaped sufficient sums to extend the boundaries of his farm and buy a Chinese lorry. But that Thursday, new zealous plainclothes officers of the Anti-Corruption Authority had driven past his special roadblock, in an aged red farmer's van.

Easy prey, he had thought. He had handed over the shakedown to one of the others. But the trap was sprung. Hearing a commotion, he had realized what was happening, and tiptoed behind the van as his fellow officers were being rounded up. He climbed up a nearby fossil-looking weeping-willow tree and stayed there all night. When he clambered down, very early the next morning, and made his way to work to attempt some damage control, he discovered that the officer commanding his division had already arranged for his transfer to the outer northern margins of Kenya.

Aaron had left without protest. He still had a job. He needed the pension to extend his banana plantation and plant guava trees.

"One day at a time," his wife, Domtilla, had comforted him.

He snapped into alertness, shifting under Nyipir's red-eyed scrutiny.

"*Ehe?*" He urged Nyipir's story out, grateful to be able to speak English in complete sentences. The stories, however, depressed Aaron. For some reason he was expected to insert himself into the narratives as "primary problem solver." Such stories invariably featured cows. He hated cows. He lifted his hand for a pause.

"Insurance?" he chided, using his teaching tone. No one here bothered with livestock insurance. But he asked the question anyway to "help locals change their behavior." Nyipir's glare rather curdled his blood. Never mind. Some people were "late adopters." "Go on," he urged Nyipir. And then the words "Wuoth Ogik" chimed like a bell inside his skull.

Hope struck Aaron. Wuoth Ogik was synonymous with his predecessor, Ali Dida Hada, in security parlance. Aaron now reached across his table to tap the 1960s radio unit. He *could* make this Nairobi's problem. Maybe Ali Dida Hada could return, and he, Aaron, could negotiate a posting to Kinangop or Masaba or Nyakach, where grass was green and streets were lined with guavas and oranges. And pineapples. And bananas. And tangerines.

Static.

He nodded at Nyipir, wrote notes—one of the few humans left in the world who give time to cursive writing. His output was like a medieval text. Shame about the Kasuku writing pad he had to use.

Thus he listed Nyipir's losses:

Missing items.

Two bulls. One red dance-ox. (Name, Jayadha)

Twenty camels, one named Ubah, the other Kormamaddo.

A hundred and eighty-two cows.(☺) Two herding dogs (names, Simba and Nyarnam). Forty-three sheep. (☺) Sixty nameless goats.

About two tons drought grass (burned).

Missing person Akai Lokorijom (wife)

Injuries, Raro Galgalu (like my son)

Recommendation: Officer Ali Dida Hada returns to lead retrieval efforts and use previous knowledge to address rustling menace.

That last sentence caused Aaron to gurgle in happiness. "Now, sir, your signature on the abstract!" he warbled to Nyipir.

Nyipir's breath caught.

His head throbbed.

He relented. He struggled to sign his name; his thumb was stiff. "What'll you do with this?" he asked when he had finished.

Aaron said, "We shall now communicate with Nairobi."

It has been two hours. The two men sit in silence while a radio wheezes static. Nyipir is clutching his head. The strain showing on his fingers.

"Maybe you should go to Omoroto?" Aaron offers for the seventh time.

Nyipir asks again, "Why?"

Aaron leans forward. "They take stolen livestock there."

The Northern Frontier Stock Exchange. Nyipir grimaces. He was one of the first to transfer rustled livestock through Omoroto more than fifteen years ago. There would certainly be a new holding area now. Rustlers were always five years ahead of the state's security apparatus.

To Aaron, "Is that so?"

Aaron nods his head like an agama lizard. "Now I shall radio ASTU. But you, you go on ahead." Aaron pulls out a large black-and-white map. He stretches it out and points at Fort Banya.

"Here!" His finger taps a black squiggle on the map.

About a fortnight's walk away.

Nyipir watches Aaron as the uniformed creature taps a ballpoint pen against his teeth, repeating, "Fort Banya, Fort Banya." Nyipir had not realized that such men existed and, more significantly, could be integral to any nation's security system.

"Hire herdsmen," Aaron suggests.

Nyipir's sigh-laden voice, "My animals' tracks go right past your rear window."

"What?" Aaron jumps up and lurches to the hole in the wall—his window. He discerns the tracks, wrings his hands. "What do we do now?" Aaron collapses into his seat. "*Aiee!* Is it the rainy season already?" he whispers.

Aaron had already experienced three rainy seasons. In two of them, a parade of raiders, rustlers, and other frightening elements strolled through his outpost, not even bothering to load their magazine clips, leading stolen livestock away. When Aaron heard the stomping of livestock, the bleating of goats, the braying of donkeys, he would ease back the cardboard and newspapers scattered on the floor, take his government-issue gun and a soft bog coat, open the trapdoor in the floor, lower himself into the bunker, shut the trapdoor, and light one of the lanterns down there.

There was also water stored in a large plastic tank, a sack of doum nuts, extra paraffin, two other hurricane lamps, two buckets, the Holy Bible, the Holy Quran, and three Elizabeth Browning anthologies—Aaron's contribution to the pile. Forty-eight hours later, he would poke his head out. If there was silence, he might pull the rest of his body out. When the old white van used to work, he would drive to the shopping center, a one-and-a-half-day trip away, and hire a room from where to prepare his field report, which confirmed that he had neither seen nor heard anything out of the norm. A year and six months ago, when he was just three months in the post, a reportedly dead six-foot-seven rustler from Suguta, with a bandolier and a Remington 870 pump-action shotgun, had barged into Aaron's office, where Aaron's shoeless feet were propped on the desk as he reread a Standard newspaper from one month earlier.

The giant at once spotted Aaron's AK-47 leaning against his desk.

He had simply pointed to it.

In his haste to give up his gun, Aaron dislodged something. Bullets ricocheted off the tin roof and Aaron dropped the gun and became a blob of jelly trying to raise its hands into the air while also attempting to stand on the tips of his toes to underline his total surrender.

The giant took the gun from the floor. He also smiled at Aaron, revealing pink gums where his two lower teeth were missing. He sat on the table, clipping and unclipping cartridges.

He complained about the weather—*Jua kali!*

"*Tutaonana*," he grunted to Aaron on his way out, we'll meet again.

Never, Aaron had vowed.

Forty-eight hours later, when he could at last speak, Aaron radioed a report to headquarters. He emphasized that he had barely escaped alive from the raid. Which was true. In the hours spent under the table, hearing the man clip and unclip cartridges, Aaron had known that fear is a cause of death. He was hoping for compassionate leave. To his sorrow, two weeks later, Aaron was made acting district security officer, with a reputation for dealing effectively with belligerent nomads.

Five months later, the new regional commandant of the Anti-Stock Theft Police had asked for his help. Tough and experienced reinforcements were needed.

Aaron had said, *"Ndio, afande!* At once, *afande."* He had smartly set off in the opposite direction, the pursuit of peace his primary objective. In this he was most successful.

Outside, the wind stirred scant shrubs, and then it barked in the lowest note of a contrabassoon.

"What do we do now?" Aaron asks, his eyes white and wide.

Nyipir's hands now prop up his chin. Head angled, eyes asquint, he sees sweat soak Aaron's clothes. *Who had said a person was best known by the questions he asked?* Watching Aaron, his bewildered humanity, his open surrender to fear, something within Nyipir at last relinquishes his wars.

Numbness creeps in.

When he can disentangle himself from Aaron's wind-haunted isolation, Nyipir leaves, hobbling homeward by way of night. He rests during the broiling day to return to his journey at sundown. Ten kilometers from *Wuoth Ogik,* Nyipir suddenly stops. He turns toward the stumpy summits he has not glanced at in more than forty years. Those silence-storing red caves with an underground stream bubbling lyrics of ill-kept secrets. Memory peers through distant thick scrub, bushes, and fallen rocks that hide a portal.

Walking again.

When he pushes open *Wuoth Ogik's* gates and sees the rusting iron cowbell that belongs to his red dance-ox, it had fallen off during the raid, instead of lifting it from the dust, he lies down next to it; his body shivering in a nameless fever.

24

IN THE CENTER OF NAIROBI, A FLOWER MAN LUGS A GIANT bunch of carnations, marigold, roses, tiger lilies, tuberoses, orange roses, yellow roses, and rosemary across the street. Somewhere outside, a husky-voiced evangelist with a faux-American accent is peddling eternal life, threat, and "Jeeheeezuz."

A visiting stranger turns from ogling unfiltered Nairobi existences though a restaurant window to browse through a newspaper filled with post-election violence, hand wringing, and nonaction. He flips through the obituary pages on his way to the sports section. He freezes. A photo. It is a man whose broken smile on full lips belies his urgent gaze. Compelling. Sculpted features, a beautiful man. He reads:

> Moses Ebewesit Odidi Oganda of Kalacha Goda. 1964–2007. Cherished son of Nyipir and Akai, only beloved brother of Arabel Ajany. Lover of water, rugby, and Kenya. Father-to-be. So deeply missed. So terribly longed for.

He shakes his head and leaps up, his hands knocking over the steel-plated salt-and-pepper shaker.

. . .

Isaiah dodges cars, keeps his eyes on approaching faces. Arms spread out. His destination: a 1970s-style office block that would slot right into Cold War Eastern Europe. He sucks in air, then enters Vigilance House's dark, humid interior, glances at the large concrete coat of arms with the legend *Utumishi Kwa Wote*—Service to All—hovering over his head like the sword of Damocles. He walks into a capsule of tight conversations, explosive, abrupt laughter, busy footsteps, and quick, squint-eyed assessing looks.

The place is packed, murmuring like a town-hall meeting. It takes fifteen minutes for Isaiah to reach an old brown desk behind which lean two men in uniform, their caps on the counter. One of them doodles in a tattered brown occurrence book. A surly "Yes?"

"Good afternoon. If you could help me, please . . . I'm here to see Mr. Ali Dida Hada." Wet palms, dry mouth. Clipped tones concealing the routine dread he felt whenever he met bureaucracy.

"ACP Ali Dida Hada," the doodler corrects; he is sketching faces and geometric patterns, coloring them in.

"Yes."

"No, his title is Assistant Commissioner of Police Ali Dida Hada. A very important man."

Isaiah waits.

"You are who?" the scribbler asks. Not once has he looked at Isaiah.

"Isaiah William Bolton . . . from England."

"Identification?"

Isaiah pulls out his passport.

The other policeman, who has been staring at him, reaches out and grasps it as if it is a dead rat. It dangles as he turns the pages.

"Bolton. Isaiah. Like the Prophet. What do you want?" he asks. Delicately handing over the document. "Why do you want ACP? He's a busy man."

"He knows about my missing father."

"You filed a missing-persons report?"

"Yes."

"When?"

"Uh . . . two years ago."

"Reference number?"

Isaiah improvises. "Mr. Ali Dida Hada worked on the case." Head throbbing, he wipes his hands on his jeans.

"ACP, ACP." A patient correction. "Who's your father?"

"Hugh Bolton."

"Last seen?"

"Don't know." He lowers his head.

"Where?"

"Northern Kenya?"

"And Afande Dada?"

"Has been looking for him."

"So he knows your father?"

And so it continues. Isaiah wonders if he should have called the British High Commission first. An hour and a half later, his mind numb and ringing, he is led to another office, and then two more, until, at last, he is clinging to the back of a chair in a semi-divided, airy, larger rectangular room packed with files, where two men are waiting for him from behind a lopsided circular table.

The older of the pair clears his throat. He is dark, almost dark violet, bespectacled, large-eyed, with a head too big for his tall body, and wrinkle lines on his forehead. He is full-lipped and droll-voiced.

Petrus Keah says, "Sit."

Isaiah sits; his eyes move from one to the other. The other man is younger, shorter, with light-brown skin, gray-sprinkled short hair, trim sideburns, two scars on one side of his face, and a thin mustache; he moves with spare gestures. His pale-brown eyes study Isaiah.

A sense of guilt seeps into Isaiah as he sweats under the man's scrutiny.

He escapes by staring at the older man.

"Are you Al Qaeda?" purrs Petrus Keah, adjusting his spectacles.

Isaiah goes mute. Sweat glistens on his forehead. Finally, he snaps, "I'm English."

"A false premise upon which to claim innocence. There *are* many English Al Qaeda."

"I look nothing like them," Isaiah huffs.

Petrus leans over the table. "Ali, my brother, does this man even look English to you?"

Isaiah glimpses the small up-and-down movement on the bespectacled man's lips, a glint in his eyes. He is being toyed with. He leans back.

Petrus cackles, "Funny, man."

Ha-ha. Isaiah scowls.

"What do you want?" Ali Dida Hada's voice is inflectionless. He had buried his slow panic at this resurrection of his futile forty-year chase. When junior officers had called to tell him that a man named Isaiah Bolton had come to see him, he had ground his teeth and prepared to escape from the office when Petrus Keah burst in, lugging old files and, anticipating his intent, said, "Were you leaving?" The challenge overt.

Ali Dida Hada had sunk into his chair as Petrus settled next to him. They had watched the files on the table while an iciness grew between them as they waited for Isaiah Bolton to walk in.

Isaiah is saying, "My father, Hugh Bolton, vanished perhaps forty years ago. I understand you've pursued the matter for a while. He paused. "Just come from Wot Ogyek." Isaiah frowns. "There's evidence he *was* there."

Ali Dida Hada's chair creaks.

Isaiah continues, "His books, art, the house itself—his signature. He was there." Isaiah pulls out the draft house sketches from inside his coat. He unfolds and spreads the paper out on the table. He points: "My father's work."

In that second, Ali Dida Hada could have slapped his own face. Patterns and clues scattered in plain sight. So obvious he had missed them. *The books!* He had touched them. He could have asked a simple question—*Akai, how did you come to be in this house?* But there were houses like this everywhere. Homes taken from colonial-era owners. After the new owners moved in, old, misunderstood household goods—books, artwork, and cutlery—were left untouched to gather dust or quietly decompose with everything else. Nobody asked why or how. Ali Dida Hada scowls.

Petrus observes Ali Dida Hada's fingers make erasing movements on the desk.

Ali Dida Hada, aware of Petrus's stare, says, "Tea?" Ali Dida Hada pushes back from the table.

A gleam in Petrus's eyes. Enigmas enthrall him.

He beams at Isaiah as Ali Dida Hada closes the door. "Isaiah Bolton, what can we do for you? We know a little bit about this case."

Isaiah's hands come together to shield his face. A release of dread knots in his stomach.

Petrus says, "Long time ago, we sent a man to look for your father."

"Yes?"

"Following a phoned-in request from an interested anonymous person."

"Yes?"

"We closed the case over two years ago."

"Why?"

"The party concerned did not renew their interest." The eight hundred pounds that were keeping the file warm had been cut off.

"Who?" Isaiah wonders. *Selene?* But wouldn't she have known where to look at once? Isaiah murmurs, "All these years of searching—nothing?"

Petrus purses his lips. "Little."

"Reports?"

"Annual updates."

"Can I see them?"

"Property of state and client."

Isaiah lowers his head. Who else would have been interested in finding Hugh?

There is a tingle in Petrus's belly as he watches Isaiah—anticipation. He looks in the direction of Ali Dida Hada's exit. Turning to Isaiah, he asks, "How can we help you?"

Isaiah leans over. "Someone knows something."

"Names?"

"Old man Oganda ... the daughter, Arabel ..." He unfolds the newspaper cutting and points at Odidi's picture in the obituary pages. "Moses invited me here. He said I'd find what I sought here. We were supposed to meet."

"Ah!"

"I'll pay."

A sniff. "A bribe?"

"No."

"What, then?" Petrus asks.

"Whatever it takes to dig out the truth."

"Truth has a price."

"I know."

Petrus watches Isaiah. Truth, truth, everyone wants truth. Few want to look at it. He lifts his hand to the back of his neck, propping up his head. "Where's Ali's tea?"

From the corridor, the sound of utensils clattering on metal. A large woman in a polka-dot apron pushes open the door, wielding a large tray.

Petrus says, "Tea! But no Ali." Petrus contrives a sigh. "He was chief investigating officer on your father's case."

"Yes?"

"Your presence has made him . . . er . . . emotional. Tea?"

"Wouldn't mind. Black, a teaspoon of sugar."

———

Rooftop view of the green city in the sun. Fewer trees every day. Dust devils on the plain, depleted animal species, their northern migration corridor being turned into a dense human settlement. Unspoken fears dart down too many alleyways and burp through the horns of far too many frustrated drivers. The post-election mood is unsettled. Accusations lurk, and there are any number of claimants who seek to be more sinned against than sinning. A mess.

Ali Dida Hada clenches and unclenches his fist. He taps his head with a knuckle. He is as tense as lightning-struck red cedar, struggling with syllables of thought. He had pursued the puzzle of Hugh Bolton for years, and as long as the money came from their anonymous client in England, the sums adjusted to inflation costs, he had been kept on the job. He had searched, but then he himself had got lost in the riddle. The best puzzle breaker of his graduating class. Then one mystery had taken hold of his will and talents. And in the end, he had lost a wife, a life, a plan, and he had not solved his only case.

After his stint in the northern lands, he was recalled to Nairobi to become a nonpracticing cryptanalyst with a high rank—assistant commissioner of police—exiled at a desk job with no defined duties. A grim smile. His achievements to date? Desert eulogist, with knowledge of water songs in seven northern-Kenyan languages, has-been chief of a thatch-roofed police post of three men at its peak. An unsolved case. A woman who owns his dreams, and a country he needs is disintegrating on him. He hunches over unbidden memories.

Wuoth Ogik, that desert house. He had examined it. Had wondered about it; its smallest details still materialized for him: soft pink of coral stone—where was that from, and how did it get here? Blue patterns on intricate tiles around a dead fountain. What did they suggest? Who chose them? The house's name: Wuoth Ogik. Why? The inhabitants.

One in particular.

She had demanded, "Herdsman, a poem." Years later, he had asked Akai Lokorijom, "Hugh Bolton?" She answered, "Just a name." "You never heard of Hugh Bolton?" he persisted. "I hear so many names." She sighed. "People are looking for him." She turned to him. "Why should it bother me?" Ali Dida Hada did not have an answer then.

Akai had disheveled his thoughts. She had mixed up his questions until driven by a yearning he had yet to name, in spite of Nyipir's presence, Ali Dida Hada reached for Akai: "Moon flowers—yellow, on the mountain in Ileret."

"So?" Akai lowered her gaze as she scratched her arms.

"I need to take you to see them."

The moon was nearer to Wuoth Ogik than Ileret would ever be. Akai gave Ali Dida Hada a sideways look. Then she moved so that their bodies connected. He could breathe her, bite her skin.

"You?" she whispered.

"Who else?"

"Now?"

"It's time."

"What kind of moon lights up those flowers?"

Ali Dida Hada had bent his head till it barely touched Akai's.

"The oldest one. It knows secrets of night."

"I need a forgetting moon," she whispered. "That's the one I want."

"I'll find it," he vowed.

But then she had turned from him, an abrupt move. Walked through Wuoth Ogik's courtyard. Left him standing, aching, wanting. No goodbye. Doors and case closed.

During his training as a cryptanalyst, one of Ali Dida Hada's instructors had warned the class about the temptations of fixation—how seeking answers to a puzzle in a quest could turn into an obsession that colored reason, confused questions, and confounded minds. Ali Dida Hada had laughed with the rest of the class.

Case closed.

.   .   .

On his Nairobi city rooftop, the sun sends light through wispy, polluted clouds.

Footsteps on narrow metal stairs. Ali Dida Hada turns. The door swings open with a creak.

Petrus. Isaiah at his heels.

Petrus booms, "Ali! Brother!" Ali Dida Hada winces. "Mr. Isaiah William *Bolton* wanted to meet you *and* our dear Arabel Ajany Oganda. He is moved by your attempts to find his father. Oh, look! A premature moon. It will be a cold night. Maybe rain."

Isaiah looks up. Petrus and Ali Dida Hada glower at each other.

Isaiah says, "I'd like to reopen the case."

Ali Dida Hada glances skyward. "I'm finished with it."

Isaiah pulls out a sliver of canvas from his coat pocket.

Ali Dida Hada stiffens, vowing that if Isaiah offers money he will arrest him for a bribery attempt. Isaiah proffers the canvas: "Would this help? My father's work. The woman?"

Ali Dida Hada takes the bookmark with two fingers, tilts it into the light. It takes him a minute to understand that he is seeing a pregnant, nude, wide-eyed Akai Lokorijom.

His mind goes blank.

A thick fog shifts.

Right there, he understands the nature of his own lunacy, why it will never leave him.

Just a name, she had said.

He had believed her.

Petrus observes Ali Dida Hada. He knows Ali Dida Hada is unaware that tears are sliding down his face.

Within Ali Dida Hada a familiar sense of homelessness. Ceaseless unbelonging. In the 1960s, he had turned himself into a Kenyan, erasing a young man's life forged in the Horn of Africa's liberation wars. Being neither pro- nor anti-communist, he had walked away mid-battle from Eritrea through Ethiopia and into Kenya. Tucking himself at the end of livestock trains, he had watered and watched strangers' camels and cows in exchange for water, meat, and, sometimes, shelter. He changed his name, he mimicked other people's deeds, cadences, histories, and movement, until he was Ali Dida Hada. Almost a year later, he had stumbled upon a Kenyan police-recruitment exercise. He was lithe and fit, his arithmetic skills were precise, and he outran everybody else. Two camel clans stood by him, creating for him a genealogy. He was recruited into the forces.

Isaiah's voice: "Does it help?"

Ali Dida Hada hands over the painting. "No."

His voice is strained. "Excuse me, I've work to do. . . . Afande Petrus will help you."

He heads for the steel door.

Petrus calls to him in Kiswahili: "Ali! We all have a case that confuses our skills—even me." A gruff laugh. "The sudden disappearance of the Nairobi lord mayor's great golden chain. Started a private investigation. A diversion. Was curious. Then it got intricate, and, yes, personal. Was all set to go to France to hunt for evidence, when, fortunately—I see that now—I run out of money." A snort of laughter. "Anyway, Ndugu Ali, your problem is this, you hunt in darkness and alone. Always a risk." Ali Dida Hada stops. "You also think truth is the same as order. Your downfall." Ali Dida Hada touches the door. "What happened?" Petrus's eyes are half closed. "Collusion? With Oganda?"

Ali Dida Hada drags open the metal door. He descends the steep steps. He hears Petrus tell Isaiah, "The search for your father cost Ali his family."

"How?"

"They abandoned him."

"Sorry to hear that."

"Why?"

"Unfortunate loss."

"No doubt."

"About the obituary."

"Yes?"

"Should we talk to its author?"

"Start the conversation."

"Where? How?"

"I draw good maps."

25

AJANY'S CONVERSATION WITH JUSTINA DOES NOT GO WELL.

Justina was shouting, "Leave me alone."

"Your money."

"Ah! Just go."

Ajany counts out six thousand shillings—Justina hesitates, then takes it and stuffs it into her brassiere.

"Let's talk," said Ajany.

"About what?"

"Odidi."

"He's dead. It's life."

"The baby . . ."

"Is mine."

"My parents . . ."

"Never tried to reach him."

"They searched for him. He was coming home."

"Home!" Justina pushes Ajany.

"*This* was a better life for him?"

"Yes."

"My brother is . . . was an engineer, a sports star. . . ."

"Did it help him?" Justina shouts.

"You certainly didn't, *slut*."

Justina slaps Ajany twice. But when Ajany lifts her hand to push Justina, a lake of red dancing before her eyes, she remembers the swelling womb beneath Justina's blue chiffon blouse. Her hand hovers in the air.

Justina offers, *"Hebu jaribu."* Just try.

Ajany touches her face, pats it. "I would, but Odidi's baby is here."

"The baby's mine."

Ajany's voice chills: "Blood calls to blood. I'll find the child."

"I'll kill it first."

"Then I'll find you."

Justina turns away, face wet, swaying in high heels. "Come near me again," she says, "I'll cut up your face."

Ajany shrugs.

By the time Jos at the guesthouse checks Isaiah William Bolton into a room with a view of the lawn, just two doors away from Ajany's, Ajany has sought out Twilight 333 again. She disappears into the music while downing Black Ice.

After midnight, after the floor show, Ajany takes to the glinting pole, remembering a woman who used to throw herself into yearning. Black curl stretch. Lights throb. Body ripple. Music swirling inside her, lengthening her. Box splits.

Remembering seasons before Odidi's death:

Phone conversations.

"You're sad," Odidi once said. "Come back home."

"You come visit," she countered.

He had confessed his fear of flying. So they spoke of rain, of drought and rock art. A hinted-at longing. "Do you miss us?" Odidi had asked.

Every day, she had thought.

"'Jany, come home." He had listened for her answer—its absence.

He should have actually told her what he needed to say.

A long-suffering brother's sigh: *"Okaay.* I'll come and see you, silly."

Ajany had started to cry.

He teased, *"Ajany yuak-yuak."*

"Odi . . ." she murmured.

He had exploded, "He's murdering you."

"N-no," she stammered.

"You're not painting?"

How had he known? "Odi . . ." Her apartment door had rattled then, a key being inserted. Bernardo was home. "He's here. Talk soon?"

Odidi, raspy-voiced: "'Jany—"

She cut him off. "B-Bernardo."

"That fungus. Leave him." His voice was soft.

Ajany had switched off the phone and pocketed it. Rearranged her face into a neutral look for the lover who had broken his guitar's stem on her arms the day before.

On the Nairobi dance floor, Ajany falters mid-crouch. She stops, seeking sensation; her hands reach for the strobe effects, swaying, moving, and winding. She stares through the smoke.

Emerging out of subtexts. What is the world like? Anguish. The dance floor is hard. Burnslide to standing. She is conscious of silver-blue lights shining in her eyes. She stumbles away from the raised floor.

Catcalls. Whistles and grunts from murky audience circles. Stench of sweat, musk, and lust-encrusted heat. A hand slams into her crotch. She claws it away, scratching back.

"*Malaya!*"—a curse.

"Skunk"—her grunted reply.

Needing air, needing sleep. She peers at her cell phone and, when the lights appear, presses out Peter the taxi man's number. Through red-lit passageways, the artificial sunset changes color from orange to yellow to pink to red and back to orange. "Peter?" she slurs on third try. "Take me home. I'm in Twilight 333. Am feeling s-s-thick." *Sick.* She vomits next to three bouncers borrowed from a rugby scrum. One in a pink shirt spits on the pavement. He sneers at her. "Useless."

His insult is a splodge between them—a blobby object from the mouth of a hulk wearing a glittery pink shirt. Ajany gives up. *Pink spangles.* She sputters in laughter. Sounds like sobbing, though.

———

He. Must. Force out. Akai.

Cut her out. He must bleed out his soul to save Akai's life, because if she appears now he will slaughter her. He knows which knife he will use, and no one will hold him accountable.

Her footsteps.
She had come to Wuoth Ogik.
She had made her decision.
Her choice had cut him off; it did not include him.
Had it ever? Nyipir wonders.
It had once, he comforts himself.

From the time when he first saw Akai Lokorijom standing on the other side of a heated watering hole, shimmering in the heat, Nyipir's life had been about that moment, that season, that second. Everything he had sought seemed to have been to anticipate this encounter.

Even at that time, he had desired to squeeze all of her into himself, hide her from the world, and contemplate her for and by himself. And later, when he could cup her face, trace its inner bones, it was in secret, and broken with long spates of dark tears. Akai Lokorijom could make him talk as if he had never spoken before. Nyipir told her where he came from, describing even the almost white shade of brown that was the colour of the loam soil of home. He described his mother and his sister to her, and how they had died. On the ground, he sketched a crooked shape of Nam Lolwe, the freshwater lake whose presence was inside his life. He told her of deep promises made, how he would one day find his father and brother and bring them home from Burma. He even whispered to her the story of Aloys Kamau, and how through the memory of his blood he could sometimes see the heart of the world. Akai had drained Nyipir of his stories before she would allow him a small glimpse into her universe.

Chon gi lala, once upon a time.

There was a dry season of such parched vehemence that even the low, pale thornbushes died. A Ndesit family crossed the lake, moved southward, and stopped at Ileret when the rains came. From there they would restock diminished herds with borrowed livestock. The vigorous incursions of hopeful administrators into that part of the country coincided with the arrival of Akai's family.

Scrambling over life's fences, traveling long distances alone to look for and dwell briefly with members of her pastoralist family, Akai erupted without patience into her teenage years. She was a consummate shirker of herding duties and a cook who always burned food, more likely to be found hunting, swimming, and challenging young men to wrestling matches.

Freshly arrived Irish missionaries had been plaguing the clan to send their children to school, a game of hide and seek, which the missionaries lost. But they were persistent. A sacrifice for peace, Akai and the other children whose families had lost their livestock were dragged into mission camps for religion and an education.

Her restless imagination thrived when it found fresh universes. A nomadic, pastoralist, sacrificial incarnate God-priest slotted perfectly into the landscape like a much-expected missing puzzle piece. With her new knowledge insights, Akai intended to seize the world. She was a mimic, and her expanding English vocabulary was tinged with the brogue of her Irish teachers. She was at the top of her class, excelling in all subjects. She expected this. Akai plagued her teachers with questions: What desire is at the heart of God? Who fills it? Where do stars go, if, as you say, they die? Where is the farthest far away?

Some teachers were charmed. Most became alarmed.

Why is what you know more truthful than what I know?

While the colony tumbled into and out of its halfhearted local war, Akai bloomed. After she menstruated, the clan shunted her off to a secluded place to learn the ways of women: manners, expectations, cooking skills, animal husbandry, pleasure, birth, how to sing, how to weep, how to raise children, how to invoke God, and how to kill a man. Akai ran away before the sessions ended, and she sought her beloved stepfather: "Initiate me into manhood!"

He bellowed with laughter.

Akai laughed with him.

Her mother covered her mouth and thought Akai had been cursed. "You have shamed me."

Akai twisted her nose. "How?"

Akai returned to school. She decided she would become a teacher and a traveler. When she came back home, she would organize proper cattle raids. She wanted to own at least ten thousand large-horned cows.

.   .   .

One school term, when the school refused to serve milk or meat but offered plenty of vegetables and plates of fish for a month, Akai organized a boycott of all the mathematics classes until the kitchens offered some meat and more milk. The protest fizzled into nothing.

Akai was suspended.

The headmaster-priest boomed: *Mutinous, indecorous, and impious.*

Big words, Akai later scoffed to Nyipir.

She was given a letter to take to her parents, who were to return with her to school to administer her public chastisement.

Akai packed her green skirt, took off her shoes, and skipped southward, in the direction of her stepfather's workplace. It was a five-night journey to the plateau where her stepfather worked for a thin, effete colonial officer as *nyapara,* supervisor of the works of other ditch-building men. He earned money to restock. He also made himself a *de facto* enforcer of cattle tax, and occasionally succumbed to temptation by adding a coveted goat or sheep to his own herds. Peaceful livestock raiding, he felt. Other men increasingly loathed him. Their opinions neither moved nor stopped him.

A day before Akai Lokorijom should have found her stepfather, she detoured, aiming for a seasonal watering hole with fragrant waters that were a mix of hot and cold, as she was. She reached the edge and saw that two people were already in the water. She increased her pace, propelled by curiosity. She hoped they had some extra fresh milk to give her.

Stillness in the day.

Heat.

I don't exist, Nyipir Oganda thinks, pinching the skin of his face.

Dusk.

Nyipir stirs.

Akai?

Sound becomes companion.

Memory reeks: longing and shame.

Things to cut away—that source of pain, his heart.

Midnight.

Nyipir wakes up and gropes the space beside him where he thought his wife lay. She is not there. She has not been there for a while. Yet tonight, when he smells smoke in the wind, he knows something essential has gone from Wuoth Ogik. Unease. A realization: he is not at home yet. A shiver. He clears his throat. His hand rests on the space where his wife used to sleep.

26

AJANY STUMBLES TO OPEN HER DOOR AFTER A POUNDING FROM the outside becomes a drilling inside her brain that forces her into wakefulness. She is in a wrinkled pink cotton nightshirt and a pair of violet shorts. Lank strands of braid cover her right eye. "It's you," Isaiah says, holding up the dreaded painted rectangle. Restless eyes, up and down Ajany's body. He restrains the urge to push Ajany's hair strands away. His voice comes from a remote place.

Ajany leans against her door. One hand reaches up and rubs her eyes open. Ache in limbs, thickness of tongue, heavy head. Isaiah. Her nose wrinkling, she examines Isaiah's tamped-down rage.

Wary step forward.

Halfhearted, "What're you doing here?" Few things surprise her these days.

Ajany touches the rectangle again.

Hesitates, would frown if it did not hurt so much.

She tries to see.

"It's you," Isaiah insists.

Idiot. She thinks.

His left nostril is whistling. The right is blocked. Sweat pools at the belt of his trousers. Knuckles are pale. Black hair bristles on his arms.

Sculptable. Drunk, she thinks.

"Well?" says Isaiah.

Ajany sways, scrabbles after phrases, hunting for clarity.

One, Isaiah is in Nairobi. Two, he is a hawk, hovering and casting *It's you* like a scourge. Three, she needs to go back to sleep.

A circling. Isaiah's eyes are black points.

Cold slithers along Ajany's spine and settles inside her belly. She shifts her arm. Tilts her head. She stutters, "N-no."

Soft-voiced: "Stop lying!"

"You're loud. . . . Look . . . when was it painted?"

Thinking is painful. But Ajany likes the sense of being right. She grins when Isaiah's gaze snaps to her face, confused lines on his forehead; he looks at the work again.

The bird of prey starts to deflate.

"I don't know. Doesn't say." Isaiah wipes his face. "Who, then?" His body blocks Ajany's way. Isaiah says, "She's pregnant."

Outside, a crow caws.

Ajany ducks beneath Isaiah's arms to re-enter her room. She dives for the bathroom and vomits into the toilet basin. Footsteps. Spine tingle. The cold in Ajany's stomach stirs. Odidi would know what to do.

A voice from behind her head.

"Are you sick?" Isaiah asks. He stands by the bathroom door; Ajany coughs into the bowl. Isaiah wrinkles his nose as he retreats into the main room and looks around. Sees Odidi's pictures on the wall. From the bathroom, sounds of water running. Two guests look in. Isaiah nods and shuts the door.

Ajany appears, damp-faced and less groggy.

Isaiah indicates the wall: "Your brother, my guide."

Ajany pads into the room.

"Who's the woman?" Isaiah lifts the bookmark up.

"My mother," Ajany says, and scowls. *Don't ask,* she hopes. *Don't ask.*

"Oh!"

Silence.

If Isaiah leaves, she can sleep.

Isaiah asks, "So—where's my father?"

"Don't know."

"What do you know?"

His books and art, she thinks.

"Why did you leave?" he asks. "Because of me?"

Ajany rubs her head.

Isaiah hesitates. Frowns. "Someone wants me dead."

"You're not worth k-killing."

"I am worth Wot Ogyek. Belongs to my father, and you know it."

Ajany splutters, tugs at her nightshirt, wipes her throat. Hears the words—entangled words—and wags a finger. "No."

"The evidence I have suggests the contrary."

Ajany moves close to Isaiah. "That's desperate, Isaiah . . . and criminal."

Isaiah asks, "Do you have a title deed?"

Ajany crosses her eyes.

"Does it even exist?" Isaiah insists.

"Ask Baba."

"Tried to. He wanted to impale me with a shovel."

Ajany giggles. "He did?"

"He did."

"He was t-trying to b-bury his son."

Sudden despair.

Hearing echoes of landscape, feeling its shape inside her, how it formed her, its earth soaking up her tears, its dust on her brother's body. Wuoth Ogik: home.

Realization interferes with drowsiness. "Bye-bye, Isaiah," Ajany mumbles.

Isaiah is unmoved. Waves the bookmark. "And this?"

Movement means a destination. The door. Her voice is grim. "*What if,* maybe, your father's dead?"

Blood drains from Isaiah's face. Eyes narrow. Voice glacial. "You tell me. If he were, given everything I've seen, I'd want to know how, who, where, and when, and how your family is involved."

"Meaning?" Ajany's chin rises.

"Cause of death, for example?"

She stares at Isaiah's clenched fists over Akai-ma's image.

She now wants the bookmark.

Isaiah says, "The house. Keeping it up is not really your family's forte." A thin smile. "Will you build apartments there? Lay foundations for another African slum?"

She moves toward the door, gestures *out* with her head.

"I'll finish this, you know. My mother's dying breath was for Hugh Bolton." He shakes his head. "Lugging his ghost into eternity."

No expression on Ajany's face.

Isaiah leans into her. "Would be worth knowing how and when your mother got to be my father's whore."

Her first effort slices open his nose. His fist deflects her arm, but the skin below his left ear is bleeding. He grabs at her hair. Her hands are around his neck. A tug, and her hair escapes from his grasp.

Isaiah wipes the thin trail of blood and gives her a sideways look.

She keeps the door open, body shivering, eyes steady.

He says, "It stinks in here." As he walks out, he lifts the painted rectangle. "Vulgar, my dear. Such pornographic attention is sordid. Wouldn't you say?"

Ajany wants to speak. She struggles for the right adjective in which to couch insults. All she needs is sound. Her mouth opens.

She spits.

It is a direct hit.

The saliva globule spatters Isaiah's face and hands.

She spits the way Akai-ma used to, then cackles as Odidi would have.

"Urgh, *shiiit!*" Isaiah howls, scrubbing his face.

"No, spit," Ajany corrects.

He shakes the gobs away.

His look.

Ajany slams the door shut. Locks it. The door shudders when Isaiah hurls himself against it. Outside, she hears him tell someone, "Er . . . no . . . no, everything is fine. No problem."

Inside the room, Ajany, crouching, breathing. She sits with a crowd in her heart. Her head aches. On the other side, Isaiah stretches out his palms on the wood of the door. Left palm, right palm, left palm. Sticks fingers into the doorjamb. Scratches his chest. *Bloody hell.* Nobody has ever spat on him before. Isaiah leans into the wall, shuts his eyes. Lies to himself: the wet on his face is not sudden tears.

27

A RECURRING DREAM PESTERS ALI DIDA HADA. HE BLAMES Petrus. The older man has been needling him about Wuoth Ogik, digging and digging about Hugh Bolton.

"What precisely did you find?"

"What did Oganda say when you asked about Bolton?"

"How is Oganda connected to Bolton?"

"What did you ask?"

"What precisely did you see?"

"All I know is in those reports," Ali Dida Hada has answered, sick in the heart.

Last night's sleep dissolved into a nightmare for Ali Dida Hada. In the dream, he was in the center of an inferno. That woman merged with the flames and was wailing at him, begging for a poem. In the nightmare, he tried to but could not speak. And the more he could not speak, the closer the fire came, and the more pitiful that woman's sobs. He had fought his way out of sleep, screaming out her name, drenched in sweat, and aroused, and furious at his need.

"Herdsman . . . a poem?"

What did he emerge with?

A half-witted tree wails in a dry wind / Crying for last season's camel's tongue / On salty, scented barks / Moon-sight stirs fragrant spells.

It had been his first true answer to Akai Lokorijom after they met.

She had laughed at his words as a delighted child might, clutching her hands and looking up at him as if he were magical. So he had danced, whirling on his heels. And when he looked at Akai again from the center of his turning, he had seen fire, and the spirit in the fire, and the fire in his heart and in the land out there. Time, space—there had been everything, and fullness. There had been Akai and he. He forgot that he used to have a wife whose name was Nafisa and that she had left him and also taken his children away.

Sometimes the anguish was a phantom limb, raw, weeping, and invisible.

Trained as a cryptanalyst in Ghana and then England, he had returned to Kenya on the day after the assassination of Minister for Economic Planning Tom Mboya in 1969. In the terrible turmoil that followed, and the deployment of security men to quell riots and rumors everywhere, one of the higher-ups tossed him the Hugh Bolton case to deal with. He fought against it, presenting his qualifications, needing a more relevant assignment.

"Just a short time," he was told.

He went to the Kenyan northern territories, grinding his teeth.

Nafisa, his wife, would write him one letter a week. He should have paid attention to her nostalgia for the English weather: "Good for my skin, which is now drying up." These letters started to spread out. Twice a month, then one every three months. *Busy,* she would tell him when he managed to get through to her on the telephone—a once-every-half-year occurrence. She said her jewelry business took up her days.

When he came home from the north, she told him in a teasing tone, "You are the smell of dust."

Ali Dida Hada had showered and perfumed his body with sandalwood. He said: "There is an ocean of lava. Mount Kulal, on the peak, there are storms even if there is drought on the ground, and the lake is always a mixture of cream and sky."

Nafisa twitched her nose, staring hard at the television showing Liverpool FC playing an indifferent game. "That's good. You still smell of ·dung." She gave him a vague look.

When he crawled into bed, her face was pancaked with a rosemary-and-lemongrass face mask, her long hair tied back. She had patted his head, then daintily pulled a duvet over his head.

Ali Dida Hada woke up thirteen times that night.

She made him *mahamri* and Masala chai for breakfast. She smiled at him, eyes coy. "Dubai gold, Ali, is selling well. Even Abdi is driving two Jaguars." And then, "Ali, let us to go back to England, for the children's sake. There's nothing here for us. These people are only good for shouting, killing, and dying. That's all they know."

The core of post–Tom Mboya Kenya had been cracked. Nothing was certain, not even hope. Citizens spoke to one another in whispers, if and when they spoke at all. When those associated with Tom Mboya and his name were hunted down like vermin, there was silence.

"We're safe," Ali Dida Hada said, reaching across the table for Nafisa's arm. "We'll leave before anything explodes."

She shrugged his hand away.

Then his children came home for half-term: "Daddy! Daddy! How lovely to find you here." His daughter said, "Do you want to hear me play the oboe?" It got worse. His son called him *Father*, in a dialect of English he had not heard before. The boy was bespectacled and fragile-looking, and he told his father it was evil to eat meat.

Ali Dida Hada tried to control the drifting. His authoritative commands generated unbearable sulks, and his meals were served burned. He applied for a transfer to Nairobi. "Personal reasons," he pleaded.

His supervising officer nodded, scribbled notes, and sent his application into a large room stacked with other dusty, pending-for-action documents.

Ali Dida Hada returned to the northern terrain to figure out both his life and the whereabouts of Hugh Bolton. The name "Bolton" was a vapor at the watering holes. Where did he live? *Somewhere.* Where did he go? *Anywhere.* When was he last seen? *Hard to say.* There were tiny, tiny story fragments linked to his presence, but these, too, merged with the lives of other British colonial officers—tax collection, road works, dead elephants, oryx, and zebra, confiscated livestock, extended pilgrimages, solitude, insanity, copper-colored hair, a fascination with cairns. False leads, one that led him up a mountain of rocks and down into a narrow valley to a crevice where a Persian hermit dwelt. If this was Hugh Bolton, he did not intend to be found or spoken to. Ali Dida Hada asked Nairobi for more details. Nothing forthcoming. He then told headquarters that the puzzle of Bolton could not be solved quickly, given that an excess of time had passed. Ali Dida Hada searched, but mostly waited to be recalled.

Six months later, a fellow officer delivered a message from Nafisa: a writ for divorce on grounds of violence, desertion, and neglect. Ali Dida Hada sprinted to his hut, threw things together, talking to himself, laced his boots, ready to retrieve his family.

The officer restrained him. Nose to nose, the man commanded him to listen. He said Nafisa was already engaged to a Jaguar-driving trader. She was also pregnant. She had left for England, with the children. He said the dalliance had been going on for a long time.

Ali Dida Hada had crumpled to the earth with his worldly goods.

Stunned, limbs shaking.

Then he had screamed once, limbs shivering.

The officer stood next to him.

They both stared into nothing.

Later.

"Nobody told me."

"No."

"Why?"

"What's to say?"

Silence.

Later.

"Thank you for bringing the message." Dizziness. He grabbed his head.

The officer told him that if he made an application, headquarters would give him compassionate leave.

Ali Dida Hada waved away the offer. "A man must be ready for anything, eh?" Then he lost his voice.

His full wits returned forty-eight hours later.

The messenger left.

Later.

Ali Dida Hada's only attempt to kill himself failed. His pistol self-destructed. He was not even scorched. Then he sent a message to Nairobi headquarters: "I'm available for any kind of work." He intended to be killed in action. That should be meaningful.

Headquarters assigned him reconnaissance duties, intelligence gathering in the much-avoided Northern Frontier District. He wandered—accompanied by an arrogant police camel with a penchant for dates, a bag of tools, herbs, the portable sanctuary of a dead mother's healing songs, a herding stick, and an AK-47.

"Who are you?"

"Bakir," he would answer.

"What are you?"

"*Duddaani-nyaatte*"—a peddler who sometimes carried goods on his back. He said he was a minstrel. He could sing, and he did. A clan elder once threatened to behead him. Ali Dida Hada replied with the first line of a lyrical formula for exorcism, "I'll uproot the djinns you keep." The elder took off. Ali Dida Hada also eulogized dead wayfarers in melodies so subtle and honeyed, near the watering hole north of Koroli, that his reputation as an accompanist for the departed preceded his steps.

This enabled him to attach himself to different arid-land clans, work as a camel handler and livestock herder, making contact with government informers, transferring information, building up relationships with people and clans while the wide skies of the northern lands disconnected him from time.

One day, he walked into an apex in the land to meet Zaman Nawfal, the Trader, who was a troublesome but key informant. A mental checklist of the Trader's known profile: dealer in all contraband, anything from ideas to blood; supplier of women, honey, and camels to the Middle East; government confidante in poaching activities; concealer—for a fee—of discomfiting corpses and the embarrassing bones of dead citizens and elephants; trader in secrets and names; snake charmer who showed up in Nairobi dressed in a white Italian-made suit and white shoes; most likely the hole down which army-issued weaponry, including tanks, vanished. There was still no evidence. People always shifted and looked elsewhere whenever his name came up.

Ali Dida Hada had been suffused with the scent of unearthly coffee. One set of the Trader's skeletal fingers played with air, communicating a story, while the other was wrapped around a flowered ceramic mug. After they took a moment to size each other up, and before Ali Dida Hada spoke, the Trader guffawed and said, *"Bambaloona!"*

Diminutive of *baabo alloona*.

Marabou stork.

"I know about you. . . . *Ka-ha-wa?*"

Ali Dida Hada stretched out his cup.

His mouth was full of a most perfect dark roast: expansive, smooth, subtle, and buttery. It had covered his palate and struck his gullet with a delicate aftertaste. The Trader saw when the flavor became a bittersweet memory that contorted Ali Dida Hada's face.

"Did you see the comet two nights ago?"

"No. What did it bring?"

"Wind, fire, water, prayers, spirits, and some tales of misfortune," the Trader said. "More coffee?" Scratching dry skin.

"No," said Ali Dida Hada. But he thrust his cup back at the Trader. "What misfortune?"

"A man made lonely."

Silence.

"What drives a person away from home?" the skeletal man asked.

"Work."

"So that's what you call it. I've a quarter-kilo of beans."

"Beans?"

"Coffee. A discount for you."

"Why?"

"You want it."

"Do I?"

"Don't you?"

Ali Dida Hada sighed. "I do."

"I like your songs."

"You know them?"

"I know your voice."

"Coffee?"

The Trader said, "Yes. What're you looking for now?"

"A man."

"Not your wife?"

Ali Dida Hada's voice started to shake.

"Name's Hugh Bolton. Englishman. What do you know?"

"Why now?"

"Someone's asking."

"Tried Wuoth Ogik?"

"Not yet."

"You should."

"Why?"

"It is there to be looked at."

"Who lives there?"

"A down-country man. But a house like that—it would know about *wazungu*."

"I'll look."

"Tell me what you find."

"Why?"

"Stories are good."

After Ali Dida Hada left the Trader, he journeyed for days. A desert hyena stalked him. His senses lit up. Acute hearing. He prepared for battle. Odd pleasure. At a dip in the track, as he was thinking about shooting the creature, their eyes met with a frisson that thrilled him. The hyena, weakened by hunger—otherwise it would not have followed a man—fled.

He found Wuoth Ogik's silhouette at nightfall.

The woman's back was to him.

Curvy thinness, like a carved Dinka cow's horns. Calves, ankles, legs—firm, feminine, long. A small waist, wide hips. She was as dark as midnight. His hands tingled, needing to touch what he knew was soft skin. He caught her scent and imagined tasting its source. Her body radiated strength; her movements were a dance. Needing to look at her, he fixated on her outline.

The rush of milk in pails accompanied hand gestures.

Akai Lokorijom milking goats.

Sensing him, she lifted her head and knocked over a calabash. The milk seeped into the ground.

She screamed, "Shit-smeared, diseased earth, greedy and foolish!"

Goats bleated. A dog barked. Her high forehead, long lashes over large, all-seeing, slanted eyes, her small nose, in a face of perfect smooth symmetry, snared Ali Dida Hada. Partially opened, moistened full lips.

He gulped down the desire to shout, "Here you are!"

A furtive hammering, because for a moment he felt the hunger in her eyes had been for him. He had wanted that look for himself more than anything else.

Akai had approached and circled him.

He stood still and thought of the hyena.

"Who are you?" she asked, arms akimbo.

Ali Dida Hada's gaze locked on Akai. He would have put out a hand to contain her if he knew it would not be cut off. His palms were wet. "I'm Bakir, a herdsman."

Akai ignored his smile.

"Bakir," he repeated, wanting to get it right. "I ask for work. I've walked a long time."

Akai rolled her eyes. She did not believe him. She said, "I like your camel."

"It's yours," he answered.

"Why?"

"It's work I need. And shelter."

"His name?"

"Kormamaddo."

Her eyes half lidded, Akai spat the name: "Bakir, you know what a goat looks like?" A laugh.

"Maybe," he said, enchanted.

She said he could start by helping Galgalu herd the livestock. He could set up his tent and share food, and in exchange for his camel, work, food, and some shillings, he could have six lambs when he left.

Akai was baiting him, expecting him to refuse.

"Yes," he answered.

She would give him a hard time.

He would take it.

A game.

He would win.

"Galgalu!" Akai had called, examining Ali Dida Hada from head to toe. Galgalu loped into sight. She turned toward her courtyard, saying over her shoulder, "Take this wanderer. Give him water for his filthy face. Work him hard. He looks like an idle one. The camel is ours."

Ali Dida Hada had suppressed a laugh.

Galgalu's chin jutted forward. He was chewing on the end of a leleshwa twig, making creaking sounds, the sloshing of saliva. He chomped on, and noted the flaring of Ali Dida Hada's nostrils. "You! Let's go," Galgalu said. "You stink," he added, safe from Akai's hearing.

Almost a week later, Nyipir Oganda appeared with thirty-five cows. Ali Dida Hada had approached the temporary thorn-fringed *boma* where the new cows were being examined for disease and bad habits before being rebranded. Nyipir sized him up. Turned his back on him, said nothing. They worked in silence.

"Nyipir!" Akai interrupted the stillness.

Both men turned, and Nyipir heard the herdsman gasp.

Nyipir ambled toward Akai. He lifted her off her feet.

She laughed a low laugh.

Nyipir asked, "Akai, now, where did you find that one?"

"He was lost."

"He has a name?"

"Bakir, he says."

"The animals like him. He sings to them. How's my wife?"

"Happy."

More laughter.

Ali Dida Hada had concentrated on examining the mouths of the cows, his hands shaking. *Stolen livestock.* Long-horned and milky white. Studied the triangular brands on the cattle's necks. *Where are they from?* He strained to listen to the lovers' murmurs. He despised the envy that had possessed him. His body slumped against the rump of a cow.

This place.

Wuoth Ogik.

Forces converged here. People left stories at springs. These were passed on from one season to another.

He heard nothing about Hugh Bolton.

In fact, he had forgotten to ask.

Later, he would meet Akai's children. A brash boy, Ebewesit Odidi, and Arabel Ajany, a scrawny girl who jumped at her shadow and followed her brother around. They were more peculiar than his children. They lived in worlds only they saw.

At first they darted past him, only to watch him from behind barriers:

fences, walls, boulders, and trees. One sunset, he was whistling a camel water song when the boy stopped him.

"What're you singing?"

"A water song."

"Why?"

"Water likes song."

"Water can't hear," he scoffed.

"Tell the camels. They come only to water that sings."

The boy pondered the matter. He nodded. "Teach me," he demanded.

Ruffian! "Why?"

"I want to know."

"My songs. My secret."

"I-want-to-know!"

"Mine."

"You work for us."

"Work, not sing."

"If I say *please?*"

"That's better."

So Ali Dida Hada had taught Odidi Oganda the first verse of a Tigrinya water song. Then, one day, Arabel Ajany sneaked over, centimeter by centimeter, until she was leaning against her brother's back, listening to their singing. The next day, as the child was waiting for her father, Ali Dida Hada overheard her sing the water song he had taught her brother. Her voice made him listen, because if he shut his eyes, he could hear his mother.

Galgalu would ask him twice a day, "When are you leaving?"

Ali Dida Hada answered, "How's my departure your business?"

He had returned to his hut one night after a long day.

He found Akai waiting for him on the steps outside.

He sat down close next to her.

Their skins touched.

They did not speak.

After maybe an hour, she left.

.   .   .

Another evening, he broke open doum nuts and gave them to Akai.

Her face turned to his, tear-streaked.

She came to his hut, sat on the steps again.

He stood behind her and told her a story:

"The lion and the fox went to live together. They put their flocks together and went on a journey until they got to a place that they liked and where they built their hut. . . ."

"Sing, herdsman. Sing, Bakir," she said, "Sing something cold."

He chanted, *"Urgessa Waaqa—nagaya nu bulci . . ."* Fragrance of God—give us peace.

Another night, she took both his hands in hers. She slipped her hands between his, warming them. Later, he turned her hands over and raised them to his mouth.

She asked, "How do you know what to sing?"

He answered in Tigrinya.

"Gudate takeme beleselasa zefenoch . . . Wounds are embroidered with soft songs, spiced prayer, so tell me, what dares barricade a heart from the oil of song?"

Whispers. She leaned into them, into him.

He turned his nose into her skin and inhaled her.

He rubbed his chin against her face.

She did not flinch.

Later.

Akai, her fingers pointing upward, sketched for Ali Dida Hada the path of the stars, speaking of them with the names she had given to them. She described the camels she loved and their personalities. She did not speak of Nyipir, nor did she mention her children. She told Ali Dida Hada, *Go away, go to your woman.* He replied, *I've no one.* She asked, *Why?* He said, *The one I had didn't want me.* She asked, *Are you cruel?* He answered, *Would I know if I were?*

Ali Dida Hada had stayed at Wuoth Ogik for more than six months when Nyipir suddenly left the ranch, "to meet with traders," he said.

Akai found Ali Dida Hada standing outside the courtyard gate at sunrise. "You're going?"

"A short while," he said, avoiding her eyes.

She stared at the ground. "What's your real name?"

He told her the one he used: Ali Dida Hada.

Akai moved closer and laid her head against his.

"Your sheep?"

"Keep them."

She bit hard into his chin.

He moaned.

She skipped away. She looked at him over her shoulder. "You'll come back."

Akai laughed at him.

Echoes of that laugh touch Ali Dida Hada's Nairobi present. *Where is she?* Ali Dida Hada stirs. *How to forget?* He used to know how. For example, he no longer thought of his mother's face. He did not even speak his original name.

28

FOG IN THE CITY. A TEMPORARY PEACE AGREEMENT HASHED out. Kofi Annan's name is enshrined in *matatus* plying the land. Since dawn, Ajany has been shading in the outline of Wuoth Ogik on art paper in red, blue, black, and green ballpoint ink. Little details. A cairn under which she writes the name *Engineer Moses Ebewesit Odidi Oganda, 1964–2007*. Four shapes to represent Nyipir, Akai-ma, Galgalu, and herself. Koroli springs. She outlines Ali Dida Hada. *Water Singer,* she writes. The backdrop is Odidi's face.

Ajany stuffs the map, three of Odidi's pictures, and a wad of money into a large, plain brown envelope. *Odidi's Baby,* she scrawls. She sits on her bed, knees drawn up, staring at the package.

Long after dusk, when the frantic traffic sounds outside have eased, she steps out her door, walks down the short corridor to where the stairs begin.

Isaiah has been waiting.

He says, "We didn't finish our conversation."

"I did."

"Apologize for spitting on me."

"I won't."

"I'm coming with you."

"You're not."

"I'll call the police. They'll talk to you."

"Please do."

"Where are you going?"

"Somewhere."

"As I am."

"Go away."

"Or what? You'll spit on me again?"

"Yes."

They jostle past the reception.

"Bye, Jos," says Ajany.

"Bye, Jos," repeats Isaiah.

"Uh," Jos replies.

The chilly evening air.

Ajany rubs her arms, adjusts her hold on her purse and envelope. They stand in the car park. Peter the taxi man sees Ajany, flashes his lights, and switches on the car engine. He says nothing when Ajany and Isaiah reach for the same door and cling to it.

"What do you want from me?" Ajany groans.

"My father," says Isaiah.

She looks up at Isaiah. "I don't know him."

A sudden sheen in her eyes.

"So tell me about your mother."

A shrug. "Go find her. Talk to her yourself."

"Where is she?"

"Don't know. Somewhere."

"Liar."

Ajany, her voice brittle, says, "My mother left the day we brought my brother home."

Isaiah pulls open the car's door.

"Twilight," she tells the taxi man.

Inside the car, Isaiah asks, "You don't know where your mother is?"

"No."

"You expect me to believe that?"

"No."

Isaiah exhales, tousling his hair.

Families are complicated organisms.

They reach the venue.

The bouncers glance at Ajany, swivel their heads at Isaiah, and glance back at Ajany. She winks back. Yesterday's man in pink is today in vivid purple.

Ajany stops to waylay Justina.

"You can go in," she tells Isaiah.

"No," he says.

"You can't keep this up."

"I will."

A quarter of an hour later, Justina approaches the main dance hall. She sees Ajany.

Justina says, "*Mavi ya kuku,* you're here to fight again?"

Ajany thrusts the envelope at her.

"What?"

"For you and the baby."

Justina fingers it, glares at Ajany, pouting.

"Who's this?" Her chin indicates Isaiah.

Ajany shrugs. "Ask him."

"He's with you?"

"No."

"Yes," answers Isaiah. He drapes a firm arm over Ajany's shoulders. She wriggles. An idea: "This is Odidi's friend Bolton."

"Oh. The *mzungu* he was meeting at Wuoth Ogik? Wasn't he an old man?"

"Yes," confirms Ajany.

Isaiah scowls. He grips her wrist.

Ajany tugs at her hand.

Justina is looking Isaiah up and down.

She asks Ajany, "Does he pay well?"

"You beat him up." She pulls free. "Then he pays double."

Justina's eyes flutter, mocking Ajany as two fingers pluck Isaiah's shirtsleeves. "I'll beat you with chains, if you want."

Isaiah lifts Justina's fingers from off his shirt. "This woman and I"—he indicates Ajany—"sewn together."

Ajany escapes.

Isaiah guffaws.

Justina joins him.

"You know Ebewesit . . . Odidi?"

"We wrote to each other. I'd have enjoyed meeting him."

She nods. "England?"

"Yes."

"You don't look English."

"What does English look like?"

Justina gestures to a part of the dance floor that is visible. There, five men of indifferent stature and shape gyrate in paroxysms of off-beat pain. One of them slides left to right and back. The music is determined to push them off the dance floor. It is also apparent that they are committed to staying on. Arms and bodies in motion, whirring like propellers ready for liftoff.

Isaiah watches the dancers. "Moses told me to come here. But then . . . uh . . ."

"Yes," breathes Justina wistfully. "That sister calls him Odidi; me, I say Odi-Ebe; you say Moses. Many people. One person."

Isaiah remembers the corpse.

"A true man." Justina wipes her eyes. She makes a face. "Want to go in?" Isaiah scans the crowd, looking for Ajany.

"She's inside," says Justina, now amused. She inserts the envelope into her shoulder bag.

They step in and are swallowed by the warmth, noise, and rhythm.

Ajany is dancing. Justina watches Ajany as she has before. Finds Odidi's stormy abandon in Ajany's gestures, in her sinuous moves. Ajany is unconscious of her complete otherness. She is not of this place. Just like Odidi Ebewesit.

A vision, a feeling.

Justina takes three urgent steps toward it. Ajany must go. She'll beg Ajany to leave before the rottenness creeps over and possesses her.

Her baby moves. *I know,* Justina soothes the child.

She turns to confide in Isaiah.

He stands frozen, his eyes fixed, mesmerized by *this* Ajany.

Justina scowls.

"You?" she prods.

Isaiah slips his hands into his pockets. He casts his eyes to the ground, lips pursed. A shudder.

One of the Twilight regulars bumps Justina's shoulders. "Sa'a Jusi?" She gestures at Isaiah.

Justina sticks her tongue out, wraps her hand around Isaiah's. "Dance with me?"

"No."

"I need you."

"You don't."

Justina giggles. "But you can't dance with her," pointing at Ajany.

"Why?"

"You are just a human being."

"So?"

"They don't really need us."

"Who are *they*?"

Justina starts to say something, but hugs her body instead. She would do anything to feel Odidi's strong and securing arms around her, even for a minute. She wants to hear again his vow to keep her safe forever.

Isaiah says, "She's human."

The DJ changes the music.

"Keep telling yourself that. You dance?"

"Mhh."

"Like that?"

Ajany is against the steel pole. Hearing melodies that had been played in Bahia, wanting to throw off the weight of her world and its realities, she dissolves like wax into the music, feels it become her body. Now she is simply Arabel, and the other side of the song is silence, and its roots are in eternity.

"No," says Isaiah.

"Dance with me?" Justina asks.

"Yes," Isaiah replies.

Ajany emerges from the vision in sound after the DJ mixes in some Hi-Life. She finds the present. She is outside the clubhouse, staring at a starry sky. She finds Kormamaddo the sky camel. Tears. She must return to Wuoth Ogik.

The taller bouncer asks, "Leaving, madam?"

Over-the-shoulder grin: from *malaya* to "madam" overnight. She peers at her phone, calls Peter the taxi man. "Need to go," she says.

"I'm praying for you," Peter reminds her.

He is worried about the state of her soul.

. . .

"Evening, Jos."

"Morning, madam. Better today?"

Ajany winces. "What time is it?"

"3:30 a.m."

"When do you sleep?"

"In the day."

"I'm checking out, Jos."

"Leaving?"

"Going home."

"Now?"

Ajany nods.

"*Woyee!* I'll miss you."

Ajany makes a face at him.

An hour later, Ajany has cleared her room, stuffed clothes, portraits, pictures, and art materials into two holdalls and three plastic bags, and left a large tip on the dresser. She pulls the door open—hinges squeak— and walks into a block of heat, Isaiah. In that moment they are alone. Nothing moves, not even breath. Not the night. A gush of fear, as if she might never find her way out. She takes a step back into the room. Isaiah follows. She propels herself forward, fighting to leave.

Isaiah had intended to be reasonable. To scold her for abandoning him at the club. Had meant to tell her he had paid Peter the taxi man to leave, that it was unfair of her to go without talking to him first. He had wanted to ask Ajany for one sensible conversation about Wuoth Ogik, finish things so they could return to their lives in peace.

Thwack!

Her handbag got the side of his head. Shock greater than the sting. Her eyes are dark with decision. She is willing to behead him if she has to. He is afraid she will spit on him again.

"*Hngngh!*" Isaiah dives to the ground, his flailing foot slams the door, he is still holding on to her.

It is possible to brawl in private silence. He can't remember locking her legs to the ground with his own. He remembers the intoxicating blend of sweat, adrenaline, soap, and woman.

Turned on.

Wanting.

He is large enough to contain her, sad enough to need to get lost inside her, with her, through her.

She kicks, aiming for his balls. Her punch catches the base of his nose. Scent of blood, screaming pain.

He could hurt her.

Hands squeeze her neck and arm.

She bites him.

Isaiah grunts and wipes his bleeding face.

Ajany reaches for his head and yanks at his hair. Bites his arm again, breaks skin. He shakes her off. Her nose is bleeding. Her teeth grasp his fingers. He drags his fingers from her mouth. He pulls back his arms to deliver a blow. She whimpers. He sees how small she is. Remorse.

Inside-out pain.

His hands fall to his sides, and he turns his face and body away from Ajany.

Breathing.

Lonelinesses spill and mix.

She wipes the blood from her nose.

Isaiah whispers, "I am sorry." For many things. Coming to Kenya in defiance of his mother. Chasing after ghosts. The solitude of walking through restless dunes into North Horr. Nobody noticing. Arriving at a place that was the same as the one left behind. How could a human being endure such infinite spaces? Causing a woman's nose to bleed—wounding another creature. What had happened to him?

Ajany listens to Isaiah breathe.

Warmth, darkness, stillness. She is lying on her stomach. Can crawl into herself. Expectations disintegrate and leach into the floor. Pain on her shoulder—is it dislocated? She chooses not to speak. She waits. She is learning how to wait.

For the next moment.

Outside, a night bird coughs and coughs.

Inside, silence.

Breathing.

Sweat, silence.

Rasping air.

Blend of blood.

In the parts where her nails have ripped his skin, a tingle.

Isaiah is motionless.

The thing that had invaded his body with heat, hatred, and fire leaves. He turns to Ajany. "I won't hurt you."

Part promise.

To life.

Ajany's eyes are solemn. Isaiah touches the drying blood beneath her nostrils and straightens her twisted arm. Wipes her face with his wrists. She watches, sees when he notices the small space between their bodies.

Contours of desolation.

She smells fear, finds that it is cold on her tongue. She tastes sadness. Shared flavor. She waits.

He licks his lips. Tastes blood.

A burned taste, like dark-roast coffee.

Dusk's light invades their space.

His right hand hovers over her.

She wonders about his touch, what it would tell her body.

He drops his hand to the floor.

A cold stone spreads from his heart, and he curls over.

A despairing admission: all losses have secret names.

Thirst is a dry scratch in the back of Ajany's throat.

And his. He squeezes his temples and blocks out the light, which pokes at his throbbing head. Could do with a cigarette, even though he had smoked for only a year and that when he was only twenty-one. Long ago.

Memory shapes.

To name something is to bring it to life.

His loss, the failures.

Bodies touch.

No one pulls away.

He whispers into Ajany's mouth.

Seeking light.

Breathing.

Slow-motion memory patchwork, the times in his life when disbelief was like certainty, illusion had become real. Once upon a time, when he was failing and being abandoned he had run and screamed and howled out a name.

Then limped home to wait for normal to return.

It never came.

Isaiah lifts his arm, touches the back of Ajany's head. She peers into his eyes. Old eyes. Her left hand frames his face. This, too, she could paint. Touch, shape, mold, and draw. Here. She could carve an outline of a man.

Isaiah says, "Life's ephemeral." Memory kaleidoscope: another face, a beach, the sea, an eternal absence.

From the light of their window, silhouettes and shadows.

Hidden things start to whisper all at once.

Ajany remembers Odidi.

Isaiah touches her face.

He says, "You're waiting for your brother. Picking up rubble from his life. You think you can rewind time." His left hand cups her face. "The Styx is a one-way bridge, honey."

Ajany stiffens.

"Will *you* return from the dead?"

She closes her eyes. She asks, "Where d-do you go?"

"War zones."

A sad sound.

"Photographing passersby."

"D-does it work?"

"Sometimes."

"And when it fails?"

"I photograph warlords."

"Why?"

"Souls that coexist with the shades of death they create: no excuses, no explanations, no platitudes. Wondered how their faces look through light."

"And?"

"I ask them to smile and photograph how their eyes disappoint their attempts."

Isaiah's fingers tug at Ajany's braids.

She flinches.

He says, "Anguish has its pleasures."

He says, "I clean up tragic houses, strip them down, sell their content, refurnish, sell for a profit, buy another house, and then another."

Distant traffic, voices downstairs, Calisto's voice, Jos's high-pitched answer.

Ajany says, "You're here now."

"Yes."

"What if *he* doesn't want to be found?"

Isaiah says, "Tell me more."

Words jam in her mind. Then an admission: "I can show you."

"What?"

"You'll see."

"I wish Moses . . ." Isaiah waits, and then: "The woman this evening, Justina, she is . . ."

"His."

"She's pregnant."

"Yes."

"His?"

"Mhh."

"What's she doing . . . there?"

"That's where they met. She's waiting for him to come back."

Outside, rustling, shuffling, knocking, tapping, twittering, and ringing. Inside, hearts beat. Something unravels.

Ajany listens.

Isaiah moves his arm over her body.

Many routes through desire.

Yearning. To *not* feel empty. Or lost.

First, they lie together side by side for a long time.

Much later.

He unzips her dress slowly, peels it off her body. He helps her unbutton his shirt, and loosen the belt of his trousers. She sits cross-legged to pull off his shoes. He watches her movements.

Wordless.

Skin to skin.

She concentrates on the quietness of this.

Inhales his waiting, his eyes needing her. A mirror, she thinks.

So she bites his ears, tastes skin, strokes his forearm, collects the feeling of his face, the bony structure, brow ridge, distance between eye orbits, shape of nasal bones, chin form. She strokes nose, eyes, ears, lips, and chin.

They will grope secrets, share unanswered questions and infinite presences. They will also dance between tombs of demoniacs. A man drinks in a woman's scent, her curves, hollows, and shadows. A woman is suspended in her body's shocked meeting with tenderness. She will use the backs of her hands to rub the texture of a man's chest hair. The man will rock to and fro inside her soul, cover her and fill her, and cling.

Somewhere outside, it becomes dawn. Inside this room set apart from the world, she breathes in the man slumped on her body, studies the muscled arm that is pale against her nakedness. She could paint just this. Nothing else. Her fingers move on their own, pinching skin to estimate muscle, fat, skin layers, and contours. They pluck at nuances that create gesture and texture. She strokes soft, hard, warm, cool, hot, wet. She'll gather and store what she needs.

Outside, a small wind and shards of washed-out red light. Outside, a cracked lamp attempts to cast light. Outside, a huge moth with feathered black wings immolates itself on glass-covered lightbulbs. Inside, stillness. Ajany tries to disentangle herself from Isaiah's hold. He clings. She pulls. He lets go.

She disappears into the bathroom.

There she touches her body.

Life markings.

Blood from a new battle dance. She listens for whisperings, the ones that suddenly promise, *You might live.*

Water. Warm. Arousing.

When she sniffs under her arms, she smells that Bernardo's odor is fading. She scrubs away what persists.

Then.

She creates a list in her head as the water runs:

Plasticine dust.

Oil-based clay.

It is for the face.

And to frame neck and shoulder, wire.

Ajany re-emerges, wrapped in a big cream towel.

Steam rushes into the room where Isaiah sits naked on the edge of her bed, head in his hands.

She stutters, "Daylight?"

His head snaps up, eyes bleary. "Yes."

She drops her towel. "Sleep well, Isaiah."

"And you, too, sleep well."

She snuggles into her pillow.

Isaiah watches Ajany close her eyes.

She is asleep.

Deep sleep's soft breathing.

He rouses himself to switch off lights, intending to return to his room. He lingers, trying to remember what it is like to be able to simply drop into asleep.

He returns to the bed, where he rests his head on the pillow next to hers. A coconut-caramel-flavored scent from her side of the bed wafts toward him—perplexing, soft, and promising. He closes his eyes, inhaling that fragrance. In less than a minute, he is snoring.

29

ON THE ROOFTOP OF A CITY POLICE STATION IN NAIROBI, THE
early morning broods over a city, a nation, that is gluing its cracked
shell together again. Ali Dida Hada and Petrus stand as if they are on a
cracked stage and are about to dance.

They were in their office that morning when Ali Dida Hada announced
to Petrus, "*Afande,* a copy of my resignation."

Petrus looked over his spectacles, and reached for his drooping
cigarette.

Leaving? An empty feeling in his belly, as if he were . . . *afraid?*

Petrus asked, "Retirement?"

"Yes, sir."

Petrus had whistled at Ali Dida Hada. "So soon?"

Until Ali Dida Hada spoke, Petrus had not known what he was
going to do.

"It's time," Ali Dida Hada answered, gathering papers from the
table.

"Then, Ali." Petrus's eyes were bright. "Together, brother, we must
erase *all* impediments to your exit."

Ali Dida Hada glanced at Petrus. *A scheming djinn,* he thought. *Could*

I shoot him? Claim a gun accident? He tipped back his head, rubbing his eyes. Men like Petrus always had contingency plans.

There is something of the look and shape of a cornered brown cat against a black-stained wall in Ali Dida Hada. Petrus watches the sky-dance of the Nairobi City Council's self-appointed mascots, the marabou storks. Petrus says, "I'll miss this city."

Ali Dida Hada waits.

"What's your opinion on a local tribunal? Will they call us to testify?"

Ali Dida Hada waits.

Petrus says, "Tomorrow, there'll be a peace march from Dandora to Kangemi."

Ali Dida Hada waits.

"Peace and goodwill for the nation." Petrus purses his lips, the cigarette dangling. "But, as a people, do we even want to live together?"

Ali Dida Hada frowns.

Petrus continues, "You and I, Ali—our terms of references include dying for the nation. Others, our 'masters' . . ." He pauses, shakes his head. "Asked to choose Kenya, fall over exits trying to save their fat buttocks." Below them, traffic. Fumes float up. Low-voiced: "Now there are those who are waiting for any excuse to light up the nation again." A snort. "Was wondering the other night . . . trying to picture one Kenyan who has given our country a dream as big as a national educational airlift. Forty years. Anyone you can think of?"

Ali Dida Hada rubs his forearms.

Petrus changes tacks, looks at Ali Dida Hada. "I met Nyipir Oganda in '69. After Mboya was murdered." His voice drifts off.

Ali Dida Hada leans back, uneasy.

Petrus continues. "His fingers?"

Ali Dida Hada recalls Nyipir's darkened, twisted digits.

"I did it," Petrus explains.

Ali Dida Hada straightens up.

"To save him. Sixty-nine . . . Were you here? Couldn't tell from your file. This chaos . . ." He waves in the general direction of the city. "We were here before—'69, when Tom Mboya died. Unfinished Kenya business, this."

Hadada ibis fly in formation above, screeching as they go.

"Bad times." Petrus's gaze is distant. "Remember?"

"I'm a simple man," says Ali Dida Hada, watching Petrus as he would a puff adder.

Petrus chuckles. "*Aiee!* This Kenya *marwa*! Makes me wonder about *soooo* many things. Small things: For example, a cryptanalyst is sent to northern Kenya, on a policeman's salary, to find out what has happened to a *mzungu*. Years later, this *simple* cryptanalyst, on a policeman's salary, has thirty-six million three hundred and fifty-two thousand shillings in six bank accounts, a *simple* car dealership in Eastleigh filled with cars that never get sold, twelve *simple* butcheries across the country, and three *simple* lorries that have been hired to transport cattle from the north to the south. All this on a policeman's *simple* salary."

Words dry up in Ali Dida Hada's mouth.

He cannot move his hands, so that, even if he had the capacity to, he cannot blast Petrus away.

Petrus pulls out a police-issue pistol from an inner pocket of his black coat. He checks the bullets. "I confess I haven't been as *simple* or as wise as you, Ali."

Ali Dida Hada opens and shuts his mouth.

Petrus says, "You *do* understand what I mean."

Ali Dida Hada does.

Petrus says, "I'd noticed thoughts of existence that bother us never seemed to touch you. Got curious. Thought we might be hosting a mystic." A sneer. "But imagine what I found, Ali? And so I ask a question Kenyans don't ask—how did you come by your wealth? Hard work?"

Ali Dida Hada closes his eyes. Voice neutral, he asks, "What do you want?"

Around Petrus, veiled, venomous presences, potent and explicit swirl. Whispered options. He struggles. He succumbs. Dread of suffering, of becoming nothinged.

No one need know anything.

Petrus drops his head.

Temporary grief—archetypal loss. As in the beginning of existence, when imagination and cowardice begat fig-leafed fear.

———

Genesis.

Ali Dida Hada remembers that the tingle from Akai's bite was as tender as a new kiss. Winds had flung white sand and dark pebbles into the air and covered the view of mountains. Even as he left Wuoth Ogik that day, he had known he would return. He had gone to his police base and dispatched a convoluted and undecipherable message back to Nairobi headquarters, buying time for himself. That night, he had driven in a white van all the way to Dukana, left the car at Puckoon Ridge, and ambled into Sibiloi Park. In a dark Somali *kikoi,* and a camouflage jacket covering a white shirt, concealing a dagger and pistol. He carried an old leather rucksack and an AK-47. He walked forty kilometers before dropping into the shade created by the merging of shadows by a *mukhi-mukha-d'ales* and *Acacia mellifera* trees. Chewing on the end of an aromatic twig, he had waited. Sure enough, a day and a half later, after noon, one of Nyipir's five hired livestock-lorries lumbered past, packed with resigned bovines.

A soft whistle from Ali Dida Hada.

Walahi! That was how Nyipir was doing it. In plain sight. Livestock standing on boxes. And inside the boxes . . .

A livestock train had approached. From what he could see, five men drove them. Ali Dida Hada moved behind a tree. Just when they would have passed him, he got up, raised a hand, and hailed them.

"*Keifilhal?*"

"*Alhamdulillah.*"

"Your family is well?"

"They are well."

"And the animals?"

"They are well."

"And you?"

"*Masha'llah.*"

"*Alhamdulillah.*"

Silence.

"And what blessings do you carry?" Ali Dida Hada asked, moving forward, and bringing his rifle forward, a finger on the trigger.

"Small things. Why anger? You can see livestock, dates, coffee, okra, khat, amber. . . ."

"You are here?" Nyipir said as he approached Ali Dida Hada's flank.

"I'm here."

"The house?"

"In order."

"Its people."

"Are well."

A direct look. "I see," said Nyipir, sweat beading his upper lip. "You are on your way to someplace?"

"In a sense."

Ali Dida Hada moved abruptly, a gesture directed at a camel and the cargo on its back. The camel spun, the bundle dropped. A box crashed to the hard ground. The spooked camel bolted. Others tried to follow. The camel keepers ran after the animals. The box's lid slipped off, and the butt of a rifle peeped out. Inside the date boxes and salt caches were self-loading pistols, assault rifles, submachine guns, AK-47s, an assortment of G3s, bullets, and two rocket launchers in long cases.

Just as he had thought. "Don't move," Ali Dida Hada ordered, covering Nyipir with his rifle.

A rumble from Nyipir: "How will you catch me?"

"Don't move," repeated Ali Dida Hada.

"And I . . . I'll go peacefully with you?" Nyipir had scorned.

Ali Dida Hada pointed the gun at Nyipir's head.

"What do you want?" Nyipir stretched out his arms.

"We'll charge you with waging a war against the people of Kenya, treason, engaging in activities that jeopardize the lives of citizens, conspiracy to murder . . ." recited Ali Dida Hada.

"So many terrible words to describe this simple trade?" Nyipir sighed.

"Consorting with the enemies of Kenya . . ."

Nyipir said, "I wondered if you were Special Branch."

Ali Dida Hada's eyes were narrowed; his finger rested on the trigger.

Nyipir said, "How far do you think you'll go with these men behind you—each one a partner in this trade? How far can you run before you die?"

Ali Dida Hada had thought of this.

He asked, "What do we do about it?"

"You let me go."

"Maybe."

"Tell me your real name."

"Why?"

Nyipir lowered his hands. "To welcome a business partner, there must be, at least, an exchange of names."

Silence.

"A quarter of profits, shares in all trading," proposed Nyipir. "And you do your part."

"What?"

"Look everywhere but where we are. We trade in information, too."

Ali Dida Hada lowered the rifle.

Nyipir said, "To start . . . twenty thousand shillings. Goodwill."

Ali Dida Hada took a deep breath.

"Cash," explained Nyipir. Added a non sequitur, "Livestock bring profits in Zaire."

Wind-borne silences seeped into sands, hills, and scrub. The sun took its time shortening and then lengthening shadows. Ali Dida Hada's silhouette shifted and twisted under the light. He inhaled the northern-frontier essence, the breath of camels, its many promises. He asked Nyipir, "Where were you taking these?"

"To friends." Nyipir leaned over to pick up a strand of dry grass to chew on.

"Where?"

Nyipir paused. "Sele Bedirru."

Ali Dida Hada lowered his rifle. "You need an escort?" It was why he was there.

An alliance among scorpions, thought Ali Dida Hada then. Watching for an unguarded moment when one might sting the other to death. But from then on, Ali Dida Hada warned Nyipir about impending military ambushes. He also misdirected government informers, restructured their messages when he dispatched these to headquarters, and provided cover for unregistered consignments.

These activities took precedence over his halfhearted search for Hugh Bolton, which he did continue. There seemed to be no records attached to his name anywhere. Was it possible for a man to erase traces of his existence?

Life had hobbled along. Ali Dida Hada now knew some peace, as if he were kept in the armpits of God.

———

Petrus drags out his crinkled cigarette pack, studies a single cigarette with its chewed-up end. Ali Dida Hada stares at blue sky, red fire. How did Petrus find me out?

Petrus insists, "We are the same, Ali, trained collaborators for shit.

Scavengers who read entrails, and then what? Mboya? Argwings? J. M.? Pio? Ouko? Ward? Goldenberg? Anglo-Leasing? The Artur scum? Parallel forces to traffic, massacre, poach . . ." He snorts. "And once a season shining tin pins and ornamental shoulder pieces to pin onto uniforms"—his hands cover his squinting eyes—"for our silence." Weariness in Petrus's voice. "What does honor mean for the men of this land?" For himself.

Cooing doves, a bristling insect, wind. Ali Dida Hada thinks, *We are the ghosts that consume us.*

Petrus swivels on his heels to glare at Ali Dida Hada. "Can you remember what peaceful sleep was?" He makes a harsh sound. "What it's like *not* to thirst for blood to spill?" He lifts his unlit cigarette to his mouth, fingers shaking. "When our type retire, we die within a year, three if lucky. You hear?"

Ali Dida Hada coughs.

Petrus stares at his shiny shoes. "Won't happen to me, understand?" Four steps left, six steps right, a swivel. "What say you?" A sly look. "Amnesia! At last, a solution." His laugh is a grunt. He rubs his chest. Unreachable ache.

"Oganda's alive." Ali Dida Hada denies Petrus's predictions.

With a downturn of his mouth, Petrus drawls, "You're bewitched by him."

Ali frowns.

"You left your wife and children for him." Petrus gestures.

Ali Dida Hada grunts, "She left me."

"You did not follow."

"She'd gone."

"You did nothing."

"Nothing to do."

"You didn't try."

"You don't know that." Ali Dida Hada sweats.

"But I do. Nyipir Oganda, a cryptologist's riddle, a seduction no discontented wife could match, mhh? I understand. Oganda made me an apostate. Turned my eyes away from the mesmerizing glower of my deathless president." A scoffing sound slips past Petrus's unlit cigarette.

Silence.

Ali Dida Hada stares at Petrus. For all his inquisitiveness, Petrus knows nothing of Akai.

"So?" asks Ali Dida Hada, suddenly unruffled and suddenly sure he would return to Wuoth Ogik.

Within Petrus, a memory deluge from his lifetime of witnessing so many blood-stained transactions, hard cash for souls to slaughter on arcane power altars. He had abhorred the low-grade crudity of the exchange, the furtive compromises. He had noticed how the chief casualties were always those whom the soul-seller had thought he loved.

An imperceptible hesitation.

Then, "Our business," says Petrus, a waver in his voice that he corrects as he pulls out a medium-sized black notebook. Inside, in neat green-ink letters, are banking details. He carefully tears out the page and, with a direct look at Ali Dida Hada, says, "Our oath of silence." Then, in broken Tigrinya, Petrus asks, *"Ezu yibehai ezi b'Tigrinya?"*— I'll forget everything I know after the money has been transferred? A slow smile. Ali Dida Hada pales. "I know. I know. But people do listen better in the language of their umbilical cord." A chortle. Petrus tucks his paper into Ali Dida Hada's pocket. "Amnesia and amnesty, you and me. We are Kenyan originals. We can use money to Sellotape our war wounds." A tiny wink. Petrus laughs.

Ali Dida Hada's face, now drained of emotion, is a void. *Dem Hira!* He curses within his mind.

Forefinger to lips, Petrus says, "Shhh." He then adjusts his glasses. "Me amnesia, you amnesty, or vice versa." Petrus salutes Ali Dida Hada. He turns around and flings open the metal door. Whistling "Sina Makosa."

Receding footsteps.

Ali Dida Hada tries to shove air into his lungs.

30

INSIDE A NAIROBI GUEST ROOM, A SKULL ACQUIRES ITS OWN eyes. Fingers mold contours and crevices, drawn from worlds of feeling that she has known and that she imagines. The light changes as she seeks its moods to offer gradations to her work. Ajany has done this before, always returning to the memory of the cave for meaning. She wipes down the plaster of Paris; her fingers shape eye orbits. More certain now of how to build the nose and mouth, she shapes the nasal opening and spine. Tingle in her arms, glow in her heart, Ajany becomes the shaping, the finding, the becoming. Later, she will adjust the skull on a black metal stand with a broad base.

First, Isaiah wipes the sandman's crusts from his eyes. Next, he waits for the bite of despair that is the companion to his waking. Third, he remembers the early morning, how it started and ended, and when he raises his body to find the woman again, a movement stops his eyes and he sees that the colors of the late afternoon have muted her being and submerged her in her story making and if he moves too soon she might disappear.

She is looking at a broken skeleton from the cave of memory. Ajany stretches clay across a plaster-of-Paris cranium.

In the midst of molding, she stops.

Glancing over her shoulder, seeing Isaiah watching her. A small smile. Soft-voiced, she says, "I need your father's photograph."

He reaches for his wallet in the discarded trousers, pulls out the photograph, steps over their clothes to reach her and give it to her, fingers touching, hands clinging.

He says, "It's late?"

"About two."

"Slept well."

She smiles.

"Here's Dad."

Ajany stares at the sepia image.

Her mind returns to the cave, and its skeleton.

She closes her eyes.

Hugh Bolton's gaze.

Obarogo.

She drops the photograph. Picks it up, hands it over to Isaiah. Not looking. Composing herself, she touches his face instead, tugging at skin.

He watches her.

She applies clay to the object's upper and lower eyelids. She touches Isaiah's mouth to learn it and transfer it to clay.

Strips of clay. A mouth of clay. She thinks of Hugh's mouth in the photograph.

When she moves again, Isaiah grabs her right wrist, catches her fingers between his teeth. Scrapes his teeth down her palms to the soft part of her wrists. She reaches up for him. Isaiah bends, kisses her, sucking, suckling, curious. Waiting for someone to move away.

The wind slams the window shut.

They pull away slowly.

She turns to her work.

Stillness.

She breathes out abruptly.

Fighting temptation—this need to cling to another, to touch and be touched, burrowing out simple spaces and escaping despair for a season.

. . .

Three days later, almost four—an imperfect face returns to the world after a full night's crafting. It is made of distance, silence, frozen time, and old light. Its essence transfixes two people, the woman who has textured him to life, and the man who would be his son who cannot speak.

"This is what I know," Ajany says, hugging herself.

Isaiah swoops her up. Squeezes her hard.

Nothing lasts.

Not hope, or pleasure. Isaiah wanted more to be in control over. He wanted a place to go to, to look and find. He had questions:

How do you know?

Where do I look?

How can you know?

Where is he?

"I don't know," she repeats.

I don't know.

"What do you know?" His fingers grab at her arm.

There's a cave made of red, she could say. But if she did, she would have to imagine how its agitated occupant got there, and if she did, she would have to start with Wuoth Ogik, and if she tried, she would hear both Odidi and her old *I swear*. The silence.

She says, "I must go home."

He suddenly asks, "Bernardo?"

She swivels her body, eyes wide. Startled.

He says, "You called out to him in your sleep—he makes you cry."

"Cry?" she asks.

Isaiah leans forward to wipe tears from Ajany's face. He shows them to her, the glistening on his fingers.

She sinks to the floor, legs crossed. Her stammer is so bad she has to pause to breathe in.

"Who is he?" Isaiah asks.

Choose.

"A man," she says.

"He makes you afraid."

Silence.

She looks to the floor.

"A hungry man I made God." *And now there's a blank.* She thinks.
Isaiah stares down at her. "Is he 'home' for you?"
"No." She shivers. "Oh no."
"Where is he?"
"Bahia. Where I live . . . lived . . . We were together. Four years. More."
"Not long."
"Long enough."
"For what?"
"To get lost." Her face is pinched.
"You're here."
"I cut myself out."
"Cut?"

An empty-eyed look, speaking with reluctance. "From him. His ghost." A wry twist of mouth. "Blood. Butterfly shaped. Like an oryx mask." She gestures.

"Oryx mask?" Isaiah rubs his face.
She nods. "Had to cut myself away. Had to."
Isaiah leans toward Ajany. "Meaning?"
She looks up at him, mute.
"What?"
"Was tied up inside him. Had to cut free."
"From Bernardo?"
"Yes."
"So? How?"

"I . . . uh . . . the knife . . . uhm . . ." No other way to put it. And there was an odd relief in speaking the truth aloud. ". . . stabbed him."

Isaiah jars his spine when he sits on the floor.
Long exhale.

Churning deep-inside turbulence. Aware of fragility, its sometimes-madness. The woman hugging her knees beside him.

He asks, "Why?"
The question he asked his warlord-photography subjects.
She repeats the same answer they gave him: "I don't know."
Quiet.
Somewhere outside; an early-evening cicada vibrates a song.
"When?" Isaiah asks.
Christmas Eve.
A woman in a turquoise dress with a flower in her hair, hips swaying

in the night. No doors open for stragglers desiring explanations for why stars twinkle when the world had fallen apart. Kormamaddo the sky camel should have fled. The song of stars became still. She would call Odidi. He always knew what to do.

"Onde Bernardo, Arabel?" Good-natured laughter, the tangle of a web made of other people's expectations.

Find Bernardo.

She would beseech him to keep her. She had taken off her shoes to return to the party that much faster, had stepped out of the lift.

Isaiah says, "You were afraid."

"No."

"Why stab?"

She says, "The knife was there. Next to the big-boobed woman's golden thong. My replacement."

"Anger," Isaiah says.

"No."

"Why stab?"

She squirms. "To loosen myself."

"You could have gone."

"He always finds . . . found me."

"What was so awful that you couldn't speak it?" He addresses other ghosts. He remembers how he fell from lofty power's altitudes.

Ajany's lips tremble.

Silence.

Isaiah smells words, hears smells, and tastes sounds. Inhales blood and sea and salt and the sound of waves that once swept away huge portions of his life.

Now.

Chin dropping to chest, refuge in the mundane. "Meet for dinner in thirty?" He gets up. No reply sought.

The room is stifling.

He slams her door in error.

Retreating footsteps. A wondering. *What if every human is born with a volume of madness to resolve?* Isaiah hunts for and retrieves his keys. *Some seize and drive those forces into an inner corral.* He enters his room. *Others are overwhelmed; they submerge and quietly drown.* He locks the door behind him.

· · ·

Good evening, Jos.
    Evening, ma'am.

He is there, head bowed, as though in prayer.
    She will color absence green.
    Like grass and life.
    His shirt.
    Black skies outside.
    Rain scatters on the red brick ledge.
    Ajany studies raindrops. That way she can postpone meeting Isaiah. There, the salve: washing blood from jagged wounds. Here, the waterfall: tumbling into fire, becoming steam, and returning as rain again. Suddenly, next to her, a pointy-nosed waiter says, "Madam, Calisto the chef recommends chicken tikka masala with a choice of potatoes, ugali, chapati, or rice." The waiter escorts her to a chair opposite Isaiah.
    Not a green shirt, more like a shade of teal.
    Eyes lowered, Isaiah suggests, "Chicken?"
    A nod.
    She counts the bamboo-wood strips of her place mat. Outside, quiet rain. He lifts his head. Between them, magnetic tension, and Isaiah's contemplation of Ajany becomes an incendiary thing. Drawn to look, she finds his voracious, restive longing. Its confusion. Blinded, she allows his hunger, revealing her own, breathing through half-open lips. Suspended seconds, soft fall of rain. On the table with its plain white cloth, fingertips touch. Stillness. Clanking plates on a tray. Footsteps. Curried steam. The food is served.

31

TWO NIGHTS AGO, HE MADE THE DECISION. NYIPIR HOVERED
outside Galgalu's *boma,* carrying a huge empty gunnysack. He needed
Galgalu's company. Bandaged and balmed, Galgalu had returned from
the medical center the night before.

Nyipir told Galgalu, "There's something in the red cave."

"It's forbidden," Galgalu replied.

Nyipir said, "For that reason, we go. . . ."

Galgalu said, "It's time?"

All the while, Galgalu had known.

They ventured into the twisted darkness, crawled on the ground
until they reached a sliver of light. They paused before entering into
the chamber of images, stories, and bones, on their knees like peni-
tents. When they re-emerged, they were burdened and changed. Nyipir
insisted on carrying Hugh's bones alone.

Three white-tailed honeyguides listen to human songs of unraveling oaths. Galgalu still prays over an Englishman's ghost, pleading for a
truce, since they are all so far from home.

—

Nyipir completes a new cairn within forty-eight hours. In that time, he has talked, mostly to human bones in a gunnysack, until his tongue is swollen. Galgalu hears some of those words, their plea for mercy.

Nyipir spoke of an almost-teenage boy running from a psychotic uncle whose head he had split with a flying hoe, a teenage gravedigger with plans to head out to Burma to retrieve family ghosts.

He spoke to the bones and Galgalu, of Hugh. "I used to be a child." Nyipir says, "Before I met a man who walked with power."

"He took me for police training. 'Can't work with "bleddy" civilians,' he said—remember? I fed and washed a grown man who could kill if he wanted to—and he did. But he showed me how not to be afraid. And work, always work with Bolton. Driving. Washing dishes, clothes. Polishing brass and boots. Fetch, carry, hunt, cook, guard, light fires, set plates, boil bathwater, and set up a safari camp, walk, hunt, talk, fight, listen. And tea. At ten and at four.

"We hunted men," Nyipir adds.

The addiction.

"This kind of thing does not end right."

Silence. Yet in Nyipir's mind, turbulence. Scarred memories of a patriot with a wire around his scrotum that would be pulled at another man's whim, for the sake of the nation. Rotting in state dungeons. Losing faith, in God, in men, in country.

He finally told Hugh, "I've lost her." Defeat.

No, he had never imagined intimate casualties, had never thought his only son would die before him in these nameless wars.

The cairn is completed before midnight. It is straight on all angles at the base, and the stones chosen to create the ramparts are perfect. When it is done, Galgalu brings Nyipir a calabash of liquid. Honey wine had medicinal and purgative values.

Nyipir had lost his Kenya on July 5, 1969, in Nairobi, when Tom Mboya was assassinated. The murder was the culmination of fears, swirling rumors, the meaning of clandestine oaths that made the rest of the country enemy territory to be owned. It was the purpose of the silences that had started before.

Nyipir and a colleague, Mzomba, had been looking across the Jeevanjee Gardens and had paused when the report of something punched the air. Then silence. They started to walk in the direction of the noise. Twenty minutes later, a woman in a green dress, barefoot, carrying white shoes, raced past them. She was crying, a horrible sound that seemed to come from all around her, and from within her.

Ka-Sehmi. Mayieee! Gi-neeeee-go Mboya.

Mboya!

Nyipir's body temperature had dropped.

Tom. Mboya.

His heart had slowed down, and he collapsed with his disintegrating national dreams.

Then.

It is a lie. Nobody would kill Tom. Nobody would dare kill Tom, because it means they would be willing to kill Kenya.

He started to stutter something.

Later, Mzomba lit a cigarette and offered it to Nyipir, who was on his knees and clinging to a telephone pillar.

This death created a fissure in the nation, as if it had split apart its own soul. The funeral cortège was more than two kilometers long. A wailing nation lined up on three hundred kilometers of road to touch the passing hearse. In the silence of everything else, in the farce of a trial, a man named Njenga, who had fired the gun, cried, *Why pick on me? Why don't you ask the big man?* Before he could suggest much more, Njenga was hanged.

After Mboya, everything that could die in Kenya did, even schoolchildren standing in front of a hospital that the Leader of the Nation had come to open. A central province was emptied of a people who were renamed cockroaches and "beasts from the west." But nobody would acknowledge the exiles or citizens who did not make it out of the province before they were destroyed. Oaths of profound silences—secret shots in a slithering civil war.

In time.

A train would stop at a lakeside town and offload men, women, and children. Displaced ghosts, now-in-between people. No words. Then one night a government man drove into town from Nairobi. He carried petri dishes of *vibrio cholerae*. He washed these in a water-supplying dam. Days later cholera danced violently across the landscape, dragging souls from that earth, pressing dessicated bodies deep under the earth.

No words.

Under the trance of fear, a nation hid from the world. Inside its doors ten thousand able-bodied citizens died in secret. Some were buried in prison sites, and others' bones were dissolved in acid.

Nyipir knew.

He saw.

He did not speak.

He hoped it would end soon.

Just like the others who had also seen, he told no one.

A hundred, and then a hundred more, herded into holding houses.

Picked up—taken from homes, offloaded from saloon cars, hustled from offices, stopped on their way to somewhere else—prosecuted, and judged at night. Guilty, they were loaded onto the backs of lorries. And afterward, lime-sprinkled corpses were heaped in large holes dug into the grounds of appropriated farms. Washed in acid, covered with soil that became even more crimson, upon which new forests were planted.

After Mboya, Kenya's official languages: English, Kiswahili, and Silence. There was also memory.

Nyipir's mind had collected phrases shouted out to those who were within hearing range:

Tell my wife.

My brother.

Daughter.

Son.

My friend.

Someone.

Tell my people.

That I am here.

Tell them you saw me.

Because there was silence, he tried to memorize names, never speaking them aloud.

Some he wrote out in a child's notebook.

In case one day a stranger might ask if so-and-so had existed.

Patrick Celestine Abungu. University professor of history, returned from Russia, bearded and bespectacled. Broad-chested and terrified. He shouted, *Tell my wife and children.* . . .

Onesmus Wekesa. Musician, composer of songs with double-meaning lyrics. A song that mocked an oafish, greedy hyena that ate up its own body had brought him to the police cells. He wept when they dragged him away. He clung to everything. He shouted, *Tell my brother. . . .*

Cedric Odaga Ochola. Engineer. Former major. Dragged out the door, he had screamed, "How can you do this?" He glimpsed a figure and shouted, *Tell my daughter. . . .*

Odd.

No one would emerge to ask after men who had been erased.

It was as if they had never been born.

Kenya's official languages: English, Kiswahili, and Silence.

But there was also memory.

Nyipir knew.

He saw.

He did not speak.

He hoped it would end soon.

Till one afternoon.

A jeering colleague.

Nyipir was braiding his horse's tail when the man sneaked up to him, spitting displaced rage: "*Nyinyi! Heee! Mambo bado. Mtaona! Mnacheza na Mzee?*"

Nyinyi. You *the other.* Not us.

Two weeks later, three men in camouflage gear, berets, and shoulder lapels watched an Ajua game in progress. In the camp near Kapedo Falls, to the south of Turkana District, the sound of the Suguta River. *Clack-clack-clack* of seed on wood. Fixed gaze of two squatting men. Two rows of rough, curved hollows on the board where stones collected. A two-hour Ajua game. Slam on board.

Nyipir collected all but four of Corporal Gakui's seed "cows." He had gloated, *"Mia dhako!"* Give me a woman!

The corporal spat, *"Kihee!"*

Silence that precedes an ambush.

Three jumpy men watched.

Kihee. Uncircumcised.

Nyipir dropped a seed into the grooved slot before turning to the man. He asked, "How does a mutilated penis make a man more of a man? *Msenje*," he said, "I've buried your testicles before, I can bury them again."

. . .

It was only when a locust whirred over a pale-brown anthill that Nyipir realized that in in this epoch of silence, he had spoken, and by speaking he had made himself a sacrifice.

He got a confirmation within five days:

Citing Acting Inspector Nyipir Oganda for indiscipline, insubordination, and criminal activity; failing to protect civilians, stealing police equipment and stock, absconding from duty; protracting military conflict . . . Verdict: dishonorable discharge.

That was 1969, the year Tom Mboya was murdered, and Nyipir lost Kenya. Often, for him, it was still 1969.

Later, despite a decree that had declared that it was not possible, somehow, the Leader of the Nation managed to die. In 1978, a lean cattleman, an inarticulate teacher, took charge, and Kenya changed again. Still, nobody dared talk about 1969 and why Tom Mboya died, not even Nyipir.

Until the day Nyipir washed his son's naked and unmoving body, and heard how a grieving Kenya, to receive a new year, 2008, had set itself on fire.

———

Ajany returns from her final pilgrimage to her brother's death scene. She had waited by the road, staring at the remains of a white flower on the spot. Later, she had gone to seek Justina, to breathe all that was in and of her that was also Odidi's. She had found herself wandering from door to door, had discovered that not one of the doors was familiar. "Justina?" she had asked passersby.

No.

Not even stout Gloria could remember that Justina had existed.

"But I saw her . . . you showed me . . ."

"Are you sure, Mami? Can I fix your hair?"

Out of Ajany, a tiny whimper.

The kiosk man had frowned. "*Ai!* Madam, Justina?" Ajany had examined the bland look on the man's face. A shield. She had turned away, taken steps toward the dusty road. Walked through the late-morning light and paused to pluck out fragments of a lily stuck on a hard black road. Odidi's flower; she would take it with her to Wuoth Ogik.

In the late day's sky, morning's wandering birds fly in array back to mountain nests.

Ajany walks into the guesthouse's reception area, limbs weighed down. Everything of life is out of focus, and she has lost her feeling for time.

Just then, a taxi driver skids in. Isaiah leaps out. He is returning from the Rift Valley, where he has experienced arcane space, color, and Great Rift Valley silences. He has also seen flamingos on Lake Nakuru.

"Hello," says Isaiah in resolute cheerfulness.

Ajany, lethargic, offers a nod, avoids his eyes.

He knows. "You're leaving."

Another nod.

She drags herself to her room.

Isaiah reaches her door in time to hear the lock turn. He waits outside, then shakes his head and walks toward his room with the caution of one traversing sliding rocks that abut a crag. Flesh and woman; delirious remembrances of intimate shadowed selves. All of a sudden, they had become afraid of each other. They were not lovers who needed words to wound; absence sufficed. Wordless, they had both fled, before dawn, to opposite portions of the land.

In the evening, on impulse, Isaiah orders Thai takeaway for two, avoiding Calisto, who is stalking him. He did not ask for his twice-a-day hot pineapple-vanilla-ice-cream crêpes.

"Arabel?"

Ajany has stuffed some clothes into an open case. She is busy removing Odidi's office photograph from its frame when she hears Isaiah's knock. His voice. She hesitates. A clock's minute hand settles into nine-fifty-two before she turns to unlock the door.

Isaiah lifts the greasy brown paper bags.

"Last Supper?" He lifts a bottle of Australian red wine. "Thai chicken, jasmine rice," he adds.

Ajany forces a smile.

What endures?

Absence.

. . .

They eat.

They start their meal in silence.

Listening to outside sounds; cars, voices, birds, drip-drip of a leaking tap; whispery wind on plants. *Tick-tock*. A woman and a man suffused by vague, steamed jasmine rice scents chewing on Nairobi-cooked Thai chicken.

Then Isaiah speaks, much too loudly: "I saw flamingos today as pink as Wot Ogyek."

"Wuoth Ogik," mutters Ajany.

Isaiah grins as he pours red wine into a coffee mug.

Fruity.

Ajany looks and looks.

The room spins.

The wine is the color of Odidi's morgue blood.

A crevasse splits open—a summons, a memory.

Appetite dissolved, Ajany falls in.

Exhausted by mysteries, of confusing answers, fuzzy thoughts, bad dreams, drowning in unknown sensations, the accumulation of silences, Ajany rises up like a creature on fire and flies out of the room. She runs past Jos, onto the lawn and through the gate.

Isaiah follows her, the wine bottle in his hand.

He shouts, "Just a minute. Wait!"

He thrusts the half-full bottle at Jos.

Light-streaked darkness.

Ajany runs blind.

Down Ngong Road, she runs and runs. She runs, and then she stops, looks left and right, crosses the road to her right, and comes to an abrupt stop outside the mortuary gate. Stands still, as if she is waiting for something majestic to appear.

The green glow of the morgue lights stains her face.

Her fingers cling to the gate wire.

Rustlings.

Vigil for a riddle.

The Old Dead gather to watch.

Rustlings.

The last time she was here, there had been radio prattle. White and pink chalked numbers on a blackboard. Green walls, creak of a faulty fan that cooled nothing and whirled in time to the ticktock of a hidden clock.

They had found Odidi's body.

Baba had groaned, then shut up and become stone.

She had bled from her nose, and from her life.

Something died.

Arguing over a body.

Then a ritual: *preparing the deceased* in a grossly understaffed morgue. She went to buy Odidi a new suit, and shoes from the mall.

Nyipir Oganda was wiping Odidi's chest when she returned, the attendant watching him, clasping a hand to his jaw.

Her father's deformed hands were gentle. He wiped Odidi's face with a cream-colored cloth. He hummed a lullaby:

Nyandolo
Nindo otere
Nindo man e wang' baba
Obi mana ka
Nindo man e wang' mama

Baba finished and gestured for the clothes.

They dressed up Odidi together. Black socks on Odidi's feet, laces on tan leather shoes, tied up just as he had taught her.

Ali Dida Hada's radio crackling, "Stand down. Calling all units." And shouting, "Oganda, leave for Kalacha now. Security forces have taken over the election center."

Dr. Mda puffed out his cheeks. *"Aieee! Ngod,"* he shrieked. "Are we *sntupid?"*

Now.

Fading voices.

Fading traffic sounds.

Delicate night-rain falls. The corroding wire of the padlocked gate cuts into Ajany's fingers. Shadows within the grevillea upon which, not too long ago, a metallic-mauve bird sang.

Memory's voice—sounds like a groan.

A choice.

She could climb over and never have to return to this side again.

Stillness.

And mutterings from in-between people: the Newly Dead.

Rustlings.

The earth is soft where Ajany stands.

Fetid scent.

Echoes.

Why does Obarogo need eyes at night?

Come.

Tug of subtle tendrils.

Come.

Whistling; breathed prelude of a shared desert song. She listens and feels Odidi as a flame without light. But when her heart should have stopped—swallowed by painful joy, she hears, *Choose,* and she is poised before a red cave's entrance. She is standing by a roadside, seeing herself inside Odidi's eyes.

Swirling fog.

Waits three seconds too long.

That, too, is a decision.

Sundering.

Cold smokelike wisps unravel, returning her to a center within other inner worlds. Mist stairs evaporate into unreachable portions of darkness. Her knees give way. Surrendering.

A lone firefly hovers.

On impulse, Ajany crawls over to scratch at a goo-encrusted plaque at the gate. *Hic locus est ubi mors* . . . The rest of the words are indecipherable. "This is the place where death rejoices to teach the living," the full plaque once declared.

Tremulous touch on Ajany's face, tender, moist, warm on skin. A hard arm around her body: she is propped up by its weight. Isaiah's head heavy against hers. Wetness slides down her neck. "You're c-crying," she says.

They take the long route back, through the city center, traversing edges of peril. She wants to stay lost. He has nowhere else to go. They walk until Ajany's toes cramp. They skirt fringes, where noise is muted and people scarce, and find themselves crossing a half-gated piazza, at the center of which looms a silhouetted cross. Hazy light outlines a side building. They approach its orange-hued stillness and discover other quiet souls, some seated, some kneeling, three with their heads buried in their arms. A monstrance glimmers on a rude table adorned with yesterday's flowers. A red light flickers on the wall adjacent to the table. It is a place to sit out the night with no risk of anyone's asking for payment or an explanation. They sink into a bench next to a small bookshelf and sit close together, like two lost children, holding hands and hoping to be found.

Later, for the first time in the years of his meanderings, Nairobi's flower man will be stopped in the middle of the street just before dawn. A stuttering woman wants lilies, rosemary sprigs, and baby's breath for all the money she has, which is two hundred and fifty shillings. Such a fresh experience; he offers her the flowers for two hundred.

Isaiah and Ajany will return to their guesthouse in the indistinctness of that time of day. In her room, they will grip each other, engulfed in mongrel plant aromas. But first, he will strip off his clothes, and then hers, crushing spaces of distance, the limits of skin. Crumbling in her bed, she will arrange his limbs around her body in order to become cocooned. Entangled, secured, and warm, they both sleep at once.

Midafternoon, Jos phones the room. "Madam, an Officer Hada's here for you."

Ali Dida Hada's eyes narrow when he sees the small, puffy-eyed woman, and the haggard, darkly tanned man next to her. He remembers the time of his first encounter with Ajany; she looked just as half-worldly then as she did now, with Odidi standing in front of her like a defense shield.

The fear and questions are huge in her eyes.

Resignation, too.

"Eh . . ." he starts, "Wuoth Ogik livestock were stolen. . . . Pole . . . Galgalu, he was hurt." Quickly, "He's safe, don't worry."

She whispers, "Baba?"

"Asking for you. I'm leaving. Police plane. Wilson Airport, fourteen hundred hours. If you want to come." He glances at Isaiah.

Outside, two crows caw—a bird quarrel in full throttle. Ali Dida Hada watches Ajany.

"She's not there," Ajany tells Ali Dida Hada. "She left us all long ago."

Ali Dida Hada removes his cap, scratches, returns it to his head. "Tomorrow. Fourteen hundred hours."

Isaiah steps forward. "Is there an extra place? I'm going back anyway. I'd be grateful for a ride back."

Ali Dida Hada turns to Isaiah with a tiny frown, offers him an imperceptible nod, and exits.

———

Somewhere in the northern frontier, a Trader marches with a new and loaded AK-47 in a frenzy fed by assorted phantoms' murmurs for vengeance. Today the man will be an exorcist in a steaming Kenyan desert.

———

Ajany, Isaiah, and Ali Dida Hada leave Nairobi the next day. They leave in an unmarked white car under cover of a blue-gray cloud with the smell of lilies and roses and rosemary sprigs. Isaiah carries Hugh Bolton's clay face. They take off from the police air wing in an eight-seater laden with supplies: six retreaded tires, newspapers, and a sack of mangoes and oranges. The other passenger is a government assistant minister. He speaks about Kenya's future, now that Article IV has been accepted—it is rosy. They speak of the state of the world—it is precarious. They say the rains are late for the second year running; they confirm that weather patterns have changed. They will land in a drizzle of locusts.

32

A BALD ELDERLY MAN WITH WHITE EARRINGS, WRAPPED IN A dark blanket, his feet in tire sandals, smoking a black pipe, walks by. Distant cowbells. A slow-sailing cloud covers a premature moon, which casts a shimmery eye over an earth amphitheater of stone and shrubs. Locusts form a small, low-hanging, moving cloud. The acacias are big-headed dryads. In the horizon is a tourmaline-shaped rock hill with etched panels. In the foreground, Aaron Chache, in creased uniform, gesturing like a marshal, guides a plane to a halt.

When it does stop, Ali Dida Hada, Ajany, and Isaiah climb down and walk into the scrawny police post.

"*Karibu, Karibu!* Afande Ali Dida Hada? You're here? You're really here?" Aaron's eyes glow, though his salute is unsteady. He detests locusts. A pre–wet season invasion; the beasts are everywhere.

Ali Dida Hada drawls, "At ease. Status update."

"As reported. Unchanged, sir. Apart from the locusts." Aaron's eyes move to the sack of fruits and the newspapers. He apologizes for the state of his uniform. "Charcoal iron, *eh!*" His finger reaches for the newspapers, eyes clinging to the sack. "Mangoes." He sighs. "And flowers." Newspapers! "How is Kenya?" he asks in Kiswahili.

"Depending on the will of God. The will of man has proved faulty." Ali Dida Hada brushes a pesky insect from his face. A bucking wind hauls in scents from a faraway lake. Ali Dida Hada exhales. A constriction in his chest dissipates. *I'm happy.*

Plane offloaded, the pilot waves and takes off, fighting for daylight. Watching the small plane circle, Ali Dida Hada says to no one in particular, "We leave for Wuoth Ogik now."

They turn to him. Aaron's mouth curves downward. The loss of company shakes him. The rich conversations he holds with himself need an audience. "So soon?"

Ali Dida Hada knows something of Aaron's dread. Those deep groans within silence. Many-layered thick darknesses, murmurs from one's soul. Unseen footsteps and other unaccounted-for night sounds. He needs to be kind. "The fruits and newspapers are yours, *ndungu* Aaron. We'll meet again soon."

Aaron clears his throat. "At least take some doum nuts with you." His voice cracks.

Night journeys have their rhythm. On the open, long, winding road, shades and shapes of blurred identities. The sound of the car's engine intrudes. They watch the moon hurry past dark clouds. They pass a euphorbia bush that emulates the leaning Tower of Pisa.

Isaiah says, "I walked this way."

Ajany glances at him.

"From Wuoth Ogik. On my way to Nairobi."

Ali Dida Hada asks, "Where did you go?"

"North Horr."

Ali Dida Hada whistles. "Didn't get lost?"

"What do you think?"

"How did you find your way?"

"By walking. And walking."

Soft laughter.

Swirl of dust.

They disturb sand grouse, which fly away in shadow. In the distance, a man-shaped form shimmers, leading two donkeys, its metal adornments gleaming. The flowers perfume the car. Ali Dida Hada warbles a song. Ajany closes her eyes. It is one of the water songs he had taught Odidi to sing. Enraptured by the almost familiar vastness, Isaiah senses how outsiders who fall out of life and end up here imagine they are the first to have ever done so.

The sound of an AK-47 going off shatters the night's peace. Ali Dida Hada stops the car.

"What's that?" Isaiah asks.

"Gunfire," says Ajany.

They listen. Then Ali Dida Hada gets out of the car and climbs on top, looking toward the west.

They resume their journey, and speed up in the direction of Wuoth Ogik. As Ali Dida Hada's car reaches a crossroad, a mad *d'abeela* slides behind a tree. The car passes by him. He jogs southward, even farther away from the scene of a crime.

Cumulous clouds and a trail of dust, and they reach Wuoth Ogik. Most of the house is coral rubble.

Ajany scans the ranch, holding her flowers.

Isaiah says, "The house is dying."

Ajany stands with one foot atop the other, staring in the direction of the cattle *boma*. To Isaiah, she resembles a thin, stripped-bare tree in an eternal landscape, or a solitary ostrich. He would have spoken but for the wind, so he shuffles to stand close to Ajany.

Galgalu approaches them, a bloody bandage wrapped around his head. He recognizes Ali Dida Hada and deliberately slows down, fingering the amethyst resting in the hollow of his chest. He distracts himself—thinks the thorn fence is thinner than usual, studies his shadow—and bends his head. *Why has that man returned?* There were an excess of curses at Wuoth Ogik. Nothing had gone right ever since Ali Dida Hada had entered into its life.

Galgalu spits sideways, depressed by the evidence of his declining powers of exorcism. He has performed arcane rituals to encourage all concerned gods to get rid of Ali Dida Hada. But here he was again.

The first time Ali Dida Hada came back to Wuoth Ogik, he had told Galgalu, "Call me *bambaloona*. . . ." Galgalu was convinced that the moment he called Ali Dida Hada "marabou stork," he would be murdered for insulting a fool. A calculating glitter had popped into his eyes. *What a silly man.*

"I know a coffee song," Ali Dida Hada had told Galgalu. "Do you want to hear it? It's from Eritrea."

"No, I don't."

Ali Dida Hada had sung anyway.

Galgalu would never admit that the voice singing *bunabuna* had transported him into a space of fine fragrance and perfect taste.

Anyway he was under no obligation to like everybody.

Galgalu turns to Ajany.

He had incanted hymns that killed lunacy. She seemed steady, even with her bunch of bright flowers.

Life in flow again.

"Ch'uquliisa!" He limps over.

Ajany hurries into his arms. *"Gaaaluu."* She touches his bandaged head. "Who?" Her flowers are crushed between them. He hears the fluttery beat of her heart.

Sweet air. She touches his face, as she did when she was a toddler. Blue flies, a buzzing cloud over him, on him. She blows them away.

Isaiah and Ali Dida Hada watch them.

Ali Dida Hada's skin gathers on his forehead as he reads the fading signs of hooves and sandals on the ground. Tracking them right, he follows until the footprints turn southwest. Dog waste. Tire-sandal marks. Cow dung, camel prints. He squats to read the ground, studies the churned soil leading out of the homestead. Ali Dida Hada's body stiffens.

Footprints.

Here is where Kormamaddo the camel took off. Here is where someone with slender feet and a light tread caught and calmed him down. Sideways motion, flowing across the ground. Every creature's footsteps have a unique rhythm. He knew the melody of these human ones. Ali Dida Hada squats on his haunches. He knows why he is here.

Hadada ibis cross the land in raucous song. Ali Dida Hada sidles up to Galgalu like a hungry apparition. Ali Dida Hada glowers at the second cairn. "Where is she?" he asks.

Galgalu lopes away, Ajany two steps behind him. She, too, notices the cairn. What did she expect? That her father would wait for her to reappear before burying Odidi?

A ghost scorpion scrambles from a long-gone predator. Isaiah's eyes follow the creature. Restrained shudder. He has heard about these creatures. How pilots who discovered the hideous hairy things aboard their planes in midair screamed all the way to wherever it was possible to land without shame. A go-away-bird holds session close by. Isaiah's shoulders sag, and he rubs the new stubble on his face. He can smell water. Can't reach it. Feeling rising bile, he leans forward, unbuttoning his shirt. Sweat drips from his face, down his back. The whirly-burr of a falling insect. *Ultima Thule,* he remembers. He returns to the car to retrieve Hugh Bolton's head. He will go into the house and sit among his father's things. He swipes at flies.

Next to the new cairn, Ajany sees her mistake. The hole her father had been digging when she left is half done. Though Odidi's coffin is not fully covered, it has been screwed shut, nailed down. She touches it, the idea of him, then she drops to the ground. Wind stirs, flings hair on her face. *One day, I'll forgive your death.* The earth is warm against her skin. Odidi's absence is now a deep-frozen clot within her heart. *One day, I'll forgive your death.* New memories. *And mine.* Soft footsteps going somewhere. *Ajany yuak, yuak, yuak.* Her head swivels. *Brought you flowers, Odi.* Upward glance—she stares into the blue; a pair of bateleur eagles. She hears, *I'll find you, silly.* A smile inches its way out of the depths of her heart.

Inside the cattle *boma,* Ajany finds and touches a bedraggled being that is the shape and texture of an aged, twisted tree bark. Bloodshot eyes, his bare feet are now cracked. The late orange light shines on his face as he contemplates the empty cattle enclosure. He is dark. At close quarters, he seems wavy, not solid, his cloak of solitude forbidding. Ajany almost drops what she is carrying, and clamps down on her lips to stop from crying out.

"Baba," she whispers.

Nyipir drops his stick and, with both arms, scrambles up and reaches out. He grabs hold of his daughter. She is alive and at home. *"Ibiro."* You are here.

She is clinging to her father. How small he has become. The wind throws dust around and covers them both.

Nyipir remembers: "Flowers?"

"Yes," she says. Then, "I found Odidi."

Nyipir's head snaps back.

Ajany unrolls Odidi's office picture.

"Here."

Nyipir receives the picture with both hands. He lifts the image to his face and presses it in, inhaling the imagination of his son's presence for a long, long time.

Later.

Voice hoarse, Nyipir says, "He looks well."

Ajany watches.

Nyipir says, "He looks well, see?"

"Baba," Ajany starts, wanting to wail about treachery.

"Yes?" He turns, eyes bright.

Hesitation. She says, "I'm happy you're here."

Later.

She tells him a little about T. L. Associates Engineering—that Odidi had left a legacy with his work in water. She tells him that Odidi's time with the gang came from heroic idealism. He had only been organizing the disenchanted youth to work for a different future for themselves. It is sad, she tells her father, that the stupid state did not have the capacity to grasp Odidi's vision and had instead destroyed him.

A vaporlike drizzle.

A large drop spatters on Nyipir's forehead. They both glance skyward. "Rain?" Nyipir whispers. Followed by a broken-up sound.

Ajany listens.

Nyipir says, "Should've told him." His eyes dart from one end of the horizon to another.

"Said something."

Ajany rubs her nose. She settles on the ground before curling up against her father's shoulder. "Baba," she says, "Odidi's woman . . . she found me. She's pregnant. His child. You'll be a grandfather."

As if the sun had all of a sudden popped into existence, everything is infused with fresh warmth and Nyipir's explosive, "A child?"

Ajany begins to smile. "Yes."

"New life?"

"Yes."

"This unknown daughter, she has a name?"

"Justina."

"Who is her father?"

"Didn't ask."

"Odidi's child, *nyara*?"

Ajany nods.

"Perhaps a son?" Nyipir huddles into his stained coat, cool tears at the edges of his eyes. But a laugh begins with a mouth twitch. When it emerges, the sound lights up Nyipir's face from within.

Later.

Ajany says, "There's another grave."

Nyipir replies, "Yes."

Silence.

Nyipir asks, "What news of Kenya?"

"A president. A prime minister."

"Two?"

"Yes."

"Together." He snorts. "What do they call it?"

"Coalition."

"Coalison."

"Mhh."

"The people?"

"Forgetting."

Nyipir scratches his chest. "That Isaiah Bolton . . ."

"Yes?"

"He left Wuoth Ogik."

"No."

"He did."

She says, "He's here." Pauses. "We came back together."

Nyipir leans back before nodding. "Good." Gripping Odidi's picture, he wipes it. "Odidi looks well. *Wuod* Oganda! Shall we go to our guests?"

Ajany helps her father up.

They veer toward the edge of the *boma*. There, Nyipir uses his walking stick to point at different parts of the earth. He says, "Akai-ma came home."

Ajany says nothing.

"At night. Here are her steps." Nyipir's voice is forcefully bland.

Ajany notes the livestock trails leading out of Wuoth Ogik as she bites down on her lips, bruising them. She stammers, "The red dance-ox?"

"It followed her," her father says on a shuddering breath.

Ajany feels hot and then cold. Golden light in the darkening sky. Ajany shivers. The air is thick with the unexpected scent of rain. No one will say anything, lest eavesdropping malicious ghouls destroy the seeds of hope.

"If I had a ram, I would . . ." Nyipir starts. "Nothing remains."

Salt in Ajany's throat.

"Nothing, *nyara*, not even a lamb."

Ali Dida Hada had stopped mid-approach, a gargling sound escaping him. Pain, both inner and outer, had convulsed his body and paled his lips: bewilderment, dread, too many battles, spiritual exhaustion. There was a time when he would have rejoiced at Nyipir's vanquishing. Now all he wants to know is the name of the one lying beneath the new cairn. Was this why Nyipir had asked for him? To reveal to him the finale of their dangerous dance?

Nyipir sees Ali Dida Hada and straightens out his stained shirt. He rubs his face, pulls at his nostrils, and clears his throat.

Ali Dida Hada seizes Nyipir's forearms. "The second grave?"

"Dead bones."

"A name."

Nyipir hears the fear in Ali Dida Hada's trembling voice. The hand on his arm is strong, hot, and pinching. A perverse impulse: *Akai*, he could spit into Ali Dida Hada's face, *it is Akai Lokorijom*, my *wife*.

"Who are you hoping it is?" he says. Half-lidded eyes.

Ali Dida Hada takes a deep breath. "Please, Nyipir."

Nyipir asks, "Do you still believe in God, Ali?"

Ali Dida Hada squeezes Nyipir's arms. He scrunches his face, pressing down grief.

Nyipir's voice is so soft: "Are you a praying man?"

Ajany's high cry, a warble, really, stops Nyipir's mischief. He is truly tired of the maze of riddles. "It's a man," he tells Ali Dida Hada. Icy-toned: "Now let me go."

Ali Dida Hada might have embraced Nyipir there and then and danced. He drops his hand, tries to conceal his relief as he asks, "He has a name?"

"Yes."

"Who is it?"

"You know."

Ali Dida Hada leans forward. A mild sense of defeat assails him. His words are clipped and odd-sounding. "Where did you find him?"

"The cave." Nyipir uses his cane to point east. "There. That red one."

"Manner of death?"

Silence.

"Cause of death?"

"No one has ever explained why death happens."

"Time of death?"

Silence.

"You disturbed the scene."

"I can take the bones back."

"Bolton?"

Nyipir shuts his eyes, blood rushes beneath his skull.

It is time.

"Yes," he says. "Yes. Bolton."

Ajany, who has been chewing her lips, now jumps.

Ali Dida Hada stares at the ground.

The air is electric.

Silence.

Then, "Who'll tell his son?" Ali Dida Hada asks.

Nyipir's eyes are fixed at distances.

Ajany watches Nyipir.

Watches for the stone Nilote's re-emergence. The sculptured man whose look revealed nothing, especially when confronted with the unknown. A visage relieved of emotion even when Akai leapt up to snarl at malevolent presences she alone glimpsed. The mobile ebony form who had twice returned to Wuoth Ogik to find Ali Dida Hada singing with his arms around a giggling Akai-ma, who had politely bowed at the pair of them before going to settle his livestock, whistling. This man was a tall, dark sentinel. Steel backed. Yet there, his hands, jagged with wounding; there, colors of damp fire lurking in his eyes. Here, his heart, a tower of secrets.

Nyipir gives Ali Dida Hada a look before shuffling to sit next to his son's unfinished grave.

33

THE HOUSE CREAKS. UPSTAIRS, AJANY PEEKS INTO A ROOM FULL of books. A pale-orange triangle of light falls on two shapes. On the floor, the clay image of Hugh Bolton's face, and on the ancient couch, a sleeping man whose restlessness tosses him from left to right. She walks over to Isaiah's inert body with a Maasai blanket. Hair strands cover his forehead. She pushes them away before she covers his body with the cloth. She glances at Hugh's books on the shelf, then leaves the room, stepping over the sculpture on the floor.

Nyipir stops by the library doorway. In the dimness, he sees Hugh Bolton's head leering at him. He grabs at his palpitating heart, holding on to the doorjamb. He waits for movement or speech. Nothing happens.

He creeps into the room—he no longer feels it belongs to him—and approaches the image. Hard clay. He lifts his head to look at the sleeping Isaiah.

Blood does call to blood.

Nyipir is also thinking of Burma: his father, his brother.

Nyipir waits.

"Isaiah William?" he whispers loudly.

Isaiah sleeps.

"Isaiah," he calls.

Isaiah leaps up with a sharp intake of breath as he sees a shadow rising from the ground.

"Isaiah, it's me," Nyipir says.

"Sir?" Isaiah rubs his eyes.

"You had questions," Nyipir reminds him. "I'll answer them."

Isaiah is swaying on his feet. "Now?" The odor of fear as Nyipir approaches him. He tenses, remembering the last night he had been here.

Nyipir sighs. "Sit down." He, too, collapses on the couch, saying, "Before you speak, hear me out."

The candlelight merges their two shadows so that on the walls, they are become one humped dark form.

Nyipir starts, "One day, Isaiah, I was on a boat in the middle of our lake. I saw neither east nor west, only water. Even though I had grown up close to water, it was only then that I thought to ask how boatmen saw passages on a sheet of water. *How do you know where to go?* The boatman said, *You carry the way.* I wondered, *How can I find it?* He said I should ask my eyes to show me where to look. I thought he was joking. Ask my eyes? *How?* He laughed at me, Isaiah. Said that question revealed my dense blindness."

Isaiah shifts.

Nyipir continues: "But after he had left me on the shore, he shouted back: *Go to the beginning. Every lake holds the memory of its mother, it is to her it strives to return, imagining roads that we follow home.*"

Outside skittering, a strangled creak. Inside, silence.

Nyipir says, "Beginnings. That's why you are here."

Isaiah asks, "My father?"

"What do you see?"

"His house, his books, his art . . . his memories . . ."

Stillness

Then Nyipir says, "He is here."

More stillness.

"Can I see him?"

Silence.

Isaiah is cautious. "Is he . . ."

Nyipir says, "Hugh Bolton is dead." Pause. "Happened long ago." He stands to point out the window. "See that grave? He is there."

Isaiah had expected this. But he had also hoped. *For what?* He repeats, "Dead?"

"Dead."

"What happened?"

The look on Nyipir's face suggests bleak pasts. Half whispered, "Accident."

"How?"

"His gun." Nyipir remembers the click, boom, the scorching.

"Where?"

"Near here." *Here.*

"When?"

Like yesterday. "Before you were born."

"How do you know this?"

"I . . . found him."

"Gun accident?" Did . . . would his father . . . self-inflicted?

Nyipir touches the back of the couch, supporting himself.

Isaiah husky-voiced: "You knew my father?"

"Worked with him."

"It *was* an accident?"

No reply.

Isaiah says, "My mother should've known. She waited for him. She cried out for him before she died."

Nyipir lowers his head.

"She paid . . ." Isaiah suddenly understands that the only other person who could have paid to find Hugh would have been his stepfather, Raulfe, who needed to be a hero for Selene, and who, like everybody else, was haunted by Hugh Bolton—even if he was the beneficiary of Hugh's absence.

"You found him." Struggling for the question. "Was he . . . did you think he . . ." *Did he kill himself?* Isaiah is unable to speak the question aloud.

The sudden quiet engulfs both men. Shadows dance on the surfaces.

Isaiah says, "My father painted your wife naked."

"Yes."

"You let him?"

A small laugh. "She wasn't my wife then."

"What was she?"

"They were . . . close."

"His mistress?"

Silence.

A grim thought. "My mother didn't kill him, did she? After she found out?"

Nyipir's abrupt, "No."

"The painting . . . Was there a child?"

Silence.

Nyipir's look is gaunt. Emptied. As the candle's light stretches his shadow over the room, he now moves toward the door. "Go to your father," he tells Isaiah. "Pray for him." He ignores the cloying scent of decay, his and Hugh's.

Hugh Bolton's cairn thrusts out of the rocky earth.

Cicadas creak.

Questions that have held Isaiah's life gather under the shadow of the coral house. *Your legacy*—Isaiah watches light make patterns on the house's disintegrating walls—*I'll rebuild it for you.*

He could unearth these bones. Request an independent forensic investigation.

Hugh Bolton is dead.

Blistering tears. *Hugh,* he says. *Father,* he corrects.

This stone grave.

This sorrow.

Weeping for Selene, with Selene.

Mother. And Raulfe, the man who could never measure up to a ghost, and for the idea of his father. He could also unearth his father's bones. He could touch them and ask for answers. Hugh Bolton is dead.

34

THE LIGHT CHANGES AS ISAIAH, COUNTING STONES, SLIPS INTO
a trance next to Hugh's cairn.

Prickling of skin.

Presence behind him.

A scent familiar to him now.

Evanescence. The feel and taste and touch of her.

Inside his skin, infusing his cravings.

Her voice: "I'm so sorry."

Ajany.

Isaiah refuses to move, to speak, to act.

Her hand on his head, fingers through his hair.

He is tempted to turn, clutch her, and cry.

He turns his face aside, lets her hand hang.

A croak as he wipes his face.

Her breath.

"What did you know?" he asks.

Ajany stares at the grave. "We saw a skeleton in a red c-cave."

"We?"

"Odidi and me."

"I see. That's what you sculpt."

She averts her gaze.

"Not the skeleton."

"What, then?"

"The feeling."

Isaiah rises. He touches her face because he needs to. He lifts her face so their eyes can connect. He wants to know. "You fooled me, Arabel."

Her body quakes. "We were ch-children, Isaiah. We were so afraid."

Behind them the house's now emptied water tank groans. A piece of building crashes inside. "You hid my father from me."

"That's unfair," she stutters. "We d-didn't know who it was."

"This death is so wrong," says Isaiah.

The pieces of landscape gathered by winds tumble into their new fractured space.

Isaiah glowers.

She steps back, hands raised, turns and hurries stiffly away.

He raises his voice. "So wrong."

Isaiah returns to staring at the cairn. *I must leave.* Kalaratri, goddess of death, again. He is drained, fed up of adventures into loss. He feels his chapped lips, swollen tongue, and a heart that was now a cutting knife. As he peers into the approaching darkness, sweat trickles down his back. But then his head drops. *What am I supposed to do now?*

———

Nyipir hears the courtyard gate creak as it swings to and fro. He is sure he had closed it earlier. *Ah!*

Ali Dida Hada turns.

"Her trail is fading," Nyipir informs him. "You know how she gets lost."

Ali Dida Hada is spellbound.

Nyipir notices. "Isn't that what you've wanted?"

Ali Dida Hada hears the offer. He moves closer. "What are you saying?"

Nyipir looks at him. "She's gone. . . ."

Ali Dida Hada's heart palpitates. "So?"

Nyipir points to the ground. "Those footsteps lead her far from me." His shoulders droop. "But you can find her."

Ali Dida Hada frowns. He looks intently at the trails, hands flexing and unflexing.

There is a quiver in Nyipir's voice: "Ali ... bring me back my animals."

Ali Dida Hada waits before he nods once.

Later, Wuoth Ogik will hear a wind-borne song that is a paean to a lion rendered in a falsetto:

Yaaya Gamo
Goofare gamme dubra
Gama dubbate
Daafana lubbuuni dufte
I sing the Solitary One
glorious mane like a girl's halo,
heard roaring from afar,
makes the fearful tremble

Ali Dida Hada the predator.

Galgalu closes his eyes. The better to imbibe this melody, and to hear the textures in the voice of its singer.

———

Ajany sits with Nyipir next to Odidi's grave.

Nyipir says, "Bolton's head is in Isaiah's room."

"Yes."

"How?"

"I made it."

"How?"

"It's what I do."

A pause.

"People pay for this?"

"Sometimes."

"How do you know what to draw?"

Ajany peers at him. "I just know."

"Even Bolton?"

"Mhh."

Nyipir nods.

Two winds clash behind Ajany.

Wrestling again with a vow of silence.

Giving it up.

"B-baba, when we were children, Odidi and I . . . we went into the red cave and saw bones and a face."

Nyipir's head sinks into his chest. His breathing is a whistle.

"Didn't know." Stillness. "Were you frightened?"

"I was. Odidi wasn't."

"Takes a long time to die, *nyara*."

She shivers.

Nyipir wonders as he glances at his daughter.

"You had an uncle. His name is Theophilus, and my father, your grandfather, his name is Agoro." He smiles. "Can you *see* them?"

A dark cloud dissolves with Nyipir's soft smile.

Ajany smiles back. She says, "Tell me more."

"*Nyamrecha!*" he says. My seer.

An unknown grandfather, an uncle visible only to her father's heart. She could draw a bridge from the bottom of a precipice to higher ground. Cairns would mark the way, stones to create bridges to connect *absent* to *now*.

Waft of decay.

Nyipir shifts to look at the half-filled cairn. "We'll talk here, and work."

The grave.

"Akai-ma's not coming back."

Ajany draws lines on the soil.

"We must allow your brother his sleep."

Sound of earth shifting: digging, shovel on stone. Alternate rhythms. Ajany's and Nyipir's.

Nyipir talks about Agoro and Theophilus.

He hunts for the right words.

"My father. Strong. Large. Perhaps it was because I was a child then. Everything looks bigger when you are a child.

"My brother, so funny. Roasted birds. Would read me stories. I wanted to be him." Nyipir paused to press his hand to his chest, where there was a niggling ache. "They are still in Burma."

Digging, shoveling.

Nyipir and his daughter extend the base of a cairn that will contain Odidi's coffin.

"You didn't go to Burma?"

Nightmares.

Should he speak of nights soaked in water-urine-blood, darkness, and nothing? Could he give voice to the terror of nonexistence, darkness's invasion, how it penetrated the soul and never left?

Nyipir chooses what he will not say. "Long, long ago, I saw a young man. A catechist. He was dead." Meandering thoughts. Nyipir sees the coagulating wound that is Aloys Kamau. How it seeps, spreads, and becomes a subterranean stream of blood in Kenya, and how its tentacles reach even the newborn, and how the wound won't close until its existence is spoken aloud, but not one person dares to.

Nyipir looks closely at Ajany.

He is looking for her brother's scars.

He continues: "My turn came. Nineteen sixty-nine. When Tom died. They wanted me to drink their oath. Couldn't."

"Why?"

"Because of Aloys the Catechist."

His crushed face.

Nyipir murmurs, "Things changed. Later, couldn't remember to go to Burma."

Three days after his discharge from service, Nyipir was summoned to headquarters. There was a fractured mahogany desk in a dim rectangular room, wood soon darkened by spattered blood. Same color as if it were soaked in tears. Nyipir wept first when four men—his colleagues—held him down and his hat—he loved the hat, a fifties film star's beige hat with a black band—fell askew. One examined his teeth as if he were a cow. Another shaved off his mustache with a razor blade, cutting into his upper lip. He waited for the snap that would confirm the splitting of bones, the death of faith. He had imagined he would stand tall. Had thought he could speak tersely and clearly about the codes of decent men, of officers and citizens. Had thought he would invoke the Name of God Almighty. Had believed he was protector of country, woman, and home. But by the end of that day, he was crawling, hatless, shoeless, and his body was twisting at the end of a sharp stick. They had brought a basket of snakes into his cell; the snakes writhed but were benign. Then they had offered to find his wife, explained to him what they would do to her. Only then had he screamed.

"Akai?" said his peer, an officer who had trained with him in Kiganjo, who beat his body and toyed with his testicles.

Creeping, crawling shame. He cannot tell Ajany that he had wailed, *"Unisamehe!"* Mercy! Can't describe the ways of losing faith. Can't speak of dread when he knew he had lost control of his death. Violence had pierced his skin, broken teeth and bones, until he could tell who a person was simply by the intensity of rage in a touch.

They had pointed a gun to his head. *Click, click, click, click, click, click.* He fell, slithered on his belly like a snake. A trail of bowel-loosened muck stained his trousers, the floor. Shit, urine, sweat, blood, tears, and shame. *"Af-f-fande, n-n-naomba un-ni-nisamehe."* I beg you, forgive me. *"Nihurumie."* Have mercy.

A boyish intelligence man, there, Petrus Keah, would joke, "I mentor delinquent citizens."

Ajany sees old seasons' shadows crisscross her father's face, she watches him shiver in front of an invisible, dreadful secret.

In 1969 Petrus had bent over Nyipir. What followed was an inventory of color, sound, and pain: the on-off small red light of a lit cigarette; the on-off red light of a switch that made electricity flow. It had gone on and on, timed at two-hour intervals. Odor of terror and blood; Nyipir's urine had pooled at his feet and seeped into the concrete.

What Nyipir tells Ajany is, "Nineteen sixty-nine was a very hard year."

Violated intimacies that men freed from conscience permit themselves, knowing that shame seals secrets in. There had been no one to tell that he existed. There had been cold, reasonable voices also devoid of truth:

"You're a good man."

"Take the oath."

"For the father of your nation." The red-eyed glare of a big-faced man in a photograph, blurred when seen through Nyipir's tears as he contemplated giving his life over to a person who growled *nyoko nyoko* as he invaded even his citizens' inner spaces. *So this was nationhood? A body freed from ordeal, a soul that would have to take care of itself.* Nyipir nodded yes. He had opened his mouth to confirm his assent, but his voice screamed, *Aloys Kamau,* and afterward he could not speak.

The past is a trance.

Ajany watches fresh crevices reshape the hollows of her father's face. Tears fill them. The overflow pierces her eyes.

"*Nyara* . . ." Nyipir entreats, "don't cry. . . . You can see, your *baba* is alive."

True.

Nyipir had lived.

Nine months later, Petrus Keah had arranged Nyipir's escape. He then commanded Nyipir: *Live. Forget. The past's behind you.* Nyipir had asked, *How?* Petrus had said, *You're a man, you'll know what to do.* Nyipir had said nothing. Petrus had asked, *So, who's this Aloys Kamau?* And Nyipir said, *A catechist. He was murdered.* Petrus said, *You'd sacrifice your life for a dead preacher?* Nyipir had stared back, numb. Petrus had lit a cigarette, given it to Nyipir, who inhaled deeply. When he gave the cigarette back to Petrus, the smoke formed an arc between them. Nyipir told Petrus that he used to collect shriveled human testicles and clean up brain matter. He told Petrus that Aloys's blood and its story were written in silence. Petrus had told Nyipir, *You are mad.* Then he added, *Kenya will survive us.* Before Nyipir could reply, Petrus added, *Amnesia is also medicine.* Then he told Nyipir, *Run.* So Nyipir ran. He ran and thought about forgetfulness, and how to create it.

On an early morning after the night of a distant day, Aggrey Nyipir Oganda had lurched into Wuoth Ogik. He had shimmered like a Nilotic ghoul. When he crossed into the courtyard, he fell to the ground. Galgalu had found him, and he had screamed for Akai to hurry.

At home in Wuoth Ogik, Nyipir had sat near a fire made near the cattle enclosure, watching day become night. Akai had waited by his side, needing him to speak. He couldn't. Galgalu had scattered healing resin into the fire every hour.

A slow season during which the outside of Nyipir knit together again. A month later, at sunset, Akai led him back into the coral house.

In their room, he clung to her. Afraid of secret things. Every night, he touched the curves of his wife's body, the places he longed to know and fill again. Every night, he understood a little more that all he could do was hold her to his body. He then watched as every night shifted her body to the edge of their bed. Their quiet tears. And he could do nothing.

His hands became stronger. He practiced writing by spelling out the names of those he had seen, some of whom he had known, the ones who had once called out to him, saying, *Tell my wife, brother, son, daughter, father, mother, friend. . . .*

He kept those names until the afternoon he met the Trader.

Desperate, three months later, Nyipir had gone out to find the man who, it was said, could return a human being to something of life. While transacting a liturgy, Nyipir had given the Trader the names. In exchange, the Trader talked to the network of people who would ensure that the name *Aggrey Nyipir Oganda* would be expunged from official records. When the name had been erased, Nyipir restarted his life.

Chirping birds, warm wind. Nyipir is shivering. Ajany examines the light-shadows around him, sometimes brightening his body, sometimes coloring it.

Nyipir tries to explain the country to his daughter. He stumbles. How to say, *We've been at war since before your birth,* when the nature of this war has been its silence?

Invisibility, a perfect camouflage for truth.

Citizens blind and deaf even when they saw neighbors being hauled away, howling. Some buried bodies of mysteriously smashed-up relatives, and addressed their anguish in riddles that only archangels might decipher. Provincial officers and chiefs passed decrees in village after village: *From now on, we shall not speak of so-and-so again. Anybody who mentions this name is an enemy of our nation.* Afterward, nobody was even willing to admit that so-and-so had ever existed.

For the sake of peace.

And if I speak, may the oath kill me.

A habit that spread across the nation.

A stark blue sky.

"Will it rain?" Ajany asks, squinting. "Odidi once told me," she says, "that volcanoes explode out of the earth to shake off men's buried deeds."

Nyipir snorts a laugh.

Ajany says, "His blood was a patch on the black road."

Nyipir listens.

"I touched it. Washed it."

Quiet.

For an intense moment, coiling infernal rage. Shared bloodthirst. Then, all of a sudden, with a guttural exhale, Nyipir grunts, "Forgive."

He twitches, also startled by the word. Hears its echo again and understands that he wills a kinder life for his child; he will sunder her from dereliction.

Her whisper. "Forget?" Ajany stares at her father, her body trembling in disbelief.

A thought. *No.*

They wait.

"Forgive." His voice wilts. The burden of this choice. He arches his back. Restless, sweating, swearing, wrestling in silence. But his daughter will not bear this haunting, she will not live her brother's suffering.

Forgive. He does not say it aloud this time because of an image that entangles him: Odidi.

I will carry you. A promise to his dead. *Alone.*

Image.

His son's body disintegrating under the weight of clay, of stones. Nyipir reaches forward and scoops hard, hot, brown-red soil. Squeezes it in his hand. It crumbles. Dust.

35

ISAIAH STUMBLES OVER A CAMEL'S SKELETON. IN THE SKY, A dark cloud marches southward. Ahead, a single weaverbird waits in a laden acacia. He picks himself up, pissed off—not at falling, but at a hideous desire to return to that woman, to purge an unreacheable wound, and also to be held on to while he howled.

All of a sudden he hears his name being called: "*Isaiaaaah!*"

Malaria hallucinations? *Now I'm going crazy.*

The sound mirage becomes Ali Dida Hada.

Later, next to a cluster of mature, flowering milkweed bushes, they stare at the southern sky.

"Maybe it will rain," Ali Dida Hada says.

Isaiah is surprised. "It rains? Here?"

Ali Dida Hada nods. "Sometimes. Where're you going?"

"Don't know."

"No destination?"

Isaiah says, "Nope." Then, "Your advice?"

Ali Dida Hada gesticulates. "About what?"

"My father."

Quiet.

Then, "You want to reopen the case?"

Isaiah wipes his forehead. An exhalation: "Don't know."

Ali Dida Hada says, "Me, I'm looking for a woman."

"Good luck," mutters Isaiah.

"Come with me."

"Why?"

"She has answers. Maybe for you, too."

Roaming.

It was something to do.

Isaiah turns.

They walk the rest of the night, until dawn unveils a kingdom of cairns, one with a headstone, ring graves, stone-encrusted spots. Stepping on ancestral bones and ancient fishes. Blend of heat and scenery encircled by waltzing shadows. In between, scraps of bush, mountains, and dik-diks.

Ali Dida Hada examines the frugal ground.

Isaiah asks, "Where are we?"

"Not so far from Sibiloi."

Isaiah dredges up images of water, while above, egrets fly in formation on a detour to the Kokoi watering hole. Later, bent-over, ramshackle cottages.

From invisible hubs, Arwyn's "Benedictus" echoes.

Surreal disbelief. "Rejoice," murmurs Isaiah.

They have reached a rusting missionary outstation.

Two grizzled nuns walk up to meet the pair; the nuns are leather-skinned die-hards with Jesus sandals who wield large wooden rosaries.

"Can we help?"

Ali Dida Hada makes introductions: "Assistant Commissioner of Police Ali Dida Hada. This one is Mr. Isaiah Bolton."

"From?"

"Kalacha."

"Chasing cattle?" A glance at Isaiah.

"Yes."

A penetrating stare. "I assume you're hungry and looking for a place to stay?"

Ali Dida Hada stands at attention. "Correct, madam."

"How many days?"

"One."

"Mhh! I'm Sister Catherine."

"A pleasure."

Isaiah follows silently.

Later.

After meditations under a kerosene lamp, seven nuns and three aides examine the visitors to the tune of Álvarez's "Plegaria" while they eat scrambled eggs and rice and a dark-green bitter-salty vegetable. Soft murmurs. Lilt in speech. Four of the nuns are Irish. Two are from the Philippines, the other a local, from Marsabit.

All of a sudden Isaiah starts to cough laughter. Ali Dida Hada nudges him. Isaiah leans over his plate, struggling with the juxtaposition of Álvarez, a woman whose face was the dusky-hued version of Vermeer's *Girl with a Pearl Earring*, Irish prayers, Filipino lilts, and two unwashed male travelers eating sensible scrambled eggs in a dark, arid landscape tormented by moaning winds. Tears from suffocated mirth flavor Isaiah's meal.

Later.

A tiny, clear-eyed nun with freckles says, "Next to the corral, there's a small room. Good for two. Someone will bring water. Use a cup to wash. At dusk, join our prayers. Then breakfast. God bless."

Isaiah and Ali Dida Hada cross the short distance to their room across a pathway lit by fireflies. The wind lowers its tone. And then, in this derelict place, a cold and fearful stone, a decrepit resident of Isaiah's soul, crumbles.

In his safari bed, listening to Isaiah's snoring, Ali Dida Hada, grateful for the presence of another human being, crosses his arms behind his head and looks into a place in his being where Akai Lokorijom has lived from the day he first saw her. He examines its contours and how it has formed him.

36

GALGALU IS SWATTING FLIES BUZZING OVER MEAT HE BARTERED
for honey when the drone of a laboring engine scatters his attention.
Few cars ever drive into Wuoth Ogik. And when they do, it is usually
someone who is lost.

A dark-green Land Rover with government number plates stops at
the gate. A man in a dark-blue suit jumps down. With the sun glancing
off his shiny Italian shoes, he strolls over and stops next to the courtyard
fence. Standing with his legs apart, he surveys everything.

When Ajany recognizes him, she ducks. She is sure that Isaiah has
officially accused the Oganda family of his father's murder. Grief. It
bothers her that this should matter.

Nyipir turns.

Stares.

Hands clinging to the handle of his walking stick, Nyipir limps
unsteadily toward the man. It takes him six seconds to toss away the
stick, and another five to rush the man and pound on every accessible
part of his body.

The visitor rolls in the dust. "*Msee*," he cajoles, "is that how to greet
a lost brother?"

Petrus Keah has come to Wuoth Ogik.

A brown bird squeals past them. Petrus narrows his eyes, adjusting his bifocals. Nyipir sweats, breathing heavily. Petrus lies on his back to consider the sky. "About the boy . . . we were betrayed," he explains, watching for Nyipir's hands. "I was late." A grunt. "But we've taken care of it." Rising, he scans the ranch, tilts his head at the crumbling house. "This is Wuoth Ogik?"

Nyipir looks at Odidi's cairn. "What you've said has not caused a resurrection."

Petrus flinches. "It's hot." He tears off his coat. "I am on a *mison* to the *mison*. Some American prayer people were supposed to have reported to their embassy five days ago. I'm here to find them and the terrorists they've spotted."

Nyipir scoffs: "A junior officer's job?"

Petrus lifts his head. "*Msee,* you underestimate its difficulty. I was heading up here anyway."

"To see me?"

"Yes. And Ali Dida Hada. Where is he? He's signed over all his bank accounts to me. Has he killed himself?"

"You've come to save a life?" Nyipir's brows rise and almost touch his scalp.

Petrus grins. "Yes."

Nyipir snarls in Luo, *"I jajuok?"*

He scoops up dirt to throw at Petrus. "Murderer!"

Petrus dodges.

Ajany has picked up a stick to wield against the invader. Galgalu circles.

Petrus, his hands raised, says, "Before you grind me into flour . . . I've a message from Odidi."

Ajany rolls her eyes, steps closer.

Petrus continues, "I was with him. He was alive when I got to him."

Nyipir stops.

"Mos, jaduong. Mos." So sorry, Petrus says. "Here, for you . . ." He digs into his coat pocket and plucks out a pile of banknotes.

Nyipir addresses the earth. "You kill everything. This was my only son." He reaches Petrus, rears up, pulls back his fist, and slams it into Petrus's face. "You kill everything!"

Petrus steadies himself, the money scattered around him. His lip bleeds. A grunt. "That, *msee,* is the last time. Next time I *soot.*"

Nyipir bows, winded.

Petrus moves, touches his wrist. *"Wuod loka,* we're too old for this. I *was* there with the boy. Before . . . before he went. I talked to him, I held him like this." Petrus cradles Nyipir's hand. "He thought I was you. A brave boy."

Nyipir shakes himself loose.

Petrus continues: "That day Oganda, I, too, found a son."

Ajany hears. Remembers the hardness of tarmac. The warmth it retained. "You were with my brother?"

"Yes."

She drops her guard.

Nyipir replies, "I've heard you. Now go." He shuffles past Petrus and reaches for his fallen walking stick.

Petrus stretches out a hand.

Nyipir stares at his own gnarled fingers.

Thwack!

Petrus's buttocks hit the ground, and he clutches his head.

"*Aiee!* This is really the last time, Oganda. What are you angry about? Nineteen sixty-nine? If I'd done less, they'd have killed you," Petrus yells. "You *sould* thank me. A stick like that can break a skull. You *sould* thank me, not try to kill me."

"Why?" yells Nyipir. An over-forty-year-old question explodes: "Did I submit to your filthy covenant?"

Petrus gets up with care, brushing his trousers.

"And if you had?"

Nyipir's voice is hoarse. "Did I?"

"No." Petrus shakes his head. "Another did."

"In my name?"

Petrus lowers his head.

Nyipir asks, "Who?"

"You want to know?"

Nyipir glowers.

"He died."

"Who?"

"He was with you."

Nyipir scans his still-grieving memory. "There were many—who?"

"Tap. Tap. Tap."

Nyipir frowns, gathering strands of memory. "His name?"

Petrus had always erased the memory of names. "Tap, tap, tap," he answers.

"Who?"

"Don't remember."

"Why?"

For Petrus, names are bothersome. "Does it matter?"

Nyipir spits out his *yes.*

Low-voiced, Petrus says, "You're alive. He's not."

Petrus had driven the man, a former professor, who had been brain-damaged, into a large farm where a hard-eyed woman in animal skin administered a stinking, bloody concoction, the vile sacrament of the oath, to men, women, and children. The man muddled through words he did not know, chewed on substances he thought was food, and sealed his will in this covenant. After this, Petrus had registered the poor man as "Aggrey N. Oganda." He had received his release-from-detention papers at once. Petrus had held on to the documents for him. But when a consignment of souls was carted away in a Black Maria, to be delivered to another farm with large sulfuric acid and lime pits, the former professor was on board.

"Going home," Petrus had explained to the man.

"Dala!" The man had grinned when he was lifted into the vehicle. "Bye-bye."

Petrus had waited for three days before presenting the letters of release to the state dungeon keepers and suggested that the highest authorities were waiting for Aggrey Nyipir Oganda. In less than an hour, Nyipir had been hustled into a hired car. Petrus drove off, speeding out of Nairobi.

Petrus stabs at his eyes to explain to himself to Nyipir: "My loyalty was always under judgment."

His name, Keah, derived by his father from the acronym for the King's African Rifles—KAR—blurred access to place of origin. Petrus was hard to place. There were Keahs of every Kenyan ethnicity. Petrus had been born in Nairobi. In the blood-hunt season of 1969, "Tribe Unknown" was a lucky thing to be. But Nyipir had been handed over to him as a temptation and an exam.

Petrus studies his shoes. "Bad times, Oganda. Had to toughen you up. A chance to live." *By the time I am through with you, you'll become another. You'll become mad and strong. You will live.*

Nyipir asks, "Why me, Keah?"

"A picture."

"A picture."

"Inside your file. A photo of you carrying the Kenyan flag on a black horse."

Nyipir frowns.

Petrus continues: "You and the horse are—*were*—my Kenya."

Nyipir wrestles a tidal flow of memory, his first contact with Petrus in the interrogation rooms. Petrus had made it a boxing match.

"Cowards run from hard touch." Petrus fists had been up. "Am I your enemy? When confronting an enemy, truth is in the fight. Blood must be spilled. Hands up!"

A blow had fractured Nyipir's jaw.

He had fallen.

"Get up!" Petrus had screamed.

"Read your enemy's eyes. Truth sets free." A blow to Nyipir's solar plexus. Nyipir had tumbled to the ground, gasping.

"Pay attention! Up!"

Nyipir, blinded, had got to his knees; scrambling about and with indifference, had thrown a punch that landed just above Petrus's boot.

Petrus had laughed. "A bull is wounded a little to give its killer advantage, but sometimes even the bull can win." He had helped Nyipir up and tried to whisper a message: "Take the oath. Go home to Akai, your wife."

Nyipir remembers how the blood from his head had blinded him, the soft swollenness of his head. "Aloys," he had spat.

Petrus, who had not heard of Aloys Kamau, had snarled, "Why sing the songs of those who can't even say your name?"

"I brought you home," Petrus now whispers.

Petrus had driven Nyipir as close to Kalacha Goda as possible. Maikona. Petrus dragged a catatonic Nyipir out of the car and said, "Live. Forget." He would not see Nyipir again until the day in late 2006 when Nyipir came to beg him to find Odidi and save his life.

Doum palms rattle in Wuoth Ogik. Inside the house, a split tank groans, and the back wall breaks. Outside, Nyipir's voice is amused. "Now I should thank you, Keah?"

"Yes."

"No." Nyipir pokes at the ground. He says, "History professor. Married to Nadezhda Grigorieva. His name, Ochieng Andronico, *wuod* Seme."

Petrus shivers, "Who?"

"The code tapper. He had a name."

Drifting white streaks cover the sky above.

Then, "I see. The boy?"

Nyipir stares at Petrus before pointing at Odidi's cairn, "He's there."

———

They all stand around Odidi's cairn. Petrus embarks on an extravagant prayer: *"Ah! Obongo Ruoth Nyasaye Nyakalaga, wuon polo kod piny, Nyasach oganda"*—O great, omnipresent, and omnipotent Governor of the heavens and earth, God of humanity . . . Petrus does not finish. He is whimpering. The sound releases what has been blocked within Nyipir.

The weight and curse of holding Kenya up for his children, his fear of Akai's fears. His questions converge in a howl that twists his body. But before Nyipir can disintegrate, Petrus gathers him up. He holds Nyipir. A trick of light makes Petrus's tears look like blood, which stains Nyipir's collar.

Ajany sobs dry tears, clutching her body. She spins away, racing to exhaust herself. Galgalu scuffs his feet. *Tears are rain. They water soil. Restore life.* Galgalu thinks he will light the lanterns early today.

The next morning, Petrus Keah leaves, with Galgalu as his guide, to go to the American mission. He leaves with Ajany's old AK-47.

37

NYIPIR IS USING STONES AND STICKS TO SHOW AJANY HOW, IN 1956, the year Kenya competed in the Olympics for the first time, he laid out Hugh Bolton's forks, knives, and spoons. "The government got tired of him, and he was annoyed with them. He said they were selling Kenya to murderers. He shouted at them until the day he was told to plan for security north of the Ewaso Nyiro River, in the Northern Frontier District."

"They expect me to refuse and resign, boy," Hugh had told Nyipir, "but I shan't, the buggers."

Nyipir remembers.

"Our lorry fell into a gully near Marigat. Did Bwana Bolton say, 'Go back'?" No. He said, 'We walk,' so we walked."

"You walked?" she asks her father.

"A long, long time."

Ajany sketches Hugh Bolton, trying to find Akai-ma in what Nyipir does not say.

Nyipir speaks of counting every twenty-third shilling he earned each month as servant and serviceman: "Money for Burma."

She glances at Baba, hand propping her chin.

"Burma," Nyipir repeats, seeing again a cold long-ago night when, mid-sleep, he heard a lake moaning for its mother, the Nile. All those years ago, he and Hugh had flailed through seven walls of heat, seen mirages for four days. Like every other outsider, Nyipir had been tempted by and tasted Anam Ka'alakol's waters. Lake Rudolf. Hugh had kicked small stones and sand into the water after he had spat out the soapy, brackish water. They had made camp there, exhausted.

A pause. "I told Baba and Theo, *I'm coming to Burma for you.*"

Nyipir had also told Anam Ka'alakol, the immense lake, that he would take her message of longing to the Nile, and promised to return with an answer.

Nyipir shuffles off toward Hugh Bolton's cairn.

He had gone neither to Burma nor to the Nile. He reads the dry land. He *had* walked past brown-and-gray elongated, treeless, desiccated, moonscape, mudflats, sweltering, *you-are-not-a-man-until-you-have-crossed* Suguta Valley. It had been greener then. Animals everywhere. Elephants. But he had gone neither to Burma nor to the Nile.

Nyipir leans over Hugh's cairn. Remembers how, in their wanderings, they had found a man lying on a stone grave who neither spoke nor responded to Hugh's haranguing in bad Kiswahili, *"Kijana utasimama sasa hivi ni nini unafanyikana hapa?"* What exactly is happening here?

Later, through a Somali trader, by way of gestured conversation, they heard that the grave hosted the man's Didinga wife.

They had bartered dried meat for a knife.

Steel plate for water and fermented milk.

In the evening, while setting out the service for Hugh's bush dinner, Nyipir saw Hugh painting the story of a man and his buried wife.

They would hunt antelopes, dik-diks, gerenuk, and oryx for food. Hugh found Abyssinian iconography and thought he had invented it. He wrote out their journey—places, facts, figures—and drew shapes on a rolled-up sheet, counted cairns, and noted a heading in his red notebook, *Vitu vishenzi*. Vile Things. These included wolf spiders, unmade camp beds, lukewarm tea, a raging bull elephant, Hugh's broken toenail, and his swelling foot—and Nyipir's applying too hot a compress to that foot. *"Umefanya kitu kishenzi!"* bellowed Hugh.

Other *vitu vishenzi*: mosquitoes and tsetse flies. *Watu washenzi.* Nairobi headquarters. Mau Mau. Colonial District Officers. Men who walked naked. Adorned women who hunted like men. Oftentimes,

Nyipir's ancestors, the Kenya Colony government, the Suez Crisis, and the Northern Frontier District were afflicted with *afya na roho kishenzi*.

Nyipir limps to the falling gate, standing on the boundaries between here and there. Why hadn't he gone yet to either Burma or the Nile?

Ajany sketches Nyipir's restlessness.

"Wuoth Ogik?" Ajany's voice follows Nyipir.

Nyipir shakes himself alert.

"Many, many days later, we made camp near a large termite mound in a corner of the Koroli springs."

Memory of ruffling winds, doum palms simulating ocean waves. A prismlike dawn and the chirping of assorted birds. A male oryx beside Hugh and Nyipir, more curious than afraid: a pale-gray compact body, clipped mane, and horse's tail, black-and-white clown-mask face.

Nyipir explains that Hugh had drawn the plans for a house in the dust, his fingers scraping the ground until they bled.

"Akai-ma?" Ajany asks.

"Wait." Nyipir suddenly smiles. "She's on her way."

Almost fifty years ago, an ebony-hued woman, as slender as the leaves of the mwangati tree, whose long, long neck was adorned with wire coils lifted off of telegraph cables, shimmered into view from across a brackish oasis. When she had waved long arms at Nyipir, who was leaning against a tree guarding Hugh, he was sure he had fallen asleep and was experiencing a revelation. When she hailed him in a low, laughing voice, Nyipir had known who she would be to him.

But Akai's gaze had moved to Hugh. Her head tilted at the sight of the pale, wiry, naked man scooping black mud and rubbing it into his face. She had stooped to laugh, holding on to her sides, and the sound had exploded light into the existence of two different men who had been lonely in their own ways until then.

Two horses and three small-bodied Rendille camels watched, their noses half in and half out of water. Akai's laughter invited everything to play. Nyipir waved her away, urged her to run off, certain he would follow her. Hugh, in the watering hole, huffed when he saw her.

Akai preempted Hugh's snarl. "What's your name, mister?" Guffawing, she pointed at his mud-encrusted face.

Hugh had straightened up from the water hole, hand in front of his balls, swiveled his head to locate Nyipir, and bellowed, *"Kijana, wapi ule mtu kishenzi? Lete hile towel haraka!"* Fetch a towel at once, boy!

Nyipir was underwater, suffocating because meaning had all of a sudden condensed into the girl in front of them. Cat-eyed sparkle, thin arms reaching toward the wrong man. Hugh gasped when the girl kicked off her shoes. Nyipir knew what would happen next, and he howled at Akai, flapping his arms to prevent it. "Go! Go! *Tokaaa!*" To Hugh, a command, "We go now, *bwana.* This is not good."

Hugh heard Nyipir. Knew his fear, and knowledge became malice.

Nyipir had prayed as Akai jumped into the watering hole and splashed muddy water onto Hugh's face. He grunted when Hugh reached forward to drag the girl to himself.

Akai came to stay. Five months later, the frame of Hugh's new house was ready. Breakfast at the site, close to the fraying tents. Nyipir had been standing behind Hugh, who was sipping black Ceylon tea.

Hugh had asked, *"Kijana, utatumia neno gani kwa lugha yako kuhusu nyumba mpya? Neno sio kishenzi."* What word can be used to name this home? Something civilized.

Nyipir, weary of the three and a half years of seeking, recording, decamping, traveling, and plotting new journeys said, "Wuoth Ogik?" He was being sarcastic.

"Na maana yake ni nini, kijana, ongeza chai?" What does it mean, boy, more tea?

"The journey ends." Nyipir had tilted the teapot into the proffered cup.

Hugh slurped the beverage. He rocked in the safari chair. "Damn good. Bleddy good. Write it out, lad, good lad."

Exactly seven months later, the Kalasinga foreman gave Hugh the hammer that would pound the last nail in a house made of desert stone, coral, crushed obsidian, termite soil, doum palm, rods, acacia trunks, and a sprinkling of cement. Above the door to an inner room with deep-set windows and a curvy roof, a workman etched the *bibas* in *Non draco sit mihi dux / Vade retro satana.* . . . Hugh smirked. "Get thee behind me, Satan."

Nyipir had asked, *"Bwana,* this says what?"

"Live-in exorcism . . . A joke, lad."

Nyipir cleared his throat. "When Madam Bolton comes, what happens to . . ."

Hugh rounded on Nyipir, face red, ginger hair disheveled, and through gritted teeth ground out, "*Mtu kishenzi*, sweep the veranda, *mara moja*."

That was then.

Silence now.

His daughter would never hear about the nightmare of a returned, wet-eyed, frantic, and newly damaged woman with a look of such death that Nyipir, without thought, threw his fate and destiny into her hell, even if it meant his damnation. Which it did. Nyipir fights his way back into the present. Something is stuck in his throat. He hurries away as he clears his throat over and over again. Thinking that, after all this time, he had neither gone to Burma nor visited the Nile.

38

A GOVERNMENT LAND ROVER LEAPS OVER BLACK ROCKS. A DOLE-
ful Galgalu sits next to Petrus, clutching the dashboard and reflecting on
life, annoyance, and his companion. He misses the livestock, traveling
with them, watching over them while they browsed. He misses the honeyguides that led him to the best honey, the honey he kept for himself.
Inundated, Galgalu touches the amethyst.

Petrus says, "Tell me more about yourself."

Right now Galgalu longs for silence.

Petrus turns. "You're comfortable?"

Galgalu stares out the window.

Petrus says, "*Eh!* This is a big land."

They drive ten minutes.

Petrus says in Kiswahili, "So—where's *your* family?"

Galgalu scowls. "Far."

"*Ehe?*" Petrus prompts, chewing on his unlit cigarette.

Galgalu lifts his left tire sandal to pull out pebbles. He leans out the
window, clears his sinuses, and blows the mucus from his nose.

Petrus grunts. "Don't do that in my car."

Galgalu looks at Petrus's suit, feels the heat. *Maybe God in His kindness will stew Petrus to death.* Galgalu smiles.

. . .

Midmorning, the car rumbles to a hasty stop, throwing dust and pebbles around. Galgalu's head hits the window. He turns to ask, *What?* And sees a man lying on the track. Petrus throws the door open and rushes over to the prone figure, who is holding on to his stomach. The ground around him is soaked. Next to him a murmuring radio offers a BBC World service signal.

A tremor in Galgalu's tone: "The Trader!"

Petrus squats close to the man. "What's happened?"

The Trader groans, "Galgaluuu! I dreamed you."

Galgalu sees what the Trader is holding on to, and blood rushes from his head. Faintness.

The Trader coughs. "Man, could you help put these things away?" His intestines are hanging out.

Soft-voiced, Petrus asks again, "What happened?" He returns to the car to re-emerge with a large, stained beige cloth, which he stretches on the ground. To Galgalu: "You! We lift him, move him into the car."

Galgalu wipes his mouth.

The Trader mumbles and coughs out phlegm. "The radio . . ."

Galgalu shuts his eyes. They lift the Trader into the car. Galgalu picks up and wipes the little radio, turns off the dial. Silence.

Galgalu says, "We're going to the mission."

The Trader says, "God and I are at peace."

"OK," says Petrus. Delirium, he concludes.

They turn the car south and set off again. The sun is high and hot. They race past a troop of baboons, the alpha male muscular, yellow-eyed, and shrewd; his troop look dried up and depressed by the heat. The Trader's voice from the backseat: "You'll find some changes at the mission."

Galgalu wonders at his tone.

They drive for another two hours. A signboard: *Light to the Nations Mission.* A termite mound outside the mission's fence has erupted with what might be read as a rude middle finger extended skyward.

Petrus switches off the car engine. Another board reads: *Light to the Nations Medical Center.* Behind that, a fenced compound with a solar-powered electrical fence. The drone of flies sounds like an electric razor. Petrus jumps out. Galgalu opens the car's back door. They lift the

Trader on the sheet, tuck his radio next to him, and carry him into the clinic.

The wind. Its empty moans. Buzzing flies. Pervading silence. The smell of smoke.

Dripping sounds within.

Unease.

The room is empty. Soot on some walls, ward beds unmade, bedpans overturned. A sinking sensation. Petrus looks at Galgalu. The Trader watches them both. Petrus asks, his face somber, "Where are the missionaries?"

The Trader giggles.

Petrus turns to study him. *Changes at the mission.* Petrus asks, "What do you know?"

"Heard something."

"Heard what?"

"You'll see."

Petrus tells Galgalu, "Wait here," and disappears through the small side gate that leads into the hanging flower garden and the house. Closed door. He knocks, waits, and then kicks the door ajar. On the clay steps leading to the door rests a new AK-47, its muzzle pointing red toward the door, its cartridges scattered, and the wall poked with bullet holes. The dripping sound seems to increase. Petrus moves toward the kitchen.

There, he sees the first corpse.

He counts the others. *What is the last shape a human being holds before death?* The question clears his mind. A black pocket Bible rests next to Pastor Jacobs. Bloody fingerprints. Petrus crouches, picks it up, wipes the blood with his hand, turns the pages, and reads: *"Since Joseph was of the house and family of David he went up from Nazareth. . . ."* He closes it and slips it into his shirt pocket, staining the shirt with blood. He picks up the AK-47, surveys the room. Steps to the entrance of a kitchen, a large, striped cat on its side, eyes staring. Stillness. What's that color? Tortoiseshell? Who would shoot an innocent cat? A tremor starts in his bones.

Meanwhile, Galgalu cleans the Trader's wounds, sprinkles a disinfecting powder in and around the opening. He wraps the Trader's stomach with bandages dragged off shelves. He looks around for anything else that might help. Galgalu tries to shake off a heaviness that is invading his body and making him drowsy. A no-name feeling.

The Trader swallows down a handful of colorful painkillers.

They wait.

Petrus reappears, waits at the door with the rifle, points at the Trader without looking at him, focuses on Galgalu, and indicates *out* with his other thumb. "Wait in the car." His voice is hard; his eyes are dark and dead.

The Trader reaches for Galgalu's fingers. "Stay!"

Galgalu wrenches free and dashes out, stumbling on debris. Things clatter and roll. He runs from the dreadful thing that Petrus had become, and the ugliness that had just looked at him from the Trader's eyes. Galgalu wavers, stares at the open door of the main house, past the pink and purple African violets hanging from white-painted rectangular buckets. The bad feeling stems from whatever is in there. He runs as if something large and fierce is after him.

Galgalu recites, "*La illaha illa 'lla Hu. La illaha illa 'lla Hu.*"

The Trader turns to Petrus, who has lifted the AK-47.

"*Ni yako?*" Yours? Petrus asks.

"In a way."

"*Wacha kunichezea akili.*" Don't mess with me.

"Same source as yours."

"Oganda?"

The Trader raises his brows—up, down; up, down.

"He knows about this?" Petrus's voice is high-pitched.

"Naw."

Petrus rasps, eyes dark. "How did the children offend you?" A vision of chaos. Petrus's head throbs, his joints ache; tiredness coagulates into a moment filled with buzzing flies.

The Trader's eyes are soft. "Didn't mean it. Then I thought, 'one for every one of mine.'"

The sun lightens the brown of the medicine bottles and throws a tainted shadow on the ground. "Why were they here?" The Trader sobs. "What are they doing here? This isn't their home."

"You should've asked them."

"I did."

Petrus shivers. Listening. *Playing life-death. All of them. With shadows.* Their reflections on shards of glass.

The Trader says, "My trade in secrets."

"So?" Petrus asks.

"The world still craves my existence."

Petrus's laugh is bereft of noise. "Yours and mine."

The Trader smiles. "Your name?"

"Does it matter?"

"I'll tell you things about yourself. Name?" A challenge.

"Keah. Petrus."

"The warlord?"

"Meaning?"

"Kenyan interrogation squad, 1968 to 1989, 1982. Your works include Nyipir Oganda."

Petrus stares.

The Trader notes, "Your gun is trembling."

Petrus lowers the gun against his thigh, observes his shaking hand. Outside, the call of ibis. Petrus digs for a cigarette to chew on.

Tears in the Trader's eyes. "Nineteen eighty-four."

"What about it?" Petrus voice cracks.

"The blood at Wagalla is not dry."

"So?"

"I saw."

"So?" Petrus's voice is thin.

"I saw you."

Petrus shuts his eyes. A 1984 northern-frontier security operation had gone out of control. Five thousand corpses later, he had been summoned to help clean things up. He had overseen the washing of the blood-spattered Wagalla runway, had arranged burials in secret sites, had terrorized would-be witnesses into what should have been eternal silences.

"My job," Petrus snarled. "Where are the other patients?"

The Trader sniggers. "Bullet-created miracles. The dying rose, life restored." The Trader squints at Petrus. "Cigarette?"

"Smoking kills."

"Light me one."

Petrus's match flares over the end of a cigarette. He almost inhales. With reluctance, he relinquishes the stick to the Trader, who immediately says, "John 3:16."

Petrus tilts his head.

The Trader says, "*Yalahi!* I asked Pastor to forgive me for what I was thinking."

"And?"

The Trader turns. "A very rude man."

Flies are filling the room.

Petrus asks, "Your belly?"

"The gentle Mrs. Jacobs. Kitchen knife."

Petrus says without zeal, "Good."

"John 3:16."

Petrus frowns. His head and joints ache. "The cat?"

"Ricochet."

"All this death."

Myriad other faces stare at Petrus, bloody shadows crawling from the past through cracks to be with him. Petrus focuses hard on the man lying broken on the bed.

The Trader says, "Correction: all this sacrifice."

"Sacrifice?"

"Ya ibada." For the liturgy.

"What?"

"You know. The liturgy that feeds nations. You're one of its slaughtering priests." Short laughter. Then a look. "Wanted to stop. Tried. Couldn't."

"You *carried in* an assault rifle." Petrus's voice is strained.

"To threaten." Murmurs, "Only threaten. Wanted to stop, *haki* . . ." The Trader allows a grimacing *"Ratatata . . .* something takes over." He exhales smoke.

Silence.

Petrus watches the flaring red end. "So—what's your death for?" he asks.

Smoke rings. "I choose one star to give it to." A snort. "You'd say *country.*"

Petrus blinks. It was true.

The Trader asks, "Intelligence?"

"Mhh."

"Ghana-trained," says the Trader. "First car, Renault Roho."

"How do you know?"

"A patriot." A giggle. "My advice? Find another god to serve."

"Kenya's my father's patrimony." A pause. "Trade unionist, like Mboya. Mombasa. Hung by the Crown. Died for this country. Yes, I'm a patriot."

The Trader wheezes, "Nobody remembers him, intelligence man.

Your country pumps biogas into other balloon ghosts to elevate and worship, *thee-thee-thee!*"

Sheen on Petrus's upper lip.

The Trader looks at his radio. He murmurs, "What to do about the world."

Petrus grinds out, "What does it need?"

"Memory loss." The Trader turns to Petrus, his face sunken. "Like me."

Petrus sets his rifle's sights, adjusts the elevation until the Trader is perfectly framed.

———

Wind flings dust. Heat boils Galgalu's body. Several heartbeats later, an explosion. Then three more in succession. The wind snatches the fireball and scatters the flames across the land. Galgalu runs out of the car. Dashes to and fro. Stops.

What a willful presence is fire. It disarrays the terrain.

Petrus reappears, the rifle dangling from his left hand. It is a little past noon, and time is an intense blue. Petrus asks, "You know where the Trader lives?"

Galgalu points northward.

They drive off.

The fire behind them falls upon life, a maniacal omnipresence.

Before the last light of day, they enter the Trader's homestead. Petrus hurries into the compound, knocking things down, kicking objects in all directions. He breaks down the flimsy entrance and from within comes the *clang-bang-tumble* of a *tukul* being ransacked. Scent of coffee blends. Galgalu follows. Petrus reaches into the roof, pulls out sealed packages. Freedom in chaos. Together, they pulverize things, they eradicate proof of existence. Galgalu—lost to the frenzied clearing, gasping, hungering, strong beyond his previous knowledge—uses his bare hands to break a wooden Lamu chest. They empty the Land Rover's three jerricans of petrol in and around the *tukul*. Galgalu is aroused after Petrus tosses three matches on the ground and fire explodes. He is ashamed, but only for a second. He laughs out loud.

Three hours later, a high-keening *d'abeela* creeps into the Trader's emptied compound. He stamps out the lingering flames. Wipes his eyes. He sniffs burned coffee remnants. Plowing through the Trader's goods, he salvages a charred guitar.

———

Galgalu says, "There was a fire; it ate everything."

Nyipir asks, "Yes?"

"Even the Trader."

"You saw him?"

"No."

"He'll return," Nyipir replies.

"I tell you, there was a fire," explains Galgalu.

Petrus Keah shivers and sweats in Nyipir's bed under the spell of malaria. His cells suffocate under a concoction made of neem and baobab and crushed roots, which Galgalu ladles down his throat. Malaria's hallucinations parade in Petrus's being, and it becomes normal for Wuoth Ogik to be shaken by his shrieks.

Tending to Petrus gives them something to do. And when his fever breaks, it is as if a soft and tender wind has visited Wuoth Ogik.

———

Petrus has taken to sitting on Odidi's cairn to watch the land. A state of partial dress—shirt buttons undone, hair uncombed, Nyipir's tyre sandals on his feet. He smiles at stones, trees, insects, birds, at clouds and at the sun. At intermittent moments his shoulders move like pistons for no clear reason. Unseen by Petrus, Ajany sketches a hazy impression of him. Galgalu crouches next to her, studying Petrus.

Ajany purses her lips. "What's he laughing at?

Galgalu suggests, "It's malaria."

He adds, voice low, "There was a fire. It left nothing. Even the Trader's gone."

Ajany tilts her green-tinged image of Petrus.

Galgalu touches it. "What else can you see?"

They watch Petrus.

Ajany's hand starts to draw outward. Lines, curves, dips, and contours become a likeness of Isaiah. Ajany sees what she has done. She stops. Galgalu watches as she scribbles the image away until there is only a dark blob on the paper. She tears out and scrunches up the paper. Galgalu hears Petrus laugh. He also remembers the fire, that it ate everything.

Nyipir sidles up to Petrus, holding two tin mugs of spiced coffee. Handing Petrus one, he asks, *"Inyiero?"* Laughter?

Nyipir stoops, scanning Petrus for evidence of lunacy.

"Life," Petrus answers. Petrus says, "Life is presence."

"Yes?"

Petrus says, "You saved me."

"You may thank me," Nyipir replies.

"But I won't, *msee.*"

Nyipir sips his coffee.

They both study the land.

What accounts for your life? Petrus asks passing clouds in his thoughts. He lowers his cup, digs out his cigarette packet, unwraps the single cigarette, sniffs it, and with a small twitch dangles it on the tip of his lips.

Nyipir steps closer to Petrus, opening his mouth to ask, *On what side of the oath do you stand?* He closes it.

Petrus then tilts his head away from the sun's glare.

He pauses mid-movement, gaze trapped by the shape of Nyipir's left hand, the twisted fingers, the protruding, black stumpy-nailed thumb. In slow motion, he raises his right hand and watches as his fingers wrap around Nyipir's hand.

Nyipir jerks backward.

Eyes wet, he faces eastward.

A hesitation.

But then his hand closes over Petrus's.

The day's hard light toasts their skin. Petrus chews hard on his cigarette end. Fresh wrinkles wreathe his face. His unlit cigarette falls and, like soft November rain beginning to fall, his tears create an inkblot on the earth's surface.

. . .

Later.

"I'm wondering," Nyipir says as he watches the regress of a column of safari ants. "Mandalay, 21° 59′ N 96° 6′ E, Rangoon, 16° 47′ N 96° 9′ E."

"Yes?" Petrus rubs his spectacles.

"Burma."

"Myanmar, *osiepna*. And Rangoon is *Yangon*."

"So my daughter says. She's very clever."

Petrus squints at the light on faraway mountains.

Nyipir says, "A place to see. Burma."

Three pairs of ibis squawk their way home. Petrus studies their flight route. Dropping rules. Escaping dutifulness, he grabs at the offer of a trail of friendship. Atonement? His eyes pop, lift, and meet thick brows. *"Msee,"* Petrus asks, surrendering to his craving, "do you have fire to lend me?"

Unknown and unseen wanderers have added stones to Wuoth Ogik's new graves. Nyipir counts these, seven. He also counts the cigarettes he and Petrus have shared in life. This last one was their second.

39

WATERING HOLES ARE LITTERED WITH MEMORY CIPHERS. CATtle bones—casualties of past droughts, a prevailing north wind. Ali Dida Hada asks after a red dance-ox. Wanderers tell him where they have seen it, marveled at its trained, polished horns, lofty temperament, and majestic amble. Following the trail, he and Isaiah reach a cross-shaped boulder in a wadi.

A pale tree stump, dry and carved by water, leached by sun, warped into a humanlike face with its nose pointing north in the direction of the water's flow. Its shorn branches point skyward. Ali Dida Hada strokes the bark. He rocks it until the loam loosens. Above, sulky clouds approach in phalanx. Ali Dida Hada murmurs, "Rain." The tree stump rolls forward. "It'll flow." He watches the wind bend the low-lying, yellowed grass.

Isaiah and Ali Dida Hada hike northward. Silent men, in the moment, in their thoughts. A *whooooo* sound stops them five hours later. A shared grin. The scent of water. The angle leaves a view of wavelets on a recently formed temporary lake, child of a flash flood. The land has split into two. The animal tracks they were following end there. Assorted birds balance on reedlike shrubs. Not yet dusk.

"So?" Isaiah asks, considering the water.

Ali Dida Hada strips off his clothes and slides into the water.

Isaiah tugs at his shoes, preparing to follow.

Ali Dida Hada says, "Crocodiles here. Small ones."

"You're joking?" Isaiah shouts.

Ali Dida Hada snorts.

"I'll build a grave of stones for your remains," Isaiah proposes, wading on the muddy shore, examining the water for reptile-looking shapes.

Ali Dida Hada submerges himself.

Later.

They resume their journey, turning northeastward, and descend into a rain-season river valley that is now dry. Ocher-tinted earth. Below, near a pale-brown monolith where a weak sliver of a tributary of the Omo River touches Anam Ka'alakol, they halt and collapse to the ground.

Isaiah, lying on his back, looking at dusk's clouds, remembers exactly how the mood changed, the electric sense of not being alone, of being watched.

Ali Dida Hada had adjusted his sarong and located his gun; he signaled stillness to Isaiah, who stiffened. They waited.

When Akai Lokorijom walks into sight, Ali Dida Hada drops his gun and gasps.

She has aged. So many lines crisscross her face. Her gaze still burns, and her mouth, though softened, still has its sarcastic twist. She smells of the land, its age, heat, and hardness. Wizened hands. And she says, "You are here."

He is silent.

"You're angry," she says.

He does not speak.

Isaiah understands that he will never again mistake Akai Lokorijom for Ajany. Here is the elemental thing that had obsessed Hugh and—he glances over—possesses Ali Dida Hada.

Her eyes skim over him. He immediately closes his.

Angular features, dark-skinned, a life form that seems to pour itself into the object of its focus. He wants to touch her skin, to know its texture. He imagines all kinds of warmth. He watches Akai Lokorijom glide over and cup Ali Dida Hada's face.

Ali Dida Hada is unmoving. "I've been looking for you," he says in Gabbra.

Behind, a volley of barks.

They turn.

One of Wuoth Ogik's herding dogs.

"The animals?" Ali Dida Hada asks.

Akai hunches, looks away to the left. "Gone."

"The red dance-ox?"

Silence.

Ali Dida Hada asks, "What do you want to do now?"

He is tired of arguing with phantoms.

Tired of losing.

He steps back and lowers his head.

Akai understands the exhaustion of bleeding life one love at a time, of trying to keep a step ahead of threat, dread, fear. Struggling not to need, not to crave more, trying to ignore the hunger to contain an other, always battling not to swallow her own.

He is here.

The only man whose stillness gives her peace.

And he grasps her world, and when he recites his poems, it is as if he can see as she does and she is not alone inside her imagining.

Akai says, "Bakir, I'm tired."

Ali Dida Hada rubs his eyes, and then his head.

"You're old," she tells him.

Silence.

A movement.

Akai pivots again.

Watches Isaiah watching her.

She asks, "Is that Abdulkadir's son? The chicken thief?"

Ali Dida Hada glances at Isaiah.

Malice. "No. That's Isaiah William . . . Bolton. Son of Hugh Bolton."

Isaiah understands the word "Bolton." He sees Akai cover her mouth. Her eyes narrow. *Are those tears?*

Ali Dida Hada feels Akai's body's heat, a thrumming force.

The smell of fear.

Isaiah shuffles under Akai's stare, scratches his arm, imagines even his pores are being probed.

She moves closer to examine Isaiah.

She walks around him.

She strokes the skin of his arm.

She says, "Your mother's in you. I see her." She reaches up and turns his head this way and that. A sly smile, a snort. "*Selena's* son." Without looking over, she asks Ali Dida Hada, "Why did you bring this one here?"

"He's come for his father."

Akai studies Isaiah.

Ali Dida Hada says, "Akai?"

She drops Isaiah's face and strides to Ali Dida Hada and looks him up and down.

Ali Dida Hada tugs at her arm, her forearms in a clinch. His jaw firms up. They are almost nose to nose. "Where is he?" Akai pulls away and spits. "Shall I tell you?"

She pivots, watching Ali Dida Hada.

"He is now buried at Wuoth Ogik. Nyipir's brought in his bones from inside a cave. He's buried next to your son."

Akai tumbles backward, shrinks, hugs her body, bends, and breathes in rhythm to inaudible sobs.

Ali Dida Hada reaches for Akai.

She slaps his hand away.

She turns to Isaiah and grabs his shirt. In her version of English, "I'm woman in Hugh pictures." *Hoo,* she pronounces it. She looks into him. "I see your mother, Selena." He waits. "She come for Hugh. But Hugh want me, not her." Isaiah is mesmerized. "Your father? He is not Hugh. OK?" She taps his face. "Your father, he someone else. Not Hugh. Look your color, see?" Akai gargles. Shakes her head. "Not Hugh. Selena— *ai!*—she's mad." Akai claps her hand. "Good revenge. Hugh . . ." She glares at Isaiah. "A bad, bad man." She sneers. "Be happy Selena mad." Another gurgle. "Or your hair be red like stupid."

Isaiah's eyes get brighter and brighter until the land blurs. He hears Akai's triumphant gloat. She is crying with laughter. "Oh, Selena!"

Akai pirouettes, half dancing toward Ali Dida Hada. With her arms outstretched, she leans toward him. "Recite something, Ali. . . ."

Ali Dida Hada will not.

But then he groans, eyes fixed on distances. "*Deluged, I breathe by praying your name. . . .*"

Akai eavesdrops.

Shuts her eyes.

Isaiah had watched Ali Dida Hada *inflate*—as soon as Akai touched him. Power like that has no use for lies. There is certainty in the spite of her laugh. With slow steps, Isaiah starts off eastward.

Promising that he will walk to death.

Wild flourishes of landscape.

Intensity of existence outside this discord.

Isaiah.

Trying to suck in air.

What do I know?

No certainties.

He has known.

Puzzle pieces falling into place.

Selene determined that he abandon his quest for Hugh.

The second and third glances of relatives.

Selene steering away the queries of those who met him.

"His father?" he once heard. "My first husband," Selene had answered in a cold voice.

Not waiting for the end of his grandmother's funeral service. "Too many nosy types around." Selene had marched him down the church steps and into their car, leaving Raulfe behind.

His skin had always been of a darker shade than the rest of the family, but, as Selene used to say—not that anyone had asked—"Throwback gene. Your great-grandfather was a Hindu."

Selene's plea: "Stay. There's nothing there for you."

Now.

Akai Lokorijom's ribald laughter.

Mocking him.

No, mocking Hugh and Selene.

What is true?

———

Months after she left Wuoth Ogik, waiting and waiting for Hugh to come back to her, Selene, gutted by stomach-aching anguish, could not sleep. She wandered naked in the echoing Naivasha house. Could not remember when low keening became an audible wail.

Needing to go home to England but not wanting to leave without Hugh. Why live? What was the point? Haunted. Wanting warmth in

July. Hurting for her husband's body, his soul, his laugh, hers. His laugh was hers. Mucus on her face. "I don't belong to anything," she told the wall. "Not even to myself." Body-shuddering weeping. *What do I need?*

A deep-voiced answer came from within the room. "I'm here, memsahib." And from that moment until the night of the next day, it was all she needed to know and touch and feel and smell and have.

Selene's plane left Kenya. She took only what she needed. Her plane circled the plains with the stragglers of the Rift Valley wildebeest migration, black pockmarks on the ground. *Migration instinct.* Selene smiled before she closed her eyes.

The baby was a boy. Selene named him Isaiah William Bolton.

Her mother, who was blind in one eye, peered at the newborn baby and said, "A significant throwback. Not as English-looking as he could be." She cackled through the opening phrase of "Flight of the Bumblebee."

"He's mine," Selene answered.

More than a year later, a divorce decree for Hugh Bolton was dispatched to Kenya.

No reply.

She waited.

And waited.

Selene forged Hugh's "no contest."

Done.

Three years later, Selene acquired a new husband. Raulfe Greenwich. A man from a popular rather than a distinguished military family that made its money illegally trading in Darjeeling tea. A diffident third-born son with a penchant for order and walking dogs in the park. In Selene, Raulfe found a foil to his blandness. In Isaiah, the son he had hoped to have. He became aware that he also had Hugh's ghost to contend with, and that he dealt with in his own way.

40

SUNDOWN. AKAI'S AND ALI DIDA HADA'S BODIES TOUCH.

Akai says, "Another song?"

Ali Dida Hada stares across the fire. "No," he says.

"A song?"

He snaps, "Only hyenas walk the same road twice."

"You're not a hyena." Her voice is a whisper.

Ali Dida Hada lifts his forefinger, touches each of Akai's eyelids. "Bring me Nyipir's red dance-ox."

The fire crackles.

A throbbing tension engulfs all.

It is the first time Nyipir's name has been mentioned.

Akai grabs dust and throws it at Ali Dida Hada.

Ali Dida Hada pushes her to the ground, his hands gentle around her neck. He says, "The red dance-ox."

Akai tears at Ali Dida Hada's hands. "Let me be."

Ali Dida Hada spits out flecks of dust.

"What do you want?" he shouts.

Akai turns away to look into the night. "How's my husband?"

Ali Dida Hada lifts himself from her. "*He* sent me to you."

Akai's head spins. Tears. She rolls over and gets up, wiping her thighs. "He . . ."

Ali Dida Hada continues: "He wants *only* his animals back."

Akai's eyes shimmer; her mouth opens and closes.

Lowers her head.

Nyipir had waited for her. He had always waited for her. She needed his waiting. She was used to his waiting. All she had ever needed to do was show up, and he would be there.

Then.

He had sent his rival to find her.

Nyipir had stopped waiting.

Quivering breath, scratchy throat.

Nyipir had stopped waiting.

The knowledge causes Akai's world to become unsteady. She sits down, stunned. *Only his animals back.* She will not cry.

Ali Dida Hada moves away.

He stops at the margins of the light.

He returns at once to her. Impatient voiced. "A poem. Do you want to hear it?"

She nods, tears in her eyes, scattered thoughts, ringing ears.

In Tigrinya, Ali Dida Hada sings, "*Seed of song hidden in the single eye of an old star . . .*"

Akai feels the end of Nyipir's waiting as if she had fallen into a bottomless hole.

Now Ali Dida Hada's forehead touches Akai's.

Gray-hair-flecked skin, wrinkles and scars.

Ali Dida Hada croons the rest of the tale into Akai's ear, and as he speaks, her head moves closer and closer to his shoulder until it reclines.

"Where's the ox?" Ali Dida Hada asks.

"Gone," she mutters.

"The car?"

"Gone."

"The animals?"

"Gone. A dog remains."

A lone jackal races to Isaiah's left, a small creature's white feathers clogging its mouth. Isaiah, still bemused, hears the water before he sees it. When he finds it, he stops. He quivers before he pulls off clothes, unbuttons his khakis. He hears the snapping of rusted chains, sees the falling to earth of a rain of ash, and smells that rancid after-burn of spent matches. There would be a moon in the sky that night. Isaiah drops into the water, submerging himself and then propelling himself to the surface.

Breathes.

No crocodiles.

Birds, plants, the scrambling of secret creatures.

The wind.

No thoughts.

Drained.

What is true?

Stark naked, Isaiah builds a cairn, piling up stones with bare and then bloody hands. The pain is a relief in the darkness. The cairn is for every illusion and lie, for questions and his personal dead. Hammering down rocks with all his might until there is nothing left to fight with.

Not even himself.

Deep night.

He sits with the warm stillness.

Sweating.

He listens to the water while shadows undulate.

At daybreak, he sees how a landscape unfurls into eternity, shimmering past origins. *How can life endure these infinite spaces?* And from nearby bushes, sounds of an impish summons—a white-tailed honeyguide has spotted a nude, hungry creature by the water who might be chirped in the direction of a freshly spotted honey hive.

———

Four nights later, a small group reaches Wuoth Ogik. Ten steps behind Ali Dida Hada and Akai-ma, Isaiah stares at the play of light on crumbling coral walls. The herding dog starts to yelp and whirls after his tail when he recognizes the boundary lines of home.

41

DUST IN HIS HAIR, MOUTH, NOSTRILS, AND EARS. DUST AND sweat inside his clothes. Isaiah can ignore it all now. So he searches faces, studies gestures. He searches for the woman he needs to hold to himself so that he can create a frame for feral, amaranthine places cleaving to his marrow, threatening to lose him.

Watching.

Galgalu's half hobble. "Mama!" he calls as he tumbles toward Akai. They cling to each other. Akai weeps as she touches the bandage on Galgalu's head, cups his face. "My poor little one," she croons, "and still just a bone."

Nyipir picks up his herding stick, cradles it on his shoulder. He waits, unmoving. He had heard the dog bark. He had stepped out, prepared for anything. He had seen and counted the new arrivals: three people, one dog. Nothing else.

Silence.

He waits.

Ali Dida Hada glances over at Nyipir, holds the look, gives a single shake of his head.

Nyipir wheezes.

Spirals. Dizzy. But he also knows if he were to reach for Akai-ma he might suffocate her and then kill himself. He sucks air in, one dollop at a time. He pivots, turning his back.

Glimpses Odidi's cairn, his promise to his son.

Above, Hadada ibis call.

Footsteps.

She appears from his left.

Akai, unkempt, her face dull, lips dry and cracked, makes a furtive gesture. She stretches out a hand to touch Nyipir's bare arm. She moves closer and closer. Tentative, she rests her head against his stiff body, his hard chest, pillowing her head.

Softer than last night's breeze, she whispers, "I'm sorry."

Nyipir does not move.

She breathes, "Please."

Straining, Nyipir swallows. Closing his eyes, he lets his right hand rest on her back.

Akai-ma exhales.

Stillness.

Then he sighs. "Why?"

Akai says, "They asked me for a sacrifice. They took the ones the river left behind."

"The river . . ."

"Is swollen. Its raining somewhere."

"Nothing's left? Not even a goat?"

Silence.

"Nothing."

"Jayadha, my red dance-ox?"

Silence.

Nyipir's broken hand covers his face. He murmurs, "I yearned for you." Nyipir sees his life drift from him.

"I longed for you. I've waited . . ."

Silence.

Akai's voice is tentative. "You sent Ali."

"Yes." He gestures at the empty compound.

Akai looks. This man, this husband, her guardian, her protector.

Today, eyes like cold stone.

A fog of sadness engulfs them both.

Nyipir tries to prevent shimmering tears from shaming him, but every part of his being hurts, everything within him longs to cry out. He says, "We've now buried Hugh."

Akai stares at the ground.

"We've buried our son."

Silence.

"Couldn't wait."

Akai looks up at Nyipir, her heart in her eyes. *Forgive me.* Nothing. No sound. Shoulders droop.

Nyipir cups her face. "Akai, remember, you also have a daughter."

She turns her face into his hands and inhales the unchanging warmth of them.

42

IN THE DISTANCE, DOUM PALMS WAIL. SHADOWS LENGTHEN. The landscape is on fire. Akai-ma finds Ajany with her head against Odidi's stone resting place. She sits down near her, forcing herself to stay, facing death, that shadow presence that hovered when this child was born. Staying put, even though she still believes Ajany is destined to abandon her. Akai's hand almost touches Ajany's head. "My child, you're here."

Ajany's body curves away. Chin on knees, she looks sideways at Akai-ma.

No answer.

Akai hears storms swirl within her being, she remembers leaving Wuoth Ogik, hearing voices shouting within her, following those voices, their alarm, into dark stillness. Like now. Sometimes the mist descended inside her, burying her thoughts. Like now. She forces herself to speak out the memory.

"My children were alone," Akai tells Ajany.

She scours the old desiccated landscape.

She makes a half-groaning noise. Churning darknesses.

The chaos that erupts and interrupts Ajany's flow of feeling when she is close to her mother grabs her, shakes her, and then she hears Akai-ma bleat: "Odidi!"

Ajany listens, imagining for an instant that there will be an answer.
"My boy," Akai cries.

Then.

Stillness.

"Ewoi-Etir," Akai calls. "Ewoi-Etir-Ewoi-Etir-Ewoi-Etir."

When Akai seizes Ajany, Ajany howls. It is a terrible strangled sound that confirms her fear that her mother is finally going to kill her.

The cry.

Nyipir, Isaiah, and Galgalu run toward it.

Nyipir rushing ahead of them. He skids to a stop.

Ajany is cradling Akai-ma, whose body is bent into a ball. Ajany rocks her. A pang and pressure dessicate Nyipir's chest. He drags himself a short distance away, the others follow, but still within earshot.

———

Skin to skin, face touching face, heart to heart, now Ajany can taste sorrows woven into Akai-ma. They have always been there; she has just not known how to look before. Feeling its hugeness, Ajany understands how much shelter it has needed. Why it had to detach from Wuoth Ogik and wander.

"Akai-ma?" Low-voiced, "Who is Ewoi? Who is Etir?"

Akai squeezes Ajany's body. "You were born hot," she says. "You should've died."

Tears spurt. Ajany stutters, "You wanted me t-to die?"

Akai-ma moans, "Nooooo."

She had separated herself from Ajany's life early, daring death to take her, vowing indifference. Yet the child was still alive. It was her brother, who was born cool, who had been snatched from her.

Akai shivers, eyes dark.

Ringing in her ears. A subdued tone: "Ewoi, Etir are your brother and sister."

Ajany coughs.

Then, "What?"

Akai says, "I lost them on the same day."

Stillness.

Her life once apportioned hope for people and places:

For Hugh.

For Ewoi and Etir.

For Nyipir.

For Odidi.

But she had not hoped-anything for her fourth-born child—this daughter. It had been like that from the start, when she found out so late that she was pregnant. The baby, a tiny girl, was born prematurely, and fevered. There were no midwives close by. Nyipir, who could have helped, was stuck in the entrails of the Kenyan state. Galgalu, so young himself, had battled to bring the creature out of Akai's womb. Akai's heavy bleeding had muddied the ground. The little thing had been born with a head full of hair and large, fathomless eyes that connected to invisible things. She also seemed to understand every uttered word.

The baby did not cry.

Akai had not named the baby.

Later.

When she was able to walk, Akai had wandered away from Wuoth Ogik, seeking news of Nyipir at watering holes and centers of trade. She had strapped the nameless girl on her back, walking in circles.

After six days, the baby all of a sudden refused to suckle.

Soon Akai had nothing left to give her. At midday, in the heat, Akai had fallen to the ground, clawed it open, and screamed and screamed out Nyipir's name. As she covered the hole with earth, a season's harbinger—a secretary bird, one with a half-eaten snake—had landed and stared straight at her.

Akai tried to again breastfeed the child.

The child bawled.

The bird stared.

Akai told herself, *At least I have a son.*

She told the bird, *Take it, then.*

She put the baby under a Mareer tree, and then she ran away.

Akai crawled into Wuoth Ogik three days later and found a way to the livestock *boma,* where she curled up next to the fire.

"Where's baby?" Galgalu had woken her up

"Where baby?" lisped Odidi. "I want baby."

Akai had stared at them blankly. "Baby?"

Galgalu had swept Odidi up and run into the landscape. Tracking Akai's footsteps, they searched every bush. Galgalu whistled for honey birds. Four showed up to lead him to honey, but not to the baby.

Four days later, as Galgalu and little Odidi walked slowly back to Wuoth Ogik, Akai saw Odidi clutching a soiled, silent bundle to his chest.

"She's dead," Akai said.

Odidi turned on her, eyes afire. He said in an old man's voice, "This is *my* baby."

Galgalu did not stop to talk to her. He went straight to his hut.

Odidi started calling the baby "Ol Arabel," after a river, for he was four and already understood thirst. He thought every river was Ol Arabel. Galgalu called the baby Arabel, which was the name of a cool, green mountain.

The feelings from that season pound Akai's mind and heart, making her body clammy. What should she tell Ajany? She glances at her.

Arabel. Ajany. Oganda. The child still listened with her eyes.

"I was also born hot," Akai says. "As you were. Odidi was born cool. Those born hot die, can even die of nothing. I was not expecting you, but you came, and when you were born, you were fire."

Ajany winces.

Nyipir eavesdrops.

Akai says, "I became Turkana, but before that, I was Dodoth. I left school to meet one man, my father. But I met two. One is Nyipir. The other, Hugh Bolton. They were together."

Ajany is suddenly cold. She rubs her arms up and down. She blows into her hands.

43

IN THE LATE YEAR HEAT OF 1956, WHEN AKAI HAD JUMPED INTO the watering hole, laughing, she dived through a portal into another way of being. Nyipir had clenched his hands, wanted to force her to leave. But her effusive life, Hugh's fascination held him back. He suppressed his fear even as it growled within him.

Akai never did deliver the message of her suspension from school to her stepfather. Instead, greedy for the promise of the bigness of life, she became Hugh's mistress.

"For me, he was the face of life. His hair was fire. He had answers. He had traveled farther than anyone I knew. Such a person was what I wanted. This is how I wanted to be."

Tell me about the world. How big is the ocean? Why doesn't it snow here, where water is needed most? Echoes. Akai now mocks her curiosity.

"But he read me things from his books. He showed me how to feel his music. Eyes shut, memory resurrects strains of what she cannot name as Chopin's Nocturne in E minor. She sways with the sounds of that past. *This is what I wanted.* She says to Ajany.

But Hugh started to fondle and toy with Akai in public. Grabbing at her in Nyipir's presence. Nyipir also started to act out. Breaking china, dropping kettles, polishing his hands. Not eating. He made himself scarce, throwing himself into carting stones for the new house. Akai began to stalk him. She would toss plates and cutlery just to watch him tense up. She undressed in his presence. Needled him to provoke a reaction. He always bowed and walked away.

A year later, during a sudden rare arid land storm, Hugh decided to sketch Akai where she had been reclining behind a boulder near the rude veranda. He commanded her to stay in the rain. She did. He sketched.

He worked all through the afternoon.

His sketch done, Akai had run in, shivering, pouting and snarling like a mad cat.

"Shut up, cow." Hugh had screamed, "Can't you see I'm painting?"

Hugh worked through the night.

Nyipir did not sleep at all.

In the morning, when he was preparing a scrambled-egg breakfast for Hugh and Akai, she walked into the kitchen, clutching her body, still trembling. "Go away." Nyipir had said.

Akai remembers, eyes glittering: "As if I were a flea. So I slapped him."

Nyipir did nothing.

Months passed.

Akai says, "Then I got pregnant. I was happy."

The buzz of flies. A striped bird, scarlet and black-beaked, whizzes past. Around Wuoth Ogik, an overbearing cloud squats over seven people. Petrus wanders along the compound's fence, looking and looking at the person who had really bound Ali Dida Hada to Wuoth Ogik.

Akai says, "Never thought about Selena. She was not of our life. Even when he brought her here and made me hide myself, even when he left with Nyipir, and I was left here alone, I was happy."

A soft chortle at youthful folly.

Moths had danced around the lanterns installed by Nyipir. Hugh got up, pulled Akai off her seat, and stripped her in front of Nyipir. She stood unclothed and round-bellied.

Nyipir dropped a tray.

Hugh sometimes tore the paper with his paintbrush, throwing the paint and staining Akai's body and clothes. He would command Akai to leave it on. And she would walk around in garish and grotesque shades.

Insults in Ngaturkana, applied by Hugh:

"Take this fat thing of yours and keep its ugliness from my sight."

"Ngilac, talononwa." Lice, bat.

Nyipir fed Akai fish soup. He stole a goat for her. He kept her from Hugh. Once, when Hugh went on a rampage, Nyipir had led her to the red caves near Wuoth Ogik to wait.

Hugh painted Akai from idealized memory.

One Saturday, Akai started to bleed.

Hugh said, "Is that the end of the bastard?"

Nyipir carried Akai to his small safari bed.

Attending to her, praying the bleeding would stop.

Three months before Akai's delivery date, Hugh arranged a sudden safari to Lokitaung. Nyipir told Akai not to go. She looked back at him, her smile faked. "We finish this," she said.

Hugh returned a week later by himself. He explained, "She's gone back to her people. Among her own kind."

He had settled into a camp chair, staring out. *"Kijana, leta Sundowner. Hiyo maneno imekwisha kabisa. Sasa tutakimya."* Bring a sundowner. That matter is done. Now silence.

Akai tells Ajany that Hugh had pushed her onto a boat with an El Molo guardsman who tied a sheep to the prow, and gave Akai fifty shillings. "You come?" she begged Hugh.

"After baby," he shouted.

Fifty shillings was good money in those days.

"I went home. They were so happy to see me. They were afraid an animal had eaten me on my way from school. They cried when they saw me." Akai stretches out her legs, holding to Ajany's hands.

Akai had told her family that the child's father was a senior officer who was preparing his army to come for her. She said he had told her to wait for him. She said it was the custom of Boltons to see the children only after they could run. To her family it was an absurd custom. Still, they made arrangements to welcome the stranger into the family.

They waited.

And waited.

They waited.

In spite of the sheep and money, the larger Akai became, the more shame-nurtured silences deepened.

Akai's beloved stepfather became a laughingstock among the elders. He started calling her section of the family "the outsiders"—this man who had fought almost to death anyone who had tried to do so before. He moved Akai and her mother out, to save face. He did so in tears. Akai said Hugh would claim her, with more cows than had ever been seen in the land.

Akai's mother set up a homestead two days' walk away from their real home, near Elemi. There were goats and sheep and a donkey. That was where Akai gave birth. She did not know there would be twins.

Ewoi, the boy.

Etir, the girl.

Caramel-skinned children with large gray eyes.

"Twins are bad."

There was a tussle, the midwife arguing with Akai and her mother about the terrible portent of this birth. "Nothing good has come today," she screeched.

"Touch them, I'll break your neck," Akai vowed.

Akai's stepfather—after a raid, on his way back home—left a red calf. It was his way of honoring the children.

Akai Lokorijom loved the calf, which took to sitting with her and following her on long walks. And as the twins grew, there were days when everything was almost good.

1960 collapsed into 1961 as a single, entrenched desiccating drought season. Everything burned. Everything struggled to breathe before drying to death.

Akai's brother came to take the red cow to join the other livestock, which would be driven to other pastures, in the heart of Ethiopia. He left them two camels, for milk.

In the heart of the drought, Akai fought with her mother over a water jug. She needed the water for her children. Words became a blow. Akai's mother slapped her to the ground. Told her to stop dreaming.

Said she was a mere curse that had tainted life from the moment she was born.

Akai did the unthinkable. She backhanded her mother.

Her mother took her by the head and spat out a dirge: "You are dead. . . ."

So Akai left, with a bundle of her few things. Her mother packed the twins, too, tied everything to the camel, and pushed them away. "Go and die," she hurled.

Akai was on her way to Kalacha and Wuoth Ogik, having circumnavigated the brackish lake, when the already fragile camel crumpled on the arid land, groaned, and died.

Akai fell where the camel lay. She spent the day cutting it up and storing its stringy pieces in the folds of her dress. She fed the children with its blood. She walked a full day with the twins, but then she hurried back to the dead camel. When she got there, she found grunting hyenas scavenging the carcass. She backed away. At a safe distance, she fled, carrying the children.

After that, she strapped her crying children, one to her back, and the other to her front. Unthinking, she hunted for liquid, pursuing mirages, trusting that at least one would yield water.

Water.

She scrambled into dried-up water holes. Her breast milk dried up. The sun seared Ewoi's and Etir's skin red. They were dry-mouthed, thirsty.

"One morning they stopped crying."

Akai's voice is cracking.

Ajany's eyes are extra wide.

Akai bit into her wrist to feed her children her blood, but her teeth slipped off her skin, her strength fading. Ewoi fell out of her arms, convulsing on the ground. Akai saw, with all her life, how truly small the baby was, how light her arms felt without the extra child. Ewoi tried to cry. Akai adjusted Etir and walked away, leaving Ewoi behind. In the near distance, a hyena howled. Akai walked on. Never looked back; the first stone veil dropped over her face. She walked the paths of hills that were dry, handsome, and still unyielding.

She stopped in the night beneath a hillock made of rocks with giraffe etchings carved into their surfaces, with their heads piercing clouds. Etir was looking into her eyes. She picked up a sharp-ended rock and started scraping her wrist. Then she managed to tear the skin at the back of her hands with her teeth. She placed the vein near the child's mouth. Etir tried to drink, but his mouth stopped moving. His eyes remained half closed; his body still. Akai placed the child at the base of that hill and walked on. She walked through the night, into the Chalbi Desert, where she collapsed and waited to die.

It was not death that came, but water. Rain had fallen in the northern hills. The desert used to be a lake. A flash flood raced through a *laga* and dragged Akai downstream for two kilometers. She crashed into a rock. She let go. The waters swept her to the edge. They paraded carcasses of the newly dead. After an hour and a half of this, the floods receded. Akai waded out of the *laga*, its sand and mud squelching beneath her feet, located Mount Kulal and the Hurri Hills, and walked southeastward. Akai showed up at Wuoth Ogik to die.

A barbet twitters. The Wuoth Ogik courtyard gate lies open and swings in intermittent phases.

Akai points. "That's where I walked through."

She had sat on the ground to wait behind the shadows of the vessels into which water poured from the roof when it rained.

The green Land Rover drove up with an antelope tied to its chassis, streaks of blood washing down the window. Hugh Bolton in drab tan khaki jumped out first and headed toward the house. Nyipir, who had been driving, reversed the car and parked it next to the *boma*.

Akai waited for Hugh to unlock the house door before she stepped into view.

Nyipir had pulled out a rifle, which he leaned against the car. He put a foot on the step, using a knife to cut down the creature. Just then he heard Hugh shout, "Whore! Whore! Whore! *Ngikakumok!* Rain preventer!"

Nyipir cocked the rifle, thinking Wuoth Ogik was under attack by rustlers. Then he saw Akai Lokorijom, swaying, shuffling, and emaciated. Heard Akai say, "My father wants his bride price."

"*Whore-whore-whore.*"

"They were two," she said to Hugh. "Their names Ewoi and Etir."

"*Liar! Liar!*"

"I leave them on the ground for you to bring."

"*Ngikakumok!*"

Akai said, "We can keep the bones."

Hugh had rushed at her with his small army knife. She fell on the ground, not defending herself. "Two babies," Akai repeated.

"*Prostitute, monkey, slut, slug. Ngikakumok!*"

Hugh's penknife slashed at her arms, shoulder, stomach, aiming for her womb. Akai stuck to him. He had raised his knife over her neck when Nyipir clicked the rifle's hammer into place and shot Hugh in the head. He reloaded the rifle, stepped back, and shot Hugh in the throat.

Akai says, "Such a man does not die easy."

Akai looks toward Nyipir.

She glances at Hugh's cairn.

Suffocating memories. Akai will not speak of how Hugh's blood spattered them.

Nyipir had pointed the rifle at her, but she had thrown herself into his arms, kissed his face all over, and pleaded in a whisper, "Help me."

The flood-of-blood night, sweating through fear. They carried Hugh's body into the car with the antelope still on its roof. They drove as far as they could before the car got stuck, moved the body between them until they reached a red hill with fissures and overhangs, where they pushed Hugh through a twisted tunnel that became a cave, took him deep into the earth, found a chamber where they could sit and breathe. It was dark. It was cool. There, Akai straddled Nyipir, tore off his clothes, covered in Hugh's blood. "Help me." Forgetting who she was, what they had become and done. Akai and Nyipir did not leave the cave until mid-morning of the next day, while what was left of Hugh bled to death next to them.

Ajany's teeth chatter, but she is not cold. Pinpricks of darkness. She senses that even Odidi is listening.

Revulsion. Fear. Terror.

Sight.

Night insects creak.

The house is still falling down.

Akai says, "Nyipir and me, we went back to the house and waited to be found. No one came."

"But then so many seasons after, when memory is dust, Ali came. But he could see nothing."

Akai then closes her eyes.

Inside Ajany, resonance from a song that was being sung as she first crossed the threshold into Saudade: "Clube Dorival." *"A morte é uma canção velha, profunda"* (Death is a deep, old song), *"braços eternos, curvados sobre as penas"* (eternal hands cupping sorrows).

And inherited guilt.

Nyipir and Akai had planted new myths about Wuoth Ogik. It was an aborted mission base. Its disappointed priest had gone back to Europe, after giving over its stewardship to his assistant and friend, Nyipir. In Kenya's pre- and early post-independence days, anything was believable. And a story repeated often enough became fact.

Ali Dida Hada paces the peripheries. Isaiah and Galgalu stand a little farther away, Galgalu translating and embellishing what he thinks Isaiah should know. Which is not much. "Mister Bolton he hears his two children with Akai-ma is died, much sorrow. So he falls on his gun and it misfires. Oh no! Much blood. Much sorrow. Mzee and Mama, they are afraid because he is died and this is a mzungu and his gun has died him. What people will say? Much sorrow. What to do? So they take his body inside a cave, far from eating animals and . . . and pray so he is never be forgotten, truly much sorrow."

Stillness.

Akai then crawls, aiming for Odidi's cairn. She rests her head on one of the stones. *God will see that you reach your place, sleep in this cool place. Giver of peace, give me peace.* Her voice is soft. *Give my children peace.*

44

SOMEWHERE NEAR THE COURTYARD, IN THE MIDDLE OF THE
evening, Petrus accosts Ali Dida Hada. "I appreciate your love."

Ali Dida Hada chokes.

Petrus asks, "All your money?"

"You wanted it."

"Not everything."

"Take it."

"And you?"

Ali Dida Hada sneers, "Concerned?"

Ali Dida Hada turns away toward the *boma*.

Petrus, in an awkward gesture, tries to give Ali Dida Hada the sign-
over papers. Rethinks, and rips them apart instead.

"A joint account?" Ali Dida Hada wonders.

"Better: I'll be your relative. I'll show up in every inconvenient
season with a long story, one thin dead chicken—stolen—and hands
outstretched to receive alms from you." A sudden grin transfigures Ali
Dida Hada's face. Petrus asks, "Is that reasonable?"

When he can stop laughing, Ali Dida Hada says, "You'll have to find
me first."

"Relatives like me have a natural radar for our targets." Petrus puts
out his hand for Ali Dida Hada to shake.

Ali Dida Hada grasps it hard.

He hesitates, then asks, "There was a fire at the mission?"

"Yes," replies Petrus.

"Casualties?"

"A few."

Ali Dida Hada looks away. "Anyone we know?"

"Yes."

"Survivors?"

Petrus blinks.

"Yes?"

"A *bambaloona*"—Petrus pauses—"might have managed to fly away."

"I see." A smile.

Later.

Around a now-roaring fire that had sustained a very long wake, four men—Nyipir, Ali Dida Hada, Petrus, Galgalu—and a woman, Akai Lokorijom, murmur in soft, soft tones. At moments what is being said has the cadence of incantations, at times sharp sounds erupt.

Slap! Akai's hand, Petrus's face—she now understands who he is.

Then silence.

Murmurs.

A high groan breaks into that night.

Nyipir.

Letting go.

Then stillness.

The intermittent chirping of crickets, muted monotones, like the dirge of sad heralds. An undercurrent of haunted silences, but now also relief.

Ajany, lying on her back, listens to the whisperings. She turns to stare at the black spaces between stars that become Kormamaddo. His nose points south, in the vicinity of her heart. She tastes the tear-flavored names of just-found siblings: *Ewoi. Etir.* Quieter tears for Odidi, fragile parents, and even Hugh Bolton. This is also the night when she has lost her home. It will return to its true heir. Throbbing in Ajany's head.

Homelessness is where Far Away is.

Small rocks hard against her back, the earth holding her weight. She turns, presses into the dust as if to dissolve into landscape.

I swear, she remembers.

Soil, fear, threat—what children they had been.

Ajany rubs her face in the soil, kneads it in desire, its aches and promises. *What endures?* Spaces in the heart that accommodate the absent. She turns over, crosses her hands across her chest, feels the stir of arcane currents of ceaseless, restless love. Kormamaddo twinkling down at illusions. *What endures?* The hard earth: her limits.

In a corner of the ranch, a changing man gathers words from around a fire. He will try to make sense of these and fill his memories with what he learns. He finds himself wandering off to the boundaries of Wuoth Ogik, looking out, looking in, trying to decide where he ought to go next, how and why. He knows it won't be England. Not yet.

Later.

From other spaces, a clear voice rings out: "Arabel Ajany!"

Ajany hugs the feeling of her name inside her mother's voice.

"Arabel Ajany!"

She lingers so she can memorize the shape her name takes in Akai-ma's mouth.

Soon.

Unsweetened porridge in a calabash. Akai-ma pours a portion out to her daughter and says, "Words are so small. They cannot show the womb of my heart." She says, "It's where I hold you." She says, "My child."

Ajany's head goes up.

Gaze-touch.

Akai-ma strokes Ajany's head, her face. "I leave now, Arabel, I must leave Wuoth Ogik."

Ajany lowers her bowl, fingers twitching. "Why?"

"Weariness has gobbled up even the words that should bridge."

Silence. A pause. Ajany is learning to look unflinching into the abyss. *This is also being.*

"We reached the end of our strength." Akai's hand supports her head. "So we turned into mutes."

Another beginning.

Night hues, ardent cravings, stomach rumble. Ajany wanting to tumble into her mother's arms and give herself the respite of temporary childlike hopes, of simple homecoming.

Ebbing of life, as normal as the tides.

"What remains?"

"Stories? When we meet again."

Quiet.

Ajany murmurs, "How will I find you now?"

Silence.

They sip porridge.

Akai-ma says, "Little to take from that house."

Wuoth Ogik in deformed shadow.

Ajany's sudden desperate tone: "Akai-ma, how does madness come? Can it arrive with the sound of wailing? It's inside." She stops. "It cries. Like a baby."

With a rapid movement Akai-ma gathers Ajany to her and presses her head to her daughter's. Lips to skin. Husky-voiced. "Tell the crying one that she has a mother. She belongs to life. She has a mother and the mother holds her. The mother forever holds her."

A burning sensation harrows Ajany's inner being.

It listens to Akai-ma say, "This is my heart, this is my breathing, and it's you. You hear?" Heartbeats. Arms tighten around each other. Time darts through them. Small contentment.

Later.

Too soon.

Ajany watches her mother's silhouette merge with the vast darkness in a slow-flow dance. On a distant hill, a pinprick of firelight. It wavers. She watches until time—or something like time—becomes seeing. After that, there is more waiting.

———

Under the waning moon, a shadow emerges. It approaches. It becomes Isaiah. He drops down next to Ajany. Above them, night-blackened clouds with starlit fringes. Isaiah shifts until their bodies touch. Ajany tilts her head, in the silver light. Mussed-up hair, frayed shirt collar, wiry arm muscles, deepened angular features, a deep gaze fixed on her. The silence. With hardening nipples and aching body, she watches light slivers dance on his skin. Her silence, their stillness.

Then.

"Hello, Arabel?" Quiet in his voice.

"Hello, Isaiah."

Isaiah reaches over. His hand on the back of her neck, he drags her to him. Rubbing his face against hers. Breathing her.

His house, she thinks. *His* Wuoth Ogik.

Bitterness.

It passes.

Echoes.

Fragrant aftertaste, this burnt-earth flavor of home.

It is this.

But it is not hers.

Not anymore.

Where will I go now? A fleeting thought.

Her head against his, readying for more absences.

"Here." He pulls out a folded square of paper from his shirt pocket. He explains, "Wuoth Ogik's title deed. Your father gave it to me."

She takes the document. Hands trembling, heart spinning. *Will you learn the faces of our stones or the passageway of old footsteps and repeat the prayers of our earth-covered dead?* She squints at the page, deciphering the words *Lieutenant Colonel (ret.) Hugh Aubrey Francis Bolton*.

Memory: a lonely, broken face inside a dark Kalacha cave.

Relinquishment.

She will *not* grieve.

Small voice. "May I still visit Odidi here?" Small tears.

Isaiah's fingers touch her face, drawing lines with her tears. "Maybe." His head resting on hers. "What can a person do with falling stones?"

The watery mumbles of a distant spring, the sheltering gaze of sky. Silence as presence. Listening, she offers, "B-build?"

"Takes time," he answers.

Myriad stars.

He says, "But *we* have time."

Stillness.

She finally hears Isaiah.

"*We?*"

"Mhh."

Silence.

Then, "Why?" Soft break in her voice.

"We're here now."

"Murderers?"

"Impostors."

"Who?"

"Me. If I remember, I'll tell you all about it."

"Amnesia?"

"Exorcism."

"Atonement."

"Sounds right."

Night crickets, cicadas, cooling earth. Another breach. Life pushing at thresholds, encircling two beings. In a shared gaze, denuded presence. Accepting all as it is, even the haunted streaks, Ajany cups Isaiah's face with both her hands. She traces its shape, its uneven edges, skin— warmth, texture. Stubble. When he clasps her to his body, her arms wrap around him. After that, everything he whispers into her ear and mouth and skin she sees in the glow of fireflies, hears in the call of night birds, the yowling of four winds, and the secret silent songs of stars that are not as distant as they first appear to be.

Later.

"Arabel," Isaiah murmurs, "where's Bernardo now?"

She recoils. A tiny shard of that strangeness is still lodged somewhere inside her. But it is working its way out. She gives Isaiah a limpid look, and her hands seek his, and his fit around hers.

Doum palms creak.

She says, "Ghosts lurk."

"We'll watch them together," he says.

"Wildlife?"

"Old friends."

Ajany's laugh is throaty.

Isaiah chuckles with her. He says, "Nothing left to run away from now. No shadows."

Her fingers stroke Isaiah's skin. "How did you find me?" she asks.

"Your mother." Ajany bucks. Isaiah's arms tighten around her. "She says I'm to *enfold* you. Like this." He squeezes Ajany to himself.

Breath squashed, she gasps, "What?"

"Or she'd *dethrone* me."

"Dethrone?"

"From the hand gesture she made, I believe it means 'to castrate.'"

Tears flood Ajany's eyes.

"I'll kiss you now," Isaiah tells her.

Ajany waits.

"Dethrone," murmurs Isaiah.

Giggles color the darkness. It pours into so many emptinesses.

45

WAVE OF DEPARTURES. NYIPIR SLIPS ON HIS OLD FEDORA, adjusts a frayed military jacket over a pale-brown shirt. A large green rucksack lies on the floor, stuffed with basics: knife, a snub-nosed pistol, rope, water bottle, a tattered black Bible, lighters, packs of newspaper-wrapped dried meat, three different passports, four identity cards, two credit cards, Maasai blankets, a rolled-up reed map, green coffee beans. From the depths of an old suitcase, Nyipir plucks out and unwraps the mouth organ.

He lifts it to his mouth and picks out chords he has given names to: Petronilla, Ajany, Odidi, Theo, Agoro. Akai, Galgalu . . . He evokes a tune.

Petrus Keah approaches the room and stops to listen. Eyes shut, he leans against the wall. Then he straightens up and saunters in, newly shaven, shirt unbuttoned, chest exposed, a white-and-gray Somali *kikoi* wrapped around his waist, red socks and gleaming black shoes adorning his feet.

Nyipir sees Petrus. His music stops.

Petrus bays an old regimental marching song off-key:

Fungua safari / Sisi vijana . . . / Amri ya nani . . .
Start the march / We young soldiers . . . / Whose order are these . . .

. . .

Nyipir accompanies him, looking him up and down. A frown of distaste spreads across his face. The music stops again.

"Keah, red socks, *sooaly*?"

Petrus turns his heels, indicates the ensemble, gestures with a finger.

"Everything 'Made in Italy,' *osiepna*."

Nothing to add, Nyipir resumes their music.

———

"B-baba?" Ajany hears the music on her way to her father, and, like Petrus, halts to listen. Here it was. The soul of Odidi's music. She tiptoes into the room. And falters. There. No lines, no contours, intensity of pale-orange light from the window shines upon dust fragments floating inside the space. Her father, Petrus, glimpses of backlit, blue-shadowed otherness, as if time had loosened its hold on the both of them. She gasps.

"*Nyara.*" Nyipir turns. He slips the mouth organ into the rucksack. "I've been waiting for you."

Ajany sees the travel packs on the floor. "You're leaving."

"Mandalay, 21° 59′ N 96° 6′ E, Rangoon, 16° 47′ N 96° 9′ E."

"B-burma."

He nods.

Her eyes widen in Petrus's direction. "With *him*?"

Petrus purses his lips.

An awful stutter garbles Ajany's words so tears show up in Nyipir's eyes. She chokes out, "B-but when will you come back?"

When she was little, she would ask him this, and when she did, he promised to be home before the moon began to smile.

Nyipir reaches for both his daughter's hands. "Today . . . today I don't know."

She stares. Huge tears floating in her eyes.

"I've something for you and Od . . . er . . ." Nyipir pulls out an old hard-covered black notebook held together by rubber bands. "Bank safety-deposit details. Odidi's name. Yours also. Gemstones. Converted from money from . . . er . . . trading. Sign in with your ID when you go. It's all been arranged." Ajany's hands hover over the notebooks.

Soft-voiced, Nyipir leans close: "Or leave it. Begin something new. Something that's yours." A pause. "You decide."

Silence stripped bare.

"Baba?"

"Yes."

Stillness.

She says, "Akai-ma's leaving."

"Yes."

"And Galgalu."

"Yes."

Ajany looks at tearstains spreading on their clothes.

What endures?

Silence.

Then Nyipir whispers. "Draw a picture for us," he adds. "Yes, shade even death in . . . use the colors of the sun and . . . and . . ." He remembers. Grunts it out: "forgiveness." Quiet. "Create room for trying again. Breathing." They wait.

"Will you, *nyara?*"

She did not understand, but his brows were puckered, eyes searching hers. In them the past, the here and the faith. She speaks to faith, she says *Yes.*

In Nyipir's age-etched eyes, new tears. So Ajany burrows her face into his shoulders.

Ajany will hold the memory of light and clouds visible from a window. She will remember her head on Baba's shoulders, hear echoes of music, smell pilgrimage, mystery, and all the worlds a father contains on musty travel clothes. She will savor this departure, the texture of old salt, and the weightless inability to say the word "Goodbye." She remembers Nyipir repeating, "Ah, *nyathina,*" a rumbling voice calling her his own, and when she glances at Petrus once more, he has become another sign of faith.

Before Nyipir crossed the threshold that separated Wuoth Ogik from the rest of the world, Ajany gave him her sketchbook. Inside were two watercolors: one an impression of his brother, Theophilus, and the other his father, Agoro, revealed in colors taken from shades of longing within

Baba's voice. He inserted Odidi's folded photograph into the pages: all the Oganda men in one place.

What endures? Echoes of footsteps leading out of a cracking courtyard, and the sound a house makes when it is falling down.

    What endures?

    Starting again.

—

Galgalu pivots sharply and moves to his left down a fire-eaten trail, which had those many years ago brought him into Wuoth Ogik. He crosses the space which takes him past the place where the Trader's *tukul* had been, where he had seen that death was also fire, and it warmed the face of life. He looked and saw that the wind still came to scatter the ash and dust.

—

Akai Lokorijom dispossesses herself even of stories she had buried in the earth. She tells these to Ali Dida Hada as they walk with slow steps. He receives them. When she stops speaking, he is still there. So they walk some more. As they walk, Ali Dida Hada tells Akai about beginnings. Tells her that if she wants he will tell her his original name, the one he had forgotten. She tilts her head so he can whisper it into her left ear. She hears it and laughs, and he with her. They walk and walk until, one day, near a gorge with secret, sweet water streams, they cross into a land where the fire makers lived, a short distance from a forge. Akai and Ali Dida Hada see pale-yellow moonflowers thriving on the shadow side of a conical green hill.

46

AJANY AND ISAIAH ARE THE LAST TO LEAVE WUOTH OGIK. THEY leave so the fire burning down the house can finish its work. The house glows. Resin-infused flames. Everything—wood, books, art, chairs, memories—turns to ash. At first the fire had mesmerized them. They watched it from their campsite, and Isaiah dragged out his battered camera to take pictures. But then, seduced by the fire's frenzied freedom, they had danced before it giddy as children, and in their dancing there was fire and the spirit in the fire found bodies stripped bare to weave into replete landscapes, into which untiring desire roared in visceral rites of exorcism. The next night—just after midnight, when it was coolest—they set out for North Horr. They walked into the morning and past the evening. If they had left even three days after the others had, or if they had waited at Wuoth Ogik one more hour, they might have escaped the weight and waves of the flash flood. The mighty water was from a deluge that had ripped apart an ancient bridge, and caused the Ewaso Nyiro to rise and spread inland over a fifty-kilometer radius for the first time in remembered history.

A rushed, endless plunge.

Later, at the tip of the water, the woman called out to the man. Her voice was smooth, as if newborn. Her eyes contained the shine that marked those who emerge out of chasms. It took an eternity before he answered. Dripping water, he asked if this was the road that led to the place where journeys ended.

Twelve days later, in the northern reaches of Kenya, rain clouds withdraw. The earth gulps down and stores water for later. A congregation of birds chirp, a raucous choir in need of a sane conductor. Transient storm-rivers disappear as the Ewaso Nyiro starts its reluctant crawl back to old boundaries. Oryx gambol; giraffes browse on the extended banks of streams, among pockets of flowering shrubs of all hues, mostly peach, a desert supernova of frozen flame, fragile blossoms, frantic in bloom, as if they were angels relishing a temporary reprieve from celestial certainty. A golden finger-of-God stirs clouds.

A hundred kilometers away, a helicopter hovers. A Cajun-accented foreigner surveys the area. The Jacobses' mission station is underwater. The helicopter drifts to where the house should have been and circles the area at least thirteen times before setting course again for Nairobi. It is assumed that the Jacobses, together with an elderly intelligence man, a local named Petrus Keah, were some of the many human, floral, and animal casualties of a sudden desert storm in Africa: *Requiescant in pacem.*

—

In this landscape, a dog and camel saunter ahead of two tall gray-haired, ebony-skinned elders, one of whom, bare-chested, traverses the land in shiny black shoes set off by red socks. The camel, separated by the storm from its herd, is a good-natured juvenile now renamed Kormamaddo II by his itinerant, self-styled new owners. The travelers approach Lake Ka'alakol, which glowers, unmoved by nature's theatrics. One of the men, with his fedora and cane, is debonair in a tattered kind of way. He has to remind the other to "Move, move." The shirtless one gawks at day and night skies. Two evenings ago, he swore he saw the amused face of Existence looking down on itself. The night before that, he heard the clamoring of wounded souls who had taken residence in his being. They had offered him a truce: the idea of peace if he would speak out their names. It was a deal. Afterward, and for the first time in a terrible and long while, he heard silence. "See those clouds," he demands of his companion.

An exasperated snort. "So now I'm blind?"

"Look again, *msee*."

"I've seen. For many years, I've seen. Move, move."

"You never told me."

A sigh.

Fourteen days later, under a pure blue sky, the travelers stumble upon a neighborhood made of neglected corrugated iron triangle-huts fringed by several giant-milkweed bushes with white-and-purple flowers in bloom. In the center of a field, a tattered red, black, green, and white flag quivers on a rusting pole. They stroll past it. Their camel scans the world in small increments, its mouth in the shape of an "O."

The desert's transitory rivers and lakes evaporate.

Within sight of what had been Wuoth Ogik, a spread-out acacia sprouts green life. In there, a colony of gossipy weavers admonish the world from nests hanging like grass fruits. Roaming winds there ambush a timeless, dense, solitary airstream heading toward the Indian Ocean and pass above a trader and his grizzled, turbaned friend slumbering on the remains of a guitar in one of the day shadows of Mount Kulal. The bluster of air currents flanking the country disturbs the quiet care of a graying midwife crouched in front of a long-limbed, panting woman who has just given birth to twins—a boy and a girl, who emerged with little arms entwined around each other. The winds blunder toward Nairobi and become the tail end of an evening storm, the suddenness of which startles a pilot whose packed plane carries a lofty man from Brazil with a jagged scar that traverses his right hand and disappears up his sleeve. The thundershower pivots, and inside of three minutes swamps a squalid, downtown bar behind River Road, where accordions belting a gritty *mugithi* compete with Fadhili Williams on tape who croons, *Hakuna mwingine zaidi yako, ni wewe, ni wewe wa maisha, moyo wangu na mapenzi yangu nimekuwachia. . . .*

Acknowledgments

This book has been breathed to life through the thoughts, words, and deeds of composite souls, creatures, and landscapes:

Thank you to the Wylie Agency and Sarah Chalfant, who sought, saw, and believed, and then turned the story's delivery into a cause. Dear Jacqueline Ko, for putting up with random ramblings with such tenderness and strength. To my brilliant, patient editor Diana Coglianese at Knopf, who peered through convoluted word thickets and shone light upon scenes while humanely killing assorted "darlings," thus infusing order into a long, long tale.

David Godwin, your wily pursuit of this story covered four continents. That this book is in existence is evidence of faith moving mountains. Thank you. Binyavanga Wainaina, for whip-wielding tough love, daring, friendship, relentless faith, and a space-to-breathe residency; Jackie Lebo, for ruthless, brilliant reviewing; Kate Haines, for scalpel-edged insight and story sense—thank you, dear ones. Thank you, RL Hooker, for the sense of colored-in spaces and gifted story-sight; James ole Kinyaga, for interpreting the book of landscape for me; and Olivier Lechien, for a thorough, hands-off review.

Soul gratitude to you, my Amazonian *comadres*—Maryanne Wachira, Ann Gakere, Sheila Ochugboju, Claudia Fontes (especially for the "*Reconstruction of the portrait of Pablo Míguez*"), Saba Douglas-Hamilton, Caroline Ngayo, Deirdre Prins-Solani, Michelle Coffey, Shalini Gidoo-mal, Andrea Mogaka, Garnette Oluoch-Olunya, Marie Kruger, Nancy

Karanja, Lucy Mulli, Beverly Singer, Doreen Strauhs, Ashminder Dhia-walla, Hildegaard Kiel.

Thank you, Marcel Martins Lacerda Diogo and Claudia (again!), for "Braziliana"; Langi Owuor, for "camel water poetry"; Jimmy Gitonga, for forensic imaginings; Amolo Ng'weno, David Coulsen, and TARA, for Northern Kenya experiences; the amazing staff at the National Museums of Kenya (Nairobi, Loiyangalani) and all those exceptional souls at the Kenya National Archives. To Chimamanda Adichie, Billy Kahora, Angela Wachuka, the Kwani Trust team. Annette Majanja, Parselelo Kantai, Keguro Macharia, Michael Cunningham-Reid, Dickson Wambari, and Michael "Kobole" Maina, my debt of gratitude.

To the many who fed my hopes and then unexpectedly crossed into unreachable realms—Mary Komen, Agnes Katama, Uncle Ben "Odidi" Winyo, Gichora Mwangi, Morris Odotte, Anthony Dzuya—supernal thank-yous.

Seed-planters: family, teachers, mentors. Daddy, irrepressible, eternal, dearly missed Tom Diju; Mummy, gorgeous great-souled story-woman, Mary Sero; long-suffering siblings who have survived some dangerous yarns, always love. Gilbert Kairo, life saver; Uncle Okoyo, who convinced a child that hares lisp and plot; Mrs. Saunders, who stuck five gold stars to a desperately shy student's first poem; Margaret Odhiambo, who lit fires in darkness; Sr. Maureen, who tore open the essence within words; Ben Zulu and the ASDF, who demanded more from the stories Africa tells; Eugenio Ferrari, CM who asked, "The book?" Then prayed.

Nick Elam and the Caine Prize for African Writing family, thank you for the flame. Chris Merrill, Hugh Ferrer, Natasa Durovicova, Kelly Bedeian, and the 2005 IWP cohort—you salvaged story sense for me. I am indebted to the Lanaan Foundation for the treasured gift of time and place, and always to Beverly Singer and Jon Davis, for dragging open New Mexico's doors for me, land of light-painted memory and enchanted friendship journeys; to all the students of the IAIA, for your beauty, inspiration, and the anvil of words; monks of the Monastery of Christ in the Desert, New Mexico: I needed the liturgy, the starkness, that silence. I needed your hearts and The Presence, thank you.

Brisbane! The 2010 Writers' Festival community, the array of zealous readers. "Didgeridoo" Joel, Carien, Theodora Le Souquet, Joe Bageant, who summoned songs from darkness, and honey-voiced Christa, who pointed out *a* way. Later, the University of Queensland and Veny Armanno, for the gift of inspired space to create unfettered, Gillian Whitlock, for order out of chaos, and Paul and Kay Bertini, who made their hearts a sanctuary for a wandering soul.

A long but still an imperfect thank-you litany: Michael Onyango, Elly Kaniaru, Ken and Pauline Mbogo, Ebba Kalondo, Rob Burnet, Munira Humoud, Mshai Mwangola, Wambui Mwangi, Bettina Ng'weno, Ngwatilo Mawiyoo, David Oluoch-Olunya, Lucia Rikiaki, Reinhart Kisaala, Joseph Ngala, Joy Muballe, Reshma Khan, Shiko Kihara, Chris and Irene Okoko, Dodo Cunningham-Reid, Ludovico Gnecci, Sarah and Tristan Callinan, Jin-Hee O, Aghan Odero, Atsango and Maureen Chesoni, Chiuri Ngugi, Giang Nguyen, Christine Bala, Kim Lee Seok, Gerry Gitonga, Kitenga Muhidin, Maina Kiarie, Georgina Okoyo, Nilofer Elias, Arthur Moke, Alphonse Ouma, Anto Poruthur, Jean-Marie Bilwala-Kabesa, Haji Gora Haji, Helen Peeks, Sammy Muvelah, Daudi Were, Guillaume Bonn, Debra Mugobogobo, Isobel Manuel, June Wanjiru, Kees van Velzen, Jane Omollo, Ntone Edjabe, Joan Vilakati, Mary Odongo, Chris Odongo, Emerson Skeens, Newton Osiemo, Musonda Mumba, Rasna Warah, Jael Alaro, Anna Okayo, Myra Mutsune, Wanjiru Gikonyo, Luhindi Sinzomene, James Murua, Alex Awiti, Emma Ganda, Onesmo ole Moiyoi, Julian von Hirschberg, Njalis ole Shuel, Salim Talib, Don Henry, Leah Gachui, Godrick Otieno, Paul Nyawade, Nestanet Tadesse, Gladys Gitau, Peter Kariuki, Pete Tidemann, Antoinette Kankedi, Tom Burke, Fiona Cunningham-Reid, Shailja Patel, Peter and Danielle Onyango, Esther Achieng, Rafique Keshavjee, Christine "Maga" Agallo, Eric Orende, Muthoni Garland, Jan Selman, Andrew Harrison, Monica Karanja, Davis Tashboya, Mercy Ojwang, Fellician Mabunda, Maryann and Marilyn Skelly, Martin Kimani, Tony Mochama, Mike Murnane, and many, many others who knowingly or unwittingly participated in this adventure.

Finally, thank you, Kenya—my canvas, haunting, rage, passion, song, impulse, yearning, love, frustration, and inspiration, and your fierce, fun, and fascinating peoples, who laugh at themselves, and muddle hard toward a good ached for. To "disappeared" Kenyans, the ones we prefer to forget. Thank you *jo' nam lolwe* and denizens of our northern lands, gifted teachers and trustees of life; I beg your indulgence. I have reshaped trails, places, words, narratives, people, creatures, landscape, and names in order to carve out this story.

A NOTE ABOUT THE AUTHOR

Yvonne Adhiambo Owuor was born in Kenya. She won the 2003 Caine Prize and is a past recipient of a Chevening Scholarship and an Iowa Writers' Fellowship. She was named Woman of the Year (Culture and the Arts) by *Eve* magazine in Kenya in 2004 for her contribution to the country's literature and arts. From 2003 to 2005, she was the executive director of the Zanzibar International Film Festival, and she has also been a TEDx Nairobi speaker and a Lannan Foundation resident.

A NOTE ON THE TYPE

This book was set in Scala, a typeface designed by the Dutch designer Martin Majoor (b. 1960) in 1988 and released by the FontFont foundry in 1990. While designed as a fully modern family of fonts containing both a serif and a sans serif alphabet, Scala retains many refinements normally associated with traditional fonts.

Composed by North Market Street Graphics,
Lancaster, Pennsylvania

Printed and bound by Berryville Graphics,
Berryville, Virginia

Designed by Soonyoung Kwon